In the
National
Interest

MARVIN KALB
TED KOPPEL

Simon and Schuster   New York

My deepest thanks go to Ted Koppel, his wife, Grace Ann, and their four lovely children, Andrea, Deirdre, Drew and Tara, without whose cooperation and encouragement this project could never have been completed.

MARVIN KALB

My deepest thanks go to Marvin Kalb, his wife, Madeleine, and their two lovely daughters, Deborah and Judith, without whose cooperation and encouragement this project could never have been completed.

TED KOPPEL

Dedicated to the memory of our friend
DARIUS JHABVALA,
a diplomatic correspondent, who did not know
how to compromise the truth.

PART
ONE

1

The only sound on the flat, hot roof was the occasional cracking of a pistachio nut. The only measure of the hours spent in patient surveillance was the growing pile of discarded shells.

Since early morning, when the sun rose over the low, parched hills in the east, the lookout had been squatting on his haunches, peering through the glare at Amman Airport. He knew every detail of the airport area but he kept rechecking. The airport, neat and unpretentious, served both the civilian and the military needs of the Jordanian capital. The lookout allowed his dark eyes to rest on a young girl lounging near the taxi stand in front of the main terminal building. She wore a tight blouse and skirt, and she smiled invitingly at one of the drivers. The lookout bit into a nut. There was no modesty in Arab women any longer.

To his right, he saw the VIP building; to his left, the control tower, topped by a jumble of electronic contraptions, including a rotating radar dish. He focused on a row of blue metal hangars with silver doors just behind the VIP building. There were no guards around them. A small fleet of unmarked private planes sat on one corner of the broad gray tarmac, which was connected to the airport's single runway by two bands of concrete. Three Boeing 727s, belonging to Alia, Jordan's national airline, were on the central part of the tarmac. They were unattended. Most of the airport mechanics were bustling around the giant 707 parked about fifty yards from the VIP lounge. Painted silver, white and blue, "United States of America" emblazoned across its fuselage, the Secretary of State's plane was almost ready for takeoff. Jordanian security troops, red berets the only splash of color in their uniforms, stood at alert, their backs to the plane, their eyes scanning the distant hills and the rooftops of the airport buildings.

The lookout smiled with satisfaction. His perch was on the rooftop of the only five-story building in the area, an apartment building. Before dawn, the security forces had run a spot-check of the roof and several apartments. Nothing unusual had caught their attention. The lookout had been hiding in a friend's bedroom on the second floor. Behind this building, along the street leading to the main terminal building, all shops had been closed, all pedestrians barred from the area. Legions of bored Jordanian police lined the route of the expected motorcade. The lookout adjusted his kaffiyeh, a black-and-white-checked headdress, and glared at the spiked Germanic helmets and the heavy gray-blue uniforms of the policemen. The lingering effect of European culture on the Arab world was a chronic irritant.

Less than a hundred yards from the lookout's position, drawn back from the main intersection, stood an American-built jeep manned by five soldiers. Mounted in the rear of the jeep was an air-cooled machine gun on a swivel-head tripod. One of the soldiers held the twin grips of the gun in both hands. Flanking him, each with an M-16 rifle cradled in his arms, sat two men, facing in opposite directions. The driver was immobile. To his right, monitoring the static from a sand-colored walkie-talkie, was a sergeant with an RAF-style handlebar mustache. Every now and then the sergeant would pick up a pair of binoculars and scan the rooftops, but he saw nothing unusual.

A terse advisory in Arabic crackled over the walkie-talkie. The sergeant murmured a soft command to his men; none of them moved. They were already on alert.

The lookout spotted the motorcade approaching the airport even before the motorcycle escort could be heard. The outriders flanked a long line of identical cream-colored Rolls-Royces, each car carrying license plates decorated with the crown of the Hashemite King.

The flags of the United States and Jordan fluttered from the fenders of the lead car as it snaked its way through the streets of Amman. Shielded by a V-shaped phalanx of motorcyclists, it attracted most of the attention. The Secretary of State and the Prime Minister rode in the second car, which was armor-plated, outfitted with bulletproof glass and equipped with a self-sustaining ventilation system that could enable the occupants to withstand even a gas attack for twenty minutes. It was an added precaution that pleased the American Secret

Service. The lookout grinned as the motorcade roared past his building toward the VIP lounge.

He was momentarily startled by the screeching whine of a helicopter passing directly over his head. Instinctively he flung himself to his knees and, with his arms outstretched, touched his forehead to the rooftop, as though in prayer. After a few seconds, he lifted his head and saw the markings on the helicopter. It appeared to be the King's; it further appeared that no one had seen him. In all probability, King Mohammed was at the controls. He often enjoyed circling the Secretary's jet during the colorful departure ceremonies; then, as the Air Force jet lumbered down the runway for takeoff, His Majesty would fly a regal escort. The lookout spat on the roof. He shot a glance at the figures of the Secretary and the Prime Minister entering the VIP lounge for their usual farewell news conference. Just beyond the lounge stood an Ilyushin jetliner. The lookout knew that it was there, but until this moment it had not bothered him. Now he felt a rush of anxiety. It would be better if no Russians were killed.

After a few minutes, the lookout saw the American and Jordanian parties emerge from the VIP lounge. The Jordanian Army Band struck up a martial tune that sounded faintly Scottish. Reporters rushed from the lounge, quickly splitting into two groups. Those who wore special passes, indicating they were members of the Secretary's traveling press corps, were allowed to follow him toward the reviewing stand. The other reporters made no effort to follow; security was too tight.

The lookout never took his eyes off the Secretary, who was by then reviewing the honor guard. The Prime Minister was on his left. Trailing them was a Secret Service man, an Uzi submachine gun off his right hip. The Secretary kept time to the lilting wail of the bagpipes, another throwback to the colonial days, as he glided past the rigid troops. It was almost time.

The Secretary and the Prime Minister strolled toward the forward ramp, chatting all the way. They grasped each other's arms and their heads bobbed together twice in a perfunctory embrace. The Secretary, with a characteristic burst of energy, raced up the stairs, paused at the top, where he turned and waved, and then disappeared from view.

Reporters and Secret Service men scurried to the ramp at the rear of the aircraft. The jet engines switched from a whine to a roar; the doors closed and the plane slowly pulled away from the apron. The King's helicopter hovered over the Boeing. The Prime Minister mumbled to an aide. Both men saluted the helicopter. The other diplomats saluted, too; then they waved at the departing aircraft, which kicked up a minor dust storm as it rumbled onto the runway.

Inside the giant aircraft, the Secretary had already shucked his jacket and loosened his tie and was nibbling absentmindedly on a cuticle. It was one of the very few overt signs of weakness or untidiness about him. Even now, with his tie at half-mast, slouching carelessly in the large swivel armchair that had once belonged to Lyndon Johnson, the Secretary exuded a certain elegance. He was in his early sixties, the sort of man whose silver hair might look tousled but never unkempt, whose trousers were always sharply creased, whose shoes seemed to repel dust. Even fatigue suited him well. The Secretary was only slightly above average in height; but because he was slim and carried himself well, he gave the impression of being tall. Although he was normally very conscious of his bearing, when he was tired he tended to slump a little.

Felix John Vandenberg possessed the lingering trace of a British accent, which had been acquired at Eton and Oxford, where Vandenberg had studied during his father's years as an international banker in Europe. To this day the Secretary of State carried a thin white scar on his upper lip—the result of a rugby accident. Foreign Service officers newly assigned to the Secretary's staff were advised to pay close attention to the color of that scar in stressful circumstances. At the best of times, when the scar was at its very whitest, Secretary Vandenberg did not suffer fools gladly. When the scar turned pink, the Secretary's staff members limited themselves to only the most essential intercourse with America's foreign minister. His temper was now in evidence as Vandenberg glanced at a cable that a young Foreign Service officer held for his inspection.

"Would it be asking too much," he said to no one in particular, "if some of the world's problems were held in abeyance long enough for me to take a leak?" He slipped into his small private toilet. "Get my Israel folder," he shouted at his aide. The Secretary ran a comb through his hair and adjusted his horn-rimmed glasses, after glancing in the mirror.

The folder was ready by the time Vandenberg walked into the "flying den," as his wife, Helen, had dubbed the private cabin that served as both office and sitting room. But instead of reading it, he brusquely pushed his way past his aide, through the compartment in which the Under Secretary of State for Political Affairs, the Assistant

Secretary of State for Near Eastern and South Asian Affairs, two members of the National Security Council and a pair of stenotypists sat, and emerged—suddenly transformed and avuncular—amidst the Secret Service agents and reporters in the rear of the plane.

"I see the King's flying escort for you again, Mr. Secretary," said the man from *Time*.

"One day that silly sonovabitch is going to kill us all," said the Secretary, smiling.

Vandenberg was now enveloped in a cluster of disheveled reporters: several crowding around him in the aisle, a few leaning over the backs of seats, others standing on armrests, braced against the overhead luggage rack, craning over their colleagues to get close enough to hear.

Darius Kane made it a point to remain seated. He leaned into the aisle and spoke softly to an Air Force steward who was capturing the scene with an Instamatic.

"Gene," he said, "it has come to my attention that the U.S. Air Force, at considerable expense to the taxpayer, caters to the Secretary's taste for Campari and soda."

The steward's face remained impassive. "You want me to dig into the private stock." It was a statement.

Many trips ago, the two men had conducted a similar conversation, but seriously. Now it had become a light-hearted ritual they both relished.

"Gene, paramount among your many admirable qualities is your ability to cut through the bullshit."

"It goes with the job, Mr. Kane."

"You may call me Darius."

"I know."

There was a wave of laughter from farther up the aisle. Only the woman from the *Washington Star* was not laughing. Her cheeks were flushed and she was visibly angry. Her voice cut through the mounting roar of the jets.

"That was terribly unfair, Mr. Secretary; and I think you owe me an apology."

Vandenberg's face suddenly looked distracted. There was a lurch as the aircraft gained takeoff speed. One of the Secret Service agents jumped out of his seat to steady the Secretary, but he was already retreating up the aisle toward his private cabin.

"I'll have you all up front as soon as I've reviewed some cables"; then, almost as an afterthought, "but I've only got a few minutes."

The reporters were all returning to their seats now. Brian Fitzpatrick of the *Washington Post* was chewing on an unlit Salem as he slipped into the window seat next to Darius.

"Gloria must be the only woman in the world who files her teeth instead of brushing them." Fitzpatrick growled rather than spoke, especially when he was rendering an opinion of his crosstown competitor.

Darius leaned over to push his typewriter under the seat.

"What was that all about?"

"Vandenberg was complimenting Gloria on the story she did out of Jerusalem; said it was eighty-five percent accurate and only fifteen percent fiction. I thought he was being overly generous."

Darius pressed a button on the inside of his armrest and pushed the back of his seat into a reclining position.

"She's right," he said. "Vandenberg needs an occasional knee to the groin to keep him honest."

"She's never right," said Fitzpatrick; but he wasn't being argumentative.

"Did he say anything?" Darius considered it demeaning to join the cluster of newsmen who invariably surrounded the Secretary of State whenever Vandenberg wandered back into steerage, but he always felt a slight twinge of guilt because he might have allowed a nuance to escape him.

"Naw!" Fitzpatrick was in an expansive mood. "He said if he had anything important to tell us, he'd pass it on through you."

"Nothing?"

"The usual bullshit."

Darius took a swallow of the Campari and soda that Gene had handed him.

Fitzpatrick squinted at him. "One of these days I'm gonna quit journalism and go to work for a television network."

As the plane began to gain altitude, the Moab mountains of Jordan receded below.

Seen from the ground, the silver, white and blue jet was just then disappearing into a bank of clouds. The Prime Minister was already headed back to the palace. The reviewing stand was being dismantled. The honor guard was scrambling aboard two waiting army trucks. The special security troops, who had been on Red Alert for the past forty-eight hours, relaxed. Everything seemed to be returning to normal.

The lookout slithered across the roof to a small triangle of shade, where a pigeon rested in a wicker cage. Tenderly removing the pigeon from the cage, he checked the band around its leg, stroked its wings and released it. The pigeon circled the rooftop once and headed toward the arid hills on the other side of the airport.

Down at the intersection an ancient bus that must have dated back to British times stopped to pick up a dozen policemen. The shops began to open. Children raced across the street and up a hill behind the apartment building. The lookout noticed that the jeep with the machine gun had left. Glancing at his wristwatch, he took a deep breath. "In half an hour, it begins . . . *Inshallah.*"

2

A 707 could have flown from Amman to Jerusalem in less than a half hour, but this 707 flew a circuitous route. The Secretary's Boeing gained cruising altitude and headed in a southerly direction, flying over rolling hills and dark valleys. Occasionally, a wadi cracked the bleak terrain. Over Aqaba, the plane banked steeply into a U-turn, turning west and then northwest, so that Darius could look down upon the Israeli port of Elath and, as always, marvel at one of the territorial anomalies of the Middle East—a Jordanian and an Israeli port side by side, peacefully exploiting the northern rim of the Gulf of Aqaba.

The pilot steered the 707 over the Negev toward Ben-Gurion Airport outside of Tel Aviv. The young Air Force major knew that he could bring the Boeing into the airport north of Jerusalem—the runway was just long enough—but the Secretary had banned such landings when he learned that the airport was located in occupied territory. It was, after all, the question of who would control the disputed West Bank that had brought Vandenberg to the Middle East in the first place. He was not about to ask concessions of either side for the sake of saving an hour or two of flying time. In fact, the roundabout flight from Amman to Tel Aviv took an hour and fifteen minutes, and the car ride from Tel Aviv to Jerusalem took an equal amount of time. This route added extra travel time to the Secretary's crowded schedule, but no one objected. It was one of the very minor inconveniences of a diplomatic shuttle.

Darius Kane appeared to be dozing. His face conveyed an impression of tranquility. In this case the impression was misleading. Churning within him, as the plane hummed into its approach pattern, was the unsettling sense that something terribly important was happening. Darius had an instinct about news, which affected his nervous system well before it engaged his mind. The less evidence that existed to confirm his suspicions, the more convinced Darius became that a crisis was developing just beyond the range of his perception. He had been neither amused nor reassured when a psychiatrist friend told him that this form of professional paranoia was a characteristic shared by some of the greatest statesmen and detectives ("and, yes," he had added, "journalists too").

"The important thing," Darius' friend had told him, "is never to lose sight of the fact that sometimes nothing is going on."

"Nonsense," Darius had argued. "*Something* is always happening." During the years that he had covered the diplomatic peregrinations of Felix Vandenberg, that journalistic instinct had hardened into a credo. His father, a New England editor, had often warned him against relying on his instincts. "Facts!" his father would insist. "A *good* journalist never depends on his instincts." Darius always had; it was one of the few bits of paternal advice he ignored—never to his regret.

Someone dropped a sheaf of papers on Darius' lap. "Is he awake?" Darius recognized the thin voice of Carl Ellis, the Secretary's press spokesman. Darius felt pity and contempt in equal measure for Ellis, a career Foreign Service officer in his early fifties, who possessed only two discernible attributes for the job: a willingness to suffer any abuse from newsmen, and an uncanny ability to parrot even the most outrageous gibberish the Secretary could produce to justify a policy. Ellis had worked briefly for his hometown newspaper after finishing college and fancied himself "an expert on the media." Since the Secretary always considered himself to be his own spokesman, he had ignored Darius' private plea that a more capable person be hired. Ellis had learned about Darius' intervention, but, like a cautious bureaucrat, he had done nothing about it. Ellis swallowed his pride easily, on the assumption that a two-year assignment as the Secretary's spokesman could be parlayed into an ambassadorship, his life's dream.

"Is he awake?" Ellis said again.

"Is there anything in this pile of crap worth waking up for?"

"No," Ellis answered in an even tone.

"Then I'm asleep." He could hear Ellis moving on down the aisle. "Hey, Carl, when is his eminence seeing us? We should be there in less than twenty minutes."

Ellis moved back, crouching next to Kane's seat. His voice dropped to a confidential murmur. "I don't think he's going to be able to make it on this leg, Darius. He's got a tremendous backlog of cables and he wants to prepare a brief arrival statement."

Darius glanced down at the papers on his lap. "If it's anything like this one, tell him not to bother." Darius saw that Fitzpatrick was scanning the same release.

> Subject: Secretary Vandenberg's Departure Statement, Amman Airport.
>
> 1. Vandenberg: Quote: On behalf of my colleagues, I would like to thank His Majesty and the Prime Minister for the characteristically warm and friendly reception we have had here. We have had very extended discussions and I gave His Majesty a very full and detailed report about the state of my talks with Israeli leaders. We also discussed bilateral relations, which are excellent. End quote.

Fitzpatrick flipped to the next sheet: "VEHICLE ASSIGNMENTS —TEL AVIV."

"This is one day when the *Post* can go with the wires."

In the row of seats behind them, the UPI's Herb Kaufman had just finished reading the departure statement. His voice had a tinge of sarcasm. "Carl, is this on background or deep background?"

Kaufman was a chunky New Yorker with thick glasses and a shock of graying hair. He was a dedicated newsman and a natural wit. He had gone from a Flatbush ghetto to Columbia College, where he was a scholarship student, and then to the Graduate School of Journalism. That had led to a job with United Press International.

Kaufman kept muttering even as he began typing. "Secretary of State Felix J. Vandenberg arrived in Jerusalem today following a round of 'very extended discussions' with Jordan's King Mohammed."

He seemed to be in genuine pain. "What do I do for a second graph?"

Darius laughed. "Has UPI ever run a one-graph story?"

"Not yet," Kaufman groaned; "but this may be the day."

He was wrong.

Darius gazed out the window, past Fitzpatrick, as the aircraft banked gently toward the airport. Tapping his nose with a forefinger, he said, "Brian, my boy, Kane's law. That sonovabitch always sees us when nothing's happening. He gets lonely. Something's broken that he hadn't expected."

Fitzpatrick grunted, unperturbed; but Darius was closer to the mark than even he realized.

3

Secretary Vandenberg and his Under Secretary for Political Affairs, Frank Bernardi, were analyzing a top-secret telex, which, during the past six hours, had been routed from Beirut, Lebanon, to Langley, Virginia. The CIA had passed the material on to the duty officer of the National Security Council. He had waited until 4:30 A.M., Washington time, to call the President's National Security Adviser, Harlan Stewart, at home. Stewart had ordered that the message be telexed immediately to the Secretary's aircraft.

Shortly after takeoff from Amman, a red light had been activated on the incoming telex machine in an alcove just behind the cockpit. The Air Force communications officer manning the machine had drawn the curtain behind him and watched the message come clattering in. He was unimpressed; but following established procedure, Lieutenant Peter Lorenzo ripped the telex off the machine, clipped the only copy into a Confidential folder and took the original into the Secretary's conference cabin.

Lorenzo handed the folder to Terence Jamieson, the Secretary's personal assistant. Jamieson had the carefully tousled look of a young Kennedy. He traveled with Vandenberg at all times, supervising the details of his personal and professional schedule. Among his many chores, none was more important than scanning the huge flow of incoming cable traffic and deciding which items deserved the Secretary's attention, and when. Before Jamieson got a crack at this job, after two tours in Southeast Asia, six other junior officers had held it, unsuccessfully. Jamieson's success lay in a special set of personal qualities: energy, devotion, intelligence, but, most important, an ability to anticipate Vandenberg's moods.

Jamieson glanced at the telexed cable and quickly handed it to Bernardi. The Under Secretary scowled. "Felix, we may have some big trouble brewing here."

Vandenberg pulled off his glasses and held the cable a few inches from his eyes.

CLASS DOUBLE A SOURCE REPORTS LIBYAN CHAIRMAN SLASH DEFMINISTER DUE DAMASCUS FEBRUARY TWENTYTHREE STOP SECONDARY SOURCES INDICATE ALGERIANS COMMA IRAQIS COMMA POSSIBLY OTHERS DUE SYRIA SAME DATE STOP
KHAMSIN

"Wasn't the Libyan just in Damascus?"

Bernardi nodded. He and Vandenberg had known each other for more than thirty years, ever since they had shared a small consular office in Munich after World War II. They had become close friends, vacationing together at the Vandenbergs' family estate near Lausanne or at the Bernardis' modest seaside house on Martha's Vineyard, whichever was more convenient. Frank had become godfather to the Vandenbergs' only child, and Felix had never missed the confirmation or graduation of any of the five Bernardi children. Of all the senior officials in the State Department, only Bernardi could take the liberty of addressing Vandenberg by his first name, or openly disagreeing with him at staff meetings. The Secretary, while appreciating Bernardi's candor and experience, rarely acknowledged his indebtedness to him.

The Under Secretary was thinking aloud now. "I don't like this, Felix." Bernardi didn't look up at the Secretary. "He was there the day before we left Washington. What the hell could be so important as to pry that bastard out of Tripoli twice in two weeks?"

Vandenberg was nibbling on a handful of candy corn.

"How good is Khamsin?"

"Damned good; but we could always cross-check it with the Israelis this afternoon."

Vandenberg flared. "Absolutely not, Frank. If they know about it, that's all I'm going to hear anyway. If they haven't heard about it, I don't want anybody panicking them."

Vandenberg reflected for a moment.

"Frank, I want you to message Khamsin. Say we want confirmation on the Algerians and Iraqis as soon as possible. I want to know if anybody has heard anything about a Rejectionist Front meeting and what could be behind it; and, Frank, emphasize that I don't want the Israelis hearing about this. Tell Washington the same thing."

Bernardi was uncomfortable. "The Israelis are going to be pretty pissed, Felix, if they ever find out that we knew about this meeting and didn't alert them."

Vandenberg's voice had taken on a pedantic tone. "That, Frank, is why the Israelis are not going to find out. First of all, they probably know about the meeting already and I'd prefer they were left with the impression that they're telling me something new."

Bernardi was still hesitant. "And if they don't know?"

"If they don't know, I may still have a slight chance to get these negotiations rolling."

It was at this moment that Ellis craned his head into the conference cabin. "The press wants to know when you're going to brief."

The look of undiluted fury in Secretary Vandenberg's eyes required no further interpretation. The full dimensions of the crisis were, even then, just beginning to unfold.

4

Security at Amman Airport was never lax; but as Secretary Vandenberg's aircraft crossed into Israeli air space, security was no longer at peak alertness. A quarter of a mile from the terminal, a lone policeman standing in a sentry box leafed furtively through a recent copy of *Playboy* that had been left by a member of the Secret

Service. He was preoccupied, glancing only occasionally up and down the empty access road.

On the other side of the airport, the four military sentries who usually guarded the far side of the runway were lying face down. They were dead. Still strapped to the back of one was a U.S. Army field radio, its long, flexible steel antenna quivering slightly in the stiff breeze that gusted across the open sand.

Moving now toward the airport, their backs to the hills of Moab, six men shuffle-jogged in the direction of the single runway. Fanning out in pairs, they jogged to within fifty yards of the asphalt, the center team waiting, motionless, until the two flanking pairs were also in position. Had anyone been watching from the terminal area almost half a mile away, he might have seen activity on the other side of the runway, but it would have been almost impossible to comprehend.

Methodically, without haste, one man in each team unslung a heavy baseplate from his back and, with a single fluid motion, slammed the plate onto the parched ground. Each partner stood by holding a thirty-inch cylinder more or less at port arms. Now the cylinders were being firmly screwed onto the baseplates, so that each attachment pointed skyward. Each team was working independently, apparently oblivious of the others, but the motions of each were identical, synchronized.

One man in each team fiddled with the ring adjustments on the sides of the mortars, slowly bringing the tubes to predetermined angles. Their partners reached into canvas satchels, removed a half-dozen shells and lined them up carefully on top of the bags.

The leader of the center team raised his arm, looking first in one direction, then in the other. He let his arm drop and the attack began. The mortar squad on the left fired first, one man bracing the cylinder, the other guiding the tail fins of the shells into the mouth of the tube one after the other. They did not pause to readjust their range; nor did they stop to watch the rounds land. Six times in the space of a minute, the dull THWOCK of mortar fire punctuated the stillness. Within seconds after the first round was launched, the sound of distant thunder began rolling back across the barren airport. The sound built with each new explosion. Even as the last rounds were fired on the far right, the first two attackers, leaving their mortar and baseplate in place, began running back toward the hills.

The entire barrage was completed in three minutes; the leader of the assault team, hesitating for a moment, watched with clinical interest as orange flames licked the gray-black columns of smoke that billowed out of the VIP lounge and two of the large blue metal hangars directly behind the lounge. Almost regretfully, he turned from the scene and began loping after his colleagues.

For a full two minutes after the last shell landed, there was no sign of life within the airport complex. An Alia maintenance crew lay paralyzed with fear under the wing of an aircraft parked some two hundred yards from the blazing lounge. Then, from a Quonset hut near the airport approach road, a few shouts could be heard, and screen doors crashed open as uniformed Jordanian troops, carrying M-16 semiautomatic rifles, ran toward a nearby row of parked jeeps. As the jeeps began careening toward the perimeter of the airport, in the general direction from which the mortar rounds had come, airport officials peered cautiously out of the customs lounge. The wail of a distant siren was swallowed up in the howl of a crash unit already racing toward the blazing hangars. Suddenly, a truck loaded with men in Jordanian Army uniforms wheeled around the VIP lounge and screeched to a halt. The men vaulted over the sides and tail gate, splitting into two groups. The first unit spread out in a defensive arc around a third hangar some one hundred and fifty yards from the two that were burning. The walls of this hangar had been punctured by shrapnel and its windows had been shattered, but otherwise the building was intact.

The second unit approached the padlocked doors at the front of the hangar. An officer stepped up to the door, motioned his men to stand back, flipped the catch of his rifle to automatic and blasted the lock away.

Two of the soldiers pushed the doors apart. Three helicopters were revealed. Within seconds, the pilot and copilot seats in the aircraft were occupied, and there was a sputter of motors coughing to life. Lazily, at first, each rotor groaned on its axis, gradually accelerating until the howl of blades spinning themselves into barely visible blurs overcame all other sound.

Outside, there was gunfire. A Jordanian police jeep had driven past the three gutted buildings to investigate the protected hangar. The jeep was caught in a sudden withering cross fire, and the bodies of its four occupants slumped haphazardly in the seats until, racing out of control in a widening circle, the jeep crashed into the wreckage of the lounge.

The troops converged now on the open hangar, forming two lines, one on either side of the open doors. As the first of the helicopters emerged, nose tilted down, hovering a scant yard above the ground, four of the soldiers from each line climbed aboard. The helicopter pulled its way cautiously clear of the hangar and, as soon as it was well clear, clawed its way into the sky, wheeling sharply to the west. Twice more the same procedure was repeated, the last of the troops on the ground backing their way in a crouch under the whirling blades and clambering aboard the third helicopter. One of the men stood balanced on the left runner, one hand gripping the open door of the chopper, the other theatrically outstretched, clutching his assault rifle. His scream could be heard above the howl of the engine. It was a cry of unrestrained triumph.

Moments after the last helicopter cleared the area, a string of violent eruptions burst through the remaining hangars and along a line of revetments that had protected a squadron of Jordanian Hunter ground attack planes. Every military aircraft in sight had been destroyed.

5

The archeologist from the University of Montana had proposed leaving Amman before dawn so that they could watch the sun rise over the fabled stone city of Petra. There was a brief, uncomfortable silence while everyone waited for Helen Vandenberg's reaction. The wife of the Secretary of State had peeled off from the shuttle to do some sightseeing in Jordan. She did not rush into an answer; she never rushed. She was a prepossessing woman who used her power and position graciously. She was not pretty by conventional standards; she never had been. Her prep school and college yearbooks showed a young girl with angular features, dark hair and, around her lips, the trace of a smile, at once playful and shy. Helen Boswick was the only daughter of a prosperous Philadelphia lawyer. At Vandenberg's side over the years, she had developed the art of conversation into a diplomatic asset. She could make even a dull Soviet bureaucrat think of himself as a sparkling raconteur.

Among Foreign Service wives, she had developed an almost legendary reputation. She led the fight for woman's rights. She wrote a monthly column for *Woman's Day*. She spoke four European languages. When heads of state visited the White House, the President always made a point of having the Secretary's wife at his side. It might have been expected that the President's wife would grumble; but Helen had anticipated the problem, and she successfully involved the President's wife in all her social plans.

Now, facing the prospect of a predawn departure, Mrs. Vandenberg reacted characteristically. "Oh, that would be just lovely," she said at last, but her eyes rolled ever so slightly toward the ceiling as she spoke. The gesture did not escape Bill Staples, the stocky ex-police captain from Chicago who ran her security detail.

"Excuse me, Mrs. Vandenberg," he said. "I hate to pull security on you, but I'd prefer that we not helicopter out of here until after daybreak."

The Jordanian officials looked disappointed, but Helen Vandenberg spared everyone a moment of embarrassment. "Isn't that a shame!" she said, adding quickly, "But if Mr. Staples says we can't leave until after it gets light, I'm sure he has good reasons."

They arrived at Ain Musa by helicopter shortly after nine, and the archeologist from Montana immediately attached himself to Helen's side. "There's no way to substantiate it, of course, but local legend has it that here the Hebrew patriarch brought forth water from a rock while leading the children of Israel out of Egypt."

Helen was still slightly groggy. "The Hebrew patriarch?"

"Moses."

"Yes, of course. Moses."

They transferred to three Land Rovers: Helen, the wife of the U.S. Ambassador, the Jordanian officials, the archeologist from Montana, a colleague from the University of Amman, a contingent of Jordanian security guards and Bill Staples.

"Normally," said the professor, "the only way to make this approach is by donkey or horse."

Helen Vandenberg leaned forward, gripping the handrail attached to the back of the driver's seat, as the Land Rover hit a large rock. "As Felix sometimes says, 'If it weren't for the honor, I'd just as soon walk.'" She was sorry the instant she said it. The professor seemed momentarily subdued.

"I don't see," remarked Helen, in total awareness of what she was doing, "anything but a solid face of rock."

The professor was delighted. "They call it el Shakk. It's directly ahead of us now; do you see it?"

The cleft in the rock was barely visible, a hairline fracture that ran hundreds of feet from the base up to the very top, bisecting the huge and otherwise impenetrable wall of stone.

Helen Vandenberg could, when the occasion demanded, be as disingenuous as a chorus girl. "We're not going in through there, are we?"

The professor could hardly restrain his enthusiasm. "This was once the crossroads of the entire Arab world. Almost every caravan that crossed the Arabian peninsula passed by here. In some ways this was the very center of commerce in the Middle East."

The Land Rovers were making their way slowly between the walls of solid rock. One of the Jordanian officials handed Helen a shawl against the chill. The professor paused only to light a pipe.

"As you can see, Mrs. Vandenberg, there would have been no way to mount an effective attack against the city of Petra. This is the only way in or out."

The fender of one of the Land Rovers scraped rock. There was no more than six inches of clearance on either side.

"The Nabataeans discovered this place three hundred years before the birth of Christ. They sent their people out from here to set up depots and to guide the caravans. Until the Romans captured Petra in 106 A.D., the Nabataeans quite literally controlled Arab trade."

Helen had become genuinely interested. "But how did the Romans ever take this place?"

"We'll never know for sure. The assumption is that some of their agents penetrated by subterfuge, killed the guards—probably at night —and that by daybreak one of the Roman legions had already slipped into the city, probably through this very gorge."

The Land Rovers bumped cautiously along a downward incline. The path widened dramatically into a broad square that introduced Mrs. Vandenberg to Petra. The square was bathed in a brilliant pink light. Directly in front of her was a massive entranceway framed by two tall Corinthian columns. The professor from Montana was transfixed.

" 'Match me such marvel, save in eastern clime,/A rose-red city half as old as time.' "

He was reciting an ancient rhyme, one that the Jordanian Tourist Agency quoted in the official brochure left in every Amman hotel room. Mrs. Vandenberg had read it in a short history of Petra that the Embassy had prepared for her, but she reacted with a sense of fresh discovery. "That's beautiful, really breathtaking." She sat in the Land Rover for an extra moment, enjoying the sight of a city rediscovered after centuries lost in the arid hills south of the Dead Sea. The columns flanked a huge structure that was literally carved out of the mountainside. A flight of stone steps, half covered with rose-colored sand, marched up to the columns and, it seemed, beyond them, into a dark interior.

"Those columns are Greek, though, aren't they?"

"Greek? Yes," the professor replied. "They've all been here, you know. The Greeks, the Romans, even the Crusaders. They built a fort here in the twelfth century." He helped Mrs. Vandenberg out of the Land Rover. She spotted dozens of Jordanian security troops on paths halfway up the mountain, all of them looking bored.

"This building," the professor continued, "is called Al-Kaznah, the Treasury. But actually it was a tomb. Look at the workmanship. Everything carved out of the pink sandstone."

Helen linked her arm in the professor's and guided him a discreet distance from the others. "Dr. Moran," she said, "I can't remember when I've felt less like playing an official role, but we mustn't forget that I am here as a guest of the Jordanian government. I've got to spend some time with my hosts. Will you forgive me?"

"Oh, my dear Mrs. Vandenberg, but of course. How terribly thoughtless of me."

Helen held his arm as they rejoined the others and walked into the dim stillness of the Treasury building. "Dr. Fawzi," she called, hearing the slight echo of her voice bouncing off the high walls. The Jordanian archeologist, who was officially Moran's host, slipped noiselessly to Helen's side.

"Madame?"

"Dr. Fawzi, it's really hard to believe that we are standing *inside* a mountain."

The Jordanian, who sported a bushy mustache, seemed delighted. "Ah, yes, madame, inside." His voice was deep, and he spoke slowly.

"The entire city is carved out of the mountains." He paused. "Petra is a wonder of the world."

"As indeed it should be." Helen rarely missed a beat.

She slowly led her party back into the clear sunlight. Dr. Fawzi gestured toward a broad, open area between the mountains. Years before, it must have been Main Street. Low-slung houses and ruins, covered with layers of fine sand, had been preserved in the dry desert climate. Helen could see a Roman amphitheater, broad and quite spectacular.

"Would that have been used for plays or athletic events, Dr. Fawzi?"

"Probably both, madame, but principally for plays."

"Dr. Moran was telling me the Romans came here early in the second century."

"Yes, madame." The Jordanian seemed to be gathering his courage. "It is curious, is it not, that Petra has existed for more than two thousand years, and yet most Europeans were totally unaware of its existence until Dame Agatha Christie used it as the setting for one of her murder mysteries."

"Why that's fascinating!" Helen turned to the wife of the U.S. Ambassador to Jordan. "Laura, did you know that this was the setting for an Agatha Christie novel?" Laura Johnstone was no ordinary Foreign Service wife; nor was her husband an ordinary Ambassador. Both had been heavy contributors to the President's successful campaign. As a reward Bill Johnstone had been appointed Ambassador to Jordan. Vandenberg had voiced his objections, insisting that the Middle East was too explosive an area for amateurs; but the President had overruled his Secretary of State. In fact, Vandenberg was later heard to admit that Johnstone had become a "good" Ambassador. High praise, coming from the Secretary. The King liked Johnstone's company, and he obviously valued his business sense. Laura crowded her husband for the King's attention. She was an effervescent woman; and Helen had discovered, much to her delight, that she carried a brain along with her good looks. They had become fast friends.

"Sure," Laura responded, fearless about topping Helen. "*Appointment with Death.* You must read it now that you've been here. I'll give you Bill's copy as soon as we get back to Amman."

"Did you have any breakfast, Mrs. Vandenberg?" the Jordanian Minister of Tourism asked.

"Just coffee."

The Jordanian official snapped his fingers, summoning a security guard who carried a wicker basket. "Then we shall have a snack here." They seated themselves on a worn stone bench in the amphitheater, from which Helen could see the rest of Petra. Jagged mountains circled the old city, much of which was undergoing scientific excavation. Several bulldozers pockmarked the landscape, along with a few campsites set up for the archeologists who dug there.

For a few moments, the small group ate and drank in total silence, each caught up in his own thoughts, absorbing the stillness of the ages.

The silence was broken by Dr. Moran. "Do you see that large vault, Mrs. Vandenberg?" he asked, pointing to the top of one of the mountains. "Way up there? Contains some of the most beautiful wall paintings in the world, dating back, in some cases"—he paused—"two thousand years."

"I hope we are going to see them." Helen stood up, and everyone quickly followed suit.

They walked around the amphitheater and then up a precarious flight of steps carved out of the rock. Spanning a deep gorge, creaking slightly in the breeze, hung a rope suspension bridge.

The Minister took Helen's arm. "Now you will truly see the finest that Petra has to offer." He called over his shoulder to the archeologist. "Fawzi!" The Jordanian was in deep conversation with his American colleague. "Come, come, come!" The Minister clucked his tongue impatiently. "This is the most magnificent section of the city; as your urbanologists would say, 'the silk-stocking district.'" He laughed appreciatively at his own humor.

Most of the security guards had already crossed the bridge. Bill Staples squeezed past the American archeologist, moving directly behind the Secretary of State's wife. He spoke to her between clenched teeth, his voice barely audible. "Let one Nabataean in and see what happens to the neighborhood."

She glanced back in mock disapproval. "Mr. Staples, you're a terrible man."

By now the entire party had crossed the bridge. They were examining wall paintings when Staples heard the first distant chatter of helicopters. He stepped out into the sunlight, squinting up at the cloudless blue sky. He looked down at his watch and moved alongside his Jordanian counterpart.

"They're early. I thought we weren't leaving for another half hour."

The Jordanian shrugged; he consulted with two of the other security officers. Staples joined the group. "They're coming from the wrong direction. I don't like it."

The first of three helicopters swooped down out of the sun. Staples could see the Jordanian Air Force markings on the tapering fuselage and he relaxed slightly. The chopper was hovering directly over the gorge, the pilot's face barely visible behind the dark sun visor that extended from his white helmet. Staples gave the pilot a thumbs-up signal; the pilot returned the salute. As soon as he saw Helen Vandenberg move into the sunlight, the pilot changed the pitch of his blades and the helicopter abruptly peeled away.

The second helicopter also dropped out of the sun; behind it, from the same blinding direction, came the third. It hovered some five hundred feet above the gorge until suddenly it swooped down on the bridge, opening a murderous fusillade of machine-gun fire. The bridge was torn in two, and the group was isolated. Mrs. Vandenberg and the others turned their backs protectively against the swirling sand kicked up by the second helicopter, which had just landed. There was the crack of two rifle shots. A Jordanian officer fell to the ground. The Vandenberg party spun sharply toward the sound of the gunfire. They found themselves facing eight men in uniforms of the Jordanian Army. Each man had his rifle pointed at Helen Vandenberg. One man, heavy-set but nimble, appeared to be out of place among his slim companions, but there was no question that he was in command. He barked out an order in Arabic, while pointing to the Jordanian officer who lay in a spreading pool of blood. Without their leader, the security troops seemed lost, and one by one they dropped their guns.

Bill Staples was rigid with fury and frustration. Cupping his left hand over his mouth, he spoke urgently into the plastic microphone that was part of a CB system linking the agents on the detail to each other.

"He's dead." For a moment Staples didn't realize that the Arab was talking to him. "If you're trying to reach the other agent, he's dead; but there's no requirement that you join him. You can, of course, if you wish; but you will *not* join us." The Arab spoke deliberately, not shouting, raising his voice just enough to be heard above the noise of the helicopters.

"Please remain quite still. One of my men will disarm you." Then he turned toward Helen. "Mrs. Vandenberg, you will board the helicopter. Don't be alarmed, you're quite safe."

Staples could see that Helen was trembling, but her voice was even. "Where are we going?"

"Please do as you're told, Mrs. Vandenberg. The longer we remain here, the greater the chance that someone else will be hurt."

Helen followed the Arab to the helicopter, glancing helplessly at Staples as she went; and with a formality that seemed slightly ludicrous under the circumstances, the Arab extended a hand and helped the Secretary's wife aboard. He seemed almost courtly. As the rotors gathered momentum toward takeoff speed, the remaining guerrillas ran toward the helicopter, covering for one another as each man clambered on board. The last thing Staples saw before he was blinded by the sand was the leader of the guerrilla unit strapping a seat belt securely around Helen Vandenberg's waist.

6

The head of the Secretary's Secret Service detail stood in the aisle next to the galley trying to block out the noise all around him. He depressed the transmit button on the phone.

"You're gonna hafta speak up. I can't hear you."

He hunched his shoulders protectively around the phone, pressing the palm of his free hand against his left ear.

Eric Thurber was prematurely bald, a freckle-faced, muscular giant who suffered from excess stomach acidity and occasional hives; but he excelled under pressure. His face revealed nothing.

"Yeah. Well, you're gonna handle that on the ground, right?"

Thurber flattened himself against the galley to make way for one of the stenotypists who was threading a path to the rear of the plane.

"Have you checked on Woodlark?" A pause. "All right. We'll talk about it when I get down." "Woodlark" was the Secret Service code name for the Secretary's wife.

Darius stopped the agent as he was returning to his seat. "Anything wrong, Eric?"

Thurber exuded nonchalance. "Wanna join the Service, Darius? I could use you."

The rear of the plane was in its standard prelanding condition of near chaos. Typewriters and flight bags littered the aisle. Reporters were retrieving their jackets from the overhead baggage racks. Some of the agents were taking their automatics out of briefcases, reinserting them in holsters. All of them were already wearing prefitted earpieces, the clear plastic wires looping over their shoulders and into the walkie-talkies clipped on their belts. Two of the agents had moved to the rear exit and were holding long canvas bags that contained sawed-off shotguns. There was nothing abnormal in all this activity, but Darius noticed that Thurber was conferring separately with each of his men as they filed to the rear of the plane.

Fitzpatrick had also sensed a change in atmosphere. "Something's hit the fan. Whyn'tcha check with Ellis." He nudged Darius in the ribs.

Darius nodded out the window. "We're almost down, Brian. It'll have to wait."

The instant the plane hit the tarmac, Darius eased himself into the aisle. He stuffed his notebook and tape recorder into a black camera bag, slung the bag over his shoulder, grabbed his typewriter and joined the Secret Service detail. He draped an arm confidentially over the shoulders of one of the agents.

"Demonstration?"

The agent shrugged.

"Come on, for Chrissake, what's going on?"

The agent twisted his body to adjust the wire under his jacket. His lips barely moved. "They hit the airport in Amman."

The aircraft shuddered to a halt. A steward heaved at the door handle, yanking the door inward and then pushing it to the side of the cabin. The ground crew was waiting for complete engine cutoff. For the first time, Eric Thurber betrayed his impatience. He waved at the ground crew.

"Get that goddamn ramp over here!"

Thurber was the first out, leaping over the closing gap as the ramp was nudged into position below the exit. Darius was on the heels of the last agent out, racing down the stairs and across the tarmac. Deployed in a tight cordon around the front ramp was a detachment of Israeli paratroopers in full battle gear. The Secretary's black limousine was parked inside the cordon. Darius had never seen paratroopers on a security detail for Vandenberg. In Israel, that was usually a police job.

Without breaking stride, Darius dropped his camera bag and typewriter, unclipped his press identification and moved briskly between two paratroopers. They made no effort to stop him. Darius reached into his breast pocket and pulled out a pair of aviator sunglasses. He possessed a chameleonlike quality that owed less to his physical appearance than to his demeanor. Whatever the occasion, wherever he might be, Darius looked as if he belonged.

Vandenberg had not yet appeared. In fact, Darius could see the stubby figure of the Israeli Foreign Minister climbing the ramp of the Secretary's plane and rushing inside. Darius walked slowly to the foot of the ramp, approaching Israel's Ambassador to the United States. Chaim Zeevi was a fidgety person, constantly pushing his heavy-rimmed glasses up the bridge of his nose or running his fingers through his bushy hair. As usual, he had hustled back to Israel in advance of Vandenberg's arrival, anxious to protect his reputation as one of the foremost Vandenberg watchers in Washington. Though he was not a career diplomat—Zeevi was, in fact, a top nuclear physicist—he had quickly become one of the best-informed persons in the capital.

"Were they trying to kill him?" Darius asked his question as though he were merely picking up the thread of an interrupted conversation. He nodded toward the plane.

The Ambassador spread both hands. "Who knows what they were trying to do. We don't even know if the attack succeeded or failed."

"I don't follow you."

Zeevi glanced nervously up the ramp. "If they were trying to kill your friend, they failed."

"But . . ." Darius was probing.

"But the failure was of such magnificent proportions that it may be presumptuous to assume we know the whole story yet."

"Was it Fatah?" Darius was referring to one of the prominent Palestinian terrorist groups.

"Only one thing I can tell you for sure; it wasn't Irgun."

Vandenberg and the Israeli Foreign Minister, Avram Cohen, were descending the ramp. The Secretary of State brushed back a silver forelock and extended a hand to the Ambassador, but he was looking at Darius. "Is he part of my security detail now or have you hired him as a technical adviser, Chaim?"

"You can't afford to have him in the first capacity, Mr. Secretary, and we can't afford to pay him in the second."

Darius was not about to be deflected. "Mr. Secretary, what happened in Amman?"

Vandenberg's expression was serious, but his voice was tinged by sarcasm. "Darius, you better than anyone will recognize how painful it is for me to admit that I probably don't know much more than you do." He kept moving, even as they spoke.

"Do you know whether it was an attempt on your life?" Darius was persistent.

Vandenberg held Darius by the elbow and murmured, "I'll try to see you later in Jerusalem." Then, pointing to the other reporters, who had been maneuvered behind steel barricades, he added, in full voice, "Your colleagues are having fits, Darius. Give them a fill-in."

By this time Vandenberg was standing next to the open door of his bulletproof limousine. Thurber was next to him, so close they were touching. The agent held an Israeli-made Uzi submachine gun.

"Avram!" The Secretary called to the Foreign Minister, who was then giving Zeevi some last-minute instructions. "Are you riding with me?"

Cohen hurried to the limousine. "You're not going to talk to the press?" He seemed incredulous. Vandenberg didn't even answer. He slipped into the back of his car and beckoned for Cohen to join him.

The motorcade moved slowly away from the plane, Thurber in the passenger seat next to the agent who was driving the limousine, the other agents running next to the follow-up car, the so-called "battle-wagon." As the cars gathered speed, the agents leaped on board, slamming the doors behind them.

Darius retrieved his bag and typewriter and wandered toward the cluster of television cameras that stood behind police barriers more than a hundred and fifty feet from the plane. He could see Jerry Blumer frantically waving one of the network's film bags to attract his attention. Blumer had pushed one of the police barricades aside.

"Can you tell me what the hell is going on here today? I've never seen security like this."

Darius slapped him on the back.

"I feel great, Jerry. Thanks for asking. Everything in Washington is marvelous. We've rediscovered sex and alcohol in the U.S. Congress. How's everything here?"

Blumer was chewing the stem of his pipe. "Patronize me later,

Darius. Something's obviously happened. If you know what it is, the morning show would love to hear about it. If you don't, perhaps you'd like to slip your overpaid ass into gear and find out."

All the while Darius had been guiding the Tel Aviv bureau chief of National News Service away from the knot of reporters that was still clustered next to the barricades.

"Look, Jerry, there was no briefing on the plane and I don't think anyone else has this yet, but there's been some kind of attack on Amman Airport. It may or may not have been an attempt on Vandenberg's life."

Blumer shook his head in bewilderment. "What does it take to convince you that you've got a story—World War Three?"

"Sure it's a story; but I've not only told you everything I know about it already, I may have told you more than I know. Jerry, I can cover the morning show with a radio circuit from Jerusalem. They'll love us both for it. You really think they wanta pay three grand for pictures of Felix Vandenberg getting into his car?"

They had begun walking through the terminal building. The cavernous baggage hall was guarded by young Israeli soldiers, slouching as usual, their eyes alert, Uzis hanging from straps over their shoulders. Darius strode to the exit, noticing, with an inner smile, that the guard at the door was already exhibiting traces of indecisiveness. Darius maintained a brisk pace. "Vandenberg," he said; then, pausing for an instant, he cocked his head in Jerry Blumer's direction. "Better check his ID."

Darius stepped out onto the sidewalk and found Paul. More precisely, the Israeli driver found him. "MIISSSSTER KANE!"

They threw their arms around each other. Their reunions always began the same way. "*Alors, Paul, mon vieux, comment vas-tu?*"

Paul stepped back and examined Darius gravely, shaking his head slowly. "Such an educated gentleman. So how come you haven't learned a civilized language, like Yiddish?" He took Darius' bag and typewriter and put them in the trunk of a massive, cream-colored Ford.

"Paul, maybe you'd better get Mr. Blumer out of custody."

"You did it to him again?"

Darius looked at his feet in mock humility.

Paul sighed. "*Vay iz mir.*"

Blumer was furious. Genuinely so. They drove out of the airport in total silence. It wouldn't last. Darius and Blumer had been friends for almost twenty years, and their first meeting had begun on a similar note.

"Washington Heights," Darius had said on being introduced to Blumer.

"Whaddya mean, 'Washington Heights'?" Blumer had growled.

"It's where you're from. Where you were raised."

"You're a smart-assed sonovabitch, aren't you?"

That exchange set the tone for what was to become an enduring friendship. Their backgrounds could hardly have been more dissimilar. Jerry Blumer was the son of an immigrant Jewish furrier. He had indeed been raised in Washington Heights, a north Manhattan neighborhood that had attracted large numbers of Jewish, Greek and German immigrants. He attended public schools and earned his B.A. degree at CCNY, in night school. During the day, he had helped his father. For reasons Blumer could never quite understand, he was drawn to a career in journalism. He began as an editor for United Press and later joined National News Service.

Darius, the son of a New England newspaperman, was born in New Delhi, and had been named after one of his father's closest friends, a gentle Parsi from Bombay, whose entire life had been devoted to Mahatma Gandhi's cause of Indian freedom. The elder Kane had known Gandhi and shared his aspirations, as well as an American Brahmin could.

A committed democrat, Simon Kane tried to resist the inescapable privileges of the white man in a colonial setting. One of Darius' earliest memories placed him at his father's side, standing at the end of a long queue in a Delhi post office. It was extraordinary behavior for any so-called "European." Their mere presence was unusual enough; whatever needed to be done at the post office could surely have been handled by a servant, but to wait meekly in line behind a crowd of natives was, in 1943, unthinkable behavior, even for an American. One of the clerks had emerged from behind his cage to dispose of the "sahib's affairs" personally. To believe in those days, as Simon Kane constantly reminded his son, that all men are created equal required more than simply an act of faith; it called for a considerable degree of imagination.

Abigail Northfield Kane, Darius' mother, had been of a more practical bent, always trying to make a comfortable home for the family in a bougainvillaea-draped villa near the Embassy quarter of New Delhi. She never understood Simon's attachment to India, and she had resisted his assignment to New Delhi with a passion rarely exhibited by the usually stoical women of Marblehead. She yielded only when she realized that Simon's lust for adventure would never be sated within the confines of New England. Restless, curious, he was in the grand tradition of the men who went down to the sea.

Their life in New Delhi was immensely stimulating to Simon, but Abigail's depression deepened in almost direct proportion to his growing excitement. If her husband regarded India's poverty as a challenge, she could see it only as a tragedy. Abigail could become, quite literally, ill if a street beggar so much as touched her. She wanted desperately to return to Massachusetts General Hospital in Boston for Darius' birth, but Simon forbade it. Such luxury would have offended him, no less than his Indian colleagues. They argued a great deal about the location of Darius' birth until finally Abigail abandoned the fight, too frail and preoccupied to continue it.

Their son was born in the Seventh-Day Adventist Hospital in Delhi; and when, as a result of some carelessness on the part of the Indian gynecologist, Abigail began to experience postbirth hemorrhaging, she seemed to lose her combativeness. She recovered, in time, but she was never the same again. She suffered periodic illnesses and stayed close to their home, which became her life. Simon was often overwhelmed with guilt. On more than one occasion, Darius could remember him toying with the idea of returning to Boston for an editorial job; but he never took the initiative. A story would break in Madras. A friend would need help. India would beckon, her outstretched hand attracting Simon's energies and passions much more than the needs of his family, at least as Abigail interpreted them. A coolness developed between Simon and Abigail, and Darius understood at a very early age that for journalists such as Simon Kane, the "story" was the consuming passion of their lives.

Even on the upbringing of Darius, an only child, there had been disagreement; but on this issue there was more of a willingness to compromise. Darius, in a sense, reflected the harmonious blending of his parents' conflicting inclinations. But if Abigail persisted in pushing Darius toward the West, Simon kept pulling him toward the East. For two hours a day, Darius would immerse himself in Indian culture, sitting with a young disciple of Gandhi's to learn not only Hindi and Urdu, but also the mysteries of the Eastern religions.

Shortly after Darius' twelfth birthday, Simon Kane was asked to return to Boston to assume the new job of foreign editor on the *Globe*, which was becoming aware of the world in the aftermath of the big war. Simon was a natural for the job, but he balked, until the publisher lost patience and ordered him home. It was a choice of a good job in Boston or no job in India. At last, India lost, and Darius was brought "home" for the first time.

The United States in the early 1950s was a strange place for Darius. McCarthyism as a political phenomenon spread through the country. Cold war governed the nation's foreign policy. Darius could remember apprehensive conversations in the Kane household. Simon had not returned to Boston to lose his sense of moral outrage. As an editor, he had the right every now and then to express his opinions on the editorial page. Among his first outbursts was a scathing attack against the junior Senator from Wisconsin. It attracted the attention of Edward R. Murrow, and the noted broadcaster asked for permission to read it on his evening report. Simon Kane won national attention. At first the *Globe*'s publisher was proud; later he became concerned when McCarthy unleashed a furious blast at Kane and demanded his dismissal. The publisher held fast against this pressure, but a logical promotion to chief of the editorial board of the newspaper failed to materialize. After several months, Simon Kane quit, a distressed and disillusioned man. He wrote a book about his experiences, but outside of Boston, it drew little attention.

"Journalism is a special calling," Simon explained one evening after dinner. "It is a summons to tell the truth as best you can determine it." Darius had asked his father why he had resigned.

"Your great-great-grandfather went to China, one of the early New England skippers. His son went to China, too, but as a missionary. He finished Divinity School at Harvard and left the next week. Stayed in a small village in southern China for thirty-eight years. That's where my father was born. He became a missionary, too. They all felt a calling." Darius loved nothing better than family stories, especially when his father told them. The elder Kane lit a pipe and stared out the window at a misty rain. He was deep in thought.

"Being a reporter is a little like being a missionary, and being a missionary is a lot like being a teacher. A reporter carries the word. It isn't sacred. There is no book of truth. He is fallible. But he doesn't write a story because some group wants him to, or even because his country says he should. He writes because he thinks he has discovered something new and interesting, and the information is liberating."

"Liberating?" Darius was puzzled.

"Yes, in the sense that the information illuminates the world and greases the wheels of a democracy. That's why freedom of the press is protected by the First Amendment. That's why journalism is such a very special calling." Darius never forgot his father's explanation. A few years later, in 1958, Simon Kane died of a heart attack. Six months later, Abigail died of complications growing out of acute pneumonia.

They left an eighteen-year-old son, mature beyond his years. During high school, Darius had been a loner, a stranger in his own country. His classmates considered him somewhat odd, different. He was naturally reserved, mixing much more comfortably with adults than with his contemporaries. His speech contained more than a trace of an Indian cadence. His skin, burnished a deep tan by the hot sun of the subcontinent, quickly set him apart from the pale-skinned Irish kids in his neighborhood. His dark good looks and studied aloofness lent an air of mystery to Darius, which he rather enjoyed cultivating, especially when he came to realize the effect the combination had on young women. Darius was almost six feet tall, wiry, with gray eyes, an excellent athlete, excelling in swimming, tennis and horsemanship—all sports where individual effort counted far more than teamwork. Scholastically, he always ended up near the top of his class, and he appeared to do it effortlessly. He was already, at the time his parents died, his own man.

Darius could have attended Harvard but chose Stanford. His years in Boston had not been particularly happy ones. A friend had recommended the West Coast, and Stanford offered a full scholarship. Darius made the dean's list by his sophomore year and Phi Beta Kappa in his junior year. In his senior year he was a quarterfinalist in the National Tennis Championships and was named executive editor of the Stanford *Daily*.

Upon graduation, Darius returned to India as a Fulbright scholar, and in his spare time he began to string for United Press International. The border war between India and China had captured front-page headlines, and Darius was familiar with the terrain and with many in the cast of characters. The UPI bureau chief in New Delhi, Swaran Raj, had known Darius as a child and respected his father as a friend of India. Darius was dispatched to the border, and his copy portrayed the fury and futility of war, highlighted by quotes from the Indian troops. Darius' knowledge of Hindi and Urdu was invaluable in covering the Indian side of the war. He couldn't get a visa to cover the Chinese side. But his reporting was so original, so fresh from the trenches, that it attracted the attention of UPI editors in New York; and as soon as the war ended, they offered him a staff job. Darius was flattered. He gratefully accepted it.

"Your father would have been so proud," Raj had observed.

Darius worked in the Indian bureau for two years, living in a small apartment not far from the house in which he spent his early years. Then the summons from New York had come.

KANE RETURN NEWYORK SOONEST FOR ASSIGNMENT ON FOREIGN DESK BLUMER

Blumer turned out to be a grizzled veteran of six years with UPI. He had greeted Darius with a corncob pipe clenched tightly between his teeth.

"OK, hotshot, I wantcha to sit down with Gromwald and take in a feed from London."

"Washington Heights," Darius had said.

"Whaddya mean, 'Washington Heights'?" Jerry Blumer had growled.

"It's where you're from. Where you were raised."

There had been a gruff affinity between them from the beginning. Now they were approaching the Tel Aviv suburb of Herzliya. Darius reached inside his jacket and pulled out a plastic pouch of English tobacco and tossed it on Blumer's lap.

"And if you're very good, there's more where that came from."

"You're a prick, Darius. You know that?"

"I know; but your wife thinks I'm cute and your kids are crazy about me."

Darius could see the driver's reflection in the rearview mirror. Paul winked. The storm had passed.

"You know they're not going to bird for this, Jerry."

"That's New York's decision. I've got some demonstration footage that Gregor shot in Jerusalem this morning. They can always lay a map of Amman over your narration in New York; but if they want the demo and the arrival, we've got it for them."

"You're an incredible man, Jerry, you know that?"

"I know, I know. Now tell me the gossip from New York."

7

The Secretary's motorcade swung off Sderot Weizmann and onto Sderot Halevi, moving past the Knesset and the Monastery of the Cross.

The Israeli Foreign Minister had been talking about the raid on Amman Airport for a solid half hour. He knew when it had happened, how many men had been killed, the number of aircraft destroyed; and he used the attack to bolster his contention that Israel could ill afford to give up any territory on the West Bank without an ironclad non-belligerency guarantee from each of the confrontation states.

There was not the slightest doubt in Secretary Vandenberg's mind that Cohen knew nothing whatsoever about the identity or the motives of the attackers. He wanted to ask Thurber about Helen's whereabouts, but forced himself to wait.

The tennis players at the YMCA heard the sirens and crowded to the fence facing the King David Hotel. Both ends of Rechov Hamalech David were cordoned off by police, and there were sharpshooters on top of the Y building. Parked on the sidewalk, directly across from the King David, was an armored personnel carrier.

Secret Service Agent Nathaniel Brady wheeled the Secretary's Cadillac into the hotel driveway. Thurber said, "I want you to stay in the car."

"I always stay with the car," said Brady.

"I said 'in' it, Nat, not 'with' it." Thurber jumped out of the limousine before it had even stopped, slamming his own door, and then waited, with his hand on the rear door handle, until four of the agents from the follow-up car had taken up positions around the vehicle.

Thurber motioned to an agent from the advance team. Pointing in the direction of a portly man who stood impatiently at the entrance to the hotel, he asked, "Who's that?"

"He's the manager, Eric."

"Ask him to greet the Secretary inside."

Vandenberg and Cohen entered the lobby side by side. There was a burst of applause from the tourists who were gathered behind long, rectangular boxes of plastic plants at the far end of the lobby. Some-one yelled, "Stick it to the Arabs, Felix."

Vandenberg was within range of the shotgun microphones, the lobby flooded in light by the television crews. The Secretary pointed into the crowd. "Is that a new member of the Israeli negotiating team, Avi?"

There was laughter, and a barrage of questions from reporters, but Vandenberg never broke stride. As he stepped into the elevator, he touched Thurber's arm. "I want to see you in my suite." Then, almost as an afterthought, he reached out of the elevator to shake hands with the Israeli Foreign Minister. "Avi, I'll see you later this afternoon."

The Secretary rode to the sixth floor in silence. Bernardi was wait-ing in the hallway. "Felix, I've got the local station chief standing by if you want to talk to him."

"Yes. In a few minutes." Vandenberg looked at his watch. "Get Stew-art on the phone for me. He should be at the White House by now." Then, turning to the agent standing behind him, he said, "Eric, come in for a moment, will you?"

The living room of the suite was filled with floral arrangements and baskets of fruit. Vandenberg grabbed a handful of grapes and stepped to a window overlooking the Old City of Jerusalem.

"Have you made contact with Mrs. Vandenberg's party?"

"No, sir; but there's no reason to get alarmed yet."

Vandenberg continued to stare out the window. "Aren't you in radio contact with them?"

"No, sir. Your wife's security detail is a State Department detail. It doesn't have the kind of communications we have." Thurber sensed that the Secretary wanted more. "State Department security has only two men with your wife. They both left Amman with her this morn-ing. Staples stays with her at all times; the other man is probably with the helicopter. The Jordanians have been trying to raise the helicopter for the past couple of hours, but they say communication with Petra is marginal at the best of times." Thurber was still talking to the Secre-tary's back. "Look, sir, I don't like it either, but Petra's more than a hundred and fifteen miles from Amman."

Vandenberg had finished the grapes and was working on a cuticle again.

"Do they know yet who was responsible?"

"No, sir."

"Ask Bernardi to come in."

The agent began to leave.

"Eric?"

"Yessir."

"Do you think they were trying to kill me?"

The agent hesitated for an instant. "No, sir."

"Thank you."

It was, Thurber would recall later, the only time the Secretary of State had thanked him for anything.

Inside the suite, the phone rang.

"Mr. Secretary, I've got the White House on the line for you."

A pause. "Felix?" The scrambling device distorted the voice from Washington. "Is Helen all right?"

"We don't know, Harlan. They haven't made contact yet, but they say that's not unusual."

"What do you want us to do at this end?"

"Where's the *Forrestal?*"

Harlan Stewart consulted a folder already on his desk. "She's at Souda Bay."

"I want her to make preparations to put to sea."

"We'll get questions."

"I want identical statements put out at the White House and State briefings. Is your secretary on the line?"

"Yeah, go ahead."

"The United States deplores these senseless resorts to violence, no matter who is responsible. The U.S. government stands ready to do everything within its power to reconcile the legitimate aspirations of all parties in the Middle East seeking peace and justice, and it will not be deterred from this goal by those who perform or those who encourage reckless acts of terrorism."

"Is that it?"

"That's it. If they get any questions on the *Forrestal*, they can just say that they're not aware of any connection. The press'll draw its own conclusions. I'll clear all of this with the President when he gets up."

"Right." Harlan Stewart had been a military man all his professional life and was not given to lengthy dialogues.

"Harlan?"

"Yessir."

"You got my message on the Khamsin cable?"

"Got it."

"Everything I said before goes double now."

"Understood."

"I'll talk to you later."

The Under Secretary of State for Political Affairs had transferred a floral arrangement and a plateful of cookies to the floor and was already engaged in fanning out an immense stack of folders on the coffee table.

"I think before we do anything else, you ought to see Pedderson."

Vandenberg shrugged. "I suppose you're right."

The CIA station chief for Israel had an academic air about him. He would not have been out of place teaching comparative religion at Michigan State, which, indeed, he had once done and hoped fervently to do again. Tall, so thin his face seemed cadaverous, Owen Pedderson was by nature a pessimist. He had rarely been disappointed. Bernardi pointed him toward the couch.

"Is the room clean, Owen?"

"Within limits."

The Secretary of State turned in exasperation. "Now what the hell does that mean?"

"It means, Mr. Secretary, that short of tearing out the floor, the walls and the ceiling, we've swept the place as thoroughly as possible. But the Israelis are very good; this is their home turf, and I would not recommend that you regard this room as totally secure."

"What do you recommend? That we use sign language?"

"No, sir, I don't think that'll be necessary. But I do think we ought to activate the gibberish box and continue our conversation in the bathroom, with the water running."

Vandenberg exploded. "Goddammit, is there no end to all this madness?" He snapped up his folder and stomped toward the large bathroom. Pedderson calmly punched the play button on a large Sony recorder and the meaningless babble of half a dozen voices, simultaneously recorded, filled the room. Pedderson followed Vandenberg and Bernardi into the bathroom. The Secretary was already sitting on the toilet, and his Under Secretary was perched on the sink. The CIA station chief turned on the cold water in the tub. A sprinkle hit Vandenberg's face. The Secretary glared at Pedderson while wiping his cheek.

"Can we start now?" Vandenberg's voice was icy.

"Yessir." Pedderson ignored the Secretary's fury.

"What do we have on the attack?"

Pedderson opened his briefcase and handed a folder to the Secretary. "Here's the initial damage and casualty report. Amman believes the OLPP was responsible, and I tend to agree."

The Secretary scanned the report. ". . . 14 Hunter attack planes destroyed . . . 37 Jordanians killed . . . 62 wounded . . . extensive damage . . ." Vandenberg's attention was drawn to a supplementary report stapled to the main document.

Organization for the Liberation of the People of Palestine. One of a number of radical subdivisions of the Palestinian leadership, it was formed in 1967, shortly after the Israeli victory in the Six-Day War. Its manifesto, published in November 1974, proclaims a policy of "no negotiation, no recognition" of Israel. It denounced the American-sponsored disengagement agreements between Egypt and Syria on the one side and Israel on the other as "a sellout of the Palestinian people" and "a curse on the soul of the Arab nation." Although it has received arms from the Soviet Union, it has often criticized the Kremlin for "collaborating" with the "American imperialists and Zionist agents."

Dr. Jamaal Safat has been the undisputed leader of the OLPP since the spring of 1976, when Syria sent troops into Lebanon to fight against Palestinian troops. Since then, he has emerged as perhaps the foremost Palestinian leader in the Arab world. Born in Nablus of prominent, well-educated parents in 1939, Safat spent most of his boyhood in Jerusalem. After the 1956 war, his father moved the family to Beirut. Safat attended the French lycée and studied medicine at American University; his classmates included future Palestinian leaders, such as Wadi Hadad and George Habash.

Safat began his underground work in Damascus. In 1963, he opened a clinic which served as a cover for the Palestine Liberation Front. Four years later, he joined the OLPP and coordinated terrorist activities in Israel. In 1968, a year to the day after the Israeli victory in the '67 war, Safat expanded his activities to include terrorist attacks outside of Israel. He participated in the hijacking of an El Al airliner to Algeria. He established contact with West German, Japanese and Latin-American terrorists. In 1970, he masterminded the hijacking of three airliners to Jordan. In 1973, he organized the hijacking of a JAL airliner, and ordered its destruction at Benghazi Airport. In 1976, he helped hijack the Air France jet, which led to the Israeli rescue of hostages at Entebbe Airport in Uganda.

Safat is considered to be highly intelligent and completely ruthless . . .

Vandenberg's attention always flagged at the word "ruthless." It
was in every CIA report, and it could easily describe every Palestinian
leader. It said nothing. Vandenberg had discovered over the years that
any leader could be "ruthless." What mattered was *how* he used his
power: his style, finesse, subtlety, his flexibility.

"Who do you think was behind it, Owen?" Bernardi asked.

"Almost certainly the Libyans bankrolled it."

"Would the Russians have known about all this?" Vandenberg's
voice sounded gloomy.

"An operation of this scope, sir? It's hard to see how they couldn't."

"Do you think they were involved?"

Pedderson was studying the tile floor. "That I can't say, sir."

"You've seen Khamsin's report?"

"Frank showed it to me before I came in here."

"What do you make of it?"

Pedderson turned the water on more forcefully.

"Well, it's a meeting of the Rejectionist Front; there's no question
about that. The timing suggests that it may be meant to coincide with
the end of your trip."

"Hmm." Vandenberg was turning the thought over. "How the hell
do they know when my trip's going to be over?" He paused reflec-
tively. "Unless they have some plan for ending it. Look, Pedderson, I
know this is going to be difficult, but I want your people to find out
whatever they can about that meeting without alerting the Israelis."
Vandenberg stopped. "No, forget that. There's no way you can find
anything out here without the Israelis knowing what you're up to. I
may need to talk to you again later tonight."

Owen Pedderson knew that he had just been dismissed. Vandenberg stopped him before he reached the living room. "You ought to
know that the President is ordering the *Forrestal* out of Souda Bay
later today."

"What'll the Russians think, sir?"

"Exactly what I want them to think. That we hold them responsible
for whatever those maniacs in the Rejectionist Front do."

"Yessir. Anything else?"

Vandenberg nodded. "On your way out, turn that blasted machine
off before I lose my goddamn mind."

8

It had begun to snow in Jerusalem. One superstitious Israeli told Herb Kaufman that it meant black days for the Jewish state and that Vandenberg was at fault. The Secretary did not believe in omens, good or bad, but he cursed the weather. He hoped Helen was all right. She hadn't wanted to come on this trip; he had insisted. He was deep in his own thoughts when his car pulled into the driveway at the Prime Minister's office. More than fifty journalists and television technicians, dressed in heavy sweaters or parkas, pressed against the vertical bars of a portable barricade that had been erected on one side of the brightly lit entranceway.

A reporter for Kol Yisrael, the state-run radio station, hung precariously over the barricade, stretching a microphone in Secretary Vandenberg's direction. "What can you tell us about the attack, Mr. Secretary?"

Vandenberg paused under the overhang approach to the ministry. "You probably know more about it than I do," he said.

"How will this affect your negotiations?"

Vandenberg recognized Herb Kaufman's voice coming from the back of the crowd.

"I suspect, Herb, that I'll be in a much better position to judge the state of the negotiations if you let me go upstairs. However—"

Another reporter began to break in, but Kaufman overpowered him. "Will you let him answer the question, for crying out loud!"

"However," Vandenberg continued, "for our part, we do not intend to allow ourselves to be deflected from the search for a just and lasting peace in this area by senseless acts of violence."

The Prime Minister's spokesman stood in the lobby waiting for Vandenberg. "Mr. Secretary, the Prime Minister would like to meet privately with you for a few minutes. He's waiting for you in his office."

Ya'acov Ben-Dor was leaning against his secretary's cluttered desk. He conveyed not only self-confidence, but power. Ben-Dor was not tall, no more than five feet eight; but he had big bones, and he had lost little of his muscle tone to the flaccidness of middle age. His arms were short and strong, and despite the unaccustomed chill in the air, he wore a shirt open at the collar. His hair popped out of the sides of his head in two unkempt ginger tufts. His voice was deep, resonant, and he spoke, as always, slowly. Even when he spoke Hebrew, he never rushed.

"*Shalom*, Felix. It's never dull when you visit us."

"It's not exactly an ocean of tranquility when I stay away." Vandenberg embraced Ben-Dor. "*Shalom*, Ya'acov. How's Esther?"

"Busy," Ben-Dor answered. He smiled and put an arm around Vandenberg's shoulders. "Come inside. It's better we talk privately for a few minutes first."

The two men had first met more than thirty years before. At the height of World War II, Vandenberg had been assigned to the Office of Strategic Services, the forerunner of the CIA, and he had spent two years in the Middle East working for the British. There was no record of it in the State Department's Biographic Register, but Vandenberg had been seconded to Great Britain's External Security Agency, known as MI 6.

Vandenberg retained his interest in the area after the war, when the Palestine mandate became an excruciating headache to the British Foreign Office. The Labour Party, which came to power on the heels of Germany's surrender, had publicly expressed its sympathy for the establishment of a Jewish state in Palestine. That, in turn, laid the groundwork for an inevitable conflict between popular sentiment, which at that time was pro-Jewish, and the British Establishment, which insisted that the country's national interest lay in re-forming old alliances in the Arab world.

Vandenberg appreciated the agony of the problem. Europe was awash with DPs, the displaced persons who had somehow survived the death camps of Nazi Germany. President Truman recommended to the British government that it issue 100,000 immigration certificates to Jews wishing to settle in Palestine. Foreign Secretary Ernest Bevin vacillated under pressure from British oil interests and a hard core of Arabists within Whitehall. Bevin countered Truman's suggestion with the proposal that a joint Anglo-American commission be created to investigate the question. Truman agreed, and among those appointed to the American half of the commission was Felix Vandenberg.

Ya'acov Ben-Dor at that time was a squad leader in a commando strike force that spearheaded the Israeli struggle for independence.

Like many other Jews born in the Holy Land, Ben-Dor believed that it was necessary to use force to re-establish the state of Israel. He and Vandenberg were brought together by a mutual friend, a British journalist who had been one of Vandenberg's intelligence contacts.

They met at a waterfront café in Haifa and talked through the night. What impressed Vandenberg above all else was Ben-Dor's doggedness. Vandenberg had met other Zionists who expressed their convictions with far greater eloquence, but the very brilliance of their rhetoric always caused Vandenberg to dismiss them as ideologues, incapable of action. To Ben-Dor, however, a Jewish state was not just a reality; it was the only reality. Ben-Dor reached across the table, grabbing the young American by both wrists. "You will see, Vandenberg," he said; "it will be history's punishment of Adolf Hitler. He will become the architect of our homeland. This commission of yours is irrelevant. The world needs to salve its conscience for what Hitler did to us. We will take what is ours, and this time the world will not refuse."

The actual state of Israel would not become a reality for almost three years, but Felix Vandenberg had become convinced of its inevitability that night in December 1945. Ben-Dor convinced him that it would happen, and that it was right.

The Prime Minister of Israel reached for a pack of Kents that lay on the coffee table. His office was small, but his wife had furnished it with a sofa, an armchair and the coffee table, in addition to the Scandinavian desk squeezed into the corner. "If somebody comes to visit, where is he going to sit? On the desk?" Ya'acov had learned to lose arguments with his wife gracefully.

"You were thinking about it, too?" Ben-Dor asked.

"Haifa?" Vandenberg replied. "Yes."

"You know, Felix, I just happened to be rereading Mark Twain's *Innocents Abroad.*"

Vandenberg raised a quizzical eyebrow.

"Twain describes his visit to the Galilee in 1867, just before the first wave of Jewish immigration from Russia. Let me read you a passage." Ben-Dor pulled the book from his shelf. Vandenberg smiled tolerantly.

"'Of all the lands there are for dismal scenery,'" Ben-Dor quoted Twain, "'I think Palestine must be the prince. The hills are barren, they are dull of color, they are unpicturesque in shape. The valleys are unsightly deserts fringed with a feeble vegetation that has an expression about it of being sorrowful and despondent. The Dead Sea and the Sea of Galilee sleep in the midst of a vast stretch of hill and plain wherein the eye rests upon no pleasant tint, no striking object, no soft picture dreaming in a purple haze or mottled with the shadows of the clouds. Every outline is harsh, every feature is distinct, there is no perspective—distance works no enchantment here. It is a hopeless, dreary, heartbroken land.'"

Ben-Dor removed his reading glasses and replaced the book. His eyes seemed moist. "Felix, I've always liked you. You know that. Within limits I even trust you. But I'm under enormous pressure. The Jews deserve this land. It is promised. It is theirs. They reclaimed it from the arid land Twain described, and today Israel is a land of hope, of energy. Don't ask me to do what I can't. This attack at Amman is just what my political opponents are looking for." The Israeli lit a cigarette. "And if I know Mohammed, he hasn't sent you over here with a caseful of concessions."

Vandenberg said nothing.

Ben-Dor sighed. He was a practical man. "Maybe the time is not ripe, Felix."

Vandenberg was studying the palm of his hand. "What do you expect me to say, Ya'acov? That I'm sorry to have disturbed you? That we'll try to reschedule our meeting for some time when terrorists are out of season? The history of the Middle East is a history of lost opportunities."

Ben-Dor smiled. "When you start quoting Kissinger to me, then I know you're angry."

"I'm not angry. I'm perplexed. You want me to tell your negotiating team what a hard bargain I'm going to drive with the Jordanians? You know I don't operate that way. You tell me what you want from Mohammed, and what you're willing to give in return, and I'll tell you whether I think it's manageable."

Ben-Dor sounded subdued. "It's a bad time to start a negotiation."

"Ya'acov, when has it ever been a good time? You think it'll be better this summer, after the next OPEC meeting? Or while we're developing pre-election fever?" Vandenberg's tone was restrained, reassuring. "I know. Your political problems are enormous. But can you guarantee that you'll have a bigger majority after the next elections? You're a statesman, not a politician."

Ben-Dor sighed. "You would have made a marvelous Jew."

Vandenberg laughed. "Who knows? On my maternal grandfather's side they were never completely sure." Plucking a date from the dish in front of him, Vandenberg rose to his feet. "Ya'acov, if your constituents could only watch you in action. I haven't been in the building ten minutes and already you've read to me from Mark Twain, you've made me feel guilty and you've maneuvered me into a position of being grateful that you're letting me meet with your negotiating team."

Both men emerged from Ben-Dor's private office satisfied with the outcome of their preparatory talks. Ben-Dor had underlined the political pressures that would limit his flexibility. Vandenberg had suggested a loss in tactical position without giving away a thing.

The two of them walked through a side door into a big, rectangular room dominated by a long table and an army map of Israel, Jordan and the West Bank. Each shook hands with the members of the other's negotiating team, taking their seats, finally, across from each other at the center of the table. Their aides arrayed themselves in order of descending seniority toward the ends of the table.

Ben-Dor began the session.

"I am happy to welcome the Secretary of State and his distinguished colleagues to Israel. He appreciates, as I know we all do, that these may be the most difficult negotiations upon which we have ever embarked."

Vandenberg reached for a handful of nuts and dried apricots and settled himself back comfortably. Ben-Dor was still talking when Terence Jamieson entered the room carrying a cable. Jamieson's face was ashen.

Jamieson stood behind the Secretary, watching him unfold the cable. Everyone's attention was riveted on Vandenberg, but the Israeli Prime Minister kept talking. The designation at the top of the cable indicated its importance. It had come from the U.S. Embassy in Berne, Switzerland, by way of the White House.

FEBRUARY 8
291345Z TOP SECRET SPECAT EXCLUSIVE FOR SECRE-
    TARY VANDENBERG
DELIVER IMMEDIATELY
FLASH WHITE HOUSE
FROM STEWART
TO VANDENBERG
HEREWITH FULL TEXT CABLE JUST RECEIVED FROM
MARKMAN IN BERNE QUOTE ORGANIZATION FOR THE

LIBERATION OF THE PEOPLE OF PALESTINE CLAIMS
TO HAVE INNER QUOTE TAKEN CUSTODY END INNER
QUOTE OF MISSUS VANDENBERG STOP UNABLE TO
CONFIRM THIS END COMMA BUT CLAIM APPEARS TO
BE LEGITIMATE REGARDS MARKMAN END QUOTE
PRESIDENTS BEEN INFORMED STOP WHAT YOUR REC-
OMMENDATIONS QUERY REGARDS
STEWART

Vandenberg folded the cable carefully and placed it in the folder in front of him. He became aware of Jamieson still standing behind his chair. "No answer," he said quietly.

The negotiations continued for another two and a half hours without further interruption.

9

Three couches were drawn around the glass-topped coffee table, forming an open square in the center of the Secretary's living room. Vandenberg was pacing near the windows; Bernardi was sprawled on a couch with his feet on the table.

"You've got to call him, Felix!"

"I know that, dammit; but if I don't have a course of action carefully plotted in my own mind, that genius will take off on his own."

"For God's sake, Felix, it's been three hours since the cable came in. How long do you think you can put off something like this?"

Vandenberg stopped pacing and stared down into the garden below. More than two inches of wet snow lay incongruously on the palm trees under the windows. Facing Vandenberg was the wall of the Old City of Jerusalem, bracketed by Dormition Abbey on the right and David's Citadel on the left. The snow was still falling. "Helen would've been entranced by this. She's never seen Jerusalem in the snow."

Bernardi said nothing, but he thought he had heard a hoarseness in Vandenberg's voice. The Secretary enjoyed a well-earned reputation for coolness under pressure, but the scar on his upper lip was turning pink and a vein over his left eye was protruding. He was, in private, beginning to show the strain. Bernardi sympathized with his friend's situation. He knew that Felix and Helen loved each other, but it was more than love that had drawn them together. It was also a deep and mutual respect. Each admired the assets of the other, choosing to ignore the faults. How would Vandenberg respond?

The Secretary's voice cut into Bernardi's reverie. It seemed suddenly brisk. "All right, Frank. Let's talk about it. We've been through tough ones before. What do we know? Helen's been kidnapped; no question about that."

"None at all." Bernardi sounded relieved at the Secretary's changed demeanor. "They found Staples in Petra. They're helicoptering him back to Amman right now." Bernardi hesitated. "Unless you want us to make arrangements to bring him over here. I could clear it with the Foreign Ministry and have him brought across the Allenby Bridge."

The Secretary shook his head. "Maybe later. I've got to resolve some questions in my own mind. Is the OLPP acting on its own? And if so, what does Safat want?" Vandenberg pulled a pad of lined paper out of Bernardi's briefcase. "Frank, tell Jamieson I want the latest information on Safat. I want whatever our intelligence has." Vandenberg's mind was racing now. "There's been no ransom note, right?"

"Right."

"Well, that'll come soon enough. What do they want from us, Frank?"

"It may be what they don't want."

Vandenberg looked up.

"They may be trying to get you out of here, Felix. The last thing in the world they want is a negotiated West Bank solution between Israel and Jordan."

The Secretary was not convinced. "I'm not ruling anything out, Frank; but it would amount to shortsightedness bordering on stupidity. What are they going to do, keep Helen a permanent hostage? And if they didn't, what would prevent me from returning to the area the minute they released her?"

Bernardi walked over to a bar that had been set up in a corner of the suite. "They may not want to keep you out of the area forever." The Under Secretary put ice cubes in a glass and poured some tomato juice out of a pitcher. "Maybe they just want to cripple you for a week or two."

Vandenberg removed his glasses and massaged the bridge of his nose. "Khamsin's cable. The Rejectionist Front meeting."

"Exactly," said Bernardi.

"It's possible. That could be it."

They were interrupted by Jamieson. "It's another message from Berne, Mr. Secretary. I thought you'd want to see it right away."

Vandenberg examined the cable.

Bernardi said, "Terry, the Secretary wants the latest files on Safat. Put a particular emphasis on where he's been and who he's seen in the past month."

"Well, this answers our first question." Vandenberg extended the cable to Bernardi.

"I recognize Bishop Carucci's name. Who are the others?"

"They're all Palestinians who were working with Carucci, smuggling weapons. I think the last three were arrested over there in the Old City." Vandenberg nodded in that direction. "They'd set up a grenade factory in the Church of the Flagellation." He stopped himself. He seemed irritated. "What the hell does it matter who they are? They're in Israeli jails and that's where they're staying."

"Are you going to ask the Israelis?"

"There's nothing to ask. It's against their policy; and more to the point, it's against ours."

"That's not quite true." Bernardi's mind was like a file cabinet, from which he was able to draw any relevant fact to buttress his case. "The Israelis swapped terrorists for some of their people back in 1968 after one of their planes was hijacked to Algeria. A year later, if I'm not mistaken, they gave the Syrians several pilots and other prisoners of war in exchange for two Israelis who had been hijacked earlier in the year. And, of course, they considered dealing with the Palestinians during the Entebbe hijacking case."

"Yes, but except for the Entebbe case, the other exchanges were done secretly, and since then the Israelis have been very tough on terrorism. Besides, Ben-Dor's in power now, and he's a fanatic on this principle of not negotiating with terrorists." A sadness crept into his eyes. For a moment he looked away from Bernardi. "But I think your initial analysis was correct, Frank." His voice was again strong, his gaze direct. "This was a major operation. I'm not at all convinced that the OLPP is alone in this. They certainly didn't blow up Amman Airport and kidnap the wife of the American Secretary of State to free a bunch of second-rate terrorists from an Israeli jail."

Vandenberg picked up the phone. "Get me the White House. I want to talk to the President right away."

Vandenberg got up and began pacing again.

"Frank, I want you to set up a meeting for me with Ben-Dor." He looked at his watch. "Make it in forty-five minutes. I want this information limited to as few people as possible. Call the Embassy in Amman and tell them to sit on this as long as they can. Make sure the Jordanians understand. What time are we scheduled to take off for Aswan?"

Bernardi pulled out his wallet and consulted a schedule that his secretary had typed on a file card that morning. "Wheels up at nine."

"Make it seven."

"What do we tell the press?"

"Use your fertile imagination."

A buzzer sounded on the phone next to Vandenberg.

"They're getting the President for you, Mr. Secretary."

Bernardi said, "Do you want me to stay?"

Vandenberg shook his head. His voice dropped half an octave, to its most soothing range.

"Good morning, sir. . . . No, it's not exactly the most propitious beginning; in fact, it's worse than we originally thought. . . . I'm sorry, I'll speak up. Helen's been kidnapped by the OLPP; you know that already. . . . About six hours ago. . . . Yes, they're demanding the release of some OLPP terrorists being held by the Israelis. . . . No, I agree, sir, we can't do that. I'm going over to talk to Ben-Dor in a few minutes. . . . I don't believe they know yet. Mr. President, I don't know what role, if any, the Russians are playing in this, but I recommend that we move the *Forrestal* out of Souda Bay. It'll broaden our options a day or two from now, and in the meantime it puts the Kremlin on notice. I've given Stewart a statement that can be released at the White House this morning. I dictated it based on the Amman attack only, but I left it deliberately ambiguous to cover all contingencies. . . . Yes, sir, it'll still hold. . . . Thank you, Mr. President, I appreciate that. . . . No, I think it best that we keep the kidnapping quiet until I've had a chance to talk to the Egyptians. . . . Well, I think we have to assume that the negotiations will continue. . . . Yes, sir. . . . And, Mr. President, thank you again."

When Jamieson entered the room a few minutes later, he found the Secretary of State sitting dejectedly in an armchair, wearing nothing but his underwear. Vandenberg's clothes had been thrown on the couch. "Terry, get me a fresh change of clothes, will you? I'm going to take a quick shower."

The snow had crippled Jerusalem. Agent Nathaniel Brady insisted on driving the jeep himself. The limousine had fishtailed badly on the ride back from the Prime Minister's office earlier in the evening, and there was no point in running that risk twice. The jeep wasn't bullet-proof, but the Israelis were going to sandwich it between two other jeeps, with armored personnel carriers front and back. It was far from ideal, but it would have to do.

The streets of Jerusalem were empty, and the city looked exceptionally beautiful.

Esther Ben-Dor greeted Vandenberg at the door of the Prime Minister's residence. She kissed him on both cheeks. Mrs. Ben-Dor was a tall, dark sabra, the daughter of a wealthy Russian merchant who had come to Tel Aviv after the Bolshevik Revolution. She had been educated in London and spoke French, German and English fluently; she was, in fact, the compleat cosmopolitan, except that she managed to retain an old-fashioned attitude toward the role of women.

"Felix, how lovely to see you. Come in. Let me take your coat."

Vandenberg took the Prime Minister's wife by the arm. "Esther, I promise you, it was not my plan to destroy your evening. If there's one thing I can't afford to do, it's to alienate the wife of the Israeli Prime Minister."

"Felix, you're so silly. Come. Ya'acov's been waiting for you in his den. Would you like some coffee, perhaps a honey bun?"

"Please." Vandenberg nodded.

Ben-Dor's den was covered with photographs of his predecessors and maps of military campaigns in which he had participated.

He was wearing bedroom slippers, blue slacks and a white shirt open at the neck. "It must be bad news," he said. "No one would come out on a night like this to tell me anything good."

Vandenberg took off his jacket, loosened his tie and dropped into an armchair. "I've had better days, Ya'acov."

Reaching over for his jacket, the Secretary removed Stewart's cable and the latest one from Berne and handed them to the Israeli Prime Minister.

Ben-Dor whistled through his teeth. "Felix, you've got *tsuris*—problems. What are you going to do?"

"We're going to refuse. It's the only thing we can do."

"Look, I don't want to tell you how to run your business, but if you'll forgive me, this is as much our decision as yours. It's a small price to pay."

Vandenberg studied the other man closely. "No one'll ever accuse you of being predictable, Ya'acov. I appreciate the gesture," he said, hesitating, "but I can't accept."

"It's not a gesture and you must accept. I won't have Helen's life jeopardized for the sake of a few miserable terrorists. We've got everything we want out of them; and to tell you the truth, the good Bishop has become a bit of an embarrassment to us."

Vandenberg was openly skeptical. "Ya'acov, only this afternoon you lectured me on your political problems. The opposition will tear you apart if you let those people go; and they won't be alone."

Esther came into the den carrying a tray with coffee and buns. The Prime Minister spoke to her softly in Hebrew. She put the tray on his desk and left. Ben-Dor filled a cup and passed it to Vandenberg.

"Felix, what will happen if we don't pay the price?"

"The negotiations will continue."

"And then what? They send us a finger or a hand and you just keep talking? Are you that strong, Felix?"

Vandenberg reached for a bun.

"What if we do things your way? You think that'll be the end of it? They still won't let her go. There'll be other demands; and you and I will have set a precedent that neither one of us can afford to live with."

"I understand what you're saying, Felix, and I don't totally disagree with you. But there are greater issues at stake here and we need to buy time. You'll have to trust me. You're too close to this, and anyway"—Ben-Dor drained his cup of coffee—"the decision is mine."

There was a long pause and then Vandenberg said softly, "I'll disclaim it." He said it so quietly that for a moment the Israeli Prime Minister thought he might have been thinking out loud.

"What does that mean, Felix?"

"It means that I may have to disassociate myself publicly from your decision."

"I'm still not sure I understand."

When the Secretary of State replied, his voice was unsteady. "I mean that it is the policy of the United States government never to negotiate with terrorist groups, and most particularly not when it comes to meeting any ransom demands. I know there are exceptions. Rules can be broken. But not this one. Not this time. If you let those prisoners go, you'll be acting entirely on your own, and I will have to make it clear, publicly, that I opposed the decision and attempted to dissuade you from it." Vandenberg took a deep breath and let it out very slowly. "I may even be forced to say that neither the U.S. government nor I, personally, consider this act to be a favor."

Ben-Dor lit a cigarette and swallowed the smoke. As he spoke, the smoke trickled slowly out of his nose and mouth. "Other than that, though, you're in full agreement with my decision?" A thin smile creased the corners of his mouth.

Vandenberg said, "You're still going to do it?"

Ben-Dor shrugged.

"Then God help you, Ya'acov."

The Israeli smiled. "So far, Felix, He always has."

The drive from Herzliya to Jerusalem had taken almost three hours. For more than an hour of that time Paul had tried to nurse the big Ford up an icy slope between one of the mountain passes that lay a few miles outside Jerusalem. An Israeli police jeep had finally pushed them over the crest. Darius had fallen asleep while they were still passing through Tel Aviv.

Paul eased the car up to the entrance of the King David with an air of triumph. Darius was still asleep. Paul reached back and slapped him on the knee. "If you want to sleep in the car, I'm going to find a better place to park."

Darius consulted his watch. "How the hell can it be midnight already?"

Paul sounded noncommittal. "It took a little longer tonight."

Darius looked out and saw the snow. "Good Lord, Paul, how'd you get through the passes?"

Paul glowed. "No problem."

Darius unfolded himself from the back of the car. By the time Darius emerged, Paul had retrieved his camera bag and typewriter.

The lobby of the King David was empty except for an Israeli security official and two policewomen sitting behind a card table. The security man stopped Darius. "Your passport, please."

Darius fished in his pocket for the press badge that the Secret Service had issued.

The Israeli moved aside half a step, pointing at the badge. "Put it on, please. Your bags over there." He gestured at the table. One of the girls unzipped the bag. The other was filing her nails. She looked up at Darius and smiled.

"Busy day?" Darius asked.

She made a face and lifted her shoulders. "No English."

Paul was standing behind Darius. "What did I tell you? Learn a civilized language." He turned his attention to the policewoman and said something to her in Yiddish. She laughed. Paul took Darius' bag and typewriter. "You see? Yiddish she knows."

Darius took the two pieces from the driver. "Where are you staying, Paul?"

"Around the corner, at the Moriah. What time do you want me?"

"Depends on what time we're leaving." Darius spotted the *Newsweek* correspondent. "Colin! What's the schedule for tomorrow?"

"Bags outside your room at two A.M. Meet here in the lobby at six."

"You're kidding. I thought we weren't leaving till midmorning. What happened?"

"Ellis said something about the snow; but we're leaving by chopper, so I can't see what difference the snow makes."

Darius turned back to Paul. "If we're leaving by helicopter I don't see much sense in your being here at all in the morning. Get a good night's sleep."

"You can never tell. I'll be here by six."

Darius picked up his key at the front desk, a heavy bronze key, and headed for the bar. Kaufman and two Israeli journalists were sitting at a corner table with the Israeli Defense Minister. Kaufman spotted Darius in the doorway.

"Did the bird fly?"

The Defense Minister looked puzzled. He extended a hand to Darius. "What's the bird?"

"The satellite, the television satellite we use to transmit pictures back to the United States." Turning to Herb, Darius continued, "No, the bird did not fly." He sat down wearily. "By the time our executive producer in New York got back from lunch, it was too late to process all the film, cut it and feed the bird."

"He's the only one who decides when the bird flies?" It was the Defense Minister. From his tone of voice, it was clear that he was just making conversation.

"He's the one," Darius said. He waved at a waiter standing next to the bar. "I'd like a Gold Star beer, please." Turning back to the Defense Minister, he opened with the obvious question. "What do you make of the attack in Amman this morning?"

The Israeli drained his cognac. "We're talking off the record now?"

The Israeli reporters leaned forward in their chairs.

"I haven't any idea," said the Defense Minister.

The reporters leaned back.

Kaufman snorted. "He's been taking lessons from Vandenberg."

"The Secretary takes lessons from me." The Defense Minister rose to his feet. "Gentlemen, it's getting late."

The Israeli reporters followed him out into the lobby.

The UPI reporter pulled his chair next to Darius. "You ought to know that Vandenberg went over to see Ben-Dor at his home tonight."

"Anybody know what for?"

"If they do, they're not saying."

Darius began peeling the label off his beer bottle. "None of it makes any sense, Herb. They attack the airport after he's gone. Vandenberg spends three hours with the Israeli negotiating team this afternoon and then goes to see Ben-Dor at home in the middle of a blizzard. And Colin told me we're taking off two hours earlier in the morning."

Kaufman snared a pretzel with his ball-point. "You know what my first editor told me?" He nibbled at the pretzel. "When you're having trouble with a sentence, throw in a period. That's the way I'm starting to feel about this story. I'm going to bed."

"Where's everybody else?" said Darius.

"Most of 'em went to bed hours ago."

"I think your editor was right. Let's go."

"I'll play you one game of liar's poker."

Darius pulled a dollar out of his pocket, scanned the serial number —C14774607A—and said, "One eight."

"Challenge!" said Kauffman.

Darius grimaced. "I should've gone to bed about six hours ago." He handed the dollar to Herb.

10

The phone and the alarm rang at precisely the same moment, but Darius was already awake. He reached over to the night table, snapping down the button on his travel clock and lifting the receiver off its cradle before the second ring.

"Five o'clock, Mr. Kane."

"Thank you, Tali."

The operator sounded pleased. "How do you know my name?"

"Because you have the only voice in the world that makes me think of sex between four-forty-five and five-fifteen in the morning. So I asked."

"Think all you like." But she still sounded pleased.

Darius replaced the receiver and stretched out to his full length, his hands pressing against the wall behind him, his feet extending over the end of the bed. He stared up at the chandelier, then down at his toes, and tried to pin down the reason for the pleasant feeling of anticipation that was swirling inside him. Then it came to him—Aswan, and Katherine Chandler.

Actually there was no reason to assume that she would be there today; nor even that she would be pleased to see him. Their first meeting a few days earlier had been inauspicious enough. It was clear from the outset that Katherine Chandler could contain her enthusiasm for the American press corps.

"I'm Katherine Chandler," she said as they came down the rear ramp of the plane. "I'm temporarily assigned to the U.S. Embassy in Cairo. If you have any questions, I'll try to help you."

She was tall and aloof. Her voice carried the lilt of a Southern accent, but there was nothing inviting about her manner. She wore blue Levi's, and Darius remembered that the top two buttons of her blouse were open.

Herb Kaufman was in a foul mood that day. "I have a question," he yelled. "Where's the UPI man, where's the telex, and when's the next plane back to Tel Aviv?"

Katherine simply ignored his outburst. She seemed to be looking beyond Kaufman, her eyes fastening on Darius. "I'm told it's important that you all get on the press bus now so that we don't lose the motorcade."

Herb was not about to be crushed. "Important to whom?" he demanded. "What's important to me is finding the UPI man and the telex."

Katherine glanced down at her clipboard. Her voice remained level, but it had an icy quality that momentarily sobered them all. "You'll find, Mr. Kaufman, that both your colleague and the telex are waiting for you in a specially constructed press room on the first floor of the old Cataract Hotel." She then turned toward an antique bus provided by the Eygptian Tourist Agency.

On the ride into Aswan, the atmosphere became even colder. Herb began disparaging the bus, the driver, the desert, the Egyptian Air Force, the hotel, most especially the food. He kept chasing a fly away from the tip of his nose, and cursing.

"Do you know," he said to no one in particular, "that the Secret Service has a highly classified scoring system for rotation out of Aswan?"

The bus became uncharacteristically quiet.

"It's a ten-point system." A couple of his colleagues began to smile. "You get half a point for drinking the water or petting a dog; one point for having relations with a camel; and nine points"—the laughter was beginning to build—"nine points for a successful suicide."

Everyone laughed—except the driver, a heavyset Egyptian who pretended not to understand English; Katherine, who stared stony-faced at the passing scenery of parched villages and sleepy donkeys; and Darius, who could not be distracted from staring at Katherine's profile. He kept looking at the curve of her neck, hoping that she would sense his interest and respond with a glance or a smile. Katherine's hair seemed honey-colored in the bus shadow; it was pulled back in a short ponytail. She wore a blue-and-white kerchief on her head, gypsy style. Once she forced a stray lock under her kerchief. Darius had been studying her for the better part of a half hour, and he still couldn't make up his mind whether she wore make-up. Through the driver's rearview mirror, he could see that her eyes were blue, so blue they looked almost violet. As they approached the hotel, she caught Darius' gaze, and she held it until, slightly flushed, he glanced away, allowing his eyes to wander toward a giant poster of

Egyptian President Naguib el-Houssan that dominated the driveway leading to both the old and the new Cataract hotels. Darius was annoyed at himself for looking away.

As the bus bounced down the driveway toward the hotel garden, Katherine stood up, and Darius began to approach her. He was about to speak to her, when Herb interrupted.

"Don't apologize for me, Darius. I write good, clean copy, and that's all that's important."

If Katherine heard Herb's comment, she gave no sign of it. The bus lurched to a stop and everyone piled out, squinting in the blinding sunlight, clutching overnight bags and typewriters, and pairing off with local reporters and stringers to exchange the latest information. Herb raced through the garden, up a winding staircase, across a veranda filled with wicker chairs and low tables, past turban-topped waiters, into a dark lobby with rotating fans, and finally down a corridor to a makeshift press room. His colleagues were close behind him. Within a few minutes they were pounding madly on their typewriters and screaming into vintage telephones trying to get lines to Cairo or London so they could file their stories ahead of their competitors. Darius watched his colleagues from the doorway, hoping to catch the eye of the fat Egyptian technician who kept wiping the perspiration from his face and calling "Cairo" with a patience that would have won Job's admiration.

"MISTER KANE!" At last Jayel spotted Darius, and, like a puffing walrus, he waddled over to his friend and placed both his arms around Darius' shoulders, already weighted down with a travel bag, a tape recorder and a typewriter. They embraced in the usual Arab way, and by the time Jayel relaxed his grip, he was twenty Egyptian pounds richer and the National News Service circuit had leaped to number one on the waiting list. Darius wrote two radio spots and glanced over at Jayel, who was still calling Cairo, the transfer point for Rome, Paris, London and finally New York. "*CHAMDULA!*" Jayel cried. "Praise be to Allah; soon the circuit comes."

And indeed it came. Within five minutes, Darius had broadcast his spots, conferred with an editor for the morning and evening TV shows, and plotted the next day's logistics. "All yours," Darius said, nodding to his network colleagues as he picked his way through the tumult and out into the sun.

He paused on the veranda until he spotted an empty table. He signaled the waiter and ordered his favorite Egyptian coffee: *"Masbut, min fadlach."* Then he settled down in a low chair and looked out at the splendor of the Upper Nile. Darius never tired of its beauty. The great river of Egypt was dark and slow-moving. There were several small islands in midstream; around them moved six or seven graceful feluccas, their white sails spread to catch the approach of the evening breeze. Immense dunes rose on the other side of the river, casting long shadows toward the distant horizon. The elaborate tomb of the Aga Khan dominated a hilltop, looking like an angry octopus. On the nearest island, a large group of laborers were lifting gigantic boulders out of an excavated pit. They worked just as their ancestors had for centuries, and they chanted rhythmically as they tugged at the long ropes. Their chant filled the air, mingling incongruously with the chatter of Egyptian and American officials sipping their drinks around the Olympic-sized pool in the lush hotel garden.

Across the garden was the modernistic New Cataract, which the Russians had built in the early sixties to house their technicians working on the Aswan Dam. It was like any other Russian hotel: the architecture was unimpressive, and things tended to break down. The quisine was its least distinguished feature. The old Cataract, on the other hand, had character. It was an ornate Victorian structure built of sandstone—rambling, solid, eternal. Darius glanced up at the whitewashed balconies and mused about the fact that nearly a hundred years before, European royalty had sat on the same balconies, enjoying virtually the same scene.

The sky, so brilliantly clear all day, had changed subtly. Layers of deepening pink clouds spread across the far horizon. Beyond the tomb, the sky had turned vermilion, a dramatic backdrop against which tall, slender minarets were silhouetted. Overhead, bands of osprey circled the hotel in deceptive laziness. Occasionally, one of the hawklike birds would swoop down to the very surface of the Nile, hover for a tantalizing moment and suddenly plunge into the river, snap its prey in its beak and then zoom triumphantly into the heavens.

"Darius, my friend. There are other, more beautiful works of nature."

Darius recognized the voice of Hamdi Mafous, the diplomatic correspondent for *Al Ahram*, Egypt's semiofficial newspaper. He was seated at a nearby table, and he was referring to his attractive companion. At first Darius didn't recognize Katherine. She'd changed into a lemon-colored dress that billowed about her legs, and she'd removed her kerchief. The breeze blew strands of light hair across her face, and she was laughing. Mafous, his dark face crowned by a shock of wavy gray hair, had known Darius since the Geneva Conference of December 1973, known him both professionally and personally.

"Meet Miss Chandler of the U.S. Embassy."

Darius wanted to smile, but couldn't.

Katherine extended her hand. "Join us," she said simply, as though the strained crosscurrents of the bus ride had never happened.

Darius ordered another demitasse of Arab coffee.

"I was just trying to win Miss Chandler's confidence sufficiently for her to tell me the Secretary's opening position." Hamdi smiled, showing a broad row of tobacco-stained teeth. "But she claims she knows nothing except wake-up calls, luggage transfers, hotel reservations and Herb Kaufman's temper."

Darius caught Katherine's eye, as though in gentle reprimand.

Hamdi continued, "Miss Chandler should have been an Arab. I doubt if there are fifty Egyptians who know more about our history and customs than this lovely lady." Katherine uttered something in Arabic, and Hamdi burst into laughter. "I see my wife fraternizing with your colleagues, Darius." Hamdi stood up. "I'd best save her from the imperialistic Zionist press." Again he smiled, and then, with an elaborate bow, he kissed Katherine's hand, waved at Darius and majestically left the scene.

"What was so funny?" Darius asked.

"I told him that if I'd been born an Arab, my father would have married me off at thirteen and I would have known nothing except washing and diapering babies."

There was an uncomfortable lull as the waiter arrived with fresh cups of coffee.

"I had no idea you spoke Arabic."

Katherine fidgeted with her walkie-talkie. Darius noticed, with an inner sense of satisfaction, that she was losing some of her glacial composure.

"How old are you?" The question had simply popped out of him, and he squirmed, even now, when he thought about it.

"Thirty-three." Her voice had softened.

"I'd like to talk to you about Herb," Darius said.

"He asked you not to apologize."

"I wasn't going to apologize. I'd just like to try to explain. He's a good man, and an excellent reporter. A real pro. But these trips terrify him. He sees Israel as the only good thing that's happened to the Jews in more than two thousand years. He lost some of his family in the Nazi camps, and he's worried sick that the same kind of thing could happen here. Every time we come on one of these trips, he thinks the Israelis are going to get shafted."

"You didn't have to tell me that." It wasn't a reproach.

"I wanted to. Herb's one of the few truly decent people I know."

Just before the walkie-talkie interrupted them, Katherine smiled at Darius and there had been a feeling of gentleness between them.

It was that feeling that stirred Darius now as he lifted himself out of bed. That and the hope that Katherine would be standing again at the foot of the ramp in Aswan later that morning.

Darius was leaning against the tiles, half dozing under the shower, when the bathroom phone rang.

"Mr. Darius Kane?" It was one of the overnight operators at National News Service. "Is this Mr. Kane?" She had an infuriatingly patient voice.

Darius collapsed in a puddle on the toilet seat. "This is Mr. Kane."

"I have Harvey Porter in New York for you."

Darius grunted.

Harvey was the overnight editor at radio news. He'd had many chances to work days but preferred nights. He was conscientious, soft-spoken and professional.

"Darius? I didn't wake you, did I?"

"No, that's OK, Harv, your call must've been delayed. I've been up for ten minutes already."

Porter said, "Do you have anything for us?"

Darius spat into the bathtub. "Yeah, wait a minute, I'll go get it."

He placed the receiver in the sink, grabbed a towel and dried himself off. Then he dried off the toilet seat, retrieved the phone and placed it on the towel. After he had combed his hair and brushed his teeth, Darius picked up the phone again.

"Harvey? I had trouble finding the script. Are you ready?"

"Can you give us a line for level, Darius?"

"Sure. Secretary of State Felix Vandenberg called an early-morning news conference here in Jerusalem today to announce his resignation."

Porter sounded offended. "All right. Give us a countdown and go."
Darius stared at the ceiling for a moment.

"Five . . . four . . . three . . . two . . . one . . . Secretary of State
Felix Vandenberg is due to leave Jerusalem before dawn today for a
round of consultations with Egyptian President Naguib el-Houssan.
Vandenberg made an unscheduled stop late last night at the home of
Israeli Prime Minister Ya'acov Ben-Dor in the wake of a three-hour
negotiating session yesterday afternoon. The purpose of the late meeting has yet to be explained, but it was apparently related to yesterday's terrorist attack on Amman Airport. That attack will almost certainly be high on the agenda of topics to be discussed with Egyptian
leaders in Aswan later today. What still remains to be determined is
whether the raid in Jordan will affect the current round of Vandenberg's shuttle diplomacy. This is Darius Kane, National News Service,
Jerusalem."

Harvey was back on the line. He sounded irritable. "That was forty-
four seconds, Darius."

"So?"

"Could you trim it by about five? We're not supposed to take in
anything over forty. We prefer thirty-five."

"Edit out the last line, Harvey. I gotta go."

Porter was reluctant. "When are we going to hear from you again?"

"I'll tell you what," said Darius, "book a circuit into the Cataract
Hotel for 1000 GMT." He picked up his watch from the sink. "Harv, if
I don't go now, I'll miss the chopper." He hung up the phone.

The helicopters were parked on the soccer field behind the YMCA.
The reporters and members of the Secretary's staff carried their hand
baggage across the frozen field. They climbed up the tail ramps, into
the bellies of the helicopters, collapsing in the canvas seats along the
inner walls of the aircraft. Within a few minutes, half of them were
asleep.

The flight to Ben-Gurion Airport was choppy, but it took only
twenty minutes. The Judean Hills were covered with patches of snow,
but the plains running down toward Tel Aviv were green. In the
dawn mist, the lights of the airport were indistinct. A light drizzle was
falling. The helicopters taxied to positions less than a hundred yards
from the Secretary's plane. Long candles of light shivered across the
tarmac.

The Explosive Ordnance Detail, three men, huddled at the foot of the rear ramp, their collars up protectively against the wind. Each man held a flashlight. The reporters stood in line, waiting impatiently for their hand baggage to be examined.

"Gene," Darius rasped as he stepped into the plane, "I don't care what it is, just so it's hot."

The Air Force steward was almost obscenely cheerful. "I got hot chocolate for everyone; and soon as we take off we got scrambled eggs and sausages."

"Hold the sausages on mine." Herb was slouching through the galley toward his seat.

"They're kosher, Mr. Kaufman. We got 'em here."

Herb smiled. "If you got any extras, wrap 'em up for me. I'll take 'em along for lunch."

"Has anyone seen Ellis?" It was Gloria.

"Are you kidding?" said Herb. "Why would he hang around us? He's the press secretary."

The press corps was beginning to wake up.

Within a few minutes, Vandenberg's helicopter settled down on the tarmac about fifty yards from the nose of the Boeing. There was some last-minute conversation between the Secretary and the Israeli Foreign Minister, and then the Secretary was bounding up the steps of his plane, waving nonchalantly at the steward. Takeoff followed within ninety seconds; all traffic to and from Ben-Gurion was cleared for the Secretary's departure.

Ellis appeared while breakfast was being served. They were all trapped behind their trays. He had an armful of papers. "These are your vehicle and room assignments."

"When's the Secretary seeing us?" someone called out.

Ellis coughed. "The Secretary's not going to be able to meet with you until after he's seen President Houssan."

Gloria was indignant. "Carl, the attack on Amman Airport was almost twenty-four hours ago, and we haven't had a chance to talk to him yet."

"He's aware of that, Gloria. He's just too busy to see you right now."

Kaufman looked up at Ellis. His face was a mask of innocence. "Is the Secretary on the plane?"

"Yes, Herb, he's on the plane."

"But he won't see us and we can't see him."

"That's what I just explained."

Kaufman went through the pantomime of typing on his tray. "Secretary of State Felix J. Vandenberg reportedly left Israel today, according to State Department spokesman Carl Ellis; however, this could not be confirmed by reporters traveling aboard the Secretary's plane."

Ellis permitted himself a tight smile. "Wise guys."

Dawn broke over the Sinai, flooding the cabin with a soft reddish glow. Some of the reporters were going through copies of the *Jerusalem Post;* others slept. Darius was watching the Secret Service agents at the front of the cabin. He slid out of his seat and wandered down the aisle, stopping next to Eric Thurber.

"No game?" Darius queried.

"Too early," Thurber replied.

"I've never known you guys to miss a game since you started heading up the detail." The agents usually played a suicidal game of three-card poker at their end of the cabin, while the reporters played liar's poker at the back end.

Thurber smiled. "Tired."

Darius squatted in the aisle next to Thurber. "Something's gone wrong, hasn't it?"

"Look, Darius, you're a nice fellow and I'm sorry if this sounds rude, but I just can't talk to you."

As Darius rose, Thurber nodded across the aisle at several other agents. "They can't talk to you either."

"That bad, huh?"

Thurber looked up at Darius. There was a nod, so slight that Darius was probably the only one to catch it.

The tropical sun burned the overcast into a fine mist as the Boeing roared south-southwest toward Aswan. Only thin lines of cloud now framed the desert wasteland. Occasionally a mountain peak broke the flatness of the terrain.

After an hour and forty-five minutes, the outskirts of Aswan appeared in the distance. The 707 banked toward the military airport north of the city, flying over the High Dam, which the Russians had taken more than ten years to complete. Darius spotted camouflaged bunkers. He assumed that these sheltered the ZSU-23-4 self-propelled antiaircraft guns and dozens of the SAM-2, SAM-3 and SAM-6 antiaircraft missiles that were known to ring the airport. On the approach to the airport, there were other bunkers, more carefully camouflaged. They sheltered Egypt's most sophisticated jet fighter planes. These bunkers were so artfully designed that the first time Darius had flown into Aswan, even from an altitude of a few hundred feet, he had been unable to spot them. Now the slightest ripple in the sand, the odd shape of a dune, alerted Darius to the military secrets that lay just beneath the surface of the land.

The Egyptian Air Force was still principally equipped with Soviet aircraft. A trickle of spare parts for the MIG-21s and MIG-23s had been resumed by the Kremlin when Naguib el-Houssan had invited a high-ranking Soviet delegation to visit him in Cairo; but Soviet-Egyptian relations remained frosty, and Houssan had ordered his Air Force to rely more heavily on the Mirage V and Mirage F1s that had been purchased from France by the Saudi Arabians and then donated to the Egyptian government.

The People's Republic of China had been able to provide some spare parts for the older MIGs in the Egyptian Air Force, but that had turned out to have been more of a political gesture than anything else.

Conspicuously parked alongside the bumpy runway, however, were six American-built C-130 cargo planes. The Secretary couldn't have missed them as his 707 landed.

Fitzpatrick poked Darius and pointed out the window. "Think he's trying to tell us something?"

Darius grinned. "He's trolling. Somebody told him that if you leave C-130s standing by a runway, you can catch Phantoms with them."

Towering next to the drab terminal building at the far end of the runway was another gigantic poster of President Houssan, resplendent in a field marshal's uniform. Waiting between two rows of Egyptian troops, equally resplendent in a gray sharkskin suit, was the Egyptian Foreign Minister, Sharawi el-Hanut. Once Egypt's Minister of Tourism, the cosmopolitan Hanut served Houssan's aim of projecting a pro-Western tilt to his essentially nationalistic policy.

"Ah, my friend." Hanut glowed as Vandenberg descended the steps into his Arab embrace. Their heads bobbed in the traditional manner. Egyptian and American cameramen and reporters shouted for the Secretary to approach their perch on the barricaded terrace of the terminal building. Vandenberg waved and smiled, but he did not move. Instead he nodded toward Thurber, who quickly motioned the Secretary's limousine into position. Vandenberg whispered something to Hanut, who told the hot and frustrated newsmen that perhaps the

Secretary would hold a brief news conference *after* his meeting with the Egyptian leader.

Vandenberg and Hanut got into the limousine from opposite sides. A dozen Egyptian motorcycle police kicked their snarling bikes into gear; they were doing forty by the time they left the airport. Struggling to keep the pace was an old jeep bearing American and Egyptian Secret Service men. The Americans looked grim, and they made no effort to conceal their Uzis. Thurber distrusted Egyptian security. He rode with the Secretary. The backup car, which appeared to be a locally rented taxi, was crammed with three other American agents, their sawed-off shotguns resting on the open windows. The driver was Egyptian.

Darius had not boarded the press bus; he was scanning the dispersing crowd.

"She's not here." The voice came from behind him. It was Hamdi Mafous.

Darius experienced a slight sinking sensation. "You don't miss much, do you, Hamdi?"

The Egyptian wore a broad smile. "I'm an excellent observer. Like you, my friend. How are you?"

"I'm tired. I'm in a rotten mood and I wish I knew what was going on."

Hamdi's smile only seemed to grow. "I can help you with the first two; and if I know you, my friend, you won't permit the third condition to exist for too long." Hamdi waved toward an ancient Chevrolet. "Come. You'll drive in with me. The car is distinctive. It may have the last functioning air-conditioning unit in all of Egypt. You can nap on the way."

Darius was feeling depressed. "That's nice of you, Hamdi, but are you driving to the hotel?"

"No. We'll drive directly to the residence."

Darius seemed reluctant. "I've got a twelve o'clock circuit."

"Twelve!" Hamdi picked up Darius' typewriter and began moving toward the Chevrolet. "That's almost three hours from now, if"—he paused significantly—"if your circuit is on time. Has that ever happened?" He didn't wait for an answer. "Oh, and incidentally, the lovely Miss Chandler is handling press arrangements at the residence." Hamdi took Darius by the arm. "I was right, no? Two out of three."

Darius felt a rush of adrenaline. "Two out of three, you sonova-bitch."

Hamdi's driver pushed the Chevrolet like a man possessed. They were doing eighty as they roared past the lumbering press bus. Darius waved at his colleagues. Settling back into his seat, he turned to Hamdi. "Tell me about her."

The Egyptian pulled a cigar from his pocket. "Sharawi gave me a few of these." He lit his cigar with a Zippo. "There's not really a great deal I can tell. She comes to Egypt only on a few occasions. I've met her several times in Geneva. She's a political officer at the Embassy in Beirut. She speaks beautiful Arabic. I don't think she's ever been married. And"—he paused, with a twinkle in his eye—"I think she lives alone." Hamdi drew on his cigar, content with a job well done. "That's all."

"That's all!" exclaimed Darius. "That's magnificent. That calls for a cigar."

Hamdi reached into his breast pocket. "You wouldn't be offended if the cigar was Cuban?"

"You're such an old friend, Hamdi, I'll suppress my sense of moral indignation."

The sweet fragrance of jasmine drifted through the open window, mixing unhappily with the cigar smoke.

Coming up quickly on the right was the old Aswan Dam, which the British had built in 1902. The lazy waters of the Nile were backed up against huge boulders. Egyptian soldiers stood in sandbagged emplacements, posing dramatically behind antiaircraft guns. They scanned the horizon.

"Are they expecting company?" Darius tried to be serious.

Hamdi laughed. "You! They've been told that the American press would be here today, and that they should look alert."

The Chevrolet rolled to the foot of the dam before making a sharp left to the presidential compound. The driver had been honking the horn imperiously every twenty to thirty seconds from the moment they left the airport. He gave the horn one final blast before bringing the car to a screeching halt.

A member of the presidential guard approached the rear window, which Hamdi had already lowered. The guard saluted; he was deferential to Hamdi, but firm. They would have to walk the final fifty yards to a swinging barricade, which blocked access to the compound. There was a further exchange in Arabic between Hamdi and the guard. Darius recognized his own name, and Vandenberg's. The guard shook his head.

Hamdi turned to Darius; he seemed apologetic. "He says you must have a pass."

Darius pointed to the wrinkled plastic diamond-shaped pass that was clipped to his coat pocket. He also reached into his wallet for his White House and State Department passes. Hamdi again conferred with the guard, but to little avail.

"He asks you to wait."

The guard spoke into a walkie-talkie.

Within a few minutes, Katherine emerged from behind a walled garden in the compound. She was back in Levi's and sandals, her hair again hidden beneath a kerchief. She held her head high, conveying an impression of professionalism. She spoke quietly to the guard; only then did she approach Darius. Her eyes seemed angry, but her voice was level and cool. "I'm sorry, Mr. Kane, but your pass is back at the hotel. The press isn't supposed to be up here for"—she consulted her wristwatch—"for at least another two hours."

Darius suppressed an obscenity and forced a smile. "I wonder if I might speak to you privately for a moment, Miss Chandler." Before she could reply, he took her by the arm and guided her toward a bench under a eucalyptus tree. "My first inclination, Katherine, is to tell you to take that walkie-talkie and stick it where the sun don't shine; but that would not only be rude"—she pulled her arm away—"it would also be counter-productive."

"Well, I'm delighted that you have such iron self-control." She was angry. But Darius knew that he had her attention.

"Let me finish," he said. "I don't know how many years it's been since I've woken up feeling that the day held something special, but that's how I felt this morning. For a while, I didn't even know why, and then I realized that I was looking forward to seeing you. You think I don't know that my goddamn pass is down at the hotel? Hamdi told me you were up here and I thought we might have the chance to talk alone for a few minutes before the whole mob shows up." He mimicked her, "'I'm sorry, Mr. Kane, but the press won't be up here for at least another two hours.' Jesus," he exploded, "two hours! I've known courtships that took less time."

Katherine still wasn't smiling, but he could tell that her anger had passed. "That might be a little too ambitious," she said. There was an awkward pause. "Want some coffee? Maybe I can get some." She walked over to the guard, chatted for a moment, then beckoned to Darius. The barricade was lifted. Katherine led Darius into the garden of one of the villas near the President's mansion. The garden was on a terraced hillside, shaded by a tall hibiscus hedge. Egyptian security men were positioned at each level.

Katherine and Darius sat down on two wicker chairs near a small table. For several minutes, they said nothing. Katherine removed her kerchief and shook her hair loose. She glanced at Darius.

"You're an arrogant bastard, aren't you?"

Darius ignored the comment and stared back at Katherine, unsmiling. "How come you never married?"

Katherine laughed. "None of your damn business. Why didn't you?"

"Too busy, and I guess I hadn't met the right woman."

"Yes, I suppose that's what I would've said if I wasn't being flip."

A black waiter in a white jacket arrived with two slim cups of coffee.

"Why are you?" Darius asked.

"Why am I what?"

"So flip, so professional."

Katherine sipped her coffee slowly, as though she was trying to decide whether to answer him at all. Then she broke the momentary silence. "Look at us, Darius. I let you con me into slipping away for an hour or so, so we can"—she glanced away—"so we can poke at each other's calluses. And then what? Later today you go your way and I go mine. But meantime I'm supposed to get all mushy 'cause you got up this morning feeling like the Scarlet Pimpernel on a new mission."

It had all come out in a rush. Darius was grinning. "You like me." He seemed genuinely surprised.

"Yes, I like you. What am I supposed to do about it? Go running into the President's villa shouting 'Lawdy, lawdy, Mr. Secretary, I cain't work fo' yo' today; Darius Kane is gonna give me an hour of his precious time'?"

Darius was feeling much better. "Would he miss you?"

"Damn right, he'd miss me. If it weren't for me, he'd never get the right amount of starch in his shirts."

"Well, I wouldn't want that on my conscience." Darius tipped his chair back. "Kathy," he said, "you're a fantastic lady, you know that?"

"Yeah, I know," she responded glumly. "Do me a favor, huh? Don't call me Kathy. Call me Katherine, call me Chandler, call me Hey, you, but I hate Kathy. It makes me feel as though I'd spilled egg on my blouse."

"How about Kat?" he said. "You like Kat?"

"First guy I ever went with called me Kat."

"Yeah? What's he doing now?"

"He's Secretary of State."

Darius just barely retained his balance. "You're kidding!"

Katherine's smile was radiant. "Yes," she said, "I'm kidding. You were starting to look so smug I couldn't stand it."

Darius reached over and put his hand over hers. He felt Katherine's fingers become intertwined with his own. Her voice was gently mocking.

"Sure," she said, "you start off holding hands, and the next thing you know he's got you in the back of Hamdi's car for some heavy necking."

"Oh, shit," exclaimed Darius, "I forgot all about Hamdi. Where the hell is he?"

"He took off the minute you went into your *macho* act back there." Katherine was running a finger lightly across the back of his hand.

Darius said, "Do you think the waiter would be shocked if I kissed you?"

She looked terribly serious. "He would not only be shocked; he would be scandalized." But her finger never stopped tracing its pattern along the back of his hand.

"He really would be, wouldn't he?"

"What?" Katherine's voice sounded husky.

"Scandalized."

She nodded.

Darius rose from his chair and approached Katherine. He held her face between his hands and kissed her very gently on the tip of her nose. Katherine had closed her eyes. He kissed her again, just as gently, on the lips. When she opened her eyes a moment later, Darius was still very close, smiling so warmly she couldn't help smiling back. Impulsively she kissed him on the forehead.

"Drink your coffee, Kane." Katherine pulled her hair back in a ponytail and smiled. "This isn't the time or the place."

There was the crackle of static from Katherine's walkie-talkie. She reached over and fiddled with the squelch knob. A voice blasted into the stillness of the garden. "Chandler, Chandler, this is Reagan."

Katherine picked up the instrument. "Chandler."

The voice sounded relieved. "Where? The press is bugging me about some meeting with the Secretary that nobody down here seems to know anything about."

Katherine wrinkled her nose at Darius.

"Start gathering your flock," she told the walkie-talkie. "You probably ought to leave there with the buses in about half an hour."

"Half an hour. Understood."

Katherine touched Darius' face for a moment and then rose from her chair. "You're a pain in the ass, Kane, you know that? Why didn'tcha pick your pass up at the hotel like everybody else?"

11

Secretary Vandenberg had informed President Naguib el-Houssan about the kidnapping and the ransom demand; now he was toying with the idea of telling the Egyptian leader that the Israelis were prepared to meet the ransom demand. He decided against it for the moment.

The two men were seated, without advisers, in a gazebo in the garden of the presidential villa. The view, overlooking the low dam, was spectacular. The six hundred miles from Cairo due south to Aswan had carried the President from the damp chill of the capital to the dry, desert warmth of the Upper Nile. Houssan suffered from bronchitis, and Aswan was penciled into his calendar every February.

"The Israelis have refused, of course." From the moment Vandenberg had outlined his problem, the Egyptian leader had been grave and solicitous. His voice was deep—"made for a Shakespearean role," as Vandenberg had once remarked to Bernardi—and his English was inflected with a German accent, acquired when Houssan had studied in Nazi Germany. Although he firmly maintained that he had been born of an Alexandrian family dating back several generations, Houssan looked Nubian; his complexion was quite dark, and his features, especially his nose, seemed almost African.

Vandenberg shrugged. "It's never easy to predict what Ben-Dor will do. In any event, he knows what my position is."

Houssan puffed thoughtfully on his pipe and raised an eyebrow. Vandenberg recognized the gesture as a question.

"My position is clear. The United States does not deal with terrorists."

Houssan was a fox. "And Ben-Dor shares your view."

Vandenberg refused to be trapped. "In principle, yes."

Even in English, Houssan did not miss many nuances. "Felix," he said, "you must be frank with me. Ben-Dor has agreed to release the prisoners, has he not?"

The Secretary of State did not show his discomfort. "Naguib, there's no point in my telling you in which direction Ben-Dor was leaning the last time he and I spoke. He had a Cabinet meeting planned for early this morning. I'm expecting word momentarily."

Houssan was bothered by the inconsistencies. "Why did you leave Israel before the conclusion of the Cabinet meeting?"

Vandenberg was back on safe ground again. "I felt it would be more appropriate if the news of Helen's kidnapping was announced here. It'll leak quickly enough after the Cabinet meeting in Jerusalem." Vandenberg paced as he spoke. "My feeling was that if the news was formally made public here, it would underscore the fact that responsible leaders in the Arab world oppose such terrorism as strenuously as we do." Vandenberg sensed Houssan's continuing skepticism. He decided to modify his tactics. "The decision to come here as early as possible was made before I saw Ben-Dor last night, but I think your instincts are right, Naguib. I also think the Israelis are going to meet the ransom demand."

Houssan was gazing out over the water. The surface was broken by sensational rock formations. "Why? Why would they do that?"

Vandenberg decided to gamble. "You understand, Naguib, I'm only speculating; but if, as we've heard, the Rejectionist Front is planning a meeting in Damascus, the Israelis could be making plans of their own. In which case, they would want to be able to demonstrate later on that they made every possible effort to avoid violence."

Houssan was tugging on the ends of his mustache. "You think there's going to be war, Felix?"

"What would any prudent man conclude? The kidnapping of my wife, Naguib—that was no random act of violence. It was carried out in force and executed with precision. The ransom demand is ridiculous. It's inconsistent with the dimensions of the act."

Houssan completed the thought. "Unless they're buying time."

"Exactly."

"But if the Israelis release the prisoners?"

"Then there'll be another demand." Vandenberg leaned forward, placing his hand on the Egyptian President's arm. "Naguib, everything we've worked for, you and I, hangs in the balance. If there's another war, your options will be severely limited. Sooner or later, you'll be dragged into it." The American Secretary of State sat back and adjusted the crease in his trousers. "Mr. President, these negotiations must not be allowed to fail."

Houssan relit his pipe. He spoke between puffs. "These days, Mr. Secretary, you may have better sources in Damascus than I do; but we have also heard about the Rejectionist Front meeting, and I share your concern. You may rest assured that all our resources will be put to the task of finding our dear Helen. I will be in immediate touch with my Jordanian brother to offer whatever counsel he may be inclined to accept."

"I shall be seeing him at dinner this evening. Shall I pass on your thinking?"

"No, my friend, I shall do so myself—by sending a personal envoy." He cleared his throat. "As always, Mr. Secretary, my admiration for your wisdom and your courage is without limits. Shall we meet with your press?"

"I'm very grateful, Mr. President. I think it best that we say nothing about the Damascus meeting."

Houssan gestured to an aide who stood waiting on a terrace of the villa. "Of course. But you will permit me to express my outrage at the senseless terrorism of yesterday?"

Felix Vandenberg smiled with what he hoped was suitable humility.

The camera crews and reporters cut through the presidential begonia beds like an assault force. They were met by a solid line of Egyptian and American security men. The jostling began to get nasty. The indignant voice of a German photographer cut through the noise of the crowd. The photographer was nose to nose with one of the American Secret Service men. "You people act like the goddamn Gestapo!"

The agent folded his arms and said nothing.

"I'm filing a formal complaint."

There was a ripple of laughter. "Do it after the press conference," someone yelled.

Several reporters and technicians squeezed past the security men and held microphones in front of Vandenberg and Houssan. The cameramen were still angling for a clear shot while trying to adjust focus.

Houssan surveyed the group. "Are you ready, gentlemen?"

Gloria's voice was reproachful. "I don't know about the gentlemen, Mr. President, but some of us are more than ready."

Neither Houssan nor Vandenberg smiled. The Egyptian President placed his pipe in an ashtray. "Please!" he said in a somber voice. "The Secretary of State has a very difficult announcement to make."

Vandenberg cleared his throat nervously. "Ladies and gentlemen, I know you're all aware of the fact that a rather major attack was launched yesterday morning on Amman Airport." The Secretary paused and coughed again. Only the whirring of the cameras disturbed the silence. "Shortly after that attack, there was a helicopter assault on Petra, where Mrs. Vandenberg was sightseeing. She has apparently been kidnapped by men claiming to be members of the OLPP." The reporters were scribbling furiously. Vandenberg continued. "The President would also like to make a brief statement."

"Questions, Mr. Secretary?"

"I'll take a couple of questions when the President has finished his remarks."

Houssan's voice floated across the garden, mellow and funereal. "We are, of course, deeply shocked to learn about the kidnapping of our dear friend Helen Vandenberg. This is not only outside the bounds of civilized behavior; it is an attempt to disrupt the peacemaking efforts of my good friend Felix. I have not only urged the American Secretary of State to continue his efforts, but I have assured him of my own cooperation in restoring his wife safely to him and also in maintaining the momentum toward a just and lasting peace in the Middle East."

There was a chorus of voices battling for the first question. Gloria's climbed above the rest.

"Mr. Secretary, you said that your wife's kidnappers 'claim' to be members of the OLPP. Do you have any doubts about the identity of the kidnappers, and secondly, has there been a ransom demand and do you intend to pay it?"

Vandenberg looked harried. "In answer to your first question,

Gloria, I'm only stating the obvious. Since we don't know definitively who kidnapped Helen, we're compelled to rely on certain communications that have come to us indirectly."

Gloria pressed the point. "Like a ransom note?"

Vandenberg nodded. "There has been a ransom demand; but I prefer, at this time, not to go into the nature of the message."

Darius forced his question above the clamor. "To follow up on Gloria's question, sir; it's always been U.S. policy to refuse to enter into any kind of relationship with, or to meet any demands of, terrorist organizations. Does that policy still hold?"

"Absolutely."

"And to follow that up, sir. Do you have any reason to believe that anybody outside the OLPP might have been involved in your wife's kidnapping?" Darius' voice was insistent.

Vandenberg caught his eye. "We're examining that possibility, Mr. Kane, but we have no reason at this time to believe that anyone else was involved."

"Do you know whether Mrs. Vandenberg is all right?" The question came from the back of the crowd.

"We know," responded Vandenberg, "that she wasn't harmed during the actual kidnapping, and we have no reason to believe that any harm has come to her since." He stood up. "I think that'll be all for now, if you don't mind."

The security men formed a corridor through which Vandenberg and the Egyptian President disappeared.

The Secretary's spokesman stepped into the gazebo. "If I could have the attention of the traveling press," Ellis shouted. "The press bus will be leaving for the airport in ten minutes!"

Darius tapped Ellis on the shoulder. "If it does, Carl, it'll be going half empty. You've got to give everybody a chance to file. We're taking the bus down to the hotel." Darius felt a tap on his shoulder.

"Follow me." It was Katherine. "I'll give you a lift."

The other reporters were already beginning to race back across the garden, the men from the wire services leading the pack.

Darius looked at Katherine thoughtfully. "Had you known that?"

"What?"

"That Mrs. Vandenberg had been kidnapped."

Katherine seemed to squirm as the Embassy car raced toward the old Cataract Hotel. She stared out the window.

"Darius, there may be times when I can help you, but most of the time I won't be able to. If we're to have any relationship at all, that must be understood." She looked at him with some of the old hardness.

"Understood," Darius answered. But he noted that she had artfully avoided his question.

The Secretary of State was approaching apoplexy. "I don't give a good goddamn if those idiots have to spend the rest of their lives in Aswan."

Ellis was weathering the storm as best he could by remaining silent. The press corps had, as Darius warned, been almost evenly divided. The reporters representing the weekly news-magazines and the specials, in this instance *The New York Times* and *Daily News*, the *Los Angeles Times*, the *Washington Post* and *Star*, *The Christian Science Monitor* and *The Wall Street Journal*, were aboard the plane. All of them had deadlines that could be met later that evening, when they returned to Amman. The reporters from the three wire services and the four networks, however, had been adamant. They had refused to leave without filing first. The wire service reporters called their bureaus in Cairo, dictating their bulletins and a few follow-up paragraphs; the men from the four networks agreed to place a single "pool" telephone call to NBC in New York, with the understanding that each of their reports would be recorded and passed on to the appropriate network with an agreed-upon release time. Placing that single call to New York, though, had taken forty-five minutes; and that, personnel from the U.S. Embassy agreed later, was a record that would likely stand for years to come.

Secretary Vandenberg, meanwhile, was in a mounting fury. "Did it ever occur to any of you half-wits that I might have more important things to do than sit on this goddamn plane waiting for those cretins to file their stories?"

Ellis turned to leave the cabin.

"Where the hell are you going, Ellis?"

"I'm going to check with communications, sir, and see how much longer it'll be."

Vandenberg snarled. "If it's more than five minutes, we're leaving without them."

"Yes, sir," said Ellis; but he was sure now that the Secretary was in the process of regaining his composure.

By the time the two Embassy cars carrying Darius and his colleagues raced onto the tarmac, the Secretary's departure had been delayed by more than an hour, and the state of agitation among American officials was so great that the ordnance detail was instructed to waive hand-baggage inspection, while four Secret Service agents were ordered to help the journalists on board with their bags.

Ellis was drenched with sweat. "You're never going to put me through that again," he said. "Never!"

Kaufman was mildly sympathetic. "Secretary give you a hard time, Carl?"

The aircraft was taxiing out to the runway.

"He is livid! He is furious! Don't you think that man is going through a difficult enough time without you people keeping his plane waiting for more than an hour?"

Darius said, "Carl, I know you've had a helluva time and nothing that any one of us says right now is going to make much of an impression on you, but you've got to get two things through your head. First of all, none of us works for the State Department. We have our own responsibilities; and when the Secretary of State announces that his wife has been kidnapped, you can't expect us to sit on that information for three or four hours until we get to our next stop."

Ellis started to say something, but Darius overrode him. "Second, it's your job to impress upon your boss that when he brings fourteen journalists along on these trips—" The thought was never completed. Sauntering down the aisle, steadying himself on the overhead luggage racks against the motion of the aircraft, came the Secretary of State.

"Ellis wanted me to leave you all behind," he said, "but I told him, 'If we don't get this information out on the networks, no one will ever know it happened.'" At that moment, to all outward appearances, Felix Vandenberg was the most relaxed man on the plane. "Did we get everybody?" said the Secretary.

"Yessir," said Ellis.

"Well, that's one problem off my mind," said Vandenberg, with only the trace of a smile. "I'll have you all up in a few minutes."

The representative of the *Washington Star* started to say something, but the Secretary cut her off. "No, really, Gloria. This time I mean it."

Midway through the flight, Vandenberg summoned the reporters to his conference cabin.

The Secretary was seated in his customary place at one end of a curved couch that wrapped around a kidney-shaped conference table.

There was a second couch on the other side of the cabin, and a huge swivel armchair was directly across the table from the Secretary.

It had become customary on these flights for the reporters to draw lots on the first leg. Each number represented a seat. The reporters moved up one number at each briefing. It was a self-imposed system that had evolved years before on the Kissinger shuttles, when the announcement of each briefing had produced an arm-flailing rush up the aisle. The interior cabin noise on these flights was such that several reporters invariably could neither hear nor be heard, therefore the need to rotate the seating equitably. The noise had also created another tradition. The Secretary of State, who always attended the briefings in the anonymous guise of "a senior U.S. official," permitted all briefings to be tape-recorded, with the understanding that the tapes were for note-taking purposes only, and that they would be destroyed, or wiped clean, as soon as the trip was over. Few, if any, of the reporters complied with this last understanding, giving rise to the anomalous situation that none of the Secretary's words were "on the record," although all of them existed on tape. The Secretary might well contradict in public something said by the "senior U.S. official" in private; but the taped evidence was useless, since the reporters had technically committed themselves to destroy it.

Secretary Vandenberg sat behind a ragged barricade of fourteen Sonys, waiting for the reporters to sort themselves out. Gloria was seated immediately next to Vandenberg.

"Mr. Secretary, I know I speak for everyone here when I say how terribly sorry we all are."

There was a murmur of agreement from those sitting close enough to hear. Fitzpatrick, seated on the far couch, growled, "What the hell are we agreeing to?"

"Gloria's expressing our sympathies," said the man from the *Los Angeles Times*.

"Thank you," said the Secretary. "Look, for obvious reasons, I'd like to keep this briefing on deep background, and short!"

There was silence for a moment, then Bernard Steinberg of *The New York Times* said, "Can you tell us anything more about the ransom demand?"

The Secretary seemed to be considering the question at some length. When he answered, he gave the impression that his words were being extracted under great pressure. "I'm in a very difficult position," Vandenberg replied, "in that the demand is not being made on us directly." He knew that it would be a matter of hours at most before the details of the ransom were public knowledge in Israel, and he had already decided to give the information to the reporters traveling with him; but Felix Vandenberg long ago had recognized that journalists place a far higher value on material that is grudgingly given.

"You mean," said Steinberg, a thin, nervous man in his late forties, "that neither the United States nor you, personally, are being asked to do anything?"

Vandenberg nodded thoughtfully.

"What are the Israelis being asked to give up now?" It was Kaufman.

"For once, Herb, your paranoia is justified."

"It's always justified," snapped Kaufman; "you just don't always admit it."

Vandenberg smiled ruefully. "The kidnappers are demanding the release of Bishop Carucci and five others whose names I don't think will mean anything to you."

Newsweek's Colin Campbell was seated in the chair directly across the table from Vandenberg. "Is that all they want?" he asked.

"That's what was in the ransom demand," said the Secretary.

"How was the demand delivered?" Fitzpatrick shouted from the rear.

"Wait a minute," said Gloria. "Wouldn't that take you off the hook? I mean, American policy may preclude the payment of ransom demands, but technically you can't prevent another government from meeting the ransom if they choose to."

The Secretary thrust out his lower lip, as though considering the question. Then he said, "I'd rather not get into that."

Gloria persisted. "Are the Israelis considering it?"

Vandenberg shook his head. "I'm not going to discuss Israeli policy."

Fitzpatrick's voice rose above the engine noise. "If Gloria's finished her private conversation, can somebody else get a question in?" He tried again. "How was the ransom demand delivered?"

"It was delivered to one of our embassies."

"Can you tell us which one?"

Vandenberg nodded. "I can, but I won't."

"Is it your feeling that the Israelis are going to release Carucci and the others?"

"I've said I don't want to get into what the Israelis may or may not do."

Darius was standing behind the armchair, leaning his notebook on the headrest. "I'd like to ask you a hypothetical question, Mr. Secretary. Let's assume that the Israelis release Carucci. Wouldn't it be logical to conclude that it was done under American pressure?"

Darius thought he detected a flash of anger in the Secretary's eyes.

"It's unworthy to suggest that the United States would pressure an ally into doing something that the U.S. government itself would refuse to do."

Steinberg asked, "Do you intend to continue the shuttle?"

Vandenberg smiled. "If it doesn't interfere too much with the filing deadlines of my traveling press corps."

There was a scattering of laughter.

Kaufman, as the senior wire service man, took the cue and ended the briefing. "Thank you, Mr. Secretary."

The reporters began filing out of the conference cabin.

Vandenberg whispered, "Darius, can I see you for a moment?" Only Ellis was left, still hovering. Vandenberg's tone was peremptory. "Alone!" Turning to Darius, the Secretary seemed to slump a little. "Let's go up to my cabin."

Vandenberg led the way to his private stateroom. The bunk was littered with books, newspapers, magazines and classified folders. Parallel with the bunk was a fold-out desk on either side of which was an armchair. Vandenberg sat in one, motioning to Darius to sit down in the other.

The Secretary removed his glasses and rubbed his eyes. "The world's gone mad," he said.

Darius said nothing.

"We're talking as friends now, right?"

"Of course."

So many times before, Vandenberg had invited Darius to his compartment for a private chat; and so many times before, the preamble had been "We're talking as friends now, right?" It was a tidy disclaimer. Darius understood that he could extract meaningful tidbits of information from the conversation and weave them into a story so long as he did not link the tidbits to Vandenberg; and of course the Secretary could disown or even disavow Darius' story because, according to the unwritten rules of the game, nothing had been transmitted officially. He was not the Secretary of State speaking to Darius, just an old friend.

Vandenberg slipped on his glasses again. "I just got a cable from Tel Aviv." Pause. "The Israeli Cabinet has decided to release Carucci."

Darius looked intently at the Secretary. "And the others?"

"All of them."

Darius lit a cigarette. "You knew that was going to happen, though, didn't you?"

There was a look of great sadness on Vandenberg's face. "I thought it was going to happen, but not because of what you said back there. It was Ben-Dor's decision. I'm only surprised that the Cabinet went along."

"Why are you telling me this?"

Vandenberg's eyes took on a hunted look. "All of this is off the record."

"Mr. Secretary," Darius said slowly, "we are friends, and it's a friendship I prize highly. But you know damned well that when you tell me something like this I'm going to have to use it. I won't attribute it, but you certainly can't expect me to ignore it."

The Secretary didn't argue the point; he continued as though there had been no interruption. "You were entirely wrong, you know."

"What do you mean?" said Darius.

"There was no American pressure. Quite the contrary. I even told Ben-Dor that if he released the prisoners, I might be forced to disavow his decision."

"And will you?" Darius asked.

Vandenberg said nothing, but allowed the faintest glimmer of a smile to appear.

Darius realized that the Secretary of State was mildly disappointed in him. "Of course," Darius sighed, "you just have, haven't you?" Darius pointed at the phone. "What does the President think?"

Vandenberg sighed. "The President operates within a rather limited horizon when it comes to foreign policy. He thinks we should either apologize, declare war or something in between."

Darius grinned in spite of himself. "Which way's he leaning now?"

Vandenberg smiled. "I haven't decided for him yet."

Darius drew on his cigarette. "It doesn't make sense, does it?"

The conversation shifted back to Ben-Dor's surprising decision to release the terrorists. "He's a complicated man." Vandenberg was musing aloud.

"But it doesn't make any sense," said Darius. "I know that occasionally the Israelis have made concessions to the terrorists, but why now? There has to be an awfully good reason to explain this. I mean, they're more adamantly opposed to making concessions than you are."

"Especially Ben-Dor," agreed the Secretary. "He's got ice water in his veins."

"Then why is he doing it?" Darius asked.

"I have no idea," said the Secretary of State.

12

Abdullah ibn-Mohammed, sovereign of the Hashemite Kingdom of Jordan, was distraught; he had said as much on several occasions throughout the evening.

"We are interrogating the security force that was guarding Helen," he said at one point during their conversation, "and if any one of them was connected with her abduction, you can be sure we will find out about it and punish him severely."

Secretary Vandenberg had replied with what appeared to be less than total conviction that he was confident that would be the case.

The discussion was not going well.

Mohammed knew of the Rejectionist Front meeting in Damascus. It was a fact that greatly disturbed him.

Vandenberg tried to impress upon the King that the Damascus meeting gave even greater urgency to the West Bank negotiations. His Majesty was noncommittal, suspecting that Vandenberg was engaging in a ploy to get him to make further concessions.

"Mr. Secretary, your energy never ceases to amaze me, but here in the Middle East we recognize that even the swiftest hawk must rest." Mohammed was trim, compact, highly intelligent. He rose.

"Your Majesty flatters me with the comparison," said Vandenberg, "but if you promise to keep this between us, I must confess I am a bit fatigued."

The meeting ended with agreement that the Secretary would return to Amman after another negotiating session with Ben-Dor.

"In any case, I'll let you know as soon as I can," the Secretary added. "And again, Your Majesty, allow me to state how impressed I am with your dedication to peace and your efforts on behalf of my wife."

Mohammed enjoyed an extra touch of flattery, and Vandenberg never failed to provide it.

Later, in one of the guesthouses near the King's palace, Frank Bernardi was analyzing the King's position.

"I don't find his behavior curious at all. For Chrissake, Felix, he thinks that you and the Israelis gang up on him at the best of times, and now he's gone and misplaced Helen . . ." Vandenberg winced and Bernardi stopped in mid-sentence. "I'm sorry, Felix. You know I didn't mean it that way; but Mohammed feels personally responsible for Helen's kidnapping, and there's no way in the world you can convince him that this won't affect your attitude as a mediator."

"Well then," Vandenberg picked up the thought, "we'll just have to find some way, won't we?" After a pause, the Secretary continued. "What if the Israelis made the first concession?"

"Why would they?" Bernardi knew he was being used as a sounding board.

"We might have to squeeze pretty hard," the Secretary agreed, "but we've got to get these damned negotiations off dead center somehow."

"You're squeezing pretty hard already, Felix." Bernardi was holding the State Department's playback report. It contained capsulized versions of newspaper stories and radio and television reports that had been monitored and transcribed by the State Department's press office and then cabled to the Secretary's plane.

"Did you feed this to Kane?" Bernardi held out the cabled transcript of the satellite report that Darius had sent to New York earlier that evening.

Vandenberg removed his glasses and examined the cable.

KANE STOP NATIONAL NEWS SERVICE COMMA TV EVENING REPORT COLON QUOTE THE REASON FOR YESTERDAYS SURPRISE ATTACK ON AMMAN AIRPORT WAS REVEALED TODAY WITH SHATTERING EFFECT AND

CLARITY BY SECRETARY OF STATE VANDENBERG HIM-
SELF STOP VANDENBERG MADE THE ANNOUNCEMENT
FOLLOWING TALKS WITH EGYPTIAN PRESIDENT HOUS-
SAN AT THE PRESIDENTS WINTER RETREAT IN ASWAN
STOP VANDENBERG COLON LADIES AND GENTLEMEN
COMMA I KNOW YOU ARE ALL AWARE OF THE FACT
THAT A RATHER MAJOR ATTACK WAS LAUNCHED YES-
TERDAY MORNING ON AMMAN AIRPORT STOP SHORTLY
AFTER THAT ATTACK COMMA THERE WAS A HELICOP-
TER ASSAULT ON PETRA COMMA WHERE MISSUS VAN-
DENBERG WAS SIGHTSEEING STOP SHE HAS AP-
PARENTLY BEEN KIDNAPPED BY MEN CLAIMING TO BE
MEMBERS OF THE OLPP STOP

Vandenberg scanned the remainder of Kane's report. A quote from
Houssan followed Vandenberg's. Then came Darius' on-camera close,
which had been filmed at Amman Airport following their arrival late
that afternoon.

KANE COLON REPORTERS TRAVELING WITH THE SEC-
RETARY OF STATE WERE TOLD THAT THE PALES-
TINIAN KIDNAPPERS HAVE DEMANDED THE RELEASE
OF SIX MEN BEING HELD IN ISRAEL COMMA AMONG
THEM THE CONTROVERSIAL BISHOP CARUCCI COMMA
WHO WAS CONVICTED BY AN ISRAELI COURT OF
SMUGGLING WEAPONS TO ARAB TERRORISTS IN JERU-
SALEM STOP NNS HAS LEARNED THAT THE ISRAELI
CABINET COMMA IN A PREDAWN MEETING TODAY
COMMA ORDERED THAT CARUCCI AND THE OTHERS
BE RELEASED STOP ALTHOUGH THE ISRAELIS HAVE
OCCASIONALLY YIELDED TO TERRORIST DEMANDS
COMMA THEY HAVENT IN MANY YEARS AND NEVER SO
COMPLETELY STOP THIS SEEMS TO REPRESENT A
TURNABOUT IN ISRAELI POLICY COMMA AND SECRE-
TARY VANDENBERG IS KNOWN TO HAVE STRONGLY OP-
POSED THE DECISION STOP THAT OPPOSITION WAS
PERSONALLY CONVEYED TO ISRAELI PRIME MINISTER
BENDOR STOP BENDOR COMMA FOR REASONS WHICH
ARE AS YET UNCLEAR COMMA NEVERTHELESS CON-
VINCED HIS CABINET TO ORDER THE RELEASE STOP
HELEN VANDENBERGS WHEREABOUTS ARE STILL UN-
KNOWN STOP THIS IS DARIUS KANE COMMA NATIONAL
NEWS SERVICE COMMA AMMAN STOP ENDIT

Vandenberg replaced his glasses with a grim smile. "Well, at least he got the story straight."

Bernardi looked exhausted. "You're pushing Ben-Dor pretty hard, Felix. He's probably reading Kane's report by now, too."

"I'm going to have to push a lot harder before this thing is over. Have the Israelis released those people yet?"

"It's supposed to have happened about six hours ago, Felix. We should be hearing something about Helen pretty soon."

"Yes, and I'm not counting on it being good news."

Terence Jamieson came into the room.

"Yes?"

"It's a message routed through the NSC."

"Right on cue," said the Secretary. "Well?"

"It's bad news, sir," replied Jamieson. "The OLPP's made a second demand."

Vandenberg's shoulders sagged, but his voice betrayed no emotion. "I can't say I'm surprised." He extended a hand. "Let me have it."

Bernardi watched the Secretary read and reread the message. Then he asked, "How bad is it, Felix?"

"Well," Vandenberg replied, "it's no worse than I expected. They're asking for five hundred million dollars in gold." He passed the message back to Jamieson. "File that carefully, Terry. It'll never be worth half a billion dollars, but it'll be an item of historical value some day." Vandenberg sighed. "Poor old Ya'acov. In some ways he's in worse shape right now than I am."

Bernardi was seated on a richly upholstered armchair. His elbows rested on his knees. His chin was cupped in both hands. "You gonna talk to the President?"

Vandenberg looked up. "That's a good idea, Frank. Why don't you get him for me. The sooner we get this next step out of the way, the better it'll be for everyone."

13

There have been great Presidents in American history, and bad ones; some have been "destined" for the job, others accidentally fell into it; but none had been dubbed the "lucky President" until John Randolph Abbott took the oath of office. He was a rich congressman from an old Establishment family in New Haven, Connecticut, blessed with flowing white hair and features that could only be described as distinguished. He had always looked Presidential, but no one had ever considered that he had the intelligence or the ambition for that high office; no one, that is, except the three thousand and nine tired and frustrated delegates to the deadlocked Democratic National Convention. The incumbent President could not win the affection, much less the votes, of a majority of the convention; and his handsome challenger from the Rocky Mountains, though he came close, couldn't either. By the time the eighteenth ballot had come and gone, and neither contender had been able to break the deadlock, the old-timers in the party decided that it was time to select a compromise candidate. He had to be someone who had never offended either wing of the party or alienated any group outside the party. Honest and innocuous.

Abbott, a twelve-term veteran, had contributed nothing to the deliberations; he had merely sat quietly, nodding or smiling whenever he thought the occasion warranted a nod or a smile, the very picture of a compromise candidate. It was two o'clock on a Thursday morning, a time when prospective voters were turning off not only their television sets but their interest in the Democratic Party.

"Abbott!" Senator Lewis Silverbox had exclaimed; "Abbott!" the others had echoed; and before an hour had passed, Abbott was the one; the lucky one who just happened to be sitting there when the exhausted hierarchy of his party concluded that anyone could indeed become President of the United States.

Abbott had been "lucky" during the campaign, too. Scandal tainted his Republican opponent's campaign. The Minority Leader was proved to be corrupt, having used and abused his power on various subcommittees to enjoy a succession of junkets with pretty secretaries and to bestow lucrative contracts on hometown friends. It wasn't that Abbott deliberately exploited these shenanigans; it was just that he said nothing while the Republicans were constantly trying to defend their actions. His silent campaign attracted more and more independent voters, who were impressed by Abbott's unimpeachable record in Congress and by his appearance of sobriety. There were columnists who wrote about Abbott's limitations, but either no one cared or everyone still wanted a respite from the agonies of Vietnam and Watergate. In November, Abbott won handily. He surrounded himself with pleasant and sometimes able lieutenants, most of them from Congress or Wall Street, and he was lucky. Time and again, during his first years in the Oval Office, when action was the crying need of the hour, Abbott had sat behind his huge desk, a drink in hand, a smile on his face, and done nothing; and surprisingly the problems got solved. No one could quite understand his process of decision-making; but the market was doing well, unemployment had dipped, there were no major wars anywhere, the campuses were quiet. Lucky.

On this particular afternoon, with the setting sun pouring through the rounded floor-to-ceiling windows behind his desk, it was clear that the President was again dawdling. He still had an enormous amount of work that had to be done before dinner. A prayer breakfast was scheduled for seven o'clock the next morning. But Whit Traynor, the President's intuitive Chief of Staff, recognized the symptoms. The President needed a break, a drink and some gossip. He sat in a Kennedy-style rocking chair with his long legs resting on a coffee table. Traynor sat down on a sofa. They chatted about the latest scandal. A prominent Mid-western senator had been charged by a columnist with faking more than ten thousand dollars' worth of travel vouchers. That afternoon's *Washington Star* had even suggested in an editorial that the senator had used the money to take one of his secretaries to Europe on at least two occasions.

The President sipped his Scotch and water. He was in a melancholy mood. "All I keep thinking, Whit, is 'There but for the grace of God . . .'"

Traynor laughed. "Don't get smug, Mr. President. There's no statute of limitation on scandal." There had, in fact, never been a trace of scandal linked to Abbott's name, but he seemed to enjoy the vicarious association.

"Well, I still feel sorry for the poor bastard. There was a time in this town when the press still operated within certain boundaries. 'Lay and get laid.'" The President smiled his locker-room smile. "Have you noticed, Whit, that all these stories get broken by young kids? They haven't been around long enough to develop a sense of tolerance."

A buzzer sounded in the telephone console on the President's desk. "Get that, will you, Whit."

Traynor was already at the phone. "Put him through. I'll get the President." Traynor held the phone against his hip. "It's Vandenberg, Mr. President."

"Goddammit!" exclaimed the President. He motioned to Traynor to pick up the extension on the side table. Somehow, whenever Abbott spoke to the Secretary of State, he felt that he should be seated at his desk. In his mind, affairs of state required a certain protocol. He ran a hand through his hair and took a deep breath.

"Felix? Where are you? . . . What time is it there?" The President's questions were the obvious ones. "Jesus, don't you ever get any sleep? What's the latest word on Helen?" Vandenberg informed the President of the second ransom demand. "Well, that's what you said would happen, isn't it? Did you say half a million or billion? . . . That's a big hunk of our foreign-aid package for the entire area. . . . Listen, Felix, hold on a second. I want to get Harlan in on this. I'm going to put you on the speaker phone."

Traynor depressed a button summoning the National Security Adviser and simultaneously switched the call to a small loudspeaker on the President's desk. Traynor nodded at the President.

"Can you hear me all right, Felix?"

"That's fine, Mr. President." Vandenberg was using his soothing voice. "But I think it would be even better if you moved a little closer to your desk."

Traynor put his hand over the mouthpiece of his phone. "That supercilious sonovabitch." The President waved him quiet.

There was a faint knock at the door. Stewart entered with apparent hesitation.

"Vandenberg's on the phone," Traynor said. "Bad news."

"Felix," the President was saying, "Harlan's here now. Suppose you bring us up to date."

There was a pause, and then Vandenberg began to summarize events since the kidnapping. His sentences, as always, were clear, precise, careful, as though he'd been honing them for hours.

"We're operating under two deadlines, both of them containing a number of intangible elements. We're now almost certain that several members of the Rejectionist Front are planning to meet in Damascus." Vandenberg's voice became muffled, but they could hear him saying, "What's the date, Frank?" Then his voice became distinct again. "That they've got a meeting planned on the twenty-third. We don't as yet know the purpose of the meeting, but I think it's safe to assume that it's not intended to be helpful. The Egyptians and the Jordanians know about the meeting, but we're not sure about the Israelis. At the moment, though, I'm inclined to believe that they know too."

The President said, "Why is that, Felix?"

"I was coming to that, Mr. President. For some reason, the Israelis have responded to my wife's kidnapping in a manner that is totally inconsistent with their past behavior."

Traynor scribbled something on a pad of paper and held it up for the President to see: "I THOUGHT HE'D FORGOTTEN ABOUT HIS WIFE."

Vandenberg's voice continued to fill the room. "Ben-Dor knew as well as I did that the release of Carucci and the others would not result in Helen's return. The price was far too low. So we're forced to assume that the Israelis have some motive of which we're still unaware. If they know about the meeting in Damascus, and think it's the prelude for war, they may be preparing for a preemptive action of their own. So far, we don't have any evidence of that. It's possible that they released Carucci because they wanted to curry favor with me, personally, or with the United States government, but that doesn't feel right.

"In any event, we've got a new ransom demand, for half a billion dollars in gold. Actually, the amount is academic. We can't change our policy simply because the Secretary of State's wife is involved."

The President sounded slightly annoyed. "I hope you'll still let me play some role in making that judgment, Felix."

Vandenberg didn't miss a beat. "If you'll recall, Mr. President, you made the final decision in formulating that policy. We agreed that even if I were kidnapped, the United States would not negotiate with terrorists."

"All right, go on." The President still sounded irritated.

"Secondly," continued Vandenberg, "the sum involved is so immense that even if it could be raised, it would take a considerable period of time to do so.

"Now that's an element that could work either for us or against us. We could buy time by saying that we were trying to raise the money.

We could even go through the motions. However, since the OLPP has close ties with the Rejectionist Front, that may be exactly what they want us to do. They could be trying to keep me preoccupied, sabotage the West Bank negotiations and push the Middle East into a new war."

"In point of fact, Felix," interjected Traynor icily, "isn't that exactly what's happening?"

"Not if we turn them down, immediately and publicly."

Traynor was scribbling on the note pad again: "IF THERE'S A WAR, HE SHOULD BE BACK HERE!"

The President read the note and nodded. "Felix," he said, his voice suddenly softening, "you're under tremendous pressure right now. Maybe you should come back to Washington. You can leave Frank over there to keep the negotiations alive; but if there is any danger of a war breaking out, you ought to be here at the nerve center."

There was a long silence, so long that the men in the Oval Office thought the line might have been disconnected. Then Vandenberg said, "Mr. President, you know I have great confidence in Frank; he's an enormously capable man. But if I return to Washington now, it'll have a shattering effect on all our friends here. Correctly or not, my leaving would be perceived here in the Middle East as evidence of panic on our part. It would play right into the hands of the Rejectionists."

"What are you proposing then?" the President asked.

"That I continue the shuttle; that we reveal the latest ransom demand and turn it down flat."

"What if they kill Helen?"

There was the slightest tremor in Vandenberg's voice. "If there's a war, Mr. President, they'll do that anyway."

"We'll discuss it at this end and I'll let you know. Now get some sleep."

There was a click at the other end of the line. The Secretary of State had hung up.

The President turned to his National Security Adviser. "Harlan, what do you think?"

"I think you've gotta go with your man in the field," said Stewart.

"Bullshit!" exploded Traynor. "That guy's a flaming egomaniac who doesn't think anyone else is capable of taking a crap without his help. Also, I think his wife's kidnapping has clouded his judgment."

Harlan Stewart was a soft-spoken man with a deceptive air of gentleness about him. "What are you recommending, Whit? That we come up with five hundred million dollars? Are you prepared to guarantee that war won't break out anyway?"

The President was tapping the bridge of his nose.

"I tend to agree with Harlan, Whit. Felix and I have been in some pretty tough spots together. He's cold-blooded, all right, but I don't see how you can accuse him of clouded judgment when he's the one refusing to pay the ransom. We can always bring him back, but let's not jump the gun until the picture gets a little clearer. Call him back, Harlan. He'll still be up brooding anyway. Tell him I said to go ahead and do it his way."

"Yessir." Stewart got up and left.

Traynor sounded bitter. "He plays you like a harpsichord, Mr. President."

The President leaned back in his chair, propping his feet up on the desk. "Yeah, well, maybe he does, Whit. But if I ever decide that I don't like the tune he's playing"—the President slapped the desk with his open hand—"I'll slam the cover on his fingers!"

Geoffrey Whittier Traynor was trim, handsome, forty-eight and a graduate of Yale. He had been recruited by the Central Intelligence Agency immediately upon graduation and served for nearly twenty years in the CIA's operations section. For a considerable part of that time, Traynor worked as liaison officer with the House-Senate watchdog committee. It was during this period that he befriended the man who was now President of the United States. When Congressman Abbott asked him to become his administrative assistant, Traynor agreed to resign from the CIA.

He was seated now, nibbling on a carrot stick, in a neat, tastefully furnished office down the corridor from the Oval Office. In a manner of speaking, he was still a liaison officer. Certainly nothing of significance that was happening at the White House did not, eventually, make its way into a CIA file.

The thought that he might be guilty of disloyalty to the President would never occur to Traynor. On the contrary, loyalty was one of his strongest characteristics, and Traynor had never wavered in the original oath of loyalty that he had sworn to the Agency more than twenty years before. The CIA was, of course, subject to the President's authority, but that did not mean that the President was not subject to the Agency's scrutiny.

Traynor dialed a private number at CIA headquarters in Langley, Virginia. Deputy Director George Tipton was at the other end of the line. Tipton and Traynor were CIA veterans from the mid-1950s. They headed a small but influential subculture within the Agency, a group that defiantly called itself "The Hard Liners."

They had pressed hard for victory in Vietnam; had bent, if not broken, the law in their crusade against dissidents at home; and had infiltrated the highest echelons of government in their vigilance against anyone who might, wittingly or not, have become involved in Communist intrigues against the United States.

Secretary of State Vandenberg ranked high on The Hard Liners' list of potential subversives. George Tipton did not share Vandenberg's belief in détente; nor did he accept his view that Peking and Moscow were implacable enemies, driven apart by nationalistic and ideological differences. He thought that the Secretary of State was encouraging a dangerous form of naïveté; and though Tipton would deny categorically that he was involved in any kind of conspiracy, he was in fact in the vanguard of a secret "palace guard," protecting the nation against its elected President and his chief foreign policy adviser.

Whenever the Secretary of State was involved in a delicate negotiation, Traynor gave Tipton a daily report on his activities. Their conversation that night was, as usual, brief and yet complete. There was, Traynor mused, as he finished his report, a certain symmetry to this arrangement. The President had appointed one of his political cronies to run the Agency; but he, Traynor, had maneuvered the President into appointing Tipton to be Deputy Director. In addition, he had easily persuaded the President that he should be responsible for keeping the Agency apprised of significant policy decisions that were being made or contemplated at the highest levels of the White House.

Traynor glanced at the note pad in front of him. A circle of arrows converged on a few words: "BEN-DOR—WHY? VANDENBERG—WHAT?" Traynor tore the top sheet off the pad, then ripped off the next three pages. There was no one in the outer office as Traynor fed the four sheets of paper into the shredder.

Traynor was so preoccupied with his thoughts that he scarcely remembered leaving the White House or getting into his car. A guard opened the gates onto Pennsylvania Avenue, and Traynor made an illegal left, heading in the direction of the Whitehurst Freeway. He snapped on the radio to WGMS, humming along softly to the strains of a familiar Chopin prelude. The midnight news came as an unwelcome distraction. A classical music station, WGMS had the previous summer become affiliated with the National News Service radio network. Traynor turned onto Canal Road. He heard without listening, disjointed phrases that seemed to dovetail awkwardly with his thoughts.

". . . release of six Palestinian prisoners . . . whereabouts of Helen Vandenberg . . . further complicates an already . . . National News Service Diplomatic Correspondent Darius Kane."

Traynor knew Kane. Now his attention was more actively focused on the radio.

". . . was a decision which Israeli Prime Minister Ben-Dor made over the explicit objections of the American Secretary of State. During a private meeting in Jerusalem late last night, Secretary Vandenberg emphasized U.S. objections to any kind of deal with his wife's kidnappers. American officials are known to be bewildered by what seems to be a complete turnabout in recent Israeli policy. This is Darius Kane, National News Service, Amman, Jordan."

Traynor snorted. "Well, you hit the bull's-eye on that one, Kane, my boy. Some American officials are bewildered as hell. But I doubt if your friend Vandenberg is one of them."

Traynor was driving solely by instinct now across Chain Bridge into Virginia. The Deputy Director had raised the same two questions that had been nagging at Traynor all evening long. Why had Ben-Dor reversed his policy? What had Vandenberg promised him?

The fact that Vandenberg had planted a disclaimer with Darius Kane only served to harden Traynor's suspicion that the Secretary of State was once again orchestrating events in the Middle East.

Traynor's car hit a patch of ice and skidded across the road. There was no traffic. Traynor lowered the window and allowed a gust of cold air to sweep across him. He took a deep breath, nosed the car back into its proper lane and concentrated on driving home.

14

Jamaal Safat, Chairman of the Organization for the Liberation of the People of Palestine, sat behind an old desk in a sparsely furnished office in West Beirut. He was, for a revolutionary, surprisingly neat in appearance, wearing fatigues that had been pressed, boots that had been polished. He had never lost his gentle bedside manner, even though he had not practiced medicine for many years. Only his black eyes betrayed the dedication, bordering on fanaticism, that had propelled him into the front ranks of Palestinian leaders; they were hard, devoid of emotion, and they rarely blinked.

With the point of a pen, Safat pushed a piece of official stationery across the desk, leaving it almost equidistant from his two closest aides, who were seated on straight-backed chairs flanking Safat and looking, for all the world, like mismatched bookends. Mohammed el-Saiqa, known to old Mideast hands as Moussa, was lean, almost effeminately graceful, immaculately attired in European clothing, the broad trouser bottoms of a Cardin suit flaring elegantly over crushed-leather Italian loafers. He had the hands of a surgeon, long, delicate fingers that busied themselves constantly in the adjustment of a wrinkle here, a crease there. Only his eyes remained still, focusing unwaveringly on the object of his attention. Those who knew the OLPP's Chief of Intelligence—and few sought such closeness—claimed never to have heard Moussa express a single word of affection or regret. His only passion was the achievement of a Palestinian state including the West Bank, Israel and Gaza. He would use any means to achieve that end. Over the years, he had won the confidence and admiration of Jamaal Safat, despite his reputation among OLPP veterans for being hotheaded.

Ibrahim el-Haj, by contrast, looked like a neighborhood butcher, his sheer bulk lending a deceptive air of lethargy to his appearance. Ibrahim's feet, shod only in fraying sandals, were wide and flat, like those of a sumo wrestler. He wore khaki slacks and a white shirt, and he used his kaffiyeh like a towel, dabbing occasionally at his glistening forehead. The last two fingers of his right hand were missing. It was believed that the OLPP Chief of Operations had lost these fingers when, as a young man growing up in his birthplace of Jaffa, he had been arrested and brutally interrogated by Israeli police. Like Moussa, however, Ibrahim was not easily engaged in casual conversation; nevertheless, the story had gained currency within the OLPP because it was reasonable and Ibrahim himself had never denied it. Unlike Moussa, however, Ibrahim had a reputation for being cool, studied in his responses, unemotional in the guidance he gave Safat.

For his part, the Chairman of the OLPP valued both advisers.

"Read it." Safat nodded toward Moussa. "It's fascinating. Yesterday's action was out of character. This more closely suits our enemy's pattern."

Moussa ignored the letter. "Carucci has expressed the wish to meet with you, to thank you personally. The others too."

Safat shook his head. "I want them all closely watched. Treat them all like heroes, but keep them under surveillance. The Zionists had their reasons for releasing them, and until we know what they were, we must remain especially vigilant." Safat poked at the letter again. "How do we respond?"

The letter bore the stamp of the U.S. Embassy in Beirut. It was signed by the Ambassador.

Secretary of State Felix J. Vandenberg has instructed me to repeat the U.S. government's well-known position with regard to acts of terrorism.

We deplore all terrorist acts wherever they occur and whatever their professed aim.

The Secretary asked me to stress that our policy with respect to terrorist demands of all sorts is firm and unwavering.

We do not pay ransom or otherwise yield to terrorist blackmail.

We do not encourage others to pay ransom or otherwise yield to terrorist blackmail.

To do so, we believe, would only encourage terrorists and increase the risks of terrorism for U.S. residents, visitors and officials abroad.

Your demands are, therefore, unequivocally rejected. The Secretary of State remains firmly committed to the goal of a just and lasting peace for all peoples of this area; however, the kidnapping of Mrs. Vandenberg is an act that not only violates all standards of civilized behavior but threatens the very objectives of the OLPP.

*The far-reaching consequences of this act should not be ig-
nored by the leadership of the OLPP and will not be ignored by
the government of the United States of America.*

"There is no need to respond," said Moussa. "The threats are
empty. What will they do, send Marines into our refugee camps?"

"No," Safat said thoughtfully, "you're a man of war, so you think
only in terms of death and violence. Never lose sight of your objective,
Moussa." Safat took the letter and smoothed it against the table. He
turned toward Ibrahim. "Your view, my brother." It was a soft command.

Ibrahim had put both elbows on the desk, cradling his chin with
folded hands. He seemed deep in thought.

"There are two courses open to us," he said finally. "Armed struggle
or this." His fingers traced the embossed seal of the American eagle.
"Armed struggle would merely be a continuation of past policy. It has
had successes, but there have been failures too, my brothers. Remember that the PLO chose armed struggle in 1970 and it was almost
crushed by Hussein's whores. It went the same way in 1976 in Lebanon. Syria almost destroyed our movement. We may need something new. The American connection has always been an option for
us, but we have never chosen to use it. Maybe this is the time."
Ibrahim paused. "In either case, we have almost two weeks before the
meeting in Damascus."

Safat smiled. "Allah has blessed me with two wise counselors." He
rose, and Ibrahim and Moussa knew immediately that he had reached
a decision. "I'd like to meet with Vandenberg. He's a subtle man, our
friend the Secretary."

Moussa exploded. "He spits in your face. He's a conniving Zionist
stooge, a pig. Jamaal, don't trust him."

Safat paced off a large circle around the desk. "Look at the manner
of his communication, Moussa. Reflect on it. Not quite government to
government, but an official communication, nonetheless.

"And examine the words carefully—'an act that . . . threatens the
very objectives of the OLPP.' This is not a man who uses words
carelessly, Moussa. He knows our objectives as well as you do. Sover-
eignty. A state. A legitimate place in the family of Arab nations. Acceptance by the United Nations."

"The extermination of the Zionists?" Moussa allowed himself a
small joke.

Safat tried to be tolerant. "There the Secretary might draw the line." The Chairman stared into space, his eyes fixed on a crack in the wall. "I will send him a personal message," he said in tones of a pronouncement. "Ibrahim, you write it down, then translate it into English." He paused for only a moment, then began. "The Palestinian people have been suckled on the . . ." Safat examined the letter again. "Put quotation marks around this. On the 'consequences' of injustice for too long. We are not terrorists. We are revolutionaries who seek the return of our homeland. We are men of compassion who are forced to resort to violence only when other options fail. We are enclosing a tape recording of your wife."

"A tape recording!" It was Moussa. He sounded incredulous.

Safat ignored the interruption. "You can tell from the tape that she is well, and I can assure you that she is being treated with utmost courtesy. We do not wish her any harm, nor are we insensitive to the principles of the American government. However, the Palestinian people cannot be ignored and will not be represented by the King of the Hashemites. In this, the OLPP is firmly supported by most of the Arab family, who are still bound and committed by the unanimous resolution of the Rabat Conference.

"As Chairman of the OLPP, which we declare to be the sole legitimate representative of the Palestinian people, I propose that we confer directly and without delay at a location of your choosing. There are other options open to us, but we prefer the path of conciliation.

"As soon as we have met, your wife will be released."

"He will refuse," concluded Moussa.

"We will have lost nothing," replied Safat.

"Why is the tape necessary?"

"It's not," said Safat, "but since we're trying the path of conciliation, it represents a gesture."

Moussa was clearly unhappy. "It suggests weakness, Jamaal."

Safat was unruffled. "Violence suggests weakness. It is only the strong who can be flexible."

15

Ben-Gurion Airport resembled an armed camp.

A few miles from the airport, in the village of Lydda, more than five thousand demonstrators lined what they believed would be the path of the Secretary's motorcade. The hourly news bulletins on Kol Yisrael stressed the security precautions that were being taken along the entire route from Ben-Gurion Airport to Jerusalem; but within the airport complex, four giant Chinook helicopters already stood by to fly the Secretary of State and his entire party over the heads of any potential troublemakers.

A sharp, gusting wind lifted the long, red ceremonial carpet and hurled it against the waiting ramp as the Secretary's aircraft taxied toward the terminal building. Four airport maintenance men scurried after the carpet and began pulling it back into place. A high-ranking police official shouted at them to roll the carpet up and take it away. The omen was too obvious to evoke much comment from the waiting press.

It was difficult to detect anything unusual in the Secretary's carriage or demeanor as he descended the steps of the ramp. Vandenberg had opted once again not to meet with the reporters aboard his aircraft, and most of them had rushed off the plane so that they would be in position to hear the Secretary's arrival statement. A microphone stand and loudspeakers had been set up near the bullpen of police barricades that contained the local press.

Israeli Foreign Minister Cohen greeted Vandenberg and escorted him almost immediately to the microphones. Protocol dictated at least a brief welcoming statement from Cohen, but he remained strangely silent, two or three feet behind the Secretary of State, gesturing toward the microphones. Vandenberg gave every appearance of not understanding the gesture. Finally, Cohen bowed to the inevitable and stepped forward.

"We welcome you back to Israel, Mr. Secretary, with an awareness of the great pressures which surround you, but ever confident that your visit will accord us the opportunity for a useful exchange of views."

The Secretary of State favored the Foreign Minister with a look of infinite compassion, nodding his head several times, as though absorbing the full impact of Cohen's statement.

"Avram, you and I, the governments of Israel and the United States, have been through many difficult periods before. When we disagree, as occasionally happens, it is in the nature of a family quarrel, sometimes sharp, even bitter, but always sheltered in the knowledge that what we seek for each other is essentially good. We may sometimes differ in our approach to a problem, but neither of us has ever questioned the other's fundamental good will.

"I remain confident that a West Bank solution lies within our grasp; that with courage and vision, we can help shape a new reality in the Middle East, the reality of a just and lasting peace. Thank you."

Vandenberg stepped back from the microphones so abruptly that he collided with the Israeli Foreign Minister; the two men grasped each other firmly to prevent a fall, instinctively smiling with the reflexes of a politician.

"Isn't it terrible?" Gloria said, turning to Darius. "I'm so suspicious of the man, I don't even believe that was an accident."

Vandenberg still held Cohen's arm, strolling casually with him toward the nearest helicopter. Certainly the still pictures that would appear on the front pages of Israel's newspapers that afternoon could reflect nothing but warmth and comradeship.

Darius ran over to the police barricades to confer quickly with Jerry Blumer. "Nothing," he said. "There's no point in my staying here. I haven't gotten a thing since we left Aswan yesterday."

Blumer said, "Go ahead. I'll call you at the King David this evening."

"How's it looking here?" asked Darius.

"Like Belfast on St. Patrick's Day," said Blumer. "Your boy's gonna be lucky if he still has a government to negotiate with."

"That bad, huh?"

"Worse. You'd better run if you wanta catch your chopper."

Darius lost fifteen dollars playing liar's poker on the short flight to Jerusalem. He went directly to his hotel room, pausing only long enough to pick up his key. He was tired, frustrated, and, he felt, inadequately informed. He needed a hot shower.

A notice had been slipped under his door.

"February 10.

"Personnel are advised that the Secretary's party will remain overnight in Jerusalem on Wednesday, February 10. Another notice will be distributed later advising of plans for Thursday, February 11." It was unsigned.

Darius dropped his overnight bag on the floor, his typewriter on the bed. As usual, the Israelis had left a folder of papers and brochures on his bed. Darius flipped through the folder.

"Tourist Guide . . . Cafés and Restaurants . . . Shopping . . . This Week in Israel . . ." Darius dropped them, one after another, in the wastebasket. This rhythm was broken when he came upon a ten-page essay prepared by the Israel Institute of Applied Social Research: "The Palestinian Problem." Darius placed it on his typewriter. He continued scanning the papers until he found the "Daily Summary of the Israeli Media, February 9." He saved that compilation and without looking further threw everything else into the basket. Darius started to read the summary. The Israeli press rarely even approached unanimity, but the editorial writers had come very close the previous day.

Ma'ariv Editorial: "The Cabinet's inexplicable decision to release six pro-Arab terrorists raises serious questions about the government's commitment to its own policies. Countless Israelis have died to preserve a strong position against terrorist blackmail. At the very least, the Prime Minister owes the Israeli people an explanation."

Yediot Aharonot: "If the Prime Minister chooses to act in total defiance of both precedent and what would appear to be the national interest, then, at the very least, it is incumbent upon him to explain to the people of Israel what lies behind his incredible behavior."

Every excerpt was in the same vein, but the most implacable assault came from the pro-government newspaper *Ha'aretz.*

"In recent years, the government of Israel has become accustomed to American arm-twisting; but for all its dependence on American generosity, the government has never surrendered its independence. Sympathetic as the Israeli people may be to the personal problems of the American Secretary of State, they cannot ignore the fact that numerous Israeli citizens have had to deal with similar acts of Arab terrorism in the past without expecting or even suggesting compromise. We are forced to conclude that no Israeli Prime Minister would have given in to the OLPP without enormous pressure from the

United States. We regret the pressure, but we cannot help but condemn the weakness of those in our own government who succumb to it."

It was, as Jerry Blumer had said, even worse than Darius had suspected.

There was a knock at the door and one of the Israeli porters entered with Darius' suitcase. "*Shalom,*" he said hopefully.

"*Shalom,*" replied Darius, sorting through a pocketful of Egyptian, Jordanian and Israeli change.

A grandmotherly chambermaid had joined them. "Please," she said, "you have laundry?"

Darius raised a hand. "Just a minute; let me take care of my friend here."

"Please," the woman insisted, "he wants Marlboro."

The U.S. Embassy customarily set aside a room in the King David in which cigarettes, liquor and a few toilet articles could be purchased by members of the Secretary's party. Since the items in the shop were duty-free and untaxed by the Israeli government, they cost less than a quarter of their price on the open market.

"I understand," Darius said. "Would you tell him I'm busy right now, but that I'm going down later on."

The woman hesitated.

"In an hour," said Darius, first pointing to his watch, then raising a finger. "One hour. OK?"

"OK." She was smiling as though Darius had just made an indecent proposal. "OK," she said again; "and maybe one Johnnie Walker." She was a little flustered. "It's for my brother."

Darius pulled out his notebook and wrote "Cigs, booze" with a flourish. "Got it," he said, moving to the bed where his suitcase lay. "Now, let me get you my laundry." He thought of telling the woman that this was by far the most useful thing he had done all day, but then he realized that even if her English were up to it, she wouldn't understand what he meant anyway.

Two floors above Darius' room, Felix Vandenberg was going through a semiprivate bout of depression.

"You realize, Frank," he told Bernardi, "we could spend the next few weeks out here playing with ourselves, and the end result might still be a war." Vandenberg fixed his Under Secretary with a melancholy stare. "Maybe Traynor's right. One of the biggest mistakes you can make is to reject someone's advice simply because you hate his guts. Maybe I should go back."

Bernardi said nothing, but he was smiling.

Vandenberg caught the mood. "Bernardi, you know you're almost as much of a bastard as I am. You just can't bring yourself to give me a word of comfort."

"You don't need comfort, Felix, you need some sleep." Bernardi was extracting some earwax with a paper clip. "If I thought there was the remotest chance of your going home, I'd help pack your bags myself."

Vandenberg looked genuinely alarmed. "You think I should go?"

"No," said Bernardi, "no, I don't think you should go home and neither do you, so what say we cut the crap?"

Vandenberg was nibbling grapes. "There's a genuine streak of sadism in you, Frank. I'd hate to have you around when things really start going badly for me."

"That may be sooner than you think." Bernardi was pointing to the half-open door behind the Secretary of State. Terence Jamieson stood hesitantly in the doorway, holding a bright-red folder.

Vandenberg twisted in his seat. "Jamieson, did I ever tell you what really happened to all of your predecessors?" He didn't wait for a reaction. "They brought me one doomsday cable too many." The Secretary sighed. "All right. Let's look at the damned thing."

For several minutes, Vandenberg seemed oblivious to the presence of the others. He read the message, stared blankly across the room, and then read it again. Finally, without a word, he handed the cable to Bernardi. "It's finally starting to make sense," he said.

Bernardi read the message once—slowly.

"Judging from the transcript, Helen's fine." Bernardi seemed genuinely relieved.

"Yes. Thank God," sighed the Secretary. Then, "What do you make of Safat's message?"

Bernardi scowled. "You think this is what he was after all along, don't you?"

Vandenberg shrugged. "I want your opinion."

"That's my reading," said Bernardi. "Safat wants legitimacy, and you can give it to him; but if that's what he wanted, why bother going through that whole charade with Carucci? Why ask for half a billion dollars? He must've known he wasn't going to get it."

"That's exactly it," said Vandenberg. "He didn't expect the Israelis to release Carucci, and for some reason, they threw him a curve." Vandenberg was up now, pacing back and forth across the room. "That's all the sonovabitch ever wanted; a meeting with me."

"And the half billion," said Bernardi. "That was just to make doubly sure that we wouldn't surprise him too."

The Secretary of State had become almost serene. He was beginning to unravel his adversary's strategy.

"When you think about it, Frank, it's not bad psychology. First you hit your enemy hard. The greater the level of audacity, the better. Then you demonstrate to him how limited his options are. We've always known we couldn't get Helen back by force, and he knows it's against our policy to buy her back; but just in case we might've been tempted, he sets the price so high that we couldn't meet it even if we wanted to. It not only forces us to start thinking in the direction Safat wants, it puts us under enormous pressure, in that we appear to have turned down what he really wants." Vandenberg rubbed a knuckle in the corner of his eye. "He's a cunning bastard, Frank. He's even offered me a legitimate reason for meeting with him."

Bernardi seemed lost, so Vandenberg walked over to where his Under Secretary sat, leaned over his shoulder and pointed to the cable. "Look at the second to last line. 'There are other options open to us, but we prefer the path of conciliation.'"

"The Damascus meeting?"

"Of course," continued Vandenberg. "If you meet with me, you'll be doing it to avoid war; and you get your wife back as a bonus."

Vandenberg was pacing again.

"How do we do it?" He appeared barely conscious of Bernardi's presence.

"You're going to meet him?" Bernardi was shocked.

"I don't know yet. The first thing we've got to figure out is whether it can be done."

"Felix, I think you're crazy." Bernardi's voice rose. "That is without question the most insane thing I've ever heard you say." Suddenly he jumped to his feet, tapping his finger against his lips. Vandenberg stopped speaking while Bernardi turned up the gibberish box and gestured toward the bathroom. When they were both seated—Vandenberg on the toilet, Bernardi on the edge of the tub—and the water was running full force, the Secretary continued.

"Crazy? Why?" Vandenberg was absolutely calm. "I'm going to have to meet with him one of these days anyway. Why not now?"

"How many reasons do you want?" snarled Bernardi. "If Ben-Dor's government survives the next forty-eight hours, this'll bring it down for sure. It'll make Mohammed think you've been playing him for a fool, and it'll give all your friends in Washington exactly the weapon they've been looking for to get rid of you." Bernardi took a deep breath. "Other than that, though, I think it's a sensational idea."

Vandenberg appeared not to have been listening. "He's left the time and the place open to me, and there's nothing about it being a public meeting."

Bernardi was becoming increasingly frustrated. "Felix, if the two of you get together, he doesn't exactly need to take out an ad in *The New York Times*."

"You don't think a secret meeting is possible?"

"You want me to tell you the obvious?" Bernardi waited for a response, got none and continued. "You're traveling with fourteen reporters. Every move you make has got to be justified. In theory, at least, that rules out any side trips to Europe. Lebanon itself is impossible for security reasons. If you were going back to the States, we might be able to arrange it there, but the chance of leaks would still be enormous. Syria's a possibility." Bernardi looked up expectantly.

Vandenberg snapped, "No, he'd have the cards too heavily stacked in his favor there. He's getting me; we can't let him control the negotiating environment as well. Anyway, I have a hunch Safat wouldn't be too crazy about letting his friends in the Rejectionist Front know what he's doing."

"How about Egypt?" suggested Bernardi.

"That's the most logical," continued the Secretary, "but I'm not sure that I want to be that heavily indebted to Houssan." Vandenberg's face suddenly broke into a look of angelic innocence. "Safat's always said he wants to visit Jerusalem."

The cacophony of earsplitting dissonance caused by the running water, the triumph of Beethoven's Ninth and the mumbo jumbo of the gibberish box still could not drown out the penetrating chants of the demonstrators who had gathered in the valley beyond the hotel gardens. With bullhorns, many were shouting: "Vandenberg, go home. Go to your United States. Vandenberg, go home. Go to your United States."

Vandenberg and Bernardi looked astonished, then exploded into laughter. "You gotta hand it to the Israelis, Felix; they've not only got you bugged, they've worked out a system for instant response."

Vandenberg was still smiling when he said, "Could it be done, Frank?" His voice was serious, expectant.

Bernardi slumped against the tile wall. "Felix, I beg you. It's insane. Outside the Communist bloc, these people have the best security system in the world." He pointed randomly at the light fixture. "Even if they don't know about it already, you couldn't possibly pull it off."

Vandenberg had stopped smiling. His voice was cold. "Let's dispense with the obvious, shall we, Frank? I want to examine whether it can be done. Can we get him into the country without the Israelis knowing about it?"

"He wouldn't come alone."

"He can bring two of his people. Can we get them in?"

Bernardi began grappling with the audacity of the problem. "How long were you planning to stay in Jerusalem?"

"This stop?" said Vandenberg. "Two days. We could stretch it to three. Why?"

"The sooner we do it, the fewer people need to know. Less chance of a leak."

"OK," said Vandenberg, "keep going."

"Obviously we can't fly him out of Beirut directly. We'd have to fly him somewhere else first." Bernardi was thoroughly caught up in the planning now. "Cyprus is too obvious. I'd say Athens or Rome. Athens is closer."

Vandenberg said, "There's something wrong with my car."

Bernardi was perplexed. "I don't follow you."

Vandenberg was scrutinizing his slippers. "Something technical; something they can't fix here. Where would they take it?"

"Probably Rome."

"That's perfect. Fiumicino Airport. We have Air Force access there, don't we?"

Bernardi nodded. "Yeah, our people come up from Naples all the time."

Vandenberg was committed. "That's how we do it. We send the transport plane to Rome with my car. If the Israelis question it"—the Secretary hesitated—"if they question it *or not*, make sure they find out that we didn't want any of their people playing with my car. Chalk it up to my paranoia; I was afraid they might bug the car. Come to think of it, that's exactly what they would do."

"And it's exactly what we would do," said Bernardi. "We've sent the car out before. It won't even strike the Israelis as being that unusual."

Vandenberg rose from the toilet and wandered over to the small bathroom window where he watched Israeli police disperse the demonstrators in the valley.

"I want them to have Air Force uniforms and some of those sunglasses that adjust to available light. Make sure each of them has one of those Air Force satchels, you know, briefcases."

"Dispatch cases," Bernardi offered.

"Don't make them too high-ranking. Just high enough so that it would be reasonable for them to be meeting with the Secretary of State. Maybe a brigadier, a lieutenant colonel and a major. Put Safat in the major's uniform. Nobody ever pays any attention to a major." Vandenberg turned to face Bernardi again. "We'd better bring Thurber in on this. Where is he?"

Bernardi left the bathroom and walked through the suite to the hall door. He peered out into the corridor. Several agents from Israel's Shinbet were clustered by the elevators. A young American Secret Service agent stood watch in front of the Secretary's suite.

"Get Thurber, will you?" Bernardi barked.

The agent appeared to be talking into his thumb. "Castle to Thurber." A few seconds later, "Bernardi wants to see you in the Secretary's suite."

When Thurber arrived, he found the Secretary of State and Bernardi seated side by side in the bathroom. He suppressed a smile.

"You used to be with the Agency, didn't you, Eric?" Vandenberg was all business.

"Yessir."

"Well, this'll be right down your alley then."

Thurber was standing in the doorway, his hands lightly clasped behind his back.

Vandenberg studied him for a moment. "What we're going to tell you requires total security. I don't even want your superiors in Washington to hear about it for the time being."

Thurber appeared ill at ease.

"You'll understand better when we've briefed you. Explain, Frank."

If Bernardi harbored any doubts about the plan, he gave no evidence of them as he briefed the head of the Secretary's Secret Service detail.

Vandenberg was listening as closely as the agent. It was, he thought, at one and the same time, deceptively simple and transparently dangerous. Thurber made the same observation.

"We can do all that easily enough, but I can't guarantee you that the Israelis won't catch on."

"How about at the airport?" Vandenberg asked.

"Ben-Gurion?"

The Secretary nodded.

"That shouldn't be any problem. The Israelis never come on the plane; we can just drive off the ramp and out of the airport. There's a checkpoint at the airport perimeter, but they know the car; and if we have one of our regular agents driving, they'll wave it right through."

The Secretary of State seemed delighted. "I always told you I had a devious mind, Bernardi."

Thurber smiled uneasily. "Where were you planning to meet with Safat, Mr. Secretary?"

"You couldn't do it here?" It was a question as much as a comment.

"No way, sir."

"How about the Venezia?" asked Bernardi.

"It's possible," replied Thurber. "But Yehuda would be your big problem."

"Yehuda?" Vandenberg and Bernardi said the name in unison.

"He's the head of your Shinbet detail, sir. He's a very sharp operator."

"But Safat and his men would be wearing U.S. Air Force uniforms," said Bernardi, "and I'm sure we could fix them up with proper credentials, couldn't we?"

Thurber was watching the Secretary of State. "Yehuda'd see right through 'em. He's a very good cop, sir. I've stood watch with him. He spots nationalities the way Johnny Bench calls pitches; and with Arabs, he's incredible. He doesn't just pick 'em out; he'll tell you what village they come from. He's got a sixth sense about them. And Yehuda would be suspicious the minute he saw three guys in uniform."

"You think the uniforms are a bad idea?" It was Vandenberg's question.

"Well, most of our military people in Israel don't wear uniforms, sir; but no, I don't think it's a bad idea. Safat would stick out like a sore thumb if he wore a regular suit. I'm just saying don't count on the uniforms to make those Arabs invisible."

Vandenberg was beginning to sound a little impatient. "Yehuda's your problem. Is it a manageable one, or does it jeopardize the entire mission?"

"No," Thurber responded, "we can handle it; but you won't want to know how."

"Understood." Vandenberg nodded. "Just keep one thing in mind. If Safat's cover is blown while he's here in Israel, it'll create the most monumental stink that any one of us has ever seen. There's a great deal at stake here, Eric."

"I understand that, sir."

"How about getting Safat and his people out again?" Bernardi asked.

"That's less of a problem," replied Thurber. "I can work something up, I think, but I'll need the Secretary's cooperation."

"No problem," said Vandenberg. "Let me have the details later." There was a pause. "Eric, who are you going to send?"

"Well, Brady's your regular driver, and he's pretty reliable. I think the other man should be Pruitt. You're his hero, sir. He'll do anything he can to protect you."

Vandenberg smiled. "I once asked Pruitt what he would do if someone tried to kidnap me, and he said, 'Don't worry, Mr. Secretary, I guarantee you I won't let him take you alive.'"

Bernardi laughed, but Thurber was grim.

"What's the matter, Eric?"

"You understand, Mr. Secretary, this means I'll never be able to work in Israel again. You can fool the Shinbet only once."

"I understand, Eric. But take comfort in the fact that if this doesn't work right, I'll never get back in here either." Thurber grinned briefly. "Send them out tonight, Eric."

"Well, that leaves the easy stuff," quipped Bernardi as the Secret Service agent left. Vandenberg began gargling. "Has it ever occurred to you, Felix, that Safat might not come?"

The Secretary blotted his lips with a towel. "No, it hasn't. He'll come. The real problem's going to be making all the arrangements without half the goddamn world finding out about it."

"Who do you want to have handle the Beirut end of it?"

Vandenberg reflected for a moment. "You're pretty high on Khamsin, aren't you?"

"She's first-rate, Felix; and she speaks good Arabic too."

The Secretary had made up his mind. "All right. Back-channel the instructions to her. Are you sure she's back in Beirut?"

"She left Aswan right after we did."

"Fine. Make sure Khamsin understands that I don't want signals flashing back and forth between Beirut and Washington. She's to limit access on the absolute strictest 'need-to-know' basis. I want Safat in the Venezia restaurant by nine o'clock Thursday evening. Get it started, Frank!"

Bernardi stood up slowly, holding his back. "How about the President?"

Vandenberg looked genuinely troubled. "I can't take the risk, Frank. If this thing fails, I'm out anyway. If it succeeds, I'll brief the President afterward." He seemed to want reassurance. "If I could talk to him privately, I'd do it; but Traynor wouldn't let him sit still for it. And if I were looking at this thing from Washington, I'm not sure that I would either. I know it's a colossal gamble, Frank; but we've got to do this one on our own."

Bernardi said nothing. Vandenberg brightened for a moment. "Don't worry about it, Frank. If this thing blows up in our faces, I'll tell the President it was your idea."

Bernardi was trying to smile. "What do you think's worrying me, Felix? I know that's exactly what you'd do."

16

Katherine Chandler, code named "Khamsin" in secret messages, had never received a back-channel cable from the Secretary's plane. On her desk at the U.S. Embassy in West Beirut a light had flashed, signaling that her private telex machine had just been activated by an incoming cable. Fortunately, she had been working late; otherwise a duty officer would have had to summon her to the Embassy. No one else could open the door to her inner office.

10224 VIA SECSTATE CHANNEL 09630 TOP SECRET EYES ONLY
KHAMSIN APPRECIATE YOUR ESTABLISHING IMMEDI-
ATE AND SECRET CONTACT WITH SAFAT FOR THE

PURPOSE OF CONVEYING FOLLOWING QUOTE PER-
SONAL UNQUOTE MESSAGE FROM VANDENBERG STOP
QUOTE SUGGEST NINE PEEYEM MEETING THURSDAY
FEBRUARY 11TH AT VENEZIA RESTAURANT IN JERU-
SALEM FOR PURPOSE OF OPENING DIALOGUE WHOSE
AIM IS JUST AND LASTING PEACE FOR ALL STATES AND
PEOPLE IN THE MIDDLE EAST STOP SECRECY AND SE-
CURITY ARE ESSENTIAL FOR ACHIEVEMENT OF THIS
AIM WHICH IS IN THE PARAMOUNT INTEREST OF
THE PALESTINIAN PEOPLE STOP ALL ARRANGEMENTS
HAVE BEEN MADE AND KATHERINE CHANDLER OF
OUR EMBASSY WILL SERVE AS YOUR CONTACT AND
COORDINATION POINT IN BEIRUT STOP PLEASE RE-
SPOND IN PERSON TO CHANDLER STOP FELIX VAN-
DENBERG UNQUOTE SECRETARY IS HANDLING ALL
CONTACT WITH WASHINGTON STOP MESSAGES RELAT-
ING TO THIS SENSITIVE OPERATION ARE TO BE
ROUTED THROUGH SECSTATES PLANE AND SLUGGED
09630 STOP DETAILS TO FOLLOW SHORTLY REGARDS
BERNARDI

Katherine had been astonished, to put it mildly, by the audacity of
the plan, and baffled by Vandenberg's purpose. She had stifled an immediate urge to cable Tipton, only because she had persuaded herself
that if Vandenberg was in touch with the White House, Traynor
would quickly learn about the Vandenberg-Safat meeting and alert
the Agency. Fifteen minutes later, her telex had carried another cable
from 09630 detailing the operation and her part in it.

Now she was seated in her Peugeot 204 opposite the main entrance
to the deserted Cercle de la Renaissance Sportive, not too far from her
apartment in Manara, a pleasant section of Beirut sitting on a high
bluff overlooking the Mediterranean. Except for a few streetlights, the
area was dark. Moussa had suggested this spot for their rendezvous.
In the old days, prior to the brutal civil war, Katherine could have
driven to Safat's old headquarters in Ras Beirut; but now elaborate security arrangements had to be made, and no one was better at this
tricky game than Moussa. Katherine had waited less than five minutes
when she spotted a lighter flick on and then off, and then a figure
emerged out of the darkness, walking noiselessly, his features too dark
to discern.

"Katherine," the man whispered. "Out of the car. If you're carrying a gun, leave it."

There was no mistaking Moussa's voice. Katherine pulled her revolver out of her purse, left it on the floor, and pushed open the car door.

Moussa had pulled a handkerchief out of his pocket. "You'll be blindfolded, and I shall assume that you left your gun in the car."

Katherine nodded and meekly submitted to the blindfold. Moussa took her by the arm and led her to a car. Katherine noted that the ride took less than ten minutes.

The blindfold was removed only after Katherine had been brought into Safat's office. As her eyes adjusted to the scene, she saw the Chairman sitting in a large leather armchair. She marveled at how unimposing, almost awkward, he appeared; shy when listening to strangers, deferential when speaking to them. It was easy to underestimate Safat, but his intelligence was wide-ranging and acute. He knew far more about Katherine Chandler than she would have imagined possible, and he treated her with considerable courtesy. Moussa and Ibrahim flanked Safat, as usual in such sessions. Katherine had handed the Chairman a typed copy of the relevant portion of the Vandenberg cable. She sat demurely, legs crossed, arms folded, waiting for a response. She was not surprised that the meeting proved to be brief and pointed.

"You are satisfied, Miss Chandler, that my safety can be guaranteed?" Safat asked the question calmly, in the manner of a prudent man taking necessary precautions.

"I am quite satisfied, Mr. Chairman." Katherine was cool, detached, professional.

"It is understood, of course," Safat continued, "that Mrs. Vandenberg will remain our guest until after my comrades and I have been safely returned here to Beirut?"

Katherine uncrossed her legs and leaned slightly in the direction of Safat. Out of the corner of her eye, she could see one of Safat's bodyguards stiffen.

"That is the essence of your guarantee."

Safat drew thoughtfully on a cigarette. He held it in the manner of an East European, the palm of his hand facing upward, the cigarette pinched between his forefinger and thumb.

"Of what value is the meeting to me if it remains a secret?"

Katherine settled back in her chair. "That, Mr. Chairman, is a matter for your consideration"—she looked at Ibrahim and Moussa—"and, of course, that of your advisers."

"And what is your feeling, Miss Chandler?" Safat studied her with a trace of amusement.

"It is hardly for me to speculate, Mr. Chairman. In this affair, I am merely the Secretary's voice." She paused. "But, if I may be allowed a personal observation, it seems to me that if you get what you want out of the meeting, you won't need the publicity; and if you don't"—she shrugged—"if you don't, it would be extremely difficult for anyone to prevent you from making it public after the fact."

"I am confident, Miss Chandler," replied Safat, "that there will be no need for that." He got to his feet, an unusual gesture for any Arab leader to make toward a woman, particularly one of lesser rank. "Would you please tell the Secretary of State that we accept his kind invitation. I will arrive at the airport in my own car. You will make all the other necessary arrangements?" He did not wait for an answer. "Yes, of course. Well, thank you, Miss Chandler."

Neither Ibrahim nor Moussa had spoken during the entire conversation.

17

Agents Pruitt and Brady viewed their charges across the hood of the Secretary's Cadillac. The interior of the aircraft was dimly illuminated with a reddish glow from the "FASTEN SEAT BELT" light over the cockpit doorway. The agents and the Palestinians had instinctively moved to opposite sides of the car upon boarding the plane in Rome.

Pruitt had not fallen victim to overconfidence. "If the Israelis are fooled by this batch, I'm bringin' my old lady in on the next trip."

Brady was by nature an optimist. "I don't know, Pruitt, the fruity one looks like an Air Force colonel to me."

Pruitt was not convinced. "Jesus, the shit's really gonna hit the fan if we screw this one up."

"Whaddya think the Israelis will do to them if they catch 'em?"

"Same thing the Secretary will do to us." Pruitt spoke without enthusiasm. "String 'em up by their balls."

The agents had no special reason for concern—yet. At Rome's Fiumicino Airport, the transfer had gone smoothly. The Secretary's C-141 had parked in a ring of American military planes at the far end of the runway. By the time the pilot had cut its four powerful jet engines, a black limousine had been driven to the rear of the plane. The driver was a woman; three men in Air Force uniforms sat in the rear. Brady had slowly lowered the "defective" limousine down the rear ramp. The woman had slipped out of the driver's seat of her limousine, after talking with the men, and held the door open for the agent.

"Good luck," she had said softly. "I'll be here when you get back later tonight."

"We shall be happy to see you," Safat had answered.

Brady had driven the car up the ramp and into the belly of the plane. It had taken only forty-five minutes to refuel the C-141, minimum time. Then it was airborne, back to Ben-Gurion Airport, a trip of three hours and twenty minutes.

For the last twenty minutes, Pruitt had felt the lumbering giant losing altitude. Finally, the plane vibrated to the shriek of the landing gear being lowered into position. Pruitt took a deep breath.

"OK, Nat, let's get 'em on board."

The two men unfastened their seat belts and edged around the front bumper of the limousine. Brady climbed into the driver's seat. Pruitt opened the rear door of the car and motioned to Ibrahim. "General, you'd better sit in the back with the colonel."

Moussa began to object. "The Chairman should be seated in back."

Safat intervened immediately. "He's right," he said quietly in Arabic, "we must observe military protocol."

There were no further exchanges. Ibrahim and Moussa settled into the back seat, while Safat moved to the jump seat in front of them.

The C-141 settled comfortably onto the runway and taxied to the southeast corner of the airport complex. The pilot cut his engines and waited for a member of the Israeli ground crew to plug into the plane's internal communications system.

"Ramp clear," said the Israeli.

"Lowering ramp," responded the pilot.

Pruitt sat in the front passenger seat of the limousine. The glass partition between the driver's compartment and the passengers had been raised. Brady was leaning out his window, watching for the U.S. Air Force sergeant to wave him off the plane. He already had the car's engine running. The sergeant whistled sharply. "Bring her down."

Brady had lowered the Secretary's four-ton bulletproof automobile down the ramp dozens of times. The three-inch clearance on each side of the specially equipped car had never intimidated him before. But never before had he carried this kind of explosive cargo. He became conscious of beads of perspiration forming on his forehead as he leaned his head out the side window; he threw the gear stick into reverse and very slowly eased his foot off the brake pedal. The car tipped backward as the rear tires caught the top of the ramp. Brady instinctively pressed down on the brake pedal, bringing the big limousine to a full stop. He breathed deeply and then allowed the car to roll down the ramp and onto level ground. He forced a grin for the sergeant's benefit. "See ya' in church, friend." He waved breezily.

Brady glanced at Pruitt, who whistled nervously. "Just drive, nice and easy." It was dark, and the airport was almost deserted. Brady threaded the car past maintenance shacks and aircraft hangars, slowing down as they approached a small guardhouse at the edge of the airport. Four soldiers were standing guard, each carrying an Uzi. A shirt-sleeved Shinbet agent aimed a small searchlight at the car, allowing the light to linger for a moment on the three figures in the back. Brady slowed the car to a crawl, extending his hand, palm up, out the window. "*Shalom,* mother!"

The Israeli doused the light and slapped Brady's hand with his own. "*Shalom,* Brady." He reached inside the hut to press a button that lifted the metal arm that still blocked the limousine's path. Brady moved the car slowly past the barricade, raising his window as they pulled into traffic.

Pruitt exhaled. "Real slow, Nat, let's not piss off the state troopers." He wiped his hands on his trouser legs. "Can you see what the Air Force is doing?"

Brady glanced into his rearview mirror. "The colonel's reading the Paris *Trib* we gave him; the general's asleep, I think; and the major looks as though he's about ready to crap in his pants."

"That's the way majors are supposed to look," said Pruitt. "Lower the partition a minute, will ya?" Pruitt leaned over the back of his seat. "Everything's fine so far, gentlemen. If I tap on the glass, though, make sure you turn off that light."

A few minutes later they passed a large green-and-white road sign:

"JERUSALEM 62 KMS." The reading light in the passenger compartment went out. Brady looked up and said, "All three of 'em are doing recon."

Brady had been right about Moussa and Ibrahim. They scanned the sides of the narrow two-lane road, irrigated fields receding into the darkness beyond. The Trappist Monastery in the Latrun Valley loomed ahead, the area of some of the bloodiest fighting of the 1948 war between the Jews and the Arabs. When they reached the Judean Hills, the road widened into a four-lane highway. Rusty relics of war marked the pine-covered hills—tanks, half-tracks, artillery pieces, each one left as a deliberate reminder of the Jewish effort to break the Arab blockade of Jewish Jerusalem, each one a monument to the dead and an incentive to the living. Safat's aides seemed to be checking out every museum piece as though each were a modern weapon of war. If Safat himself saw them, his eyes betrayed no sign of emotion. They seemed instead to be glued on some distant vision; he had returned to Palestine.

Brady reached into his shirt pocket and pulled out a cigarette.

"I thought you quit," Pruitt remarked.

Brady didn't take his eyes off the winding highway. "I just unquit."

The limousine hummed along at a steady sixty miles an hour, occasionally speeding past an old sedan but more often being overtaken by yellow Mercedes taxis crowded with tourists heading toward the Israeli capital. "Crazy bastards," muttered Brady. "They're beginning to drive like Arabs."

"Think the Jews and Arabs will ever get together?" Pruitt sounded almost philosophical.

"Yeah, like the Hatfields and the McCoys."

Pruitt chuckled. Deep down, he hoped Vandenberg could succeed. The agent had been traveling through the Middle East for many years, and he had always admired the intelligence and industry of the Jews, the mysticism and hospitality of the Arabs; and he had also come to appreciate the strategic importance of the Middle East, especially after the oil embargo following the October 1973 war. He glanced at the Palestinian leaders through the rear mirror. "Goddammit, the Secretary's a gutsy sonovabitch, bringing Safat here."

When they were still fifteen minutes away from Jerusalem, Pruitt picked up the receiver on the car radio. The conversation was terse.

"Pruitt to Thurber."

A pause.

"Thurber."

"We're fifteen minutes out. You want us to go to the King David or the restaurant?"

"The restaurant."

"That's a ten-four."

They continued for a few more minutes in silence. The big limousine climbed effortlessly through the Judean Hills. The lights of small villages twinkled in the distance.

Pruitt turned to his colleague. "Let me talk to them again."

Brady lowered the partition.

"Gentlemen," said Pruitt, his voice taking on a firm but respectful tone, "when we get to the restaurant, you will wait until I open the door for you. I want the general to get out first, then the colonel, and you"—he turned to Safat—"you get out last, sir. If anything goes wrong, I want to be sure that we can at least get you to the U.S. Consulate."

Safat seemed to be in a kind of trance. The car had come to the crest of a hill. As they rounded a curve in the road, they could all see the brilliance of Jerusalem.

"Did you hear me, sir?" asked Pruitt.

"I heard you," Safat replied softly in English. He had both hands resting on the partition, and he was looking at the approaching landscape with a mixture of sadness and wonder. He was recalling the days of his youth, when Jerusalem was his backyard, but at first glance it all seemed so new that for a brief moment he seemed nonplussed.

"Excuse me, sir." Safat seemed momentarily startled. "Just want to raise the partition," Pruitt explained. Safat leaned back and watched the glass rise slowly in front of him.

As they drove past Jerusalem's bus terminal, there was a loud explosion some distance off.

"Right on schedule," breathed Pruitt.

Brady pressed down slightly on the accelerator. "Where'd they do it?"

"Right behind the Y," said Pruitt.

"I hope they didn't screw up the tennis courts." Brady gave a tight smile.

"Never mind that. I just hope Yehuda goes to check it out."

Brady snorted. "Are you kidding? They couldn't keep him away with a tank."

"OK, coach," snapped Pruitt, "we'll find out in a minute."

As they turned onto Rechov Shimon Ben Shettach they were stopped by a police barricade. Brady lowered his window and pointed to the pin in his lapel. Pruitt had picked up his Uzi from the floor.

A police officer waved them through.

Brady slowed down. "What happened?" he yelled.

"Don't overdo it," Pruitt muttered out of the side of his mouth.

"We don't know"—the policeman spread his arms—"boom . . . we don't know."

Brady waved and gunned the car past the barrier. The street, one of Jerusalem's smallest, had been cleared of other cars, but there were many Israelis there, anxious to catch a glimpse of the controversial American diplomat. They had been hustled by the police to the other side of the street. Vandenberg's limousine, the backup, was already parked in front of the restaurant, which was located on the ground floor of a rather dingy building. "VENEZIA." The neon-lighted sign cast a yellowish glow over the scene. An Israeli television crew had camped near the Secretary's car. The cameraman instinctively started filming, his lightman already having cast his spotlight in the direction of the approaching car, even before Brady had brought the limousine to a full stop. Pruitt was out of the car in an instant. The rest of the group froze.

"Where's Yehuda?" Pruitt called out to a Shinbet agent blocking the doorway to the building.

"He goes to check out the blast," said the Israeli.

Pruitt pointed at the television crew. "Maybe you oughta get them on the other side too." He waited until the Shinbet agent approached the cameraman. There was a brief scuffle, some shouting, but the crew moved. Pruitt opened the rear door. "I'll lead the way, gentlemen." Pruitt and the three Palestinians moved into the restaurant, passing two American agents on the way. An Israeli agent sat at a small table immediately inside the dining area. He raised his hand in recognition of Pruitt. The American interposed himself between the Israeli and his three uniformed charges. Pruitt rested his hand on the Israeli's shoulder, inclining his head toward the Arabs. "They're OK; they're here to see the Secretary."

Vandenberg dined there quite regularly. He claimed to love Italian food, but his loathing of the food at the King David was far more of a factor. The Venezia had a small bar and a seating capacity of thirty-eight. Half the restaurant could be closed off behind sliding doors.

Pruitt threaded his way between the tables. "If you'll follow me, General."

Four Secret Service agents sat at a table in front of the closed partition. Each man had a Coke in front of him. One of the agents rose to open the partition just wide enough for Pruitt to catch the Secretary's eye and get a nod of approval. The agent stepped back and gestured to Safat and his aides to enter the closed-off area of the restaurant. Pruitt then shut the sliding door behind the Palestinians and latched it.

"Is there anything else I can do?" The owner of the restaurant was a slim Italian Jew who had come to Jerusalem after Mussolini's rise to power.

"They're not going to be eating," Pruitt responded, taking up his position in front of the latched door.

The Secretary was accompanied only by his interpreter, Ismail el-Houssany, a Beirut-born Arab who had worked for the U.S. Embassy for more than twenty years and had won Vandenberg's confidence during the course of many difficult negotiations. Vandenberg enveloped Safat's right hand in both of his own, politician style.

"Chairman," he said, "I'm very glad that you came. You're a man of considerable courage."

Safat tilted his head slightly, acknowledging the compliment, but he said nothing. He did not introduce Ibrahim or Moussa.

"Shall we sit down?" Vandenberg motioned to a table. "I thought it would be preferable that we not have any interruptions." He pointed to several trays of pastry, a basket of fruit and carafes of coffee. "You've had a long and tiring journey; if there's anything in particular that you'd like, it would be a small matter." The interpreter was only three or four words behind the Secretary.

"*La, la. Shokran.*"

Houssany hesitated for an instant. He knew that Vandenberg spoke reasonably good Arabic and that Safat's English was passable, but obviously neither man was prepared to make even a gesture in the other's language. He translated dutifully. "The Chairman says, 'No, thank you.'"

Vandenberg took off his glasses, held them up to the light and squinted. "Very well, then. Let's begin." He replaced the glasses. His voice was almost toneless. "Mr. Chairman, we are meeting at your request. I'm prepared to listen."

Safat removed his sunglasses, folded them carefully and placed them on the table. Moussa and Ibrahim sat down at the next table, Safat's Chief of Intelligence fidgeting with his jacket.

"Not too long ago, Mr. Secretary, your own country celebrated the bicentennial anniversary of the American Revolution. Yours has been perhaps the most successful revolution in history." Safat smiled. "Perhaps it has been too successful. You no longer recognize yourselves as the descendants of revolutionaries. It's tragic, but America, which has served as the model for so many revolutionary experiments, is now, in many ways, the most reactionary country in the world." He poured himself a tiny cup of Turkish coffee. Vandenberg's expression was impassive.

"There is scarcely a corner of the world," Safat continued, "that remains untouched by revolution: Soviet Russia, China, Latin America, Africa. Some European countries are even experiencing their second revolutions. Here, in our region of the world, there has been great progress, in Syria, Iraq, Libya, Algeria, Lebanon, Egypt. Certainly the Zionists prosper. When they feel cold, the whole world shivers. When they experience hunger, the world clutches at its belly in sympathy. When they mount campaigns of territorial expansion and wage wars of aggression, they, the aggressors, are treated with concern and compassion, while their victims are condemned." Safat blinked several times, took a deep breath, and when he continued, his voice was lower, softer.

"We are outcasts, Mr. Secretary, not outlaws. We do not seek to destroy the family of nations; we want to join it. And how do the great-great-grandchildren of America's revolutionaries respond? They deny us our existence." Secretary Vandenberg listened, immobile. "My people are tired of war, Mr. Secretary; but they will fight, and they will fight, and they will fight, because we are a nation without a country. The Zionists wait for us to take root somewhere else; in Lebanon or in Jordan. This will not happen. Palestine is here. It is a part of this land."

Safat leaned across the table, staring directly into Vandenberg's eyes. "You are not my enemy. America is not my enemy. There should be understanding between us." He slumped back in his chair and waved a hand in front of his face as though he already realized that Vandenberg's reply would be too painful to hear.

Vandenberg answered in deliberate tones, pausing often, to give his words added emphasis.

"Mr. Chairman, much of what you say has great merit. The Palestinian people must and, when certain conditions have been met, will have an independent sovereign state. But the United States will never disenfranchise one people in order to create a home for another. Neither one of us can ignore reality.

"Would I have met with you now if there was not imminent danger of a war that would be disastrous to everyone? Almost certainly not. Does my wife's safety enter into the equation? Yes; but probably less than you think. I love her very deeply. She is, without question, the most important single person in the world to me. But would I betray the lives of millions and my country's honor to secure her safety? You'll have to accept my assurance that I would not."

The Secretary sipped at a glass of water, watching Safat over the rim of the glass, as if he were sizing up the impact of his words on the Palestinian. "We can opt, Mr. Chairman, for rhetoric or reality. Words are cheap; and in this context, nothing would be easier than for me to tell you what you want to hear. You want formal recognition from the United States? Done. You want to become party to the negotiating process? We'll impose it on the Israelis. You want to create a nation on the West Bank of the Jordan River? I can't promise anything, but we'll try." He paused. "But what would I accomplish if I said these things? A short-term gain and a long-term disaster. Congress would not permit us to grant you diplomatic recognition. The Israelis need our help, but they are hardly as vulnerable to American pressure as either their closest friends or their bitterest enemies believe. The Israelis may be more flexible than their public posture suggests, but they will not negotiate with an entity that denies their right to exist.

"If you want rhetoric, Mr. Chairman, you've come to the wrong man. It's an aid, a useful device, and occasionally I employ it as such; but it is no substitute for reality. I can offer you my good offices. At the appropriate time I will tell Ben-Dor that we have met, and that we will meet again. I will examine with him and with you the parameters of a possible agreement. I caution you now, it will be less than you demand and more than he is prepared to give, but that's the ultimate shape of all good agreements."

There was absolute silence in the room. Finally Safat responded, "What does that mean, 'at the appropriate time'?"

Vandenberg gave a small shrug. "When I have evidence of your good will."

Safat smiled without humor. "You mean when I have returned your wife to you."

The Secretary of State allowed himself a thin smile in return. "That would certainly constitute evidence of good will."

"And your 'good offices' would still be available?" Safat's smile had a touch of sadness now.

"As I said, Dr. Safat," Vandenberg replied, his voice barely audible, "I don't seek short-term gains at the expense of a long-term disaster."

"Would our second meeting be public?"

Vandenberg seemed to consider it for a moment, then he said, "No."

For the first time, Safat's smile was genuine. "If you had said anything else, I would not have believed you. Very well, Mr. Vandenberg, I will place my trust in you, and we will see how you repay it."

The meeting had lasted less than fifteen minutes. Even before Safat rose to his feet, Ibrahim and Moussa were standing. They had touched neither the food nor the coffee, and neither one had spoken a word.

Vandenberg and Safat were facing each other across the table. Vandenberg said, "You're a man of great intelligence, Mr. Chairman. It's surely not necessary to spell out the obvious."

Safat's face grew blank as the interpreter completed the translation.

The Secretary continued. "I'm no magician. Before we can even discuss the framework of a negotiation, the Israelis and the Jordanians . . ."—he paused—"and the OLPP will have to make some very fundamental changes in their present positions. If this meeting or the next one should become public knowledge, the chances for such flexibility would be radically reduced, possibly even eliminated."

Safat extended his hand across the table. "You are quite correct, Mr. Secretary, it is not necessary." He had spoken these last words in English.

Safat put on his glasses and Air Force cap.

"Ready?" the Secretary asked.

"Ready," the Palestinian leader responded.

Vandenberg tapped gently on the sliding partition; Pruitt opened it just enough for him to slip inside and shut it behind him. He approached the Secretary. "Sir, you remember what you have to do now." It was a statement, though it sounded like a question.

Vandenberg nodded. "You want me to provide a distraction while the Chairman is leaving."

"Yessir."

Pruitt then turned to Safat. "Sir, the Secretary's going to be leaving the restaurant first, and I'm going to escort him outside. Another agent will pick him up there. You should follow within fifteen seconds. You're going to see some bright television lights out there. That's part of the plan." Pruitt waited for the interpreter to finish. "Is that clear to everyone?"

Safat spoke to Pruitt in English. "Where will our car be?"

"It'll be just to the left of the entranceway. But don't worry. I'll be waiting for you." Pruitt discovered that he had everyone's full attention. "If there are no further questions, let's move out, gentlemen."

The Secretary's car was already idling in front of the restaurant; so was the backup car, with Brady at the wheel. A crowd of more than a hundred Israelis had gathered on the other side of the street, fretting against the restraints of a half-dozen policemen. It was not an angry crowd, but a couple of young men with long sideburns carried anti-Vandenberg placards. The Israeli television crew retained some flexibility, roaming in the middle of the street, ready to pan from the crowd to the Secretary. A reporter stood near the cameraman, holding a microphone. There were four American agents around the Secretary from the moment he left the restaurant. Vandenberg headed for his car; then he seemed to hesitate for a moment, as though acting on impulse, before striding around the car and toward the crowd. The single light from the television crew followed Vandenberg, casting harsh shadows across the street. Many of the Israelis began to applaud, and the Secretary waved.

Pruitt paused next to Eric Thurber in the doorway to the restaurant. "Is Yehuda back?"

Thurber nodded in the direction of the crowd. "Right where he's supposed to be."

Instinctively Yehuda had positioned himself behind the television light so that he could see the Secretary and scan the crowd that quickly surged toward him. Vandenberg began shaking hands. The Israeli reporter, sensing his opportunity, posed several questions to the Secretary of State, who responded as though he had all the time in the world.

"Now!" barked Thurber.

Safat and the other two had reached the doorway. Pruitt tapped Moussa. "Let's go."

No one paid the slightest attention as the three Air Force officers got into the second limousine. Vandenberg was still answering questions across the street. Pruitt cautioned, "Take it nice and slow, Nat."

The car nosed gently out into the street and past the police barrier a full minute before the Secretary of State finished his interview and entered his limousine.

The ride out of Jerusalem was blessedly uneventful, but Pruitt seemed edgy. He leaned across the front seat and watched the needle of the speedometer edge toward seventy-five.

"You're pushing it kinda hard, aren'tcha, Nat?"

Brady nodded. "Yehuda was sniffin' around the car like it was a bitch in heat."

"You think he made us?"

Brady accelerated slightly into a curve. The heavy car barely swerved.

"I think he knows he's been had."

"Yeah?" Pruitt twisted in his seat to look out the rear window. The road was empty. "What'd he say?"

"Just suckin' around. 'Did you have any trouble getting the car fixed? How long is the General staying in Israel?'"

"What did you tell him?"

Brady's eyes remained fixed on the road, but they gave off a malicious glint. "I told him no, it turned out to be just a carburetor problem."

Pruitt grinned. "You're gonna love it here. The Shinbet has a special place for smart-ass spies."

Brady grunted. "Whaddya think I told him? Nothing. But he knew something was wrong."

"Lemme talk to the turkeys in the back." As soon as the partition had been lowered, Pruitt said, "Gentlemen, when we get to the airport, I think it might be a good idea if you were all asleep."

They rode in silence the rest of the way.

The Shinbet agent at the checkpoint was friendly, as always, but he clearly was in no hurry to raise the barricade. He stood with one hand resting on Brady's open window, playing his flashlight over the three figures in the back of the car. "Who are your friends, Brady?"

"Same stiffs I brought in three hours ago."

"They must be pretty important."

"We just haul 'em; we don't check their pedigrees."

The Israeli seemed reluctant to break off the conversation.

"You don't know who you take in the Secretary's limousine?"

Brady lighted a cigarette.

"Sam, I was just makin' the same point to the Secretary about an hour ago. I said, 'Mr. Secretary, it doesn't seem right, me takin' just anybody in your car. I wanna know who they are and what you were talkin' about.' And you know what he told me?" Brady reached out and gripped the Shinbet agent by the elbow, drawing him closer. Brady lowered his voice almost to a whisper. "He said, 'Brady! Fuck off.'"

The Israeli still looked suspicious but snapped off his flashlight, inclined his head in the direction of the barricade and muttered, "Go on."

Brady asked, "You want me to go under it or through it?"

The Israeli didn't smile. He merely raised his eyes to heaven, as though in supplication, and stepped over to the hut, reached in and pressed the button that raised the barricade.

As they approached the rear of the C-141, Pruitt couldn't restrain his enthusiasm. "Brady, you're beautiful."

Brady braked the car to a smooth halt next to the ramp. "Ain't it the truth." He smiled, wiping his moist forehead with his jacket sleeve.

Vandenberg returned to the King David Hotel and walked through the lobby with an air of long-suffering tolerance. Grudgingly, he paused near the microphones extended over the plastic plants. He looked and sounded tired.

"Is it true," one of the Israeli reporters asked, "that you warned Prime Minister Ben-Dor not to release the terrorists?"

Vandenberg appeared to sag a little. "I think you can understand my dilemma." The lights of the television crews bounced off the rim of his glasses as he tried to frame his response. "If I agree to answer questions like that, then no matter what I say will only further complicate what is already an excruciatingly complicated situation. I recognize that the Cabinet's decision was not taken lightly. It would be ungracious of me to express anything less than my most heartfelt appreciation."

Darius was standing behind the cameras and the lights. He knew that Vandenberg couldn't see him.

"Mr. Secretary, you've been here for nearly forty-eight hours now, and unless you've been holding some top-secret meetings we don't know about, it's difficult to detect even the slightest movement in your negotiations. Has your shuttle ground to a halt?"

Vandenberg's gaze flitted over the knot of news people and camera crews. "Let's say it's idling," he quipped, a Chekhovian smile creasing his face.

Gloria was unimpressed. "Mr. Secretary, you seem particularly down this evening."

"I can't imagine why." Vandenberg had intended to let only a trace of bitterness show in his voice but it came out sounding harsh.

"Are you going back to the United States?"

Vandenberg had started to turn away from the microphones without answering. Gloria blocked his path. "Are you?" she repeated.

"Eventually," he replied.

Ellis, who had waited for the Secretary's return, stepped between Gloria and Vandenberg. "That's enough," he said, casting a disapproving glance at Gloria. "Mr. Secretary, you're wanted upstairs."

Vandenberg smiled at Gloria. "Everyone's got a boss." The Secretary patted Gloria on the shoulder and walked briskly down the corridor toward a waiting elevator, leaving an aura of almost palpable gloom in his wake.

Gloria was dissatisfied. She attached herself to Darius. "What do you make of it?" she asked.

Darius was noncommittal. "He's got a lot to be depressed about."

"I think we're going home." Gloria was hunching it.

"He sure as hell tried to convey that impression." Darius headed toward the revolving doors that led out of the hotel. Gloria stuck with him.

Darius looked exasperated. "Gloria, I've learned to examine what that man says so carefully that all he has to do to completely mislead me is to tell me the truth."

"So . . ." Gloria was eager to continue, but Darius suddenly felt claustrophobic. He needed air and room, to move and think. He excused himself and darted outside. The snow that had fallen a few days earlier had melted, but there was still a brisk snap in the air. Darius stuck his hands in his pockets, his shoulders hunched against the nighttime chill. Jerusalem, 2,500 feet above the Mediterranean, always seemed perfumed by fresh breezes off the northern slopes of the Judean Hills. Darius couldn't shake the nagging sensation that he was tiptoeing around a major story without recognizing it. He knew of no man in the world who was better able to camouflage his moods, and conceal his tactics, than Felix Vandenberg. Darius' instincts told him that he was being set up, an unwitting actor in a drama that Vandenberg was directing. But, aside from his instincts, he had no evidence to support his suspicion.

The Secretary of State was back in the bathroom, perched on the edge of the tub. Bernardi sat on the closed toilet. The strains of Brahms' "Tragic Overture," echoing from a speaker in the living room, alternately overpowered or gave way to the noise of gushing water from the tap.

Vandenberg stared at the tile floor. "Anything from Thurber yet?"

Bernardi gave a shrug. "It'll come," he said. "Now all you've got to do is call Washington and tell the President that the line was busy when you tried to reach him yesterday."

Vandenberg permitted himself a rueful smile. "I intend to revel in my success for a full five minutes before I start sounding penitent."

Bernardi grinned. "It really went well?"

"I only wish some of our formal conferences could be handled as smoothly." The Secretary of State could barely check his enthusiasm. "It went magnificently," he began. "Superbly. In the long run this nightmare may turn out to have been the best thing that could have happened to us. Safat's rhetoric was predictable but restrained. The man's ready to deal, Frank. It's remarkable. You know, he actually has some rather statesmanlike qualities." Vandenberg was beaming. "He's going to release Helen tomorrow morning. With any luck she should be here by early afternoon."

Bernardi was very pleased. "That's wonderful, Felix. I know how much of a strain this has been on you, and I want to tell you very frankly how much I've admired the way you've handled yourself. You set an example for all of us."

The Secretary seemed genuinely touched. "That's very decent of you, Frank. It wouldn't have been possible without your help and support, and I appreciate it, I really do."

Both men seemed a shade embarrassed. Finally, Vandenberg broke the awkward pause. "You realize, of course, Frank, that it would have been absolutely impossible for me to have made that admission if I thought there was the remotest chance of our being overheard."

Bernardi chuckled. "I'll include it in my memoirs."

Vandenberg shrugged. "I'll deny it in mine."

Bernardi returned to his nagging worry. "D'you want to call the President now?"

Vandenberg shook his head. "First I want to reconstruct the conversation, so that we both have it fixed in our minds. These are the key points. He started off by lecturing me. Standard Marxist boiler plate; totally predictable. What he wants was also predictable; recognition, a

Palestinian state. What's fascinating and significant is that he now seems to recognize that we're the only ones who can get it for him."

"Do you think he knows what the price will be?"

Vandenberg nodded. "I made that very clear. I told him that we're not going to sell out the Israelis, and he should have no doubts that we expect the Jordanians to be involved in any agreement."

"He bought that?" Bernardi's forehead was furrowed in disbelief.

Vandenberg's patience, which, when the occasion demanded, could be inexhaustible, was notoriously finite in the sheltered company of aides and subordinates. "You know, Frank, with a superhuman effort on both our parts, we might manage to elevate you to the dizzying heights of mediocrity."

Bernardi flushed but said nothing.

"He," the Secretary of State went on, "wasn't buying, and I wasn't selling. This was purely an opportunity for us to feel each other out, to determine if we had any common meeting ground at all. The fact that I agreed to talk with him was a huge concession; and to Safat's enormous credit, he not only recognized that but responded in rather admirable fashion."

Vandenberg pulled a tortoiseshell comb out of an inside pocket and guided a few silver strands of hair back into place.

"Each of us knew before the meeting where the other stood. The critical fact is that the meeting itself took place and that there can be no misunderstanding about the parameters within which future meetings and discussions can be held."

The Secretary examined his reflection in the mirror without any evident pride. He saw the diminished figure of his Under Secretary in a corner of the mirror and turned to face him. There were deep pouches of fatigue under Bernardi's eyes. Vandenberg's tone softened sufficiently to suggest regret for his earlier sarcasm. "It could've been a disaster, Frank. Instead, we've established an essential contact without compromising either security or our basic position. If Safat was really committed to the Rejectionists, if he really wanted war, he never would've proposed the meeting in the first place."

Bernardi reached over to the toilet paper, unrolled a few sheets, folded them neatly and blew his nose. "You don't think he's trying to throw you off guard; buy time?"

It was a good thought. Vandenberg said nothing for a long moment. Then he shook his head slowly. "No," he responded in a voice so soft it was barely audible, "no, I really don't."

Both men became aware of Terence Jamieson who had quietly materialized in the bathroom door holding a slip of paper.

"Now what?" snapped the Secretary.

"Just got this from Pruitt. He said you'd probably want to see it right away."

Vandenberg took the slip of paper. It read simply "Package airborne." He fixed Jamieson with a playful scowl. "Do you realize this is the first time in almost a week that you've brought me a piece of news that is not a total, unmitigated disaster?"

Jamieson permitted himself the shadow of a grin. "I'm sorry, sir. I'll try not to let it happen again."

Vandenberg shouldered his way past Jamieson into the bedroom. "Comedians," he muttered. "Everyone in Hollywood wants to be a diplomat; and what do I have in the Foreign Service? Nothing but a bunch of goddamn comedians."

Jamieson and Bernardi followed the Secretary of State through the bedroom into the living room. A jumble of nonsense syllables rushed from the gibberish box, while music from a second tape recorder continued to roar out of the bedroom.

Vandenberg gestured helplessly. "Is this really the only way? I feel as though I'm in a goddamn nut house."

Neither Bernardi nor Jamieson replied. They had been through these outbursts of exasperation too many times in the past. Evidently Vandenberg had not expected an answer, because he continued with barely a pause for breath. "Get the President for me."

John Randolph Abbott was, if truth be told, slightly intimidated by his Secretary of State. Not that Vandenberg was ever less than deferential in his dealings with the President; never overbearing, Vandenberg was always the model diplomat: courteous, tactful, wise, helpful. It was just that Abbott always suspected that Vandenberg was deferring to the Presidency while holding the incumbent himself in less than the highest esteem. At this particular moment, though, some inner sense prompted him to believe that he had the Secretary at a disadvantage, and he wanted to assert his constitutional authority. Vandenberg had just told the President about his meeting with Safat. Extraordinary in many respects, but especially in Vandenberg's decision to proceed without prior Presidential approval.

Whit Traynor, who was on an extension, as usual, was in a state bordering on apoplexy. Abbott hardened the tone of his voice. "Felix, you had absolutely no right to make that decision without consulting me first."

Felix Vandenberg lay on the sofa with both feet resting on the coffee table. He held the telephone with one hand while massaging the temple over his left ear with the other. He said nothing.

"Did you hear me, Felix?"

"Yes, Mr. President."

"Then would you perhaps favor me with a reply."

Traynor scratched a message on a note pad: "FIRE THAT BAS-TARD!" Abbott ignored his aide.

"I'm sorry you feel that way, Mr. President. I was only acting in what I believed to be your best interest."

The President's voice rose in pitch. "Run that one by me again, will you, Felix? How in the name of sweet, bleeding Jesus did you think you were acting in my best interest by making a major foreign policy decision without letting anyone in the White House, let alone the President, know what the hell you were doing?"

"Mr. President, the meeting had to take place." Vandenberg's voice was low but firm. "We're facing a possible outbreak of war, and I thought the only way to defuse it was by establishing some kind of dialogue with the OLPP."

"Dammit, Felix, that's not the issue." The President's voice had become strident. "I'm not saying that you shouldn't have met with him. What infuriates me is that you did it on your own, without checking."

Vandenberg smiled. He knew he had won the argument. "Mr. President," the Secretary said, sounding almost disingenuous, "if I understand you correctly, it's not the decision you're questioning, but the manner in which it was reached."

"You bet your ass," bristled President Abbott with total conviction. "That's exactly what I'm questioning; and I don't recall hearing any answer yet, Felix."

"Mr. President, if security had been blown on the meeting, it would have been an explosive political issue back in the States. Now, if you had made the decision, a man of your integrity would have lived with the consequences. You could've blamed a subordinate; but I think I know you, sir. You wouldn't have done it." Vandenberg leaned back on the sofa, like a poet composing his next couplet. "This way, Mr. President, you had complete deniability. That's all I meant when I said I thought I was acting in your best interest. If the Safat meeting hadn't worked, I would've been finished anyway. You could've fired me and placed total responsibility on my shoulders without compromising your own integrity in any way."

"You're fulla crap, Felix; you know that, don't you?" shouted the President, but there was no longer a sarcastic edge to his voice. Abbott had the feeling that once again, as Traynor was so fond of telling him, Vandenberg had just been playing him like a harpsichord.

Vandenberg began rubbing an itch that was burning between his toes. He sat up with the phone trapped between his head and right shoulder, pulled his left foot across his right knee, and gently massaged his toes.

"I'll send you all the details in the overnight cable, Mr. President." There was a grunt from Washington. "That's essentially it from here for now. Good night, sir."

"Keep in touch, Felix." The President had intended to issue an order, but it had emerged sounding more wistful than peremptory.

"Yessir, I certainly will"—Vandenberg made sure that the receiver was securely nestled on its cradle before adding—"you incompetent moron."

Under Secretary Bernardi slouched in a blue-velvet overstuffed armchair, his head lolling back, his eyes tracing a crack in the ceiling. "One of these days you're gonna say it to his face."

Vandenberg had finished his bout with the itch. He was leaning back on the sofa again. "When you think about it, Frank, it's really a tribute to the system. How many other countries can you name that continue to thrive under such mediocre leadership?"

Bernardi closed his eyes. "Have you figured out what kind of a con job you're gonna do on Ben-Dor yet?"

The Secretary of State's lower lip was extended in a thoughtful pout. "Do you realize, Frank, that at this moment I'm so bereft of inspiration that I'm toying with the idea of telling him the truth?"

Bernardi was unimpressed. "Yeah. Now what are you really going to tell him?"

Vandenberg was heading for the bathroom. "*I'm* not telling him anything. *You're* going to call him to let him know that Helen is due here tomorrow." Vandenberg was washing his hands. He could sense Bernardi behind him. As he turned off the water in the sink, he heard Bernardi's voice rise above the music.

"There are times, Felix, when you can be a pluperfect sonovabitch."

The Secretary of State rewarded him with a beatific smile. "Then, Frank, you are going to reply to his next question by saying that while you are not in a position to explain *how* the release was obtained, you can, and indeed you do, give him your strongest personal assurance that the *United States government* did not pay a penny to obtain the release of my wife."

"But you want to leave him with the impression that someone else might have."

Vandenberg shrugged. "*How* he misinterprets a deliberately ambiguous answer is his problem."

"And what if he doesn't bite?"

"I don't expect that he will, but it's all he's going to get out of us for the next few days. Even if he doesn't believe it, it'll be almost impossible to prove that no one paid the ransom."

Bernardi was trying to delay the inevitable. He stood silently for a moment gazing at the red, white and blue folders neatly stacked on the Secretary's bed. "What if he asks me about your visitors this evening?"

"He won't," replied Vandenberg. "But if he does, tell him the truth, as far as you can. The visit dealt with the circumstances surrounding Helen's release." Vandenberg was heading back to the living room. "But don't volunteer that. Make him drag it out of you." Secretary Vandenberg was suddenly brimming with energy again. "Make the call from your room, Frank; and on your way out, send in one of the stenographers. I want to dictate the overnight cables."

Vandenberg walked toward the small bar in a corner of the living room. He rarely drank anything but Campari and an occasional glass of wine, but he poked playfully among the bottles. "Why not?" He pulled a bottle of Courvoisier out of the standing rack and poured himself a small tumblerful of the golden brandy. He carried it to the window overlooking the skyline of Old Jerusalem. He could see his reflection superimposed on the glass. Felix Vandenberg smiled at the image and drank a quiet toast to himself, and to the way things seemed to be going.

18

"Everything all right, Mr. Kane?"

"Fine, Nahum, thanks."

Nahum was a pudgy Viennese-born waiter who had survived the Nazi death camps to fight in three Israeli wars against the Arabs. His past was not, however, written on his face, nor was it evident in his manner. He wore a gentle smile on almost all occasions; and unlike most of the other waiters at the King David, he seemed to exude a certain air of cosmopolitan gentility, as though he were genuinely enjoying his work. And indeed he was, and never more so than when he waited on Darius Kane, whom he had come to regard as a kind of supercelebrity, an insider who would occasionally share a secret with him.

"The usual this morning, Mr. Kane?" Nahum was brushing imaginary crumbs off the fresh white tablecloth and fussing with the setting he had placed for Darius. "Fresh orange juice, two poached eggs on a single slice of toast, strong tea made from three tea bags, and a soft bun." Nahum ticked off Darius' breakfast menu with a sense of deep pride. He smiled when Darius nodded, but he didn't linger. Most times, a brief political exchange would follow, but this time Nahum sensed that Darius seemed uneasy, somewhat downcast.

Nahum withdrew, while Darius picked up his copy of *The Jerusalem Post.* Its banner headline reflected the same questions that had kept him from a restful night.

VANDENBERG EXTENDS JERUSALEM STAY INTO THIRD
DAY, BUT NEGOTIATIONS STILL SEEM STALLED

Darius did some private calculations as his eyes wandered over the busy dining room, pausing occasionally on one of the pretty, miniskirted Israeli policewomen.

We arrive in Israel on Wednesday. Vandenberg sees Ben-Dor. No big news. Not unusual, really, at this stage of the negotiations. The Secretary ought to be moving on to Aswan, Riyadh, Damascus or back to Amman on Thursday. But no. He spends the entire day, we're told, in his hotel suite working on details of the negotiations, as well as other international business. No meetings with Ben-Dor, or with Cohen. Now that's unusual, but Ellis says it isn't. No leaks from anyone, not even Shlomo Dubin, leader of the political opposition. We find out, after the fact, that the Secretary goes to dine at the Venezia, by himself. Bernardi explains, off the record, that he's depressed about Helen's kidnapping. Wants to be alone. OK, fair enough, but somehow not convincing. Nothing for Thursday evening news, either. Two nights in a row with no satellite.

There had been no complaints or queries from New York, but Darius was becoming increasingly edgy. No matter how often he told himself that he was not in the TV business *just* to appear on the tube, he was almost always overcome by a wave of insecurity and depression when he was off the air for two days in succession. Goddammit, what the hell was going on?

Two tall glasses of fresh orange juice flashed into focus, breaking into the haze of his calculations. "Eggs'll be ready in a moment, Mr. Kane." Nahum was gone before Darius was even able to grunt his appreciation. He sipped his orange juice, enjoying its pulpy taste, and read the editorial in his newspaper. It mirrored a widespread Israeli concern about Vandenberg's real intentions, and it ended on an accusatory note.

> . . . and therefore we cannot escape the conclusion that once again the American Secretary of State is prepared to sacrifice the interests of Israel for his long-range goal of insuring a flow of Arab oil and of improving his tattered policy of détente with Russia. It almost seems as though morality plays no role in this global strategist's policy.

"May a working stiff join you, sir?" Herb Kaufman was approaching Darius' table with two notebooks tucked under one arm, the *Jerusalem Post* under the other, and both hands full, as he tried to balance several plates and a small glass of canned orange juice.

"Yeah, but don't mess up the clean tablecloth."

Nahum was at that moment placing Darius' poached eggs between his neatly spaced knife and fork. He paid absolutely no attention to Herb. "I'll have your tea in just a second, Mr. Kane."

"And if it's not too much trouble," Herb hissed, "maybe you could bring me some silverware." Herb managed to drop one notebook into his eggs. "Goddammit, why wasn't I born beautiful instead of brilliant?" Like most of the other guests, Herb had to get his own breakfast from a long, rectangular table groaning under the weight of every conceivable kind of herring, lox, bagels, buns, juice and eggs. Although the shuttle was only a week old, Herb already looked as if he had been on the road for a month. Pouches had formed under his eyes, and his paranoia was intense.

"Goddamn editors!" Herb was hunched over the table, shoveling eggs and buns into his mouth in one continuous movement, as though fearful that at any moment there'd be a call that would tear him away from his meal. "They woke me three times in the middle of the night. And for what?" The question was rhetorical. Darius did not interrupt; he was cutting into one poached egg with surgical care, watching the yolk yellow the toast. "Once on a Reuters callback about a coup in Chad. Did Vandenberg have any reaction? 'Sure, shmuck,' I said, 'I'll wake him as soon as we hang up.' Once about UPI radio wanting some actuality about the Knesset debate. I didn't bother telling the idiot it was four in the morning. And finally at five-thirty . . ." Herb rolled his eyes toward the chandeliered ceiling. "At five-thirty, I'm finally getting off to sleep again, and I get a call from the sports editor in London. He wants a piece on the Sunday soccer match."

Darius was dabbing his mouth with a linen napkin, thinking of coining a solicitous phrase, but Herb had paused only for a sip of coffee. "And now this editorial!" He pointed to the *Jerusalem Post*. "That sonovabitch friend of yours, Darius, is at it again. Screwing Israel so he can kiss the Arabs' ass."

Darius had his doubts about Vandenberg too, but they were private doubts. "Herb, he may be screwing Israel. That's always possible, but we've got no evidence. And let's be fair, for Chrissake. His wife's been kidnapped by some fanatical Palestinians. He's upset."

"Bullshit!" Herb's nostrils flared. "He's making a deal, Darius. He's using Helen's kidnapping to make a deal. I can feel it. He's making a deal at Israel's expense."

That particular possibility had also occurred to Darius. "Let's say you're right, for a minute." Darius was trying to pacify Herb. "But can you imagine Ben-Dor, with all the troubles he's already got, allowing Vandenberg to succeed?"

"Maybe Ben-Dor doesn't know yet."

Darius sympathized with Herb's passionate feelings about Israel's survival, but he refused to believe that Vandenberg would participate in a betrayal of Israel. He knew the Secretary too well. He decided, for the sake of argument, to revert to basics.

"Herb, do you have any evidence that Vandenberg is making a deal against Israel's interests?"

Herb shook his head.

"Who led the fight in Congress to boost military aid to Israel?"

Herb nodded, as though answering "Vandenberg."

"Has Vandenberg ever, ever shown an anti-Israeli bias?"

Again Herb shook his head.

"Then let's try to give him the benefit of the doubt." Herb was about to interrupt, but Darius continued in a slightly louder tone of voice, tinged with a touch of genuine compassion. "Herb, the essence of a deal in the Middle East is a compromise, a compromise between Israel's right to exist and the Arabs' right to reclaim occupied territory, including the setting up of some kind of homeland for the Palestinians."

"Fuck the Palestinians." Herb pushed his chair back from the table and crossed his legs. "Screw them. What have they done?" Herb didn't wait for an answer. "Slip into Israel in the middle of the night. Blow up schools, kill kids. Leave bombs in theaters. Pledge themselves to destroy Israel. No way, Darius. No way. I agree with Ben-Dor. Let's settle it on the battlefield."

"To what end, Herb? Another war, more killing, more chance of another Soviet-American confrontation? The Palestinians must be accommodated. That's what Vandenberg is trying to do. That's what's in America's interest. You must see that, Herb," Darius concluded on a plaintive note. He noticed that the dining room was almost empty, and even Nahum seemed eager to clear the table.

Herb was oblivious to the sudden quiet. "Darius, do you know what Israel means to Jews? Do you know that six million Jews—six million human beings—got killed during the Holocaust? That hundreds and then thousands of Jews finally came out of the sewers and the death camps to come here, actually to *return* here? To reclaim land given by God? Are we now to be asked to give it all up, piece by piece? When will Houssan, or Mohammed, acknowledge that Israel even exists? I mean, is that too much to ask?"

Nahum, standing to one side, nodded in agreement.

"It isn't, Herb." Darius' voice was soft. "It isn't at all. But we've got to go for a compromise."

"Fine," Herb agreed. "Which one?"

"I don't have one." Herb could barely hear Darius. "I just know there must be a compromise, and I believe Vandenberg will come up with one." He tried to smile. "Herb, this land has been soaked in blood, and it hasn't all been Jewish. The Christians feel strongly about Jerusalem; so do the Moslems."

"So what does that mean? That we get kicked out of here again? That Nasser rises out of his grave to lead a holy war against Israel? Shit, Darius, when does it all stop? We're entitled to our little acre too."

"Right. That's what I meant about compromise."

The tone in Darius' voice was so doleful that for a moment Herb seemed deflated. His anger and frustration subsided, like air leaking out of a balloon. The two friends looked at each other but couldn't speak.

"Mr. Kane." Nahum had approached the table. "May I offer a suggestion?" He began clearing the table. "Jerusalem is especially beautiful today. You know the old proverb?" He didn't wait for an answer. "'Ten measures of beauty came into the world: nine measures for Jerusalem, one for the rest.' Jerusalem is truly a city of gold. Go sit in the sun. You could use a rest."

"And can I join him too?" Herb was again sarcastic, again normal.

Nahum smiled. "Mr. Kaufman, we Jews are not used to such luxuries."

Darius snapped to his feet. "Meet you at the pool in twenty minutes." He started toward the double French doors.

"Make it thirty. Got to call the office first."

Darius got to the pool first, cutting through the hotel's carefully manicured garden. The hibiscus bushes seemed on the verge of budding, and tall palm trees swayed gently in the morning breeze. The air was brilliantly clear, almost crystalline, lending a very special quality to the sky over Jerusalem. He stretched out in a lounge chair, and within a few minutes, he could feel the warmth of the sun, which hung over the turrets of the Old City. The day itself seemed to sparkle.

There was only one swimmer in the pool—an off-duty Secret Service agent. Darius doubted that the temperature had reached seventy. An Israeli soldier, one of dozens stationed around the hotel, leaned casually against a date palm; he was holding a machine gun in one hand. In the distance Darius could hear the noisy chatter of a group of middle-aged American women who were seated in a semicircle of lounge chairs at the far end of the pool.

Herb pulled a chair over to Darius and dropped into it. He gripped the armrests and lifted his face toward the sun. "Hmmm. Feels good." Herb could feel the tension ease out of his body.

"Darius?"

"Yeah."

"Sorry."

"'Bout what?"

"Getting so emotional before. I try to stay cool about Israel, but . . ." He didn't finish the sentence.

"Herb, you're one of the great men of our time. I love ya. Forget it." There was a pause. "Besides, who knows? You may be right."

The two friends sat in the sun for a few minutes in silence. Suddenly Darius asked, "Why are we the only ones here?" He got up on one elbow. "And how come you're not nervous?"

"Whaddya mean 'not nervous'? I ran a bed check before coming down here." Herb lay flat on his back with his eyes closed. He held up his fingers as he spoke. "You got four tennis players, three shoppers, three late sleepers and two I-don't-know's."

"Who are the I-don't-know's?" asked Darius.

"*Time* and *The Wall Street Journal.*"

"You're fantastic," said Darius. He closed his eyes and leaned back to enjoy the warmth of the sun. Suddenly he felt a shape pass between him and the warmth. He waited for the shape to pass. Instead, it spoke. "Channel Five, am I right?"

Darius squinted at the shape. It wore a broad-brimmed hat and at least forty excess pounds. "No, ma'am," replied Darius. "You're confusing me with that newscaster. It happens all the time."

The shape returned to the group at the far end of the pool, where it was welcomed by a triumphant voice. "Did I tell you? Did I tell you it wasn't him?"

The shape was bitter but unyielding. "Gertie, you're wrong. I've seen him a million times. He just don't wanta be bothered."

"KANE!" The voice came booming across the garden. It was Carl Ellis. "DARIUS!" Then, "Herb, is that Darius with you?"

Kaufman yelled back, "Darius isn't here! This guy's just sitting in for him."

Darius snorted. "God's punishing me for something, Herb."

Ellis walked toward them, carrying his jacket over one shoulder, a finger hooked through the loop inside the collar. Otherwise he was dressed for work. He stopped between their chairs, looking down at the two reporters. "How come Darius has a tan and you're still so pale?"

Kaufman scarcely moved. "I work for the wires."

Darius chuckled. "Pull up a chair, Carl."

The shape's voice floated along the length of the pool. "Bastard! I knew I recognized him."

Ellis appeared confused. "I can't stay. I just wanted to alert you. The press buses are leaving for the airport at noon."

Darius and Herb sat bolt upright. Darius looked at his watch. "What the hell are you talking about, Carl; it's almost eleven now. Where are we going?"

Ellis backed off a step. "I don't know, Darius. I was just trying to be helpful."

Herb's voice took on the reassuring, slightly patronizing tone of an overworked cop trying to dissuade a would-be suicide. "Caarrrl"—he stretched the name into several syllables—"I think the point Darius is trying to make is whether we should pack a suitcase or a picnic lunch."

Ellis was in genuine, visible distress. "Look, all they told me was to round you guys up and make sure you got to Ben-Gurion by one-fifteen at the latest."

Darius kept his voice level. "Carl, do *you* know why the Secretary's going to the airport?"

"No." It was not an admission Ellis enjoyed making. "Fellas, I gotta go. If you see any of the other guys, spread the word, will ya?"

Darius and Herb watched Ellis cross the lawn.

"There are times," said Darius, "when I could almost feel sorry for him."

"Sorry!" Kaufman's indignation shook the Israeli soldier out of his reverie. "How the hell do you feel sorry for a guy who's an intellectual eunuch?"

Darius poked a foot under the deck chair, groping for his sandals. He tucked his copy of the Paris *Trib* under his arm. "D'you see Red Smith this morning? The guy's incredible. He really writes beautiful copy and he's been doing it since before you and I were old enough to read."

Kaufman was wiping his glasses with the bottom of his T-shirt. "What the hell does Red Smith have to do with Ellis?"

"Herb, consider what you and I are about to do. We're going to race upstairs, get dressed, pack an overnight bag—just in case—race downstairs, hop on a minibus, drive for more than an hour and then probably wait for at least another hour before we even find out what we're doing; and all because that thirty-eight-thousand-dollar-a-year eunuch told us to. Now considering all that, I'd just as soon talk about one of the world's greatest sportswriters." Darius paused. "Come to think of it, I'd just as soon *be* one of the world's greatest sportswriters, because this sure as hell is no way for a grown man to earn a living."

The woman in the broad-brimmed hat rose from her chair at the other end of the pool and aimed a blood-red fingernail at Darius, as though she were pronouncing a curse. "As long as you live, you'll never be a David Brinkley."

Darius clutched at his throat in mock horror.

Herb grinned. "I think she's trying to make up with you."

Dan Sapir, the Prime Minister's articulate spokesman, leaked the news of Helen Vandenberg's release to his favorite newsman from *Davar,* a Histadrut newspaper, exactly five minutes after the reporters traveling with the Secretary of State had piled into three minibuses for the hour-and-fifteen-minute ride to the airport. The news spread through Israel's journalistic grapevine within thirty minutes. Kol Yisrael broke into its regular programming with a news bulletin. The driver of Darius' minibus, who had been listening to a portable radio tucked between the window and the dashboard, smiled broadly at an Israeli soldier who was leaning against the door.

"What happened?" Darius asked the soldier.

"He speak no English," said the driver, still smiling. His accent carried the inflection of an East European background. "Mrs. Vandenberg released. Radio says she come soon Israel."

Darius muttered "Sonovabitch" and prayed that Blumer had sent a crew to the airport. NNS's Tel Aviv bureau always monitored Kol Yisrael. If Blumer was in the office, then there would be no problem. If he was at lunch—Darius, glancing at his wristwatch, noted that it was almost twelve-thirty—would his secretary be able to alert him, or, failing that, would she dispatch the crew on her own? Darius' stomach tightened into a knot, though he retained his outer composure. By the time the buses reached the airport, speculation abounded, but there was no more hard information. Darius spotted the press bullpen near the VIP lounge, and he sighed with relief when he saw the NNS camera standing among a dozen others crowded into a corner of the bullpen, already overpopulated with anxious reporters, producers and photographers. Among them, sullen, stood Blumer, biting into his pipestem. Normally, the "Vandenberg press" was spared the humiliation of bullpen stakeouts and was allowed to wander among the VIPs and officials; but this time they were herded unceremoniously into the jammed enclosure.

"Moshe!" One of the Israeli reporters yelled at the superintendent in charge of security. "There's been a terrible mistake. You've put the Secretary's press in with us common people." He spoke in Hebrew. There were a few snickers among the Israelis.

A Kol Yisrael reporter approached Darius; he was holding a microphone. "Mr. Kane, we're on the air live. Do you mind if I ask you a few questions?"

Darius shrugged. He did not like the idea of reporters interviewing other reporters, particularly in the Middle East, where those traveling with Secretary Vandenberg were often regarded as quasi officials; even the Israelis dismissed any arguments to the contrary with smiles of infuriating tolerance. The reporter's introduction of Darius was brief. The NNS diplomatic correspondent was, in fact, better known in Israel than in the United States. His reports were frequently carried on Israeli television and radio, and many of his stories were reprinted in Israeli newspapers.

"There is one question in particular," the Kol Yisrael reporter was saying, "that is on the minds of all Israelis this afternoon. What was the price for Mrs. Vandenberg's release?"

For an instant Darius was tempted to admit his ignorance, and voice his suspicions. But he restrained himself. "I'm afraid you've overestimated the Secretary's interest in a free exchange of information with reporters." Darius smiled. "In all honesty I can't tell what, if anything, has been paid for Mrs. Vandenberg's release. But I can assure you that I'll be as interested in finding the answer to that question as you are."

"You mean," the Israeli asked, "that no one in the American party has given you even a hint of what was given up for Mrs. Vandenberg?"

"That's exactly what I mean."

The Israeli reporter looked skeptical, but before he could pursue his line of questioning, the attention of both interviewer and interviewee was drawn to the din of two approaching Chinook helicopters.

"Thank you," the Israeli said, "for your highly informative responses." He barely concealed his sarcasm. The Israeli turned toward the helicopters and, without missing a beat, launched into a narrative description of the quickly changing scene at the airport.

Herb Kaufman was watching Darius with a look of bemusement. "I'll tell you something, Kane. You've sure got *chutzpa*. I've been with you all morning and I *know* how ignorant you are; and you're giving interviews?"

Darius wrapped an arm around Kaufman's shoulder. "The price of fame, m'boy. You wanta know the funny part? I told him I didn't know anything, and now he's pissed off because he's sure I'm holding out on him."

The helicopters landed, the noise of their rotors drowning out all other sound. The backwash from the spinning blades sent gusts of warm air swirling across the tarmac. Only the cameramen, hunched over their Auricons and Arriflexes, faced into the wind. The others, including the men on the security detail, looked away, protecting their eyes, so that for the moment, the landing of a U.S. Air Force DC-6 went unnoticed. Then, as the helicopter pilots shut down their engines, the noise of the approaching propeller-driven plane slowly filled in the vacuum left by the dying sound of the turbojets.

The timing was impeccable. A ring of American and Israeli security men with Secretary Vandenberg and Foreign Minister Cohen at its nucleus reached the side of the DC-6 no more than a minute after its propellers had traced a final languid circle. An El Al ramp was pushed to the door of the plane. Vandenberg bounded up the steps, taking two at a time. Darius and the other reporters pressed against the police barricade, less than fifty yards away.

The man from *Time* observed, "Any guy who's that eager to see his wife can't be all bad."

"You're sweet, but dumb." Gloria smiled. "He just wants to get to her before the Israelis or any of us do."

Vandenberg had disappeared inside the plane. The Israeli Foreign Minister stood at the foot of the ramp, clearly ill at ease. Once he placed a foot on the bottom step, as though he were about to board the plane; then he hesitated and bent over to tie a shoelace. Five minutes elapsed; to those outside the plane, it seemed much longer. Finally, standing side by side, Felix and Helen Vandenberg appeared at the door of the plane, smiling broadly. He thrust one hand into his coat pocket, lightly clasping his wife's elbow with the other. Mrs. Vandenberg waved in the general direction of the cameras; then, as she spotted familiar faces among the group of reporters, she broke into a wide grin and waved more energetically. In spite of themselves, several of the news people cheered and waved back.

Brian Fitzpatrick snapped, "Dammit, I'm glad she's back!" as though daring anyone to disagree with him. The Secretary gently led his wife down the ramp. They hesitated for a moment and then walked over to the microphones that were bunched together outside the press bullpen. The automatic triggering devices on a dozen Nikons and Leicas exploded into a barrage of clicks and whirs as the Vandenberg couple posed somewhat awkwardly. Finally, the Secretary broke the ice. "I told you she couldn't stay away from me." His words were amplified through two huge speakers, so that for an instant Vandenberg recoiled from the unexpectedly loud sound of his own voice.

"How are you feeling, Mrs. Vandenberg?" It was a British reporter from the London *Daily Express.*

"I feel very well indeed, thank you."

"Were you well treated?" It was the same reporter.

"Well, I think I would have preferred making the trip from Petra to Jerusalem by a somewhat more direct route." Helen Vandenberg appeared to have completed the thought, but her husband whispered something to her and she continued. "But all things considered, I was quite well treated. Yes."

A jumble of questions struggled for attention. Secretary Vandenberg leaned into the microphones. "Ladies and gentlemen, I'm sure you can understand that my wife is extremely tired. She has a brief statement to make, and then I hope you'll permit me to take her back to the hotel."

Helen Vandenberg seemed almost relaxed, self-assured, as she spoke. "As I've already told you, I was well treated. I never felt that my life was in danger; but, by the same token, I have absolutely no idea as to where I was held, and although I've since learned that I was kidnapped by the OLPP, I couldn't, quite honestly, from my own experience even testify to that. Now, I'm sure Felix will answer any further questions you may have."

Vandenberg smiled broadly at his wife, turned the full glow of his enthusiasm toward the cameras and said, "No, I won't. At least not now. We're going back to Jerusalem."

As the couple turned away from the microphones, an Israeli reporter flung a final question at Vandenberg's back. "Mr. Secretary, did you pay the ransom?"

If Vandenberg heard the question, he gave no evidence of it.

Jerry Blumer stood behind Darius. "OK, hotshot, what's it all mean?"

"It means I'd better get my ass in gear and find out what Felix paid to get his bride outa hock."

They were walking through the customs lounge when suddenly Blumer stopped and sat down on the edge of a luggage conveyor belt. "Come here." He pointed to a spot on the belt next to him. "All right, now I'll tell you whatcha gonna do." Blumer consulted his watch. "It's one-forty. The film's on its way to the lab. With any luck, Gideon'll have it out of the soup by two-thirty. I've got the studio fired up, so you can count on a live camera. In just thirty seconds, you and I are gonna get up and walk to the car. Then you're gonna take your little typewriter, and by the time we get to Herzliya, you will have written a script, which I will then give to Gideon so he'll know what sound bites to pull and I'll call New York and feed them the script. I've ordered the bird for two-forty-five our time; that's seven-forty-five in New York. That's fifteen minutes before the *Morning News* takes air. If any of this crap takes longer than I've figured, we've just blown three grand. Is that clear?"

Darius raised his hand.

Blumer snarled, "Don't get cute with me. What?"

"Now can we go?"

They were up and walking toward the exit. Blumer, who was half a step behind Darius, raised his voice. "Do you know that you give me acid indigestion? I go months without so much as a sour burp, and then you come into town and my stomach feels like Hurricane Hilda."

They were on the sidewalk elbowing their way through a group of touring American Baptists. The tourists and their bags were similarly emblazoned with tags that read: "HOLY LAND TOURS, FIRST BAPTIST CHURCH, DEMOPOLIS, ALABAMA." Seated to one side of the exit, two Orthodox Jews, ringlets of dark hair curling from underneath their broad-brimmed black hats, were engrossed in a game of chess. One of the tourists nudged his wife. "Will you take a look at that, Millicent."

Darius couldn't resist. "What'sa matter," he said to the man, "haven't you ever seen a Yankee before?"

Blumer and the Alabaman wore almost identical looks of disbelief.

Blumer grabbed Darius by the arm. "Will you, for cryin' out loud, just once, stop horsin' around?"

Darius was grinning broadly as he allowed himself to be dragged across the street to Paul's waiting car. The engine was already running. "It's the classic old joke, Jerry. About the rabbi's son who marries a gentile girl in Alabama, and—"

Blumer opened the car door. "Some other time, huh?"

Darius shucked his jacket, handed it to Paul and slipped into the back seat. He was already unzipping his Olivetti case by the time Blumer got into the car. Darius balanced his typewriter on his lap while guiding a two-carbon "book" of NNS copy paper behind the carriage. Then he stared at the blank page as though waiting for divine guidance. None came immediately. He stared out the car window, hardly noticing the rushing landscape of farms, fields, buildings and cars. The speedometer needle hovered around the seventy mark. Darius reached into his back pocket for his notebook. As he flipped through it, he underlined several quotes. Next to a few of them, he drew asterisks. They were fully halfway to Herzliya before Darius began typing, but then his fingers flew over the keys with such fury that even his jaw muscles seemed to flex and unflex with the intensity of the effort.

Darius was still typing when the car pulled into a narrow driveway leading to the satellite station. The guard hit a button, lifting an iron barrier, so that Paul did not even have to stop the car. "*Shalom*, Arik," he shouted; the guard, a young, bearded Israeli, waved at the passing car. Paul eased it to a stop in front of a low railing. He turned off the ignition and glanced at his watch. "Thirty-four minutes," he marveled, expecting a compliment. He got none. Darius kept typing, pausing for a moment as though searching for a final burst of inspiration.

"You finished?" Blumer asked, trying to sound matter-of-fact.

Darius shook his head irritably. "Quiet!"

Another moment of reflection was followed by a final, furious assault on the keyboard. Then he read the script to himself, mumbling so no one else could hear him. He stripped the copy paper out of the typewriter and, handing the script to Blumer, exclaimed with a broad grin, "Sometimes I wonder how I keep surpassing myself!"

Blumer squinted over the bowl of his pipe. "Considering the level at which you started, it must have been easy."

Darius had begun walking along the gravel path that led to the film-editing rooms. "The second I said that, I knew I shouldn't have opened my mouth."

Gideon, the film editor, was leaning against the doorway of the one-story building. He was a big man with bushy hair and remarkably quick, delicate fingers. "*Shalom*, Darius!"

The two men embraced. Darius took the paper cup of coffee that Gideon was holding out of his hand and drank from it. "Gideon, it seems to me that you're taking this far too seriously." Darius spoke in a tone of mock confidentiality. "I don't want you to be tense. Just because you have this once-in-a-lifetime opportunity to cut an important story for a major American television network, you don't have to get uptight."

Gideon resumed his casual pose, leaning against the doorway. "I thought I was cutting *your* piece."

Blumer was getting genuinely nervous. "I hate to break up your routine, but what time is the film getting out of the lab?"

Gideon consulted his watch. "In about fifteen minutes."

Blumer groaned. "What happened?"

"What do you think happened?" Gideon shrugged. "The NBC courier made it here first. You should hear how the ABC and CBS producers are screaming. There's *no* way they can make their morning shows."

Blumer indulged in his first smile of the day; he patted the film editor on the cheek. "Do you realize, Gideon, that it's moments like these that make life worth living? But if you don't get us on the air in time, I will personally circumcise you." Blumer paused dramatically.

Gideon said, "You're twenty-eight years too late."

"Again!" Blumer added.

Darius waved to the girl behind the reception desk. She was not a particularly pretty girl; but whenever she smiled, she was instantly transformed into a beauty. She smiled at Darius, but he didn't break his stride. He kept walking toward the NNS editing room. "Come on, Gideon," he said, beckoning, "leave that barbarian alone. I wanta go through the script with you." Then, as an afterthought, he called out the door, "Jerry, will you get my call through to New York?"

"It's in the works, Mr. Kane." Blumer's voice was fat with sarcasm, but he was feeling no pain. Blumer was in his element, facing a deadline that seemed improbable to meet, cajoling international operators, screaming at film editors, manipulating correspondents and producing pieces of instant history for television viewers. He thrived on deadlines, each one a new challenge. At this moment, his sense of excitement was almost boundless because he knew that two of his richer, more prestigious competitors were about to be beaten by a deadline. He floated on his own cloud.

A telephone rang in the editing room. "Fast enough for you, sir?" Blumer was still doing his act, but his contentment seemed to coat the walls. Darius grinned at Gideon and picked up the phone.

"Yes, it is," he told the New York operator. Darius could hear her on the line with one of the desk assistants. "Tell Mr. Schubert I have Darius Kane for him in Tel Aviv." Charlie Schubert was the overnight editor on the television assignment desk, the central nervous system for NNS's national and international coverage. Schubert was an old-timer who had been a fine wire service reporter before he had been seduced into joining NNS in its early days by what had then seemed a magnificent increase in salary. Now he was miserable; the producers ran each news broadcast as though it were an independent fiefdom, and his role on the assignment desk often struck him as being more symbolic than substantive. He had begun to think of himself as a high-priced errand boy, and of television news as a contradiction in terms. But he had a family, a mortgage and he was fifty-four years old. He could no longer afford to leave. Darius had always respected his professionalism.

"Charlie, you'd better get someone from the *Morning News* on with us right away. We don't have a helluva lot of time."

"Bert's already on the line."

Bert was Bertram R. Ross, executive producer of the NNS *Morning News*, thirty-four years old, a graduate of Phillips Exeter and Harvard, and a Fulbright scholar at Oxford, who had gone directly from a staff job at the White House to "executive responsibility" at NNS, never stopping for journalistic experience along the way. The word at NNS was that "Bert has a rabbi," and the phrase was always accompanied by the gesture so meaningful in any bureaucracy: a thumb pointing upward. Ross, acutely aware of his fortuitous grip on power, never removed his jacket and rarely smiled. One day, he was convinced, he'd run NNS, and he wanted to project the proper image from the start. Charlie, seated behind a cluttered desk, his sleeves rolled up above his elbows, bifocals resting on the diminishing thatch of graying hair just above his forehead, was not his type.

"What do you have for me?" Ross's voice was flat, suggesting objectivity.

Darius forced back the word "contempt"; instead, he assumed a brisk tone of self-assurance that he knew would preempt any argument from the young producer. "Bert, we're gonna have less than ten minutes to put this piece together. I won't have time to put any narration on track, so the voice-over and the on-camera close will have to come out of the studio live. I'm gonna give you the background of the kidnapping and the ransom demands over film of Vandenberg's helicopter arriving, Helen's DC-6 pulling in, some of the security at the airport, Vandenberg boarding the plane and the two of them getting off the plane together." Darius barely paused for breath. "Then we'll lead into the brief news conference they held at the airport. The on-camera close will be fairly long because there are a number of critical questions surrounding the release that have to be raised."

"How long?" Ross asked, as though he were a bookkeeper.

"Three and a half to four minutes."

Ross gasped. "Darius, all I want is a news spot, not *Gone With the Wind*."

Before Darius could reply, Jerry Blumer had cut in on the extension. "Bert, this is Blumer! A: We don't have time to argue with you. B: This is not only the *major* story of the day, it's the *only* story. C: ABC and CBS aren't going to be able to get their film out of the lab in time, so they're gonna have to go with straight studio pieces. Now why don'tcha quit jerkin' everybody off?"

Ross sounded petulant but resigned. "All right; but see if you can cut it to three. What time are you gonna be able to feed the bird?"

Blumer's voice dropped an octave. He could sense that Ross had been thoroughly intimidated. "If we're lucky, we should be able to start feeding about ten to eight, your time."

"Darius, are *you* still on?" Ross was trying to sound businesslike.

"Yeah."

"How do you want us to lead into you?"

"You wanta take it down?"

"Yes. Go ahead."

"Helen Vandenberg has been released by her Arab kidnappers. She was flown into Tel Aviv today, apparently none the worse for the experience; but the intentions of her kidnappers and the circumstances surrounding her release are still shrouded in mystery. NNS Diplomatic Correspondent Darius Kane has a report."

Gideon raced into the room waving a round film can at Darius.

"Bert, I gotta go; the film just came out of the lab." Without waiting for a reply, Darius dropped the phone on its cradle. He squatted next to his camera bag, groping through its contents until he retrieved a stopwatch. "Gideon, I'm gonna need about three or four shots for the voice-over intro. I'll give you exact times in a minute. I want you to pull the entire sound bite, starting where Vandenberg says"—he flipped through his notebook—"hold on a second, where he says, 'I told you she couldn't stay away from me.' Then go through the whole thing. Pull everything you've got on sound. Vandenberg'll walk away, and then some reporter says '. . . did you pay the ransom?' We'll go from that directly to the live close."

The editor was scrawling the cues on the blue top of the editing table with a yellow crayon. Then, as Kane timed the opening that he had typed in the car, Gideon pulled the film out of the can and, using special tape, fastened the tail of the film to a plastic core which he dropped onto one of four spindles on the table. Gideon's fingers were quick and sure. He spun the spindle quickly, so that within seconds all the film had been neatly sucked into a flat roll on the editing table. He then fastened the head of the film to another core on a second spindle. The film dangled in front of him like a celluloid bridge. Deftly he inserted the film into sprockets on the round side of a counting machine and rotated the clock to zero. His Steenbeck table operated smoothly. Gideon was ready.

"Go ahead and fast forward." Darius rapidly traced a circle in the air. "I'll tell you when to stop." The film sped from one spindle to the other, activating the speaker. The voices coming from the speaker rose in pitch until they were indecipherable. Through a small viewer, Darius could see Vandenberg wheeling away from the microphones and turning his back sharply to the camera. "Right there," Darius said, "find the cue I gave you."

"Got it." Gideon was unflappable. "D'you want to give me the times for the top?"

"Yeah." Darius consulted his script as he dictated scenes and times. "Open the piece with a three-second shot of security. Then give me seven seconds of the choppers landing. Helen's plane landing is going to have to be very short. Make it three seconds of her plane pulling to a stop, then throw in a two-second cutaway. We can take six or seven seconds of Vandenberg bounding up the stairs. Then three or four seconds of Cohen tying his shoelace; eight seconds of Felix and Helen in the doorway waving and coming down the stairs, then three or four seconds of the tourists waving back and we go into the sound bite."

"Are you sure you don't wanta throw in a few more scenes?" Gideon sounded slightly annoyed.

Darius conceded the implied criticism. "I know, it's a helluva lot of stuff. Can you make it?"

Gideon had already begun selecting shots. "I can make it. Go powder your nose."

Blumer had been standing behind both of them, gnawing at his pipe and fidgeting with his Zippo lighter, but he said nothing. He knew when it was important to keep quiet; it was one mark of his professionalism. "I'm going into telecine, to call New York." Blumer glanced at the clock. It was nineteen minutes to three. "You all right?"

Darius nodded. "I'll be in the studio in a minute, soon's NBC is finished feeding," he said, running a comb through his hair.

"Gorgeous you already are." Gideon smiled. "Go! Millions of Americans are waiting for you." The Israeli was making splices for Darius' film package.

"Don't get nervous, Gideon. This is your big moment." Darius picked up his script and headed down a long, narrow corridor toward the far end of the main building, which was reserved mostly for editing, lab work and offices. The facilities at the satellite station were adequate, but hardly imposing. Darius strode across an open courtyard littered with refuse and beer cans; he could hear the waters of the Mediterranean slapping against the beach a few hundred yards away. For Darius, Herzliya was nothing more than a studio; for Gideon and other Israelis, it evoked powerful memories of the resistance to British rule. In 1939, more than eight hundred illegal Jewish immigrants had landed on the Herzliya beach, some ending up in jails but most joining in the struggle for a Jewish homeland.

Darius entered another building that at one time had been an army warehouse but which now served as the actual broadcast studio. It was a cavernous, barnlike structure with enormously high ceilings and a pair of antiquated color cameras. The only furniture was a bare desk and a chair placed on a raised platform. Alex Francilli, the NBC correspondent, was seated at the desk facing the camera. Darius heard a disembodied voice booming from the rafters. "OK, Al, New York says they got that last take fine."

Francilli tossed a breezy salute in the general direction of the voice. "If they're happy, I'm happy." He saw Darius. "You going back to Jerusalem?"

"Don't know yet," Darius responded. "If you want to hang around until after I do my feed, I'm gonna call New York and see how they wanta handle the show tonight."

Francilli had lighted a cheroot. "Naw, I think I'm gonna leave. If you get back give me a call; we'll have dinner. *Ciao.*"

Darius seated himself behind the desk. An Israeli technician wearing a headset rested one foot on the camera pedestal. He yawned. Darius tried to ignore him. He reread the on-camera close of his script, committing it to memory.

The voice of the Israeli director came from a speaker mounted just outside the control room overhead. "Would you give us a line for level, please?"

Darius clipped a small microphone to his tie. "The reunion took place under top security and with—"

"Thank you," the voice interrupted.

"Is the film up?" Darius asked. He tried to conceal his impatience. The studio clock read two-forty-six. There was no answer from the control room. Darius addressed himself to the cameraman. "Can you find out if the film is in telecine yet?"

The cameraman murmured into the mouthpiece of his headset. There was a pause; then he shrugged. "They say they let you know."

The minute hand on the clock jerked up a notch. Two-forty-seven. Darius closed his eyes and ran through the close of his report again.

At two-fifty, the director's voice broke the silence. "All right, we try it in thirty seconds."

Darius watched the television monitor that stood next to the camera. A card flashed on the screen: "NATIONAL NEWS SERVICE— TEL AVIV." The academy leader that had been edited onto the head of his film report flashed a reverse series of numbers on the screen. "8 . . . 7 . . . 6 . . . 5 . . . 4 . . ." At "3" the numbers disappeared and the screen went blank for three seconds. Then, out of the corner of his eye, Darius could see a jeep with several Israeli paratroopers on board. He began to read.

"The reunion took place under top security and with military precision. An Israeli helicopter—"

"Hold it!" It was the director again. "We'll have to start over. New York says the picture is breaking up."

Darius took a deep breath. A frown creased his face.

"As soon as they rerack the film, we'll go again. Just relax." Blumer had seen the frown. It was now two-fifty-five, seven-fifty-five in New York, and Darius could picture the frenzy in the video-tape room at NNS.

There was a hint of irritation in the director's voice, perhaps reflecting the tone of his conversation with his New York counterpart. "The film is ready. If we don't get it this time, we lose the satellite. In thirty."

Darius watched the monitor and tried to quiet the churning in his stomach. He could see the numbers again on the television monitor. When the jeep appeared, he began reading once more.

"The reunion took place under top security and with military precision. An Israeli helicopter landed Secretary Vandenberg at Ben-Gurion Airport precisely as his wife arrived aboard a U.S. Air Force DC-6." Darius sensed, rather than saw, the image of Vandenberg mounting the steps of the plane as he continued reading. "The Secretary literally bounded up the steps to share a few moments of privacy with Mrs. Vandenberg, while Israeli Foreign Minister Avram Cohen waited discreetly below. From the moment Helen Vandenberg appeared in the doorway of the aircraft, it was apparent that she had withstood the strain of the past few days well. Secretary Vandenberg was clearly in a buoyant mood."

The film cut to a medium close-up picture of Vandenberg, who was saying, "I told you she couldn't stay away from me."

During the exchange of questions and answers, Darius tightened the knot in his tie, smoothed his hair and looked directly into the camera. Darius saw the images of Felix and Helen Vandenberg turning away from the microphones. The Israeli reporter's question was insistent, demanding some form of comment. "Mr. Secretary, did you pay the ransom?"

It was almost time for Darius' on-camera close. The retreating figures of the Vandenbergs were suddenly replaced by Darius Kane, who was looking earnestly into the studio camera.

"That question," Darius began, "was pointedly ignored by the Secretary at the airport today, but it is a question that simply will not go away. Now that Mrs. Vandenberg has been safely returned, the Israelis, in particular, will insist on knowing what was given up to secure her release. Earlier this week the Israeli government defied its own policy by freeing six convicted terrorists, as demanded by Mrs. Vandenberg's kidnappers. That decision succeeded in raising a storm of domestic protest here in Israel, but it did not bring about Helen Vandenberg's release.

"There have been unconfirmed reports of a second ransom demand calling for a payment in hundreds of millions of dollars, but there is no evidence of that money having been raised. So the questions, rather than having been resolved today, now—themselves—occupy center stage. Why did the Israelis violate their own ground rules for dealing with terrorist demands? Did the United States pay a ransom; and if so, what was it? Because ultimately it all boils down to this. Helen Vandenberg was released this morning, but no one seems either able or willing to explain why. This is Darius Kane, National News Service, Tel Aviv."

The monitor went blank. Darius looked up at the clock. It was two-fifty-nine. The director sounded slightly weary. "New York says 'Thank you, nice job.' "

Darius pointed at the clock. "They're just gonna have enough time to rewind that tape before they have to go on the air."

The cameraman was unimpressed.

By the time Darius reached the control room, the technicians had all left, but Blumer was still on the phone with New York.

"What's up?" asked Darius.

Blumer waved him off. "Look, I know Seagram," he was saying, "and I know he's gonna want to handle this story chronologically." Blumer was holding the phone with his left hand; with his right hand, he was covering both eyes, as though shielding them from an intense light. "Charlie, of course we're going to follow up on the ransom; half the goddamn world is going to be following up on the ransom. But I'm just telling you, it's already three o'clock here. Felix and Helen are probably makin' out like a coupla rabbits; and even if they aren't, we sure as hell can't expect to see either one of them again today. But—" Blumer spluttered in frustration. "Will you let me finish? Darius is right here. He's gonna drive to Jerusalem and see what he can dig up; but I'm just tryin' to explain to you, Charlie, that by the time he gets there, it'll already be four-thirty our time. He's gonna have a maximum of four hours before he has to turn around and drive back here again. I just want to alert you guys to the very real possibility that we might not have a helluva lot more film this evening than what we just fed you." Blumer was biting down hard on the stem of his pipe, but he was nodding. "Good," he said, "good. I'm glad you like it." He pressed the mouthpiece of the phone against his chest and told Darius, "Charlie said your piece was just on and to tell you it was great."

"D'you want me to talk to him?"

Blumer shook his head. "Now, Charlie, just listen to me for a minute. Get one of the associate producers in early, and have them pull every bit of film that we've sent out of here over the past week. Make sure they get the Amman footage from the first day, and the Vandenberg-Houssan news conference out of Egypt. Have Seagram call me here as soon as he gets into the office. That'll be . . . what? A couple of hours from now, right?"

Blumer held the phone at arm's length and pantomimed the act of wringing the phone's neck. Then he returned the phone to his ear and said in a normal voice, "OK, Charlie, we'll be in touch. He says what?" Blumer turned toward Darius. "Bert Ross says to tell you it was a first-rate piece."

"Tell him I said thank you." Darius extended the middle finger of his right hand in a rude gesture at the phone.

"Darius says thanks. Talk to you later." Blumer delicately dropped the phone on its cradle.

"All right, Jerry, before I start hauling my ass up to Jerusalem, tell me what you have lined up."

Blumer relit his pipe. "We've got three crews in Jerusalem. One is staking out the King David. That's yours. The second crew is at the PM's office. There's a chance that Ben-Dor will make a statement around four. Andy'll cover that." Andy Wasserman was an American-born Jew who had emigrated to Israel in the early 1960s and who normally worked as a stringer for the National News Service radio network.

"What's Cleve doing?" Cleveland Denison was based in Israel for NNS as the network's staff correspondent.

"I sent him over to talk to Dubin." Shlomo Dubin was the leader of Israel's primary opposition party. "He's got a crew with him, but I don't know if he'll get anything worthwhile." Blumer pulled a crumpled envelope out of his shirt pocket and consulted some scribbled notes. "One of Dubin's people called me this morning with some crap about a secret West Bank deal that's supposed to be in the works already. Actually, it sounds less crazy this afternoon than it did when I talked to him this morning."

"Are you planning on a second piece out of here tonight, or do you want me to use it as part of my story?"

Blumer shrugged. "It depends on what all of you get. We'll make that decision later."

Darius smiled. "You're doin' a helluva job, Jerry."

Blumer nodded unhappily. The morning show was already history. The brief euphoria of a successful satellite broadcast had already passed. The pressure of a new deadline was building. "Call me here around six, will you?" Blumer's voice sounded weary.

"Will do. Listen, if Cleve calls, have him try to reach me at the King David. Nothing bothers Vandenberg more than a rumor he didn't plant. Dubin might be on to something, and maybe I can use it to flush our friend out of his suite."

Blumer scrawled another note on his envelope as Darius left.

Paul was waiting in the lobby holding a brown paper bag. He was seated in a straight-backed wooden chair, his feet straddling Darius' typewriter and camera bag. The instant he spotted Darius coming down the hall, Paul picked up the Olivetti and the bag with one hand, extending the paper bag with the other. "Here, sir. You should eat something."

Darius felt enormously grateful. He took the bag and walked toward the car. "Paul," he said, "you are a very dear man."

The driver was slightly flustered but pleased. "I don't like people to starve in the back of my car. It creates a bad impression."

During the entire trip from Herzliya to Jerusalem, Paul sang Yiddish folk songs. Darius first ate, then dozed and finally slept.

Darius was stripped to his shorts, lying face down on the floor of his hotel room. He had just completed twenty push-ups, and he didn't think he could do a twenty-first. A film of sweat had formed in the small of his back. Far from being habitual, the exercise was Darius' way of working off the frustration of indecision.

Among the messages waiting for him on his return to the King David was one from Katherine Chandler. "Flew in with Mrs. V. Call me when you get the chance."

Darius forced his weight away from the floor with a heavy grunt. The sudden jangle of the telephone sent a shiver of anticipation down to his toes. Darius flung himself across the bed, face down. As he picked up the receiver, he rolled over on his back. "Hello!" The exuberance in Darius' voice faded; he heard the static of a transatlantic phone call.

"Darius?" It was radio news. "Pete Harrigan in New York."

Darius suddenly felt exhausted. "Yeah, Pete?"

"What do you have for us?"

In the rush of the satellite feed, Darius had, in fact, totally forgotten about radio. Such oversights, however, were acceptable only insofar as they were never admitted.

"Pete, I'll get back to you within a half hour. I can't talk to you right now. I'm waiting for a call from Vandenberg."

Harrigan's voice sounded almost wistful. "Can't you give us anything? We haven't heard from you since the release."

"Half an hour, Pete. Promise. I don't wanta tie up the line right now." He hung up.

Though Darius would never admit to being a superstitious man, he had developed a grudging respect for "fate" during his early years in India. He did not like to concede that it played any role in his own decision-making, but every now and then he became the victim of its power. A few moments earlier, Darius had been toying with the idea of calling Kat before he finished his work—perhaps for a drink; but he had been torn by indecision. Now the call from radio news had settled the matter. The lovely Miss Chandler would have to wait.

Darius grabbed the phone and asked to be connected to the Secretary's suite. The phone rang only once. "Secretariat." The voice was brisk, thoroughly businesslike.

"I wonder if you could help me?" Darius affected a British accent. "I'm alone here in Jerusalem, and I've been told that there's some rather smashing crumpet up there on the sixth floor."

The voice on the other end of the phone mellowed, but it was still cautious. "Is that you, Darius?"

"Actually," Darius continued, "I'd be quite content to just sit in the corridor and peek in occasionally. I understand you Americans specialize in long-distance lusting."

"That's not always true, sir." The secretary's voice had become cloyingly sweet. "To borrow a slogan from one of our *major* networks, some of us prefer it 'up close and personal.'"

"Ouch!" Darius dropped the accent. "Score one point for the gorgeous lady with immediate access to the Secretary of State."

"You're wasting your time, Darius. He's not taking any calls."

"For Chrissake, Lois, he's had four hours. What is he, some kind of pervert?"

"I'll put your name on the list, but seriously, I've been told to hold all calls."

Darius sighed. "Look, Lord knows I don't want to interfere with the one constructive thing that sonovabitch has done over the past few years; but if he does come up for air in the next half hour or so, I'll be in my room, OK?" Darius remembered what Blumer had told him about the Likud party's suspicions. He decided to gamble. "And, Lois, if you do see him, tell him I need to talk to him about some secret negotiations."

"I'll tell him."

Darius cut the connection. For a moment he stared across the room; then he picked up the phone once again and pressed the button for an outside line. Without waiting, he dialed the one-digit area code for Tel Aviv and the number of the satellite studio. It took the operator at Herzliya a couple of minutes to find Blumer. When he got on the phone, he was clearly irritated. "Hey, hotshot, will you, for cryin' out loud, call radio. Those assholes have been driving me crazy all afternoon."

"I know. I talked to them. Didn't Andy feed 'em anything yet?"

"Sure he fed 'em. But you know that goddamn sausage factory; they used up all his stuff in the first two hours. Besides, they really want to hear from you."

"I'll call them first chance I get. Have you heard anything from Cleve?"

"Hold on." There was a slight pause. "Gideon, close that door, will you?" Blumer's voice had dropped to a confidential whisper. "Dubin told Cleve some cockamamy story about Safat dropping out of sight and maybe even leaving Lebanon for a few hours yesterday. He's supposed to have flown to Aswan for a top-secret meeting with Houssan. Dubin claims that the Egyptians acted as intermediaries; that Vandenberg sketched out a new West Bank proposal through Houssan, something that would give the OLPP an active role. If you ask me, it sounds like a lot of crap."

"What does Cleve think?"

Darius could almost imagine Blumer shrugging. "You know Cleve. He thinks they oughta put a straitjacket around the whole goddamn country."

Darius was scribbling notes on the message pad by the phone. "Did he get Dubin saying any of this on film?"

Blumer snorted. "What? Are you kidding me? Dubin may be nuts, but he's not crazy."

"Are you going to use it?"

"Not unless you get something more to substantiate it."

"I haven't had any luck yet getting through to Vandenberg, so I'm just going to sit tight here in my room and I suggest you sit tight too. I'll knock out a few spots for radio and get them off our backs."

"Please!" Blumer sounded relieved.

"What about Ben-Dor?" Darius glanced at his watch. It was past five-thirty. "Did Andy get anything over there?"

"No," replied Blumer, "and it doesn't look as though he's going to. The PM's office released a one-line statement saying that the government of Israel is relieved and gratified by the safe return of Mrs. Vandenberg."

"That was it?" Darius asked.

"That's it."

Darius was sitting on the edge of his bed. "Look, unless I get something out of Vandenberg, I don't see much point in my coming back to Herzliya. I'm going to be losing light here in another hour or so. I could do my stand-up close with the Old City as a backdrop, then call you later and you could give me a shot list of what you've pulled, what New York has, and then I'd do a voice-over narration here. I could then send one of the drivers to Herzliya with the track."

Blumer's voice carried a note of finality. "I'd rather have you here."

"My union says I don't have to work more than twenty hours a day."

"Stuff your union."

Darius laughed. "Well, as long as you're willing to be reasonable about it, I'll see you later."

Darius sprang from the bed, pulled on a rugby shirt and a faded pair of jeans and sat down at the desk. His typewriter had a blank sheet of paper in the roller. Fifteen minutes later, Darius was completing his fourth radio report when the phone rang.

"Darius?" It was Lois in the Secretariat. "The Secretary says if you come up right now, he can give you two minutes."

"I'll be right up."

Darius was kept waiting in the corridor outside the Secretary's suite for only a moment. When the door opened, he could see Helen Vandenberg sitting on a couch, her legs tucked beneath her and her husband standing in a corner by the window studying a folder. Darius strode over to Helen, leaned down and gave her a peck on the cheek.

"You have no idea," he said, "how delighted we all are to have you back safely." Darius was holding Helen by the hand. "Most importantly because we're all terribly fond of you; but in part, at least"—Darius glanced over at Vandenberg—"because your husband has been absolutely intolerable without you."

Helen was beaming. "How very sweet. Can I fix you a drink?"

In the corner, Vandenberg had closed his folder. "He violates our privacy, insults your husband and you offer that insolent bastard a drink. Sit down, Darius, I'll be right with you."

"Drink?" Helen asked again.

"No, thanks very much." Darius knew when he'd pushed things far enough.

The Secretary's wife rose and headed toward the bedroom. "In that case, I'll leave the two of you alone. I've got to pack anyway; Felix is sending me home tonight."

Vandenberg took his wife's seat on the couch and motioned Darius to an armchair. "Do me a favor. Don't use that until she gets to Washington. Now what's on your mind?"

"We're getting reports, Mr. Secretary, of a secret negotiating session." Vandenberg's face remained impassive. He waited for Darius to continue. The silence began to gather a force of its own.

Finally Vandenberg asked, "What kind of a session?"

Darius understood that as soon as Vandenberg realized the limits of his knowledge, he would lose whatever psychological advantage he enjoyed at the moment. So he said simply, "Safat."

Vandenberg's voice became tinged with impatience. "What about Safat?"

Darius sensed, rather than knew, that he was being maneuvered into revealing his ignorance. "We've heard that he flew secretly to Aswan for a meeting with Houssan."

Vandenberg didn't waste an instant. "Absolute and utter nonsense!" he snapped.

"How do you know?" Darius asked the question with seeming innocence, and it appeared to throw Vandenberg. For a fleeting moment, the Secretary of State seemed flustered.

"Because I'd know, that's why." Vandenberg had recovered his composure almost instantly. "I know you give us absolutely no credit for knowing what goes on in this part of the world; but believe me, if the Chairman of the OLPP flew to Aswan, I'd know about it."

Darius persisted. "You haven't been in direct or indirect contact with Safat?"

The Secretary wore a smile of limitless forbearance.

"Darius, I hope you don't take this personally, but you must understand that I was able to restrain my enthusiasm for seeing you just now. I agreed to see you partly because you're an old friend and partly because I don't want any crazy rumors about secret deals or secret meetings complicating what is already an excruciatingly complicated round of negotiations." Vandenberg paused; he then continued in his most reassuring tone. "To the best of my knowledge—and I like to believe that I'm reasonably well informed—there has been no secret meeting between Safat and Houssan."

Vandenberg rose and Darius knew that the session had ended. He decided to try one more tack anyway. "You mean Safat released Helen without getting anything in return?"

The Secretary of State had picked up his folder once again and, with his lower lip extended in a thoughtful pout, appeared to be lost in its contents.

Darius left without exchanging another word with Vandenberg. The conversation had made him uneasy; but, though he re-created the interview as he walked to his room, he couldn't pinpoint the exact reason for his uneasiness. Darius reached for his key as the phone began ringing insistently, as though the caller were challenging Darius to open the door more quickly. Darius took his time.

It was Harrigan in New York. The tone of his voice carried equal measures of reproach and apprehensiveness. "Hey, Darius, guy, it's been almost an hour."

Darius sensed that Harrigan must have been under pressure from one of the radio news executives. "Yeah, Pete, I'm sorry."

"What do you have for us?"

"I've got three and a half spots for you. If you want to wait a minute, I'll finish the fourth." He didn't wait for an answer; he dropped the phone on the bed and walked over to the desk to get his typewriter. When he had his Olivetti settled comfortably on his lap, he picked up the phone again.

"Pete?"

"I'm gonna switch you into one of the studios. Vic'll take you in."

Darius resumed typing while Harrigan transferred his call to a recording studio. Each of his four radio reports was a condensed rehash of his earlier television report. The only new element was contained in the last lines of the fourth spot.

. . . Secretary and Mrs. Vandenberg returned immediately to Jerusalem and retired to their suite. They have remained there in total seclusion. The Israeli government, which is undoubtedly eager to learn more about Mrs. Vandenberg's release, has, for the moment, limited itself to expressing gratification at her safe return. This is Darius Kane, National News Service, Jerusalem.

"Give us a level, will ya, Darius?"

Darius read the lead of his first spot directly into the mouthpiece of the phone. "OK?"

Vic Lazlo, the operations editor, was dissatisfied. "You using your Sony?"

"No, hold on a minute." Darius reached into his suitcase on the floor and pulled out a larger tape recorder than the miniaturized M-101 Sony that he carried in his camera bag. Zipped into a small pouch attached to the recorder's carrying case was a short electric cord with a single-prong plug at one end and a pair of copper clips at the other. Darius unscrewed the mouthpiece of the phone and attached the two clips to a pair of tiny prongs inside the phone. Then he slipped the other end of the wire into the monitor outlet of his recorder. Next he removed a trim microphone from the pouch and inserted the plug at the end of the microphone wire into two of the remaining outlets on the tape recorder, depressed the record key and flipped the microphone switch to on. Attached to the telephone in this fashion, the tape recorder acted as an amplifier, with mixed results. "All right," he said, "let's try it again." Darius read another line of copy. "Any better?"

"We'll live with it," replied Lazlo. "Give us a countdown and go."

Darius read the four reports in order, pausing briefly after each one to give the radio technician enough space on the tape to separate them without losing a word. When he had finished, Darius said, "That's it, friend."

"Not yet, Darius. Do number four again, would you? And this time say 'returned immediately *here* to Jerusalem.'"

Darius stifled an impulse to argue. He reread the spot. Lazlo came on the line again. "Beauty. Hold on, Darius, the desk wants to talk to you."

Harrigan sounded slightly embarrassed. "The TV desk wants to talk to you; but before I switch you over, do you know anything about this AP report?"

"What report is that, Pete?"

"They quote an 'informed Israeli source' as claiming that Vandenberg authorized President Houssan to act as intermediary with the OLPP, and that Safat flew to Aswan yesterday for a secret meeting with Houssan. That was supposed to be the payoff for Mrs. Vandenberg's release."

Darius groaned inwardly. "Look, Pete, anything is possible; but first of all, the 'informed Israeli source' is Shlomo Dubin."

"Who the hell is he?"

Darius sighed. "He's the head of the major opposition party. That doesn't mean he's wrong, but he's not exactly your most unbiased observer. Secondly, I just talked to Vandenberg and raised that issue with him and he denied it. Now that doesn't mean it's not true either, but I'd handle it very carefully if I were you."

"Don't you think you ought to give us something on it?"

"Well, I wasn't going to," Darius said. "It doesn't make much sense to report a rumor only to knock it down again, but I guess it all depends on how much play the AP story is getting."

"No," Harrigan conceded, "they're not pushing it too hard."

"Then let's leave it alone. If the story builds, I'll try to get back to you."

"All right." Harrigan wasn't convinced, but he lacked the necessary confidence to argue with Darius. "Hold on; I'll switch you over to television." The transfer took only a few seconds.

"Darius?"

Darius recognized the voice of Phil Strong.

"*Maggiore!*" Darius had first met Strong in Vietnam. Strong was then a major in the Marine Corps. He had resigned his commission after a second Vietnam tour to take a job running the NNS bureau in Saigon. His phlegmatic manner concealed an incisive mind and a dry sense of humor.

"Has Felix done a no-no?" Strong was now foreign editor on the television desk.

"You mean the AP story?" Darius asked.

"That's the one."

"I couldn't swear to it, Phil, but I think that story is hyped up. I just saw Vandenberg and he denies it."

"You believe him?"

"Let's put it this way, I know where the story came from and I'd hate to go with it without more evidence."

"Are you gonna knock it down in your piece?"

"I don't know, Phil. I just went through the same routine with radio. I'm not sure we ought to be in the business of running unsubstantiated stories and then killing them in the same piece."

"We'll look awfully silly if it turns out to be true."

"I know."

"Seagram says he'll go with your judgment." David Seagram was executive producer of the *Evening News*. From the point of view of day-to-day decision-making, Seagram was the most influential executive in the entire television news operation.

"You know what that means, don't you?" Darius asked dryly.

"Yeah," answered Strong. "It means your pecker's on the block if Felix is fibbing."

"Right on the money." Darius looked at his watch. "I'd better get cracking. Tell Dave how much I appreciate his confidence, will you?"

"I'll tell him." Then as an afterthought, Strong added, "Listen, there's nothing unethical about covering your ass. You could always throw in a graph at the bottom of the story."

"I know. Thanks."

Darius depressed the button on the phone long enough to break the connection with New York. Then he dialed the operator again.

"Would you get me the Secretary's suite, please?"

Again the phone rang only once. "Secretariat."

"Lois," urged Darius, "I need to talk to himself again; just for thirty seconds."

"I'll see if I can get him."

"Hello." Vandenberg's voice conveyed more than a trace of impatience.

"Mr. Secretary, AP has just put out that story I was telling you about. Before I write my report for tonight, I wanted to be absolutely sure that I didn't misunderstand you in any way."

Vandenberg spoke deliberately. "Darius, I give you my word: Houssan was not authorized to speak in my behalf; and to the best of my knowledge, there has been no meeting—or even any contact that I'm aware of—between Houssan and Safat." Before Darius could say anything else, Vandenberg ended the conversation with the perfect excuse. "Look, I've got to get off; the President's calling me on the other line." The connection was broken.

Darius hung up the phone, carried his typewriter back to the desk and wrote a straight, chronological account of the attack on Amman Airport, Helen's kidnapping, Israel's surprise decision to release Bishop Carucci and the others, and then a descriptive passage on Helen Vandenberg's return to Israel. In his on-camera close, Darius alluded to a rash of rumors and unsubstantiated reports that had already begun to circulate; but although he suggested that the United States must have made some concessions to obtain Mrs. Vandenberg's release, he made no specific reference to any secret meetings that might have involved the Chairman of the OLPP. As he reread the script, Darius again felt uneasy, but he knew that his report was as comprehensive, accurate and clean as the available facts, as he knew them, would allow. He also knew that if Vandenberg was misleading him, no one in New York would give a damn about Darius Kane's sense of journalistic integrity.

19

It was almost one o'clock Saturday morning. The four American network correspondents had just completed their reports for the evening TV news broadcasts. The bird had flown frantically but uneventfully. Blumer looked exhausted. It had been a long day, but New York seemed content. "Right on time, Jerry," the producer said. The satellite line to New York had already been cut when Blumer muttered, ". . . and what about the story?" The CBS and ABC correspondents had included references in their reports to the Likud-inspired rumors of a secret Safat journey to Aswan; Alex Francilli had ignored the rumors. In all other respects, there was little to distinguish from among the four pieces. None of the correspondents had broken any major new ground.

Darius invited Francilli to share the late-night ride back to Jerusalem, but there was little conversation. Francilli was bone-tired. No sooner had Paul steered his limousine through the flourescent-lighted suburbs of Tel Aviv than Francilli fell into a deep sleep, snoring so evenly that Darius could keep time to the rhythm. The headlights of the car carved a narrow corridor through the otherwise total darkness. Darius tried unsuccessfully to doze. Almost against his will, he kept returning to his conversations with Vandenberg—to the decidedly unsettling feeling that he might have been had.

"*You* haven't been in direct or indirect contact with Safat?" His question had been that direct.

Vandenberg had responded by denying that there had been a *Houssan*-Safat meeting.

"Sonovabitch!" Vandenberg had swivel-hipped right past him.

"Is anything wrong, sir?" Paul half turned to Darius.

"No, Paul; just thought of something I should've done." It was possible that Vandenberg had misunderstood his question, but Darius doubted it. He had seen the Secretary employ the same tactic too many times in the past. It was an artful way of dodging a question, and Vandenberg had executed it with precision and brilliance.

"Son-of-a-bitch!" This time Darius accented each syllable. Darius looked at his watch. One-fifteen. It would be past two by the time they reached the King David. Past seven in New York. Too late to do anything about his piece. Too late to call Vandenberg. "I'll get that bastard in the morning," he mumbled.

Darius slouched in his seat and closed his eyes. For a few minutes he was conscious only of the sound of the engine and the occasional squealing of tires on the macadam road. He might have dozed, or even fallen asleep, were it not for a gentle tapping at the fringes of his memory. The tapping became more insistent, a warm sensation that seemed to radiate from the pit of his stomach. Katherine!

Kat.

Darius recalled the lines of her face; the extraordinary color of her eyes, almost violet in the bright sun of Aswan; and her long-legged, confident and yet fully feminine stride. This was a very special girl, and Darius allowed his mind to fantasize a relationship only lightly touched by reality, uncomplicated by the objective demands of his life, or her own. He wanted to remember them sitting in wicker chairs overlooking the Nile, but all he could imagine was the two of them lying naked in a big double bed, teasing, joking, fencing, embracing, kissing and finally loving each other. He felt a surge of well-being bordering on euphoria as he teetered precariously on the outer rim of sleep.

Their arrival at the King David came as an intrusion. Paul jumped out of the car and retrieved the reporters' typewriters from the trunk. Darius and Alex stumbled into the predawn chill, their faces lined with exhaustion. Francilli groped for his pass, hesitating in front of the Israeli soldier who stood near the iron grille that had been drawn halfway across the hotel entrance. The soldier glanced at the pass and then grunted. Alex, groggy with sleep, made his way into the lobby.

"Do you want me in the morning?" Paul glanced at his watch.

Darius forced himself to focus on the question. "I don't think so, Paul. No. Just leave a message in my box so I'll know where you are."

"*Shalom*, sir. I'll be here at eight sharp."

"Ten will be fine, Paul. Sleep late."

Darius dangled his pass in front of the soldier's impassive face, smiled, and then, upon entering the lobby, surrendered his typewriter and shoulder case to a policewoman seated behind a bare table. He wandered over to the reception desk while she unzipped his case.

The hotel clerk, a short, bareheaded man, had already placed Darius' key on the counter. Darius picked up the key. "Do you have a room number for a Miss Chandler?" He tried to sound casual. "She's with the Secretary's party. She arrived this afternoon."

"Chandler. Chandler." The clerk muttered the name while consulting a typewritten list in a special folder. After a few moments, he spotted the name among a group of four others added to the bottom of the list in pencil.

"Chandler," he said in triumph. "602."

The policewoman had finished examining Darius' typewriter and case. She smiled at a plainclothes Shinbet agent who was slouching against a pillar at the other side of the lobby. He was looking at Darius. Having picked up his things, Darius walked toward the elevator, down a long, empty hallway, his footsteps echoing in the silence. He felt the first twinge of apprehension. It was, after all—he looked at his watch—almost two-thirty. He recalled his last meeting with Katherine. He *thought* it had gone very well. Now, suddenly, he doubted his instincts. Maybe he was exaggerating her interest. The elevator ride took an interminable twenty seconds. When Darius reached his room, he realized that his hands were freezing. After opening the door and dropping his typewriter on the sofa, he sat down on the edge of his bed and studied the phone. He was conscious of a rapid heartbeat and a tightness in his chest. "Either," he told himself, "you care one hell of a lot about this lady, or you're about to have a heart attack." Finally he dialed Katherine's room. The phone rang once, twice—Darius considered hanging up—and then a third time. The ringing stopped, and Darius could hear the receiver at the other end clatter against something hard. Katherine's voice sounded muffled. "Hello?"

"Kat?"

There was a pause and the sound of movement. "What time is it?" Her voice sounded clearer.

"Quarter of three."

"What are you, some kinda nut?"

Darius chuckled. "I just got in."

"That's terrific." She didn't sound as though she meant it.

"Can I come up?"

"Darius, it's . . ." She seemed to be groping for something. "It's almost three o'clock, for cryin' out loud."

"I know, I just told you."

"That's terrific," she said again. "I'm on the same floor as the Secretary. If you come up here at this time of night, someone'll probably shoot you; which"—she was fully awake now—"would be nothing more than justifiable homicide, but it might wake up the Secretary and then there'd be hell to pay." She paused. "Where are you?"

"Room 420." Darius wanted to add something, but nothing appropriate came to mind.

"Darius?"

Darius was certain that she was going to change her mind. "What?"

"D'you know this is how the Russians conduct their interrogations? Wake people up in the middle of the night?" She hung up without waiting for an answer.

Darius felt a rush of excitement. He dialed room service. The phone rang interminably. Finally someone answered. "Yes?" In one word the man conveyed both boredom and resentment.

"I'd like to order some champagne." Darius sounded almost apologetic.

"The bar is closed."

"Is the kitchen still open?"

"The kitchen is closed."

"What *do* you have?"

"Cheese and apple juice."

"That's *it?*"

"You want it?" asked room service.

"Have you ever thought of going into public relations?" Darius' sarcasm was wasted.

"Pardon?"

"Forget it."

Darius changed back into his jeans and rugby shirt. He went into the bathroom to brush his teeth. He examined himself in the mirror. "You devil!" He grinned broadly and returned to the bedroom. He spotted his open suitcase on one of the twin beds and quickly shut it and shoved it under the bed. He snapped off the overhead light. Except for a rectangle of light coming from the bathroom through the door left slightly ajar, the room was in darkness. Darius walked over to the doors leading to a small balcony overlooking the garden and the Old City. He unlatched the doors after pulling open a heavy pair of curtains and stepped onto the balcony. He stood there for a while, both hands thrust into his back pockets, his eyes scanning the wall and the turrets and minarets beyond, until a chill ran up his back. He shivered and retreated into the room.

The tap on the door was so light, so tentative, that for a moment Darius was not even sure that he had actually heard it. He opened the door, half expecting to find an empty corridor. Instead he found Katherine leaning against the doorway. She seemed smaller, more petite, than he had remembered her.

"You sell peanuts here?" She was carrying a bottle of Jack Daniel's by the neck. "I assume that a gentleman of your bearing and background drinks only bourbon." Her voice carried a mocking tone, but it seemed slightly unsteady.

Darius drew her into the room, and into his arms, in a sweeping motion, kicking the door shut with one foot. He held her very gently, feeling every curve of her body pressing against his. Their embrace was tender and total. For a full minute or two, neither of them said a word. Finally Katherine whispered, "This bottle is getting heavy." Darius ignored her complaint. He was conscious of a suggestion of perfume, almost lost in a smell of mint, probably from toothpaste. He ran his hand in a broad oval up and down her back. He kissed her forehead, while cradling her face in his hands.

"You are beautiful, Katherine." Darius could hear a hoarseness in his voice, and he knew it wasn't deliberate. "Come"—holding her hand, he led her to the desk, where earlier he had placed two bathroom glasses.

Darius poured an inch into each glass. He handed Katherine one glass, clicking the top of his against the bottom of hers. It was only then that he noticed Katherine was also wearing jeans. A faded blue shirt was knotted around her slim waist. She was barefoot. Around the corners of her mouth Darius could see the beginnings of a smile.

"Darius?"

"Yes."

"What the hell are we doing?" She took a sip of bourbon.

Darius put his drink down on the desk. He stood in front of her. Because she was half leaning against the desk, she seemed even smaller. Darius leaned down and brushed his lips against the corners of her eyes, the tip of her nose, her upper lip and then her lower lip, all the while nudging her feet apart with the toe of his sneaker until he had finally insinuated his thigh between hers. Katherine rose to the tips of her toes and, wrapping her arms around his neck, locked her body against his. She could feel his excitement rise, and for a few moments she seemed to lose herself totally. She regained a small degree of consciousness only when she felt Darius' hand slipping under her unbuttoned blouse and caressing her breasts. Almost against her will, she recoiled, perhaps no more than an inch, but Darius could sense a change in her mood.

"Time out." Her voice sounded apologetic.

Darius looked hurt.

"Please." She burrowed her fingers in his hair and kissed his cheeks.

"What's wrong?" Darius seemed annoyed.

"Please," she repeated, speaking very softly. "Please don't be angry."

"I'm not angry." But she could tell that he was.

"I'm not teasing you." Katherine kissed the palm of one of his hands. "I want you very much. I want very much to make love with you." She hesitated for a moment. "I just don't want to get laid."

Darius smiled grimly. "I'm pretty good at nuances," he said, "but I've got to admit that one escapes me."

"I don't think it does." Katherine moved away from the desk and seated herself cross-legged on the bed. "We really don't know each other, Darius. If we led normal lives, we could count on some kind of relationship evolving naturally; but that isn't going to happen with us." Katherine took a deep breath. "If we just hop into the sack together, we may never even have the chance to find out if we like each other."

Darius had straddled a chair. "If you want to get technical about it, we haven't even been formally introduced."

"Don't." Katherine's voice was husky. "I'm trying to tell you something about myself, and you're not making it very easy. Has anyone ever suggested to you that I might be an easy lay?"

"No!" It came out a shade too forcefully.

"Or that I might be queer?"

"Come on, Kat."

"Well, sooner or later, somebody will. People are always a little uncomfortable with unmarried women in their thirties; especially where I came from."

Darius had sat upright during the brief exchange. Now he rested his chin on the top of the backrest. "Virginia?"

"No'th Ca'lina"—she exaggerated the drawl in a self-mocking way—"and I mean Ol' South No'th Ca'lina—old line, old stock. My great-great-granddaddy was a slave owner. My grandmother still used to call the hired help 'darkies.'" Katherine had resumed her normal speech pattern. "I was born on a plantation that's been in the family for more than a hundred and fifty years. For the first seven, eight years of my life, I was raised by a black woman; and I never knew her name. Everybody just called her 'Mammy.'"

"You don't sound all that Southern anymore." Darius didn't feel like talking at all, but he felt he had no alternative.

"I used to love it, but now I have trouble even remembering what it was like." Katherine was looking at Darius, speaking to him; but somehow he had the feeling that she was talking as much for her own benefit as his. "It was another world. We lived about a hundred miles west of Durham; and when I was about twelve, I went to a private school in Greensboro. It was a Presbyterian school—very WASPish. No colored, no Jews, no Catholics; nothing but the future flowers of Southern womanhood." She smiled with a small, helpless shrug.

"What happened?"

"Kennedy. Split the family right down the middle. The Chandlers had always been Democrats, but Daddy said he'd vote for a Jew before he'd help put the Pope in the White House. So he voted for Nixon. But my mother—she was charmed by the Kennedys; 'specially Jack. So in the spring of '63, she decided that I should go to Radcliffe. My father was against it until Radcliffe turned me down. Then it became a matter of family pride. He was furious. I think he must have cashed in every political chip he had. Didn't make any difference though. I had lousy grades; I'd never studied a lick in my life. I didn't tell my father, but I applied to Boston U. and they took me. I think I worked harder those first two years than I'd ever worked in my life. I made dean's list the first year and straight A's the second. I didn't think it'd do any good, but I applied for a transfer to Radcliffe." Katherine paused for a moment, savoring the memory. "When they accepted me, I couldn't believe it. It was the single most exciting thing that had ever happened to me."

Darius was tempted to interrupt, but he was reluctant to spoil the mood of exhilaration that seemed to have taken hold of Katherine.

"That was the first time I'd ever done anything important for myself; the whole thing—getting into Boston and then doing what Daddy, with all his political clout, hadn't been able to do."

"Mmm." Darius gave a noncommittal grunt.

"I'm boring you."

"No," Darius said flatly. "What happened after Radcliffe?"

"Oh, we had a big fuss. Mother wanted me to come home and get married." Katherine was still sitting cross-legged on the bed, and now she closed her eyes. "I went home that summer, after graduation, and we had some terrible fights. I told them I was going to graduate school. First they tried to bribe me. They were going to send me to Europe; I could spend up to a year there if I wanted to." She opened her eyes again. "You want to hear something funny? They said I should go to Europe and learn French. I told them I already spoke French. They didn't even know."

"When did you learn Arabic?"

"In graduate school, later that year." Katherine was leaning backward on the bed, supporting her weight on rigid arms. She was looking up at the ceiling. "God, when I think of some of those fights. Daddy'd been a pilot in the Second World War. He couldn't understand what was happening in Vietnam, or what was happening at home. The whole antiwar thing just drove him wild. Not that I was really into all of that; but I said something about the demonstrators, in their way, being just as patriotic as he was. That brought it all to a head, all the bitterness and the hurt and the frustration. He all but threw me out of the house; said he wouldn't give me another nickel to go on to school, that I'd soon find out what made the world go 'round." There was a thin film over Katherine's eyes, but her voice was almost toneless. "That's when I told him I had a scholarship and I didn't need his money . . . or him. I shouldn't have said it that way, but I was angry too." She clicked her tongue a couple of times, perhaps to hold back her tears.

"So you went back to Radcliffe?" Darius was prompting now, sensing that Katherine had been working up to this period in her life.

"I went back to Radcliffe and within a week I was hopelessly involved with this guy."

Darius held up a cautioning hand. "Let me guess. A Saudi?"

Katherine smiled. "You're close. He was an Egyptian working on his doctorate at Harvard. Very bright. Very intense. As a matter of fact, he was wrapped up in the antiwar movement. He had a little flat just north of Cambridge, in Medford. Two weeks after we met, I moved in with him."

"Daddy must've loved that."

"Daddy never knew. I think it would have killed him. I don't think I've ever been so thoroughly involved with anyone in my whole life. It was only a few months after the Six-Day War, and Saled was just torn up. He wanted to go home, but he had less than a year to go for his Ph.D. I sometimes wonder now whether the whole thing wasn't just a colossal act."

"What do you mean?"

"Oh, he was almost thirty, kind of old to still be going to school. I wouldn't be surprised if somehow he had been linked up with Egyptian intelligence. Anyway, he sure did get wrapped up in the peace movement. I guess at the time that struck a chord with me—hearing him talk about the hundreds of thousands of Palestinian refugees; how what was happening in Vietnam was all part of the same thing that was going on in the Middle East."

"You believed that?" Darius asked.

"No, not that part. In fact, eventually, that's what led to our breaking up. Saled turned out to be just as pigheaded in his opinions as my father was in his." Somewhat wistfully, Katherine added, "Except Saled lacked my father's good manners."

"What do you mean?"

Katherine sighed. "Oh, I don't know; it's all so long ago now. Saled was convinced that U.S. imperialism—I don't think he could *say* one without the other—that U.S. imperialism in Vietnam and in the Middle East were one and the same thing. He got really steamed up one night; claimed that my father was a war profiteer, that most Americans lived off the misery of the underdeveloped world. He really believed it. He said it was all part of a Zionist conspiracy to keep some kind of war going somewhere in the world at all times. God knows, I didn't like what we were doing in Vietnam, but Saled couldn't understand that it was possible for me to oppose the war without hating America. One thing led to another. He called me a 'spoiled bitch.'" She was recounting the story very matter-of-factly.

"I started packing. Maybe we were just getting tired of each other anyway. But he got physical; he began slapping me around. That was it. When he saw that I was really serious about leaving, he got terribly emotional and apologized; but I'd had it. I never said another word to him. I just walked out."

"How long did you live together?" Darius asked.

"Not long. Three or four months. But it left a mark on me. For the first few weeks, I was so wrapped up in that man I just couldn't stand to be away from him. Then, after it was over, I felt nothing. It was just as though I'd been drunk or high for those few months. I *knew* I didn't love him, but I couldn't even remember if I'd ever liked him."

"Bingo," said Darius.

"Yeah," she echoed, "bingo. I got very involved in my studies again, and then this girl friend of mine got me a job with the government."

Darius poured himself another drink. He held the bottle toward Katherine, but she shook her head. She seemed determined to finish what she had to say.

"I've had boy friends; I've dated a fair amount. But until you, I really didn't ever want to get involved again."

Darius looked as though he was searching for something in the bottom of his glass. "And now you do?"

"Would it frighten you terribly if I said yes?"

Darius said nothing for a long time. Then he swallowed what was left of his drink. "Katherine, would you mind very much if I join you on my bed?"

"You're avoiding the question."

"No, I'm not. I'm just afraid that you might think I was being less than serious if I dozed off in the middle of my answer."

She laughed. "I really did go on, didn't I? Come on." Katherine patted a place on the bed next to her. Darius stretched out full length, his hands folded on his chest.

"D'you know how old I am?" he asked.

Katherine shook her head.

"In a couple of weeks I'll be forty, and for the first time in my life, I'm feeling very, very mortal."

Katherine was resting on an elbow, smiling at him. "Someone should've told you."

"Don't be a wise ass." Darius reached down for Katherine's arm and drew her toward him, until the two of them lay on the bed side by side. Katherine curled up against him.

"Until a few months ago, I never questioned what I was doing, and I never seriously considered doing anything else. I've been bouncing around the world for almost twenty years, and with minor reservations, I've enjoyed every minute of it. A friend of mine says that journalism is the only career in the world that lets you be an adolescent past the age of forty."

Katherine remained very still. "So what's the problem?"

"I'm beginning to wonder what I'm gonna do when I grow up." Darius kissed the top of her head. "The sum total of my responsibilities for the past umpteen years has been to reduce some of the world's most complex problems to an easily digestible minute-thirty on the tube."

"You do it well, though, don't you?"

"I do it brilliantly," Darius said, with only the trace of a smile. "That's just the problem. I could probably go on doing it for the *next* twenty years, and then I could spend my retirement browsing through my old scripts."

"Why don't you quit and do something else?"

"What? Teach the process to a new generation of adolescents?" Darius was stroking Katherine's hair. "My father really believed in this business. He was convinced that being a good reporter made a real difference in the scheme of things."

"And you don't?"

"I just don't know. The other guys who do the same kind of work I do—they're all good. Maybe I catch an extra nuance every once in a while, but the people who watch our stuff every night on the air—I don't think they even know the difference."

Katherine tilted her head toward Darius. "You still haven't answered my question."

"Yes, I have. There was a time, genius"—a flicker of a smile crossed over his face—"when the thought of getting seriously involved with someone like you would've scared me half to death. Now it may be the only thing that can save me from being scared."

Katherine rolled on top of Darius, allowing the front of her blouse to open and her hair to form a soft curtain on either side of his face.

"I like you, Darius." She kissed him very gently on the lips, and then she began to nibble on his earlobe. "And now not another word."

"Ah, all you want is my body," Darius whispered; but as he began to remove her blouse, he added with almost boyish innocence, "I like you too, Kat."

Darius struggled to focus on the pleasant sensation that was sending tremors from the base of his spine to the back of his head. Katherine was tracing small circles between his shoulder blades with her tongue. He groaned with pleasure. The tracing stopped.

"What happened?" Darius tried to raise one eyelid.

"The light woke me up."

"No. I mean, why'd you stop?"

"Close the curtains."

"I'll flip you for it."

Katherine reached under the blankets and drew her fingernails very lightly up and down the length of his thigh. Darius lay very still until the hand stopped.

"You don't fight fair," he complained.

"The curtains," she repeated.

"Fascist!" He slid out of bed and stumbled toward the window. He drew the curtains and staggered past the bed.

Darius had made it to the bathroom and was brushing his teeth when the phone rang. The sound bounced angrily off the tile walls. Darius scooped a handful of water from the tap, rinsed his mouth and glared at the phone. "Shove it up your nose!" he told it.

The phone was still ringing as Darius slipped into bed next to Katherine. "I think they mean it," she said.

Darius sighed and picked up the receiver. "What do you want?"

"Darius? Phil Strong."

"Yeah, Phil."

"Are you sitting down?"

"I'm *lying* down. I try to do it for three or four hours every other night."

"I'm sorry, friend. I wouldn't have called you if it weren't important." Strong sounded subdued.

Darius reached over to the night table for a cigarette and his lighter. "Go ahead, Phil. I'm awake."

"Your boy screwed you."

"What do you mean?"

"I mean he's gonna be lucky if the Israelis don't lynch him."

"Phil, what the hell are you talking about?"

"*U.S. News and World Report* has just released the advance text of a story that's gonna be in their next week's edition. Somehow they got hold of a tape. They've got the full transcript of a conversation between Felix and Safat."

"Holy shit!"

"That's not the worst of it. I don't know what he's trying to pull, but he caved in totally to the OLPP. I mean he gave them everything they've ever wanted. He promised them formal recognition by the United States; he said he'd bring them directly into the negotiating process. What the hell else did he say? . . . Hold on a second."

Darius felt a wave of nausea rushing to his throat. Strong came back on the phone. "Yeah. And here's a beauty. He promised that the U.S. would try to create a state for the Palestinians on the West Bank."

Darius tried to clear his mind. "Are you sure this thing is genuine?"

"What can I tell you? *U.S. News* claims to have heard the tape."

"Where and when is this supposed to have taken place?"

Strong gave a short, bitter laugh. "That's the kicker. Somehow they snuck Safat right into Jerusalem. About the only thing *U.S. News* doesn't have is how they did it. It seems to be the genuine article though."

"Can you telex me a copy of the story?"

"It's on the way."

"When did the story break?"

"We just got it."

"All right, Phil. Let me get my thoughts together and I'll call you back in a little while."

Strong chuckled. "I was gonna say it could be worse, but I'm not sure it could be."

"You're a source of great comfort to me, Philip. I'll talk to you."

Darius dropped the phone and sank back onto his pillow.

"What happened?" Katherine asked.

Darius stared at the wall opposite the bed. "That goddamn sonovabitch bastard!"

"Our Secretary of State?"

"*Your* Secretary of State!"

Katherine pulled back the covers. "I'd better get dressed."

Darius mashed his cigarette in an ashtray. "I don't think it's gonna make any difference. The best thing we could do is lock ourselves in here for the next week."

"Do you want to tell me what happened?"

"Felix and Safat had a meeting here in Jerusalem. *U.S. News and World Report* got a tape of the conversation. About the only thing our boy didn't give away was the Knesset building."

Katherine sat speechless on the edge of the bed. Then she crawled across the rumpled blankets until she knelt next to Darius. "I think we both have to get back to work." She brushed a strand of hair back from Darius' forehead and kissed him in that exact spot. "Love you, Darius."

"Goddamn him!" exclaimed Darius. It took him a few minutes before Katherine's words cut through the confusion and disappointment that had so recently absorbed him. By that time she was gone.

PART TWO

20

Gloom seeped out of the Secretary's suite like an invisible fog, curling its way down the corridor in both directions. Conversations were terse and conducted in whispers.

Inside the suite, the Secretary and Bernardi, still clad in their pajamas and bathrobes, sat on the sofa. They looked crushed, their faces creased with sleep. Vandenberg spoke in a weary monotone. "Where's the damned transcript, Frank?"

"They're sending it, Felix. Should be here any minute."

"Those morons aren't putting it in code, are they?"

"I can't imagine they'd be that stupid"—Bernardi wrinkled his brows—"but I'd better check anyway." The phone rang before he reached the door.

"Get it, Frank, will you?" Vandenberg seemed to be in a trance.

Bernardi picked up the phone, listened for a moment and then said, "No, this is Bernardi." Pause. "Ask him if I can talk to him." Longer pause. "Keep him on the line; I'll get right back to you." Bernardi replaced the receiver. "Felix, I think you're going to have to handle this one yourself. The Prime Minister's calling. The girl says he's madder'n hell; won't talk to anyone but you."

Vandenberg exhaled softly, ballooning his cheeks in resignation. "All right." He tightened the cord on his bathrobe. "No point in delaying the inevitable. Put him on."

Bernardi pressed an intercom button. "Put him through, Maggie." He picked up the telephone by its cradle, flipped the wire over and past an armchair and handed the phone to the Secretary of State.

"Ya'acov—" began the Secretary.

Bernardi could hear the voice of the Israeli Prime Minister hissing through the receiver which Vandenberg held loosely to his ear. "Mr. Secretary, I would never have believed you capable of such out-and-out treachery." Ben-Dor's voice rose in indignation. "This is not simply a sellout; this is a betrayal of historic proportions!"

"Mr. Prime Minister—"

Ben-Dor ignored the interruption. "It is only because of our long-standing friendship—perhaps 'relationship' might now be more appropriate—that I am even bothering to call you first. Mr. Secretary, if the report I have before me is true, I would ask you to leave Jerusalem immediately, and I will hold any further discussion that might be necessary with the White House directly."

Vandenberg's voice was calm, level, reassuring. "Mr. Prime Minister, first of all, you have me at something of a disadvantage. I haven't seen the full text of the report yet."

Ben-Dor's voice resonated with contempt. "Mr. Secretary, save your pathetic little evasions for your friends in the media. I expect a straightforward answer, and I expect it now."

"Ya'acov, there'll be ample opportunity for indignation after you've heard what I have to say, but at least do me the courtesy of listening first." There was total silence at the other end of the line. "From what I've seen," Vandenberg continued, "the report is a total and absolute distortion. The *only* part of it that is true—and I give you my sacred word of honor that it was my intention to tell you about this—is the fact of the meeting itself. It took place, and it took place here in Jerusalem. Everything else, however, is a malicious distortion." Vandenberg strung his sentences together, as though to prevent further interruption. "Now, Ya'acov, I'm prepared to come to your home or office immediately if you insist, but I would really prefer to read the full transcript of the U.S. *News* piece first. May I come to your office in two hours?"

The silence at Ben-Dor's end continued for a moment. Finally the Israeli Prime Minister said, "Two hours." His voice still carried an angry edge. The connection was broken.

Felix Vandenberg bit down hard on the web of flesh between his thumb and forefinger.

Bernardi spoke with uncharacteristic bluntness. "Felix, I think you've been had."

Vandenberg studied the tooth marks on his hand. "Yes; but I don't think it was Safat. He's a conniver, but he's also a man with an historic mission. This isn't going to serve that mission. Putting out a distorted version of the conversation doesn't serve any constructive purpose. It's a piece of very effective sabotage."

There was a knock at the door. Terence Jamieson came into the room carrying a slim red folder. "I've got the full text of the report, sir."

The Secretary of State instantly immersed himself in the contents of the folder. He read in silence for a few moments; then he began to shake his head. "Oh, Lord," he sighed, "somebody's really done a job." He reread the last page of the text and handed the folder to Bernardi. "You can skip over the first couple of pages. They didn't touch Safat's monologue, but they really sliced me up."

Bernardi skimmed over the first two pages. Page 3 began:

SAFAT: You are not my enemy. America is not my enemy. There should be understanding between us.

VANDENBERG: Mr. Chairman, what you say has great merit. The Palestinian people must and will have an independent sovereign state. Neither one of us can ignore reality. Does my wife's safety enter into the equation? Yes. You want formal recognition from the United States? Done. You want to become party to the negotiating process? We'll impose it on the Israelis. You want to create a nation on the West Bank of the Jordan River? I can't promise anything, but we'll try.

You're a man of great intelligence, Mr. Chairman. It's surely not necessary to spell out the obvious. If this meeting or the next one should become public knowledge . . . (PAUSE)

SAFAT: You are quite correct, Mr. Secretary, it is not necessary.

Bernardi threw the folder on the coffee table. "You want to know my opinion, Felix?" He went on without waiting for an answer. "This is such transparent nonsense that no one could take it seriously."

Vandenberg looked at his Under Secretary with what seemed to be almost a touch of compassion. "People tend to believe what they want to believe, Frank." The Secretary's voice was composed. "This piece of nonsense, as you put it, could very likely spell the difference between war and peace; and as someone who's always prided himself on having a healthy perception of reality, I'd have to say that war has now become by far the more likely of the two."

The explosion ripped through a third-floor rest room in the main building of the State Department at approximately seven-forty-five,

Washington time, Saturday morning. A homemade bomb tore a gaping hole in the wall, rupturing several water pipes and flooding most of the Middle East Affairs section of the Agency for International Development. There were no casualties.

Kenneth Dawson, one of the State Department correspondents for the Associated Press, was at home in Germantown, Maryland, talking by phone with an overnight editor at the AP office in Washington. Dawson was being briefed on the *U.S. News* story when the editor got word of the State Department explosion over the police radio. Dawson consulted his notebook for the home telephone number of the weekend duty officer for the State Department press office, called him and learned that Frederick Lassiter III was, characteristically, unaware of either event. To his enormous credit, however, Lassiter immediately grasped that a mounting public interest in both stories would be likely to develop during the course of the morning. He promised to be available at his State Department office within an hour.

In a quarter of that time, Dawson had dressed, grabbed a hunk of cheese and a raw carrot from the refrigerator, and had guided his car through the secondary roads of rural Maryland. Now he was speeding down highway 270 toward downtown Washington. He kept flipping his radio dial back and forth between WRC and WTOP, two of Washington's major all-news stations. The story of Vandenberg's meeting and conversation with Jamaal Safat was repeatedly headlined, but neither station had been able to provide any additional information. By eight-twenty, WTOP made its first mention of the explosion at the State Department, very tentatively suggesting that it might be linked to Vandenberg's apparent sellout.

"Asshole!" Dawson flared at the radio. "What the hell d'ya think it was—a protest against the food in the cafeteria?"

As he passed the police station between Gaithersburg and Rockville, Dawson was doing eighty miles an hour.

The first demonstrator appeared outside the United States Mission to the United Nations in midtown Manhattan shortly before nine A.M. He wore a plain gray overcoat over a black suit and a white shirt buttoned at the neck. He had stapled a piece of brown cardboard to a broom handle. It was marked with bold, black letters: "VANDENBERG! NEVER AGAIN!" A red swastika had been crayoned over the second N in Vandenberg's name. The demonstrator, who was bearded, wore a black homburg; he walked resolutely back and forth in front of the U.S. Mission, attracting little or no attention.

By nine-thirty, however, almost a dozen other men and women had taken their places behind the homburg; by ten o'clock, other demonstrators had drawn five cars across First Avenue, blocking all uptown traffic. One young man, wearing a World War II aviator's jacket, climbed to the roof of one of the cars and, using a battery-powered bullhorn, began leading a chant: "VANDENBERG MUST GO! VANDENBERG MUST GO!" It echoed for several blocks.

Patrolmen Anton Schweitzer and Jesús de Cruz tried, with infinite patience, to unsnarl the traffic jam by themselves. By the time they realized that the younger demonstrators, at least, were determined to provoke a confrontation, it was too late. They called for a Tactical Force Unit just as the first television camera crew arrived on the scene.

By ten-thirty, the crowd of demonstrators had grown to more than five hundred; traffic on First Avenue was backed up for five blocks; and several dozen young demonstrators had prostrated themselves in front of the original five cars, preventing police tow trucks from removing the vehicles.

At ten-thirty-eight, Police Captain Carlton Willis brought instructions from the mayor's office to cordon off a two-block area in front of the U.S. Mission. The demonstrators were to be left alone unless they provoked violence endangering life or property.

By noon, a microphone and loudspeakers had been set up, and many prominent New York politicians and show-business personalities were leading a crowd of more than ten thousand in a call for Felix Vandenberg's dismissal from office.

Only the sound technician from the State Department's audio-visual section enjoyed relative freedom of movement. He sat on a raised dais in a corner of the Press Briefing Room. He controlled a battery of Ampex tape recorders and a panel of knobs that could activate any or all of the two dozen or so microphones built into the four tiers of tables routinely used by the reporters covering the State Department. Normally, during any of Secretary Vandenberg's overseas trips, even the weekday briefings were sparsely attended. On this particular Saturday morning, however, the room was jammed. More than a hundred reporters and television technicians waited with mounting impatience for the spokesman's arrival.

The spokesman had meantime barricaded himself in Carl Ellis' office down the corridor. The telephone consoles twinkled with incoming calls. If the secretaries looked harried, Lassiter looked frightened. He was receiving last-minute instructions from Ellis, who was on a special hookup from Jerusalem.

"I'm not particularly interested in what you think," Ellis was bellowing. "You will read the statement I've given you just as I've given it to you, and then you will stonewall."

"Carl, we've got a mob of angry people in that briefing room. They aren't going to be satisfied with this kind of kiss-off."

Ellis, whose role as a buffer between the Secretary of State and the press regularly taxed his self-restraint to its outer limits, wasted little patience on his subordinates. "Tough!" he said, and hung up.

Lassiter wiped the palms of both hands on his trouser legs, took a deep breath, opened the door and headed toward the briefing room.

Two stenographers sat to one side of the podium. Lassiter stepped up to the rostrum that stood in front of a relief map of the world, opened a manila folder and, looking up from behind horn-rimmed spectacles, asked, "Is everybody ready?"

"Go ahead." It was Dawson.

"I have a brief statement. I will not be taking questions."

There was an explosion of protest. Lassiter raised one hand and leaned into the microphone. "Do you want me to read the statement or not?"

One of the television reporters in the back of the room yelled, "Let him read the statement, for cryin' out loud!"

Lassiter began. "Secretary of State Vandenberg did recently hold conversations in Jerusalem with the Chairman of the OLPP, Jamaal Safat. The Israeli government has been advised of the nature and content of these conversations. An account of the meeting, released earlier today by *U.S. News and World Report,* is a total and irresponsible distortion."

There was a long pause. Lassiter closed his manila folder. "That's it."

Someone shouted, "What do you mean, that's it?"

"Precisely what I said." Lassiter began to move away from the podium. "Thank you."

"Hold it, Fred." Dawson sounded exasperated. "*You* don't end these briefings. We do." Pause. "Whom do we attribute this garbage to—you?"

Lassiter took one step back toward the podium. "This *statement*," he responded icily, "is attributable to the Department of State."

The man from Reuters was more polite. "Fred, that's not very helpful."

"I'm sorry, but that's all I'm authorized to say."

"When did the meeting take place?"

"No comment."

"Were the Israelis advised before or after the meeting?"

"No comment."

"If the *U.S. News* account is a total distortion, what *was* discussed?"

"No comment."

"Fred, what about the explosion here this morning?"

"What about it?"

"Was it in any way related to the meeting?"

Lassiter paused for a beat. "You can address all questions regarding the bombing to the Metropolitan Police Department."

"I'm addressing them to you."

"No comment."

"Has the White House asked for Secretary Vandenberg's resignation?"

Lassiter glared at the questioner and swallowed an angry answer. "That's obviously a question that you should address to the White House spokesman."

Kenneth Dawson closed his notebook, stood up and said, "Thank you, Fred." He didn't even pretend to mean it.

President Abbott, Harlan Stewart and Whit Traynor slumped in armchairs, staring balefully at a row of television monitors. It was six-forty-five, Saturday evening, Washington time; and to all intents and purposes, the four network news broadcasts might have been prepared by a single producer. Each anchorman began with an account of the *U.S. News* story. Each correspondent satellited a report out of Israel, focusing on Vandenberg. Francilli scored something of a coup for NBC by uncovering the fact that the secret meeting had taken place at the Venezia. He quoted Israeli sources as claiming that three U.S. Air Force officers had joined the Secretary of State at the restaurant that previous Thursday evening; Francilli inferred correctly that

Safat had been smuggled into Jerusalem in the guise of an American officer.

An image of Darius Kane appeared on one of the monitors; he was leaning against the edge of a balcony overlooking the Old City of Jerusalem.

"Turn it up, will you, Whit." The President was pointing at the NNS monitor.

The volume on Darius' report rose in mid-sentence. ". . . reaction has been one of disbelief mixed with outrage. Secretary Vandenberg met this afternoon for more than an hour with Israeli Prime Minister Ben-Dor. Neither Israeli nor American officials had any comment on the tone or content of the discussions; however, well-informed sources claim the meeting went surprisingly well. The Israeli Prime Minister is described as satisfied with Vandenberg's assertion that his conversation with Safat was reported out of context and has been grossly distorted.

"It should be noted, though, that there is no hard evidence to support this claim and, publicly, Israeli reaction continues to be one of undiluted fury. Darius Kane, National News Service, Jerusalem."

Darius' "well-informed" source had been none other than Secretary Vandenberg himself. Vandenberg had invited Darius to his suite. Without apologizing, the Secretary conceded that he had been forced by events the night before to "misdirect" Darius, but, he insisted, he had not "lied." Then, oozing sincerity, the Secretary had asserted, "Ironically, Ben-Dor is considerably less upset about the meeting than you seem to be."

Darius expressed skepticism.

"Look, I don't blame you. I was surprised too," Vandenberg continued. "I'm not suggesting that Ben-Dor was happy about the meeting; but he was far more understanding than I had expected him to be, and I'm convinced that he accepts my version of the conversation."

"What *is* your version?" It was an obvious question.

Vandenberg merely smiled and, shaking his head, escorted Darius to the door.

Darius had been tempted not to use the information. It was clear that Vandenberg was using him. Still, the Secretary had seemed surprisingly self-possessed during their brief conversation; somewhat grudgingly, Darius was forced to concede that Vandenberg had not, in fact, ever specifically denied meeting with Safat. He, Darius, had neglected to frame his questions with the necessary precision. Darius kicked an imaginary can across the room. "That sonovabitch is doing it to you again." Yet, despite his anger, Darius had used the information, but this time he protected himself by noting in the final line of his script that there was no hard evidence to support the contention that Vandenberg's meeting with Ben-Dor had gone well.

Whit Traynor sat on the arm of the President's couch, shaking his head in grudging admiration. "You gotta hand it to Felix," he said. "He's got those idiots eating out of his hand."

The images of four anchormen formed a solemn chorus line across the row of television screens. The newscasts continued to unfold as though directed by a single hand: four reports on the demonstration outside the U.S. Mission to the United Nations; four reports on the bombing at the State Department; four more reports on the formal statement issued by the State Department spokesman; and then the anchormen again, gravely intoning a litany of worldwide reaction. The volume was still up on the NNS monitor.

"For the most part," said the gray-haired anchorman, "foreign governments are approaching the subject cautiously. The governments of West Germany and Great Britain say they will have no comment for at least another twenty-four hours. In Paris, the French Foreign Ministry issued a statement praising Secretary Vandenberg for his 'statesmanlike conduct' and his 'bold recognition of reality' in the Middle East. From Moscow, National News Service Correspondent Colin Lake reports that the Kremlin has produced an uncharacteristically swift response. By and large, reports Lake, the Soviet statement was noncommittal, but it took advantage of the opportunity to hammer home their long-standing support for the establishment of a Palestinian state."

The President turned to his National Security Adviser. "Harlan, are we getting anything directly from the Israelis?"

"No, sir. I just checked with the Department and they haven't heard anything all day; but that's not surprising. Their Ambassador's in Jerusalem, and I doubt if they've even bothered to cable any instructions to the Embassy here." Stewart got up. "I'm going to check in with Langley and see what the Agency's got."

Traynor waited until Stewart had left the room.

"Mr. President, I hope you'll forgive my saying this, but I think if we let things take their normal course, we're never gonna get to the bottom of this affair." President Abbott remained silent. "Nothing against Harlan, sir. He's a good man."

"But?" the President prompted.

"But he's Vandenberg's man. I'm not suggesting that he's disloyal to you; but if Felix is dirty on this one, I can't see Harlan being the one to drop the ax on him."

"What do you want to do?" asked the President.

Traynor tried to keep the excitement out of his voice. "I've still got a couple of contacts at the Agency. Just let me run a very low level investigation through back channels."

The President shrugged. "Go ahead."

Traynor strode over to the television sets and began switching them off.

"Hold it," said the President. Traynor stiffened. "Leave one of 'em on, will you, Whit. I want to catch the scores." Abbott yawned. "We're going about this in the right way, aren't we?"

"Absolutely!" replied Traynor, with genuine conviction. "I think you're handling this exactly the right way."

Darius was acutely aware of the fact that he was skating on the edge of professional disaster. He sat on the edge of his bed with the telephone pressed tightly to one ear, the palm of his hand blocking out extraneous noise from the other. He forced himself to keep any trace of impatience out of his voice.

"Bill, I *do* understand what you're saying and normally I'd agree with you completely, but I'm convinced that Vandenberg has no more idea of how that meeting was leaked, or by whom, than you or I do."

William O'Conner, senior vice president of National News Service, remained pointedly silent. O'Conner had left a message with the television assignment desk that any call from Darius was to be transferred to him immediately. Although he made no specific reference to Darius' script of the evening before, it was clear that he felt Darius had been taken in by Vandenberg. If Darius needed evidence, O'Conner's frosty silence provided it.

"Look, Bill, I'm the one who got burned. If anyone is supersensitive right now to Vandenberg's evasions, it ought to be me."

"That's true." It might have been the tinny quality of the overseas line, but Darius was unable to find even a touch of levity in O'Conner's voice. There was another awkward silence.

"Bill, I know you're pissed off and disappointed. So am I. But whether or not Vandenberg misled me is totally irrelevant at this point. The question is, What *did* he tell Safat and who leaked it?"

"What do you think?" O'Conner's tone remained unyielding, but Darius sensed a subtle shift of mood.

"I think Felix got his hand caught in the cookie jar. I think he was getting ready to screw the Israelis and someone blew the whistle on him."

"Maybe the Israelis themselves?"

"Maybe. If they got some inkling of what Vandenberg was up to, the most effective way they have to nip it in the bud is to leak it." Even as he was speaking, Darius developed a new insight into the case he was making. "But that's exactly my point. That's why I think you should put someone else on the shuttle for the time being and let me sniff around here."

O'Conner was not in good humor. "Darius, NNS has a very expensive bureau in Israel. You let Blumer and Denison worry about the Israeli angle." There was a pause, and Darius knew that O'Conner was lighting a cigar. "You think the *U.S. News* story is essentially correct." It was a statement, not a question; but Darius acknowledged it anyway.

"Right."

"I want you to prove it."

"How?"

"You're a brilliant fellow, Darius. You'll think of something."

Darius lit a cigarette.

"You understand I can't talk as freely over this phone as I'd like." Darius was thinking of the Israeli military censors who were assumed to be monitoring all calls that involved members of the Vandenberg party.

"Go ahead."

"I'm pretty sure no more than five people were involved in the meeting."

"Vandenberg, Safat and who else?" O'Conner prompted.

"Two of Safat's people and Vandenberg's interpreter."

"Where's the interpreter?"

"He lives in Beirut. I think he's gone back there."

"That's where Safat is now too, isn't it?"

"That's right."

"Then that's where I want you to go."

Darius examined the lengthening ash on his cigarette. "I still think I can do us all more good here."

O'Conner appeared not to have heard him. "I want you to call me personally as soon as you find anything. You have my home number, don't you?"

"I have it."

"I'll look forward to hearing from you then." O'Conner hung up.

Darius looked at the receiver for a few moments. Then he dialed the NNS office in Tel Aviv. A woman answered the phone. Darius recognized the voice. "Dahlia?"

"Yes."

"It's Darius."

"Darius! Why don't you come to see me?"

"I'm trying to cut down on all my vices. Dahlia, my love, I need your help. What's the most direct way for me to get to Beirut?"

"Beirut? Why do you want to go to Beirut?"

Darius sighed. "I don't. Bill O'Conner thinks I need to broaden my horizons. He's probably jealous of you and me. Now be a sweetheart and book me on the next connecting flight, will you? Oh, and Dahlia, tourist is all booked up, you understand?"

Dahlia's voice took on a slightly patronizing air. "Darius, my darling, I don't think there's been a tourist-class seat available anywhere since you began flying."

Darius gave an appreciative chuckle. "That's why I love you so. Do you have an airline guide handy?"

"I'm already looking." Her voice trailed off into silence. A moment later she came back on the line. "You can either take a flight very late tonight into Athens, overnight at the airport and then catch an early flight on to Beirut in the morning, or you can fly out to Nicosia first thing tomorrow morning and make a connecting flight forty-five minutes after you land there."

Darius made a quick decision. "Book me on the Cyprus flight."

Dahlia snorted into the phone. "I don't even know who she is and already I hate her."

"I respect you far too much to even respond to a ridiculous suggestion like that. Dahlia, you're fantastic; I'll see you in a few days."

Darius tried to rest, to force his mind to go blank, but the sounds of voices and laughter from the garden below intruded into his effort. Darius decided to pack.

It was early evening in Jerusalem. Darius had tried unsuccessfully all afternoon to reach Katherine by phone. He had been reluctant to leave his room, hoping that she would call him. Shortly after six, Darius dressed for dinner; but before leaving the hotel, he decided to retrieve his passport from the Secretariat on the sixth floor and advise Vandenberg's staff that he was getting off the shuttle. It was in the corridor that he, almost literally, bumped into Katherine.

"I'd like to talk to you," he said, loosely tapping his passport against the thumb of his left hand. "Can you come down to my room in a few minutes?"

Katherine shook her head. "I can't. I'm leaving for Beirut in a couple of hours."

Darius grinned in amazement. "You're kidding. What are you gonna do in Beirut?"

Katherine smiled tolerantly. "I live there."

Darius slapped his passport against the wall. "I love it!" he exclaimed. "I'll be in Beirut in the morning."

A slightly hurt look crossed Katherine's face. "I wish you wouldn't joke about it. If there was any way I could've stayed here another night . . ." She didn't finish her thought.

"Who's joking? I really am coming to Beirut in the morning. What do you think I'm doing with this?" Darius held up his passport like a trophy.

Katherine placed her hand on Darius' arm. The gesture had an air of such intimacy about it that Darius rolled his eyes in the direction of the security men flanking the elevators. Katherine dropped her hand. "Where are you staying?"

"I don't know yet. Where do you want me to stay?"

"Oh, no." Katherine was smiling, but she shook her head. "The Foreign Service does insist on at least a modicum of discretion. Why don't you stay at the St. Georges?"

"I thought it was destroyed."

"It's been rebuilt, more or less. It's a lot better than the Holiday Inn and only five minutes from where I live."

Darius slipped the passport into his inside pocket. "I've always said that location in a hotel is everything. I'll meet you in the bar at three."

"Make it four."

Darius' gloom had totally vanished. "That, lady, is a date!"

21

From one thousand feet, at least, Beirut seemed to have lost little of its former beauty. Darius' Middle East Airlines Boeing 727 was making its approach over the harbor before cutting south and hugging the coastline, a ribbon of sand separating the blue Mediterranean from the snow-covered mountains. Darius felt a rush of nostalgia. Like dozens of other foreign correspondents covering the Middle East, Darius had once lived in Beirut. For him, it had been as beautiful a city as Hong Kong or San Francisco; in many ways, even more so. Beirut was the only city in the Middle East that blended French and Arab culture, and the Christian and Moslem religions, into a mix that was at times breathtaking and appealing and at other times volatile and dangerous.

For thirty years, the Lebanese had lived by the rules of the Covenant, a French-conceived plan for dividing political power between the Christians and the Moslems. The President was to be a Christian; the Prime Minister, a Moslem; but the economy remained essentially in Christian hands. The rules were broken when the Palestinians began to ignore governmental authority. They played on festering Moslem-Christian differences. They used Lebanese bases to launch guerrilla raids against Israel, thereby provoking Israeli retaliation against Lebanon; thus Lebanon, against its own wishes and interests, was drawn into the bitter Arab-Israeli dispute. The social, religious and political mix proved to be too combustible, and in the spring of 1975, events got out of control. Christian rightists, fearing a gradual left-wing Moslem take-over of "their" country, went on the attack, staging surprise raids against Moslem villages and Palestinian camps. Bloody retaliation quickly followed, producing eighteen months of devastating civil war. Finally, the Syrians, backed by Saudi Arabia, intervened. Thirty thousand troops crossed the border and slowly smothered the fighting. In the process, Lebanon lost its vitality; the Palestinian movement lost its mandate of heaven; and Syria draped a heavy, khaki-colored cloth over the country that had once been known as the Switzerland of the Middle East.

Darius saw Syria's presence the moment he got off the plane. It was in the form of a Syrian soldier, wearing the emblem of the Arab Peacekeeping Force, who was helping a Lebanese security officer check the passports of incoming passengers. Except for occasional pockmarks on the walls, the airport itself seemed to have been repaired. It bustled with life. Announcements of incoming and departing flights in English, French and Arabic echoed through the noisy building. Darius grabbed his bag and hailed a taxi for the twenty-five-minute ride to the St. Georges Hotel in downtown Beirut. The ride itself provided Darius with a confusing kaleidoscope of impressions of a city—and a country—struggling to regain some sense of its former vitality against formidable odds.

He spotted a Syrian tank first; it was hiding unsuccessfully behind a Middle East Airlines billboard. Within a few minutes, the taxi passed a sprawling Palestinian refugee camp, overcrowded with desperately poor and unhappy people. The sea glistened to his left, and Darius rolled down the back windows of the taxi to catch the swift breeze. A few fishermen were bent over their nets on the beach. "SPAGHETTERIA"—Darius could see the sign of the finest Italian restaurant in the Middle East. He had heard that it had reopened. He made a mental note to take Katherine there for dinner some evening. Marines stood guard at the American Embassy, still an imposing symbol of Western power. The American University of Beirut, looking as if it had never been closed, still seemed America's best long-term investment in Lebanon. This particular neighborhood appeared to have escaped the worst ravages of war.

But as the taxi got snarled in downtown traffic, Darius could see both the reminders of the devastation and the signs of rebirth. Many houses were no more than hulls, destroyed by the murderous cross fire that had cut down thousands of Lebanese. Many cafés, however, were open for business; chic women sat cross-legged at small sidewalk tables sipping Campari and soda with young Lebanese who yearned to recapture the past. The cab passed the harbor, weaving through dense, honking traffic; up close, the harbor looked utterly demolished. The Phoenician Hotel looked as though it had been reopened; so too the Palm Beach Hotel, once the favorite of the British. The Crazy Horse Saloon, though, had been destroyed; only the outside sign remained, hanging askew.

Darius admired the pluckiness of the Lebanese; if any people in the Middle East could rebuild their city by attracting foreign capital and talent, it was the Lebanese. But Darius could see that it was going to be a long and difficult chore. He was, thus, in a rather somber mood when the taxi pulled to a stop in front of a new hotel.

"The St. Georges," the driver said flatly.

Darius did a double take.

The St. Georges had been a landmark in Beirut, and his home for more than two years. It had always had a slightly rumpled look, like an aristocrat in old tweeds; but it had been a magnificent, proud hotel, serving journalists, diplomats, Saudi princes, spies, couriers and courtesans with equal elegance, taste and discretion. Now, from Darius' first impression, it looked as though it had been redesigned by bookkeepers, correct and comfortable in the bloodless fashion of a small Hilton.

But as he entered the lobby, he spotted the gray-haired concierge leaning over a ledger, and his spirits soared. Darius literally tiptoed over to the desk. "A large suite, boy; sea view, double bed with firm mattress, and a Lebanese whore with big tits."

The concierge glared up from his ledger. He was clearly on the edge of a massive temper tantrum until he saw Darius sporting an enormous grin.

"Mr. Kane!" he exclaimed, racing around his desk and all but leaping into Darius' embrace.

"It's so good to see you, Mansour." Darius was beaming. "I thought for a moment that all was lost." Mansour Brady was the concierge's concierge, easily the most knowledgeable contact in Beirut. He was, in addition, one of Darius' oldest friends in the Middle East. His father had been an Irish poet; his mother, a French-educated Lebanese aristocrat; their offspring had grown up to be an institution, though not of the kind his parents, in their innocence, had envisioned.

"I am serious about the large suite, the sea view, and the double bed, Mansour." Darius, after ten minutes of intense reminiscing, had felt a wave of exhaustion sweep over him, and his friend had seen the change in him.

"Room 412." Mansour waved to a bellhop.

Darius paused. "That was my old room number."

Mansour smiled. "The old number but not the old room. No need to fill out a registration card, Mr. Kane. I have your old one."

"Laundry?"

"Same system. Just leave everything on the bed."

"Bottled water?"

"Same system."

"Thanks."

Darius walked toward the telephone switchboard, located behind a half door in a small room off the main lobby. He put a twenty-dollar bill in an envelope and placed the envelope in front of the chief operator, a swarthy matron in her mid-fifties. "Madame," he said, "I have come to apologize for the inconvenience."

"Inconvenience? Monsieur . . ."

"Kane." Darius filled in the blank.

The operator flipped through the names of hotel guests.

"You won't find it there yet," Darius added hastily. "I've just checked in."

"Then I don't understand." The operator looked puzzled.

"I'm speaking of any future inconvenience I might cause you or any of your colleagues. Unfortunately I'm forced to make a great many telephone calls, and some of them may be overseas. I know how difficult it is for you." Darius' face wore a disarming smile. "I hope you'll permit me to stop by occasionally and offer my apologies personally."

Several lights flickered unattended on the switchboard. Darius noticed that the envelope had vanished.

"Mais, bien sûr, Monsieur Kane." The chief operator gestured grandly. "Avec plaisir."

Darius nodded slightly and left.

In less than fifteen minutes, Darius had unpacked, ordered an omelet and a beer from room service, and placed a call to the television assignment desk in New York. The call came before the omelet. He gave the desk his hotel address and room number and asked that Bill O'Conner be advised of his arrival in Beirut.

"Two o'clock," he murmured to himself as he stepped into a hot shower, "and all's well."

The bar at the St. Georges had always been a reporters' hangout, the place in Beirut where a visiting journalist could be assured of a friendly drink and the latest news or gossip. The barman, a trim, balding Lebanese in the employ of at least five intelligence networks, excluding his own government's, had served, among other things, the finest Bloody Mary in the world, along with tidbits of information that could be purchased and that eventually worked their way into some of the most prestigious newspaper columns. The bar itself had been the centerpiece of the room, a carved piece of oak trimmed with a brass footrail that glistened in the semidarkness; and cushion-covered benches had fit against the pine-paneled walls, surrounding small square tables and chairs.

Darius hoped that the bar had somehow survived the war, and the bookkeepers. As he entered the room, he tried to restrain his nostalgia. But there was no need. The bar had been restored; even the carpet still looked frayed. "Goddammit," Darius said, "even bookkeepers have souls."

"Mr. Kane!" Antoine recognized Darius a split second after Darius had seen him. He had been polishing glasses behind the bar; his diploma from the London Bartenders Association still hung proudly on the wall. The two friends shook hands. Antoine escorted Darius to one of the bar stools.

"No, Antoine, in the corner, please."

"She must be special."

Darius nodded, looking from table to table, as though searching for a familiar face.

"None of the old gang returned, Mr. Kane." Antoine brushed a few crumbs from the table. "This is a new group, younger, different."

At just that moment, Katherine appeared in the doorway.

"Two of your Bloody Marys, Antoine." Darius rose from his bench. Katherine doffed her cape and slowly walked toward Darius' table, conscious of every man's eyes measuring her progress.

"You look incredibly lovely."

Katherine curtsied. "I should. I spent almost an hour primping."

"You're not supposed to say that." Darius held out both hands. "I think you're always beautiful."

Katherine sat down on the bench. "That, dear Darius, is the sweetest, most heartwarming pile of unadulterated crap that anyone has handed me in years." She was still smiling as she added, "However, I've been giving it a great deal of thought, and I've decided that I love you." Darius was still standing, so she patted the bench seat beside her. "Are you going to sit down or are you working here?"

Darius remained standing. "Do you really mean that or are you just being cute?"

Katherine stared at him for a moment. "Of course I mean it." She shimmied a few more inches along the bench. "Here"—she pointed—"right next to me."

Darius slowly sat down, shaking his head. "That ain't funny McGee."

Katherine linked arms with Darius and pressed the length of her body against him. She spoke softly, with a quiet intensity. "You know very well that I mean it; but you also know that it scares the hell out of me to say it." She nestled her head on Darius' shoulder. "What are you doing here, anyway?"

Darius gently disentangled his arm from Katherine's. "Hold it, dear heart. My head doesn't move quite that fast. Hi-how-are-you-I-love-you-no-I-really-mean-it-what-are-you-doing-here-anyway?" He studied Katherine carefully. "When we're cuddling in a corner like this, what are the ground rules? Am I talking to my girl or am I being debriefed?"

"That's a low blow, Darius."

"Is it?" Darius reached for a cigarette. "If it is, I apologize. I really do. But you've got me at a helluva disadvantage, Kat. You know who I am and what I do. All I know about you is that you're supposed to be a political officer in Beirut and that you show up all over the Middle East."

Katherine had placed both hands palms down on the table. She seemed to be studying them intently. A few minutes passed. Darius could see the tightening of her jaw muscles, and he assumed she was fighting back tears. Finally, Katherine spoke, in a very low, even tone.

"I am the political officer here," she said. "I am also involved in some things that I couldn't discuss with you even if you weren't a reporter. But I am not debriefing you, or pumping you"—her voice rose slightly—"and I don't give a shit why you're here." She was collecting her purse. "And now, if you don't mind, I'd better get back to the Embassy."

Darius remained seated. "I *do* mind; and I *am* sorry." He took her hand. "Katherine, I love you. I love you very much. This isn't the first time I've ever said that, but it's the first time I've meant it."

Katherine was rubbing the top of her thigh in a desperate back-and-forth motion with her free hand, as though consoling herself. When she turned to look at Darius, he could see that she was crying. "Damn you," she muttered. "Damn you, anyway."

"I know," whispered Darius. "We're both too old to be playing games, and neither one of us wants to get hurt." He struck a match and touched the flame to his unlit cigarette. "I'm here because my office wants to know whether Vandenberg and Safat said what *U.S.*

News claims they said; and assuming that is the case—which I do—to find out who blew the whistle on Felix." Darius drew deeply on his cigarette and exhaled the smoke in a thin stream across the table. "There!" he proclaimed. "And I'm sorry I didn't say that three minutes ago."

Katherine hadn't bothered to wipe the tears from her face. "You really mean that—about loving me?"

Darius took a cocktail napkin from the small pile on the table and blotted Katherine's tears. He nodded.

Katherine nestled against him again. "I really do, you know."

"Do what?" asked Darius.

"Give a shit that you're here." She took a sip of her drink.

Darius ignored her comment. "Listen, I hope we can have dinner and spend the evening together, but I need to make a couple of phone calls first." Katherine powdered her nose. "But I may need your help. You know Felix's Arabic interpreter?"

Katherine looked startled. "What about him?"

"I want to talk to him. He was in Jerusalem the other night. You knew that, didn't you?"

"You can save yourself the time." Katherine looked troubled. "He's dead."

"What do you mean, he's dead?"

"He was killed this morning in a traffic accident."

Darius looked at Katherine intently. "What kind of a traffic accident?"

Katherine sighed. "I don't know. We're looking into it." She took one of Darius' cigarettes. "I know. I don't think it was an accident either, but for God's sake, don't go blurting anything on the *Evening News* yet. No one's even supposed to know that he's dead. Why don't you go make your other call."

Darius cradled his chin on his upturned hand. "I need your help on that one too."

Katherine raised an eyebrow.

"Safat." Darius allowed the name to slip out casually. "I want to see him."

"Oh, is that all?" Katherine dropped her hand on Darius' thigh, tracing an irregular pattern on the material with her nails. "I'll see what I can do," she said.

"I had to take a suite," Darius said.

"That's nice."

"Do you want to see it before dinner or after?"

"Both," said Katherine.

"I'll get the bill."

Katherine had rejected Darius' offer to take her home; she left his hotel suite shortly after two in the morning. When the phone rang, eight hours later, Darius was still asleep.

"Mr. Kane?"

"Yes." Darius did not recognize the voice.

"Would you please be in the lobby in fifteen minutes?"

Darius was still not fully alert. Before he could ask a question, the line went dead. For a moment Darius lay immobile on his back, wondering whether he should tell Katherine about this call. He decided against it.

It took Darius less than ten minutes to shave, shower and dress. As he left his room, he instinctively took his notebook and tape recorder; but as he was closing the door, he hesitated for a moment and then tossed the tape recorder on his bed. If this was to be what he expected, the tape recorder would be an impediment.

By the time Darius reached the lobby, he was beginning to have doubts. He knew neither whom he was meeting nor precisely where he would be going. More to the point, if he did get to see Safat, Darius was unsure about the proper approach. If the Palestinians themselves had leaked the story, Safat would have no reason to admit it. If the Israelis leaked it, Safat would know little more than Darius knew.

"My dear Mr. Kane, how delightful to be able to welcome you to Beirut." A hand cupped Darius' left elbow. Darius turned and found himself face to face with Dr. Abdul el-Rafid, the representative of the Arab League in Washington. For just an instant Darius was uncertain whether this meeting was coincidental, or whether, in fact, Rafid was his contact. The Arab maintained a gentle but firm pressure on Darius' arm, steering him in the direction of the front door.

"I apologize that we could not give you more notice, but then we didn't receive your request for the interview until a couple of hours ago." Rafid maintained a breezy line of banter as they walked into the street. "I, myself, only left Washington a few days ago. You can imagine what a pleasure it is to feel the soft Mediterranean breezes after the harsh winter climate of Chevy Chase. Ah, but then the joys of springtime are all the more readily appreciable on the heels of a

North American winter." Rafid never actually looked at Darius. His eyes were on a late-model Chevrolet parked about fifty yards from the hotel entrance.

"Please." Rafid had released Darius' arm. They walked swiftly toward the Chevrolet, where Darius was motioned into the back seat. The moment Darius was seated, Abdul el-Rafid closed the door, from the outside, and, with a cheerful wave, turned into a busy flow of pedestrians. The car had already joined the noisy traffic. Darius took a deep breath. The driver wore a red-and-white-checked kaffiyeh, held in place by a plaited black headband. Seated next to him was a dark-skinned man with a Prussian-style crew cut, little more than a stubble. Neither he nor the driver had even acknowledged Darius' presence; however, as the car made a sharp left turn, the second man, who had the thick neck and heavily muscled shoulders of a wrestler, turned awkwardly in his seat and locked the door near Darius.

At one point Darius felt that the driver was watching him in the rearview mirror; but he was actually searching for something beyond Darius, through the back window of the car. Darius turned and saw an open jeep carrying three men: a driver and two other Arabs holding AK-47 assault rifles.

The car stopped at a roadblock not far from American University. The two Arabs handed what appeared to be identity cards to an armed guard who grunted and then tapped impatiently on Darius' window. Darius lowered the window.

"Your press card!" the guard snapped.

Darius gave his White House and State Department credentials to the guard.

"Your Lebanese press card." The guard looked annoyed.

The driver murmured a few words in Arabic.

"Your passport." The guard was beginning to run out of patience.

Darius pulled his passport out of his inside jacket pocket and handed it to the guard. Two other guards approached the car. One of them carried a long metal pole with a rectangular mirror attached to one end. It looked like a gigantic dentist's mirror, and it was used to search the underside of the car. His companion reached past the driver for the ignition key, with which he opened the trunk. The search lasted for a full three minutes. Tires and tools were removed and replaced.

Finally, the guard who had taken Darius' passport said, "When you come back, you get it." Then he slapped the roof of the Chevrolet with the passport. "Go ahead."

Darius turned to look for the jeep. It was gone.

Their ultimate destination proved to be a modern seven-story apartment house. The muscular man directed Darius to a small elevator in the foyer. It was a French model, little more than a cage with a folding metal-grille door. The guard pressed 3 on the panel; but before the elevator reached the third floor, he pushed the stop button. The elevator squeaked to a halt. They were now suspended between floors. Without speaking, the man indicated to Darius that he wanted him to turn around and place his hands against the elevator's rear wall. Darius complied, noticing, as he turned, that on the staircase, level with the elevator, another guard stood, holding an American-made M-16 loosely trained on the elevator. Darius' companion had a remarkably deft touch. He ran his hands lightly through Darius' hair, ran a finger along the inside of Darius' shirt collar and then, beginning at the shoulders, frisked his quarry for concealed weapons, examining even Darius' pens and shoes. Only when the search was completed did the elevator resume its laborious journey to the seventh floor.

Two more guards waited on the landing. As Darius got out of the elevator, an apartment door opened. The foyer, inside the door, was unfurnished, with the exception of two straight-backed chairs. Darius remained standing for a few moments until another door opened and a well-groomed young Arab, dressed in European clothing, appeared.

"You are Mr. Kane?"

Darius nodded with a smile.

"The Chairman will see you now."

The Palestinian leader was seated behind a plain metal desk. Two of his aides sat on a couch. Darius assumed they were Ibrahim el-Haj and Moussa el-Saiqa, who had accompanied Safat to his meeting with Vandenberg. A guard, wearing a holster that appeared to contain a .45-caliber automatic, stood near the door. The young man who had escorted Darius into the room left immediately. Jamaal Safat motioned to a chair in front of the desk. "Do you speak Arabic, Mr. Kane?"

"No, I'm afraid I don't."

"Ah." Safat made a self-deprecatory gesture with his hands. "I regret my English does not suffice. We can use French, or my colleague here"—he pointed at Moussa—"can interpret."

"I suspect that your English may be better than my French, Mr. Chairman."

"Very well." Safat directed a few words in Arabic to Moussa, who picked up a chair from a corner of the room and brought it to the side of Safat's desk.

"You had a comfortable journey?" Moussa's translation was consecutive rather than simultaneous, but there was no pause. His English was flawless.

"Yes. Thank you. No problem at all."

"Would you care for some coffee?"

"Yes. That would be very nice." Darius had always found that any kind of refreshment helped to prolong and sometimes even lighten the tone of what might be a difficult interview.

"How can I be of help to you?" Safat sat very still, his hands folded in his lap.

"Accept my congratulations." Safat raised an eyebrow but said nothing. "You appear to have been enormously successful with our Secretary of State."

Again Safat said nothing.

"Only one thing puzzles me, Mr. Chairman. What did you gain by publicizing the conversation? Surely it would have been more useful to have allowed the Secretary enough time to implement his promises. In fact, if I remember the text correctly, you acknowledged as much at the end of your discussion."

"With commendable economy of words, Mr. Kane, you have outlined, far more effectively than I could have, precisely why it would not have been in my interest to leak either the meeting or the substance of the conversation. Why then do you begin by assuming that I am the culprit?"

A door opened quietly behind Darius; a man entered carrying two cups of Arabic coffee. He placed them on the desk and backed out of the room.

"Because, Mr. Chairman, it makes even less sense for the Secretary of State to leak a conversation that to all intents and purposes ends his usefulness in this part of the world; it may even cause the President to ask for his resignation."

Safat smiled tolerantly. "Come now, Mr. Kane. You're a resourceful reporter. The conversation took place in Israel. Certain political elements in Israel would like nothing better than to sabotage Mr. Vandenberg's efforts, especially if they found him to be cooperating with the OLPP. Has it not occurred to you that the Israelis themselves might have released this information?"

Darius decided to take a stab in the dark. "Why would the Israelis have bothered to edit the tape?" Something in Moussa's translation of his question bothered Darius. It seemed to be a shade too long, and there had been a subtle change in the tone of his voice.

Safat looked directly at Darius. "First of all, Mr. Kane, if you know of the existence of a tape, you know more than I do. Secondly, would it surprise you if I told you that the conversation as published by *U.S. News* is not accurate?"

Darius took a sip of coffee, making a conscious effort to appear relaxed. "I would consider that an extraordinary admission, Mr. Chairman. You're telling me that Secretary Vandenberg did not promise you recognition by the United States and an independent state for the Palestinian people on the West Bank?"

Safat did not even wait for the translation. "I am saying nothing of the kind. You have the reputation of being a careful journalist, Mr. Kane. Please don't disappoint me. I conceded that certain details of the conversation were not accurately reported in *U.S. News*. I have no intention of violating the confidentiality of my discussions with your Secretary of State. I am, however, interested in convincing you that while someone obviously *is* trying to cause Mr. Vandenberg serious embarrassment, I am not that person."

"You're saying it was the Israelis."

Safat smiled. "You'll have to draw your own conclusions, Mr. Kane. More coffee?"

Darius covered the cup with his hand. "It would, of course, also be to your advantage, if you believed the Secretary incapable of living up to his promises, for you to manipulate events so that the Israelis were blamed for something they didn't do."

Safat steepled his fingers and raised them to the bridge of his nose. He seemed to be struggling for control. "Mr. Kane"—he sighed—"I have been trying for years now to arrange a serious discussion with a senior member of your government. Difficult as you may find this to accept, I not only believe in the Palestinian cause with every fiber of my being, but I would also like my people to gain recognition without further bloodshed. The American government could be very helpful in this regard. Do you think I would arrange a discussion with your Secretary of State for the express purpose of sabotaging any useful role that the United States might be able to play?"

Darius nodded. "I agree. I don't think you'd do that. But if, as the result of your meeting with Vandenberg, you felt that there had been absolutely no change in American policy, wouldn't that call for a change in tactics?"

Safat slammed his hand on the desk. "I am not a fool, Mr. Kane. The meeting went well. I left Jerusalem filled with a greater optimism than I've known in years. Perhaps Vandenberg was only humoring me, but I had every intention of patiently awaiting further developments." The Palestinian leaned across the desk, lowering his voice. "Tell me, Mr. Kane. Did you know that Secretary Vandenberg's interpreter was murdered here in Beirut yesterday morning?"

"I knew that he died in a traffic accident. Was he murdered?"

"He was," Safat said, "and not by any of our people."

"The Israelis?" guessed Darius.

"On occasion they have been known to use such tactics." Safat got to his feet and walked around the desk. "And now, you must forgive me, but I have a great deal of work to do. It's been a great pleasure meeting you, Mr. Kane. I hope it's been useful for you."

"Very useful, Mr. Chairman. Thank you for your patience."

The interview was over.

The return trip to the St. Georges Hotel took place without incident. Darius scribbled furiously in his notebook for much of the ride. Two conclusions seemed all but inescapable. Vandenberg had been telling the truth when he told Darius that his conversation with Safat had been distorted, or at least reported out of context. What was still unclear, of course, was how much Vandenberg *had* promised the Palestinian leader. Secondly, all evidence seemed to point to the Israelis as the ones who had released the story. Some Israelis, anyway. Safat, Darius was convinced, was genuinely disturbed by the leak. It was an extraordinary story, but it needed further exploration.

When Darius returned to the St. Georges, he couldn't help but notice that the lobby seemed to have been turned into a quasi-military post. In command stood the towering, slightly ludicrous but unmistakably aristocratic figure of Desmond Castleberry, editor of *U.S. News & World Report.* Simultaneously, in three languages—English, French and Arabic—he was issuing instructions to the concierge, who had emerged from behind his desk, and to a small corps of bellhops, who had been assembled for his service, in the proper handling of his luggage, which included three large suitcases, three small ones, two garment bags, two typewriters and a tennis racket.

Darius had known Castleberry ever since they had covered the Indochina war in the sixties. Desmond's father had been a wealthy publisher. His political and financial clout, and Desmond's own instinctive intelligence, had propelled the younger Castleberry into the front ranks of those foreign correspondents who hobnobbed with prime ministers and became expatriates. Despite his eccentric behavior, Castleberry always managed to come up with one exclusive after another, incurring the admiration or envy of his peers; and, to his credit, he never shied away from danger, covering every war from Vietnam to Angola, always with a fresh rose in the buttonhole of his jacket lapel.

Castleberry, upon spotting Darius surveying the scene in the lobby, gave a theatrical cry of delight. "Darius, my dear boy." He had affected a British manner of speaking, and his voice, always high-pitched, lent an added air of foppishness to his manner. "I thought you were with his eminence." A momentary look of concern crossed his face. "Felix isn't in Beirut, is he?"

Darius shook his head. "No, he gave me a couple of days off to check on some crap that *U.S. News* is running."

Castleberry smiled appreciatively. "One of my better stories, even if you do force me to say it myself. Listen, are you free for dinner?"

"Not sure," responded Darius, thinking of Katherine. "I have to make a couple of calls first, but I could certainly meet you for a drink in about forty-five minutes."

"Look forward to it, old chap. Oh, for God's sake, that isn't a sack of oranges." Castleberry abandoned Darius and leaped after a bellboy who was dragging one of his leather garment bags along the floor.

Darius knew that Castleberry would be late. It was not a malicious aspect of his nature; it simply suited his self-image. Darius deliberately stalled in his room for an hour and a quarter before going down to the bar. Castleberry arrived ten minutes later.

"I am most dreadfully sorry. Have I kept you waiting long?" He didn't wait for an answer. "The Ambassador called just as I was leaving the room, and I couldn't get the poor bastard off the phone." Castleberry managed to convey by virtue of a long-suffering smile the enormous burden of being constantly in demand.

Darius decided to begin with a massage. "You can't blame him, Des; I'm sure he gets a far more comprehensive briefing from you than he does through official channels." For an instant, Darius was concerned that he might have allowed an edge of sarcasm into his voice. There was no reason to worry.

"Oh, absolutely," cried Castleberry. "The man has no idea what's going on. If he had even a shred of pride, he would have resigned long ago. Ah, well, 'There but for the grace of God.'" Castleberry paused significantly. "Did I ever tell you that Felix wanted me to take the ambassadorship here?"

Darius nodded. "You would've been superb."

Castleberry did not disagree.

"Diplomacy's loss is journalism's gain." Darius permitted himself a slight smile. "That was one helluva story, Desmond."

"Felix and Safat?"

"Mmm." Darius nodded. "How'd you do it?"

"Rather impressively, I thought."

Darius didn't flinch. "No question about that; but since you obviously weren't there, how could you be so sure of the dialogue? I mean, someone could've fed you a pure fabrication."

"That's unworthy of you, Darius. You know me better than that."

"No, no. I'm not questioning your integrity. It's just that a transcript can be made to say anything."

Castleberry smiled. "Nice try, old boy."

Darius appeared to miss the point. "I'm serious."

"Oh, I know you are. I also know that what I had in my story was a verbatim transcript."

"How can you be sure?"

Castleberry motioned to a waiter. "I'm sure."

The two men gave their orders. After the waiter left their table, Darius said, "The only way you can be that sure is if you had a tape."

Castleberry shrugged.

"It could've been faked." Darius was leaning across the table, keeping his eyes fixed on Castleberry's.

Castleberry turned away. "I really can't talk about it."

Darius' voice was low but insistent. "There *was* a tape, wasn't there?"

"Darius, you're an old friend, but this really is becoming a trifle annoying."

Darius hadn't moved and, if anything, his voice had become even quieter; but there was something in his manner that caused Castleberry to pay close attention the instant Kane spoke again.

"You're absolutely right, Desmond. Of course"—he paused for a moment to be sure he had the other man's attention—"the Solzhenitsyn affair was 'a trifle annoying' too. Or had you forgotten?"

It was dark in the bar, but Darius could see that Castleberry was flushed. "You really are an unprincipled bastard."

There was no humor in Darius' laugh. "Me, unprincipled? You're a born revisionist, Des. I saved your cute little aristocratic ass on that one; and what's more, I've never said a word to anyone about it. But you're beginning to make me reconsider the wisdom of that."

Years earlier, Darius had obtained an exclusive interview with the Soviet novelist and dissident Alexander Solzhenitsyn. He had allowed Castleberry to read his notes and had given him permission to quote from the interview, but only on the condition that NNS would be given proper credit. Castleberry wrote the interview as though it were his own, fabricating a number of quotes that gave his story considerably greater impact than the one Darius had sent back to the States. Castleberry had blamed the mix-up on his editors in Boston, but both Kane and Castleberry knew that was a lie. Darius had been furious at the time, but reluctant to add fuel to Soviet government charges that both interviews had been inventions. He had allowed the issue to die.

"What I want to know, Desmond, is whether there was a tape, and if so, where it is now."

"I don't know."

"What do you mean, you don't know?"

"I don't know where it is."

"Don't play games with me, you supercilious bastard. You don't leave a tape like that lying around in your hotel room."

"I'm not playing games. I never had the tape. I heard it only once."

"Who's got it?"

"I don't know."

"Then who *had* it?" For the first time Darius allowed his voice to rise.

"I can't tell you that."

Darius' voice was as soft as velvet. "Oh, I think you can."

Castleberry was deflated. "I'll never be able to use him as a source again."

"Don't worry about it, I'll protect you."

The *U.S. News* editor stirred a piece of ice around his glass with a finger. "His name's Tivoli; Gustav Tivoli."

"What does he do and where do I find him?" Darius was still pushing, but gently.

"He's one of the very few Italian bankers in Zurich."

"How does he tie in?"

"I'm not sure. I've never pressed him on it. His bank used to do a lot of business with my father, and now I think it does a lot of business with Arabs, and with Jews too. He's been a very useful contact over the years, and I've always found him to be extremely reliable. He's not the kind of man you push around though."

"No," Darius agreed, "of course not." He got up and threw a bank note on the table. "Desmond, I don't know how to thank you. You've been extraordinarily helpful." His smile was radiant. "We must have dinner sometime."

Castleberry kept stirring his drink, not looking up at his colleague.

Darius went directly to Mansour Brady and inquired about flights to Zurich. There was one that left Beirut the next morning. "Book a first-class seat for me, please." Darius slipped the concierge a five-dollar bill. Then he returned to his room and booked a call to O'Conner in New York.

It was seven-thirty in the evening, Beirut time, when the NNS operator found O'Conner lunching at the Four Seasons.

"Bill, we may be on a party line here," Darius cautioned, "so I'm going to be a little oblique." Darius could hear the conversation swirling about O'Conner, who said simply, "Go ahead."

"The man from Berlitz has gone on to his reward."

"No shit!"

"Yup; and that's just the beginning. There was a tape and one of the gnomes has it."

"Gnomes?" O'Conner was confused.

"You remember that book I gave you a few years ago, when we were thinking about that show on the multinationals?" The book, *The Gnomes of Zurich*, dealt with the Swiss banking industry.

"I gotcha."

"I'm going to pay him a visit tomorrow."

"I think you should."

"The other guy I came here to see?" Darius most especially did not want to mention Safat's name.

"Yeah."

"He also says the conversation was distorted."

"You've got enough for a story right there."

"Not yet, Bill. I want to see the gnome first."

"I'll have a crew meet you. Where are you staying?"

"How about the Dolder?"

"I'll have Sally book you. The crew'll meet you there."

"Fine. I'll talk to you tomorrow."

Darius hung up and fell back on the bed. He was feeling very good. The story was falling into place, and at a pace that dazzled even him. Suddenly, though, his professional elation was tempered by personal disappointment. Leaving Beirut would mean leaving Katherine. Darius turned to the phone again with sudden urgency. He dialed the Embassy. Miss Chandler was in a meeting and couldn't be disturbed. Would he care to leave a message? Darius hesitated. He couldn't shake the feeling that for some reason it would be better if no one knew they were seeing each other.

"Tell her that Doug Kittering called. I'm at the St. Georges." He hung up, feeling foolish.

Darius pushed Katherine to the back of his mind and pulled a couple of sheets of hotel stationery out of the desk. It was time to try to sort out what he knew, what he suspected and what he had yet to find out. He drew a vertical line down the center of one page and wrote "KNOWN" at the top of the left-hand column and "SUPPOSITION" above the one on the right.

Under the first heading, he wrote, "Vandenberg says transcript distorted.

"Safat partially confirms.

"Both insist they had nothing to do with leaking the meeting.

"Three other witnesses. Two of them Safat's people—third man dead.

"Castleberry heard tape through Swiss banker with Arab *and* Jewish connections. Someone doctored the tape.

"WHO? HOW MUCH DID THEY CHANGE THE ORIGINAL MEANING? WHY?"

Darius then began scribbling in the second column.

"Vandenberg always swore he'd never meet with Safat until OLPP recognized Israel.

"Just because tape was doctored doesn't mean he didn't sell out Israelis. BUT—sellout couldn't have been worse than transcript, so Vandenberg gains nothing by faking text and leaking it.

"Safat? Possibly. If Vandenberg *was* tough, Safat could use tape to destroy him.

"OLPP *did* kidnap Helen. That could've been plan all along."

Darius reread what he'd just written. He started writing again.

"The Israelis? If they discovered Vandenberg sellout, they'd want to sabotage U.S.-OLPP contact ASAP. Destroy Vandenberg too!"

Darius pushed the paper away and threw his pen on the desk in frustration. On the one hand, it didn't seem logical for Vandenberg to engineer his own destruction, but the meeting with Safat wasn't logical either; and he'd been misled by Vandenberg too often to dismiss totally the possibility that the Secretary of State was somehow wrapped up in this operation too. In short, he was no further along in finding out who had bugged the meeting, or why. The death of the interpreter nagged at Darius too. There were enough people in Washington who'd like to see Vandenberg toppled. It wasn't likely, but it could even have been one of the Secretary's rivals in the Administration using the interpreter as the inside man.

The telephone startled Darius. He pushed his chair back and went over to the bed again.

"Hi." It was Katherine.

"Hi, yourself."

"Why the mystery?"

"Stupid, I guess. I didn't want to compromise you."

"That's adorable."

"Yeah." Darius was becoming acutely embarrassed. "Listen, I'm flying out of here tomorrow morning. Can I see you tonight?"

"Oh, Darius, I can't." She sounded genuinely torn. "Why do you have to leave so soon?"

"I can't tell you over the phone. No way you can make it tonight, huh? Not even late?"

There was a long pause. "I just can't. This Vandenberg-Safat thing is developing a life of its own. The cable traffic is unbelievable. I don't think I'm going to get out of here at all tonight."

"Well, I'm flying to Europe in the morning. I imagine I'll be back in the area before too long. Do you have my number if you get to Washington?"

There was silence at the other end.

"Kat?"

"I'm here. It's just that we're starting to sound like a couple of people at the end of a summer interlude."

"Oh, bullshit! We both knew it was going to be like this. It's no interlude, and we are going to see each other again."

"Sure. When?"

"I don't know. I love you."

"I know."

"Take care of yourself, OK?"

"Darius?"

"Mm."

"Please come back." There was a click and then the buzz of a disconnected line.

22

The turrets of the Dolder Grand Hotel sat like enormous witches' hats on top of the ornate old building. The hotel was an institution that presided over the Dolder Quarter of Zurich, overlooking the city itself; imperious, exuding a sense of hauteur that soothed the rich and denied the existence of anyone else. To the Swiss, poverty is a communicable disease. The Dolder was well quarantined.

It was snowing lightly when Darius reached the hotel. A film crew, dispatched from Paris, waited in the lobby. Darius told the cameraman, a Russian émigré, to remain at the hotel, even though it was unlikely that there would be any work that evening. "If you do go out, André, just make sure that I know where to reach you."

Darius went to his room. The view was, as usual, breathtaking, the snow adding majesty to the Alps. He immediately looked in the Zurich phone book for Gustav Tivoli. Only one was listed. The phone rang several times before a woman answered. *"Ja?"*

"Entschuldigen Sie," said Darius. *"Sprechen Sie Englisch?"*

"Moment bitte, ja?"

Another woman got on the phone. "This is Mrs. Tivoli. What do you want, please?"

"My name is Darius Kane, Mrs. Tivoli. I'd like to speak to your husband if he's home." There was a long pause. For a moment, Darius thought that she'd hung up.

"My husband is dead, Mr. Kane."

"Good Lord. I am terribly sorry, Mrs. Tivoli. I didn't know."

"No. Well"—the woman's voice was flat—"if there's nothing else . . ."

"I need to talk to you, Mrs. Tivoli. It's extremely important. I know this must be a very bad time for you; but if I could just stop by to see you for a few minutes."

"I'd really rather not, Mr. Kane."

"Believe me, I wouldn't be imposing on you if it weren't terribly urgent."

"Are you—were you a friend of my husband's?"

For just an instant, Darius considered lying. "We had a mutual friend. Your husband and I never actually met."

There was another long pause. Finally Mrs. Tivoli asked, "Can you be here at nine o'clock?"

"I'll be there. Again, I'm terribly sorry."

The banker's widow did not say goodbye.

Darius stood at his hotel window, looking out at the snow-covered golf course below, mulling over the latest development. He glanced at his watch. It was almost seven. He suddenly realized that he didn't know whether Mrs. Tivoli had meant nine that evening or whether she had intended him to come the following morning. He dismissed the thought of calling her back. If she had meant the morning, Darius could explain the misunderstanding. Darius undressed and wandered into the bathroom. As a torrent of steaming water gushed out of the heavy brass fitting, Darius thumbed open a small cardboard package of Spanish soap that lay on a separate towel table.

"There's a nice touch of symbolism for you," he mused as he sniffed its fragrance. "Black soap."

The neighborhood was unfamiliar to Darius, but it was unmistakably upper crust. The Tivoli residence was particularly opulent. High sculptured hedges covered by undisturbed snow flanked a brick archway. The driveway curved down a slight incline, past an elaborate rose garden, a gazebo and a tennis court, and then looped back around a marble fountain. A Jaguar was parked in front of a two-car garage; a Mercedes 450 SEL stood near the main entrance of the house. From the fresh tire tracks in the snow, it was clear that the Mercedes had just arrived. The house itself was mainly stonework. Massive. Enduring.

Darius told the taxi driver to wait. He spent a moment searching around the oak doors for a bell. There was none. Then he pulled the heavy iron ring that passed through the nose of a lion's-head knocker, and he heard chimes in the hallway. A maid answered the door. She held the door with both hands, as though guarding it against an unwelcome intruder.

"*Mein Name ist Kane,*" said Darius, smiling. "*Ich habe vorhin mit Frau Tivoli gesprochen.*"

"*Ist in Ordnung, Hilde,*" said a woman from behind the door. "*Lassen Sie den Herrn hinein.*"

Darius hadn't known quite what to expect of Mrs. Tivoli. She was, in several respects, something of a surprise; younger than Darius had judged from her voice, she was strikingly attractive. She appeared to be in her mid-thirties; elegant, carefully groomed. She did not, Darius thought, look like a broken woman.

"I'm sorry that I was so abrupt with you on the telephone before." She moved across the foyer toward Darius with the controlled warmth of an experienced hostess, extending a slim hand in Darius' direction. "As you can imagine, it's been a very difficult couple of days."

"Of course." Darius shook her hand. "I'm very grateful that you agreed to see me."

Mrs. Tivoli guided Darius toward an open door. "We'll sit in the library. I hope you don't mind, but I've asked our family lawyer to join us. It wasn't clear to me just what your business with my late husband was." She spoke English with only the slightest trace of a German accent.

Darius winced inwardly at the news of the attorney, but he said only, "No, that was a very wise thing to do. In fact, your lawyer might be extremely helpful."

The room was fitted with ornate rococo furniture and was lined with floor-to-ceiling shelves that held thousands of leather-bound volumes. Much of the room's pegged oak flooring was covered with an enormous fawn-colored Taiping carpet. In front of a stone fireplace lay a ruby-bright Persian carpet on which three overstuffed leather armchairs and a huge matching couch were arranged.

"Kurt von Marbod, I would like to present Mr. Kane." The lawyer was somewhat corpulent, but dapper. He struggled to get out of his chair.

"Please," said Darius, "don't get up." But the feat had already been accomplished. Von Marbod stood with his left thumb hooked in his vest pocket, holding out a plump, pale hand. He looked about sixty. His hair, which was combed straight back without a part, was amazingly black. Darius thought he detected the faint odor of pomade.

"Mr. Kane." Von Marbod bowed an inch in Darius' direction.

Mrs. Tivoli gestured to the couch. "May I offer you a drink, Mr. Kane?"

"Whiskey and soda would be very nice."

Mrs. Tivoli gave an almost-concealed sigh and seated herself demurely at the other end of the couch. "Have you just arrived from the United States, Mr. Kane?"

"No." Darius hesitated for a moment. "Mrs. Tivoli, I know it must be extraordinarily difficult for you to receive guests at a time like this, and you're being far more gracious than I have any right to expect. But clearly, this is not a social call, and I don't want to impose on you more than is absolutely necessary. So, please, there's no need to make conversation or to feel that you have to entertain me in any way. I think it would be best if I got right to the purpose of my visit." Darius glanced at Von Marbod, who nodded nonchalantly from his seat near the fireplace.

"I'm a diplomatic correspondent for National News Service. That means that I spend much of my time traveling with Secretary of State Vandenberg." The maid was standing at Darius' elbow with a silver tray holding a glass, a crystal decanter of Scotch and one of the old-fashioned siphon bottles that squirt soda from a stainless-steel head. Darius fixed himself a short drink and then settled back into his corner of the couch. "As you can imagine, the meeting between Vandenberg and Jamaal Safat has created absolute chaos in the Middle East. For the moment, at least, Vandenberg is staying in the area, but I think he'll have to return to Washington any day now. He could even be forced to resign."

Von Marbod, after lighting a long cigar, seemed to derive genuine pleasure from blowing the end into a dull red ember. Mrs. Tivoli looked at Darius with polite attention.

"The story of that meeting was broken by Desmond Castleberry." Darius waited for a moment to see if the name produced any reaction. It did not. "Castleberry heard a tape of the conversation. The man who played that tape for him was your late husband." The only sound in the library was the popping and crackling of the fire. "Forgive me for asking, Mrs. Tivoli, but how did your husband die?"

It was Von Marbod who answered. "Mr. Tivoli's car went out of control. It skidded on a patch of ice and crashed into a tree."

"There's no reason to believe it was anything—"

Von Marbod cut in. "No reason whatsoever. Now, Mr. Kane, forgive me if I seem rude, but I fail to see how we can be of any help to you."

"The tape that Mr. Tivoli played for Castleberry. Where is it?"

Mrs. Tivoli had clearly removed herself from the conversation.

"As I said, Mr. Kane, I don't want to be rude, and I admire your enterprise; but even if I knew the answer to that question, I still don't understand what possible business it could be of yours."

"The tape was fixed, Mr. von Marbod; doctored, edited. I'm sure Mr. Tivoli didn't know that; but the end result is the same. We've only begun to see the repercussions of that tape. It's not stretching things to suggest that the failure of Vandenberg's peace mission, under these circumstances, could lead to another war in the Middle East. If that tape still exists; if we can find it"—Darius gave a small shrug—"there's considerably more at stake, sir, than a reporter's enterprise."

Von Marbod pulled a pocket watch out of his vest. He was looking at the watch as he spoke. "I'm sorry, Mr. Kane. We can be of no help to you."

Darius made no move to leave. He sat in silence, gazing at the fire, collecting his thoughts. "Mr. von Marbod, I appreciate your position. I know that your first responsibility is to your client; and I understand that you don't want to do anything to violate that trust, or to hurt Mrs. Tivoli, or, for that matter, to do any damage to Mr. Tivoli's memory." Darius couldn't be sure, but he thought for an instant that Mrs. Tivoli had smothered the beginning of a smile.

Von Marbod rose from his chair. "Mr. Kane, I must insist. Your visit has been most inappropriate; and I'm sure if Mrs. Tivoli had known why you wanted to come here, you would not have been invited in the first place."

Darius remained seated. "You didn't let me finish, Mr. von Marbod. I was about to say that this matter is far more than a matter of journalistic enterprise. Knowingly or not, Mr. Tivoli was involved in something that was intended—in fact, something that has succeeded in totally undermining an American peace initiative. You're quite right, of course. You don't have to deal with me. But if I can find that tape, there's no reason whatsoever for me to involve the Tivoli family. I can and would protect my sources. If I don't get the tape, I still intend to tell as much of the story as I know, up to and including the late Mr. Tivoli's involvement. At that point, Mr. von Marbod, you will be dealing with an entirely different proposition. Do I make myself clear, sir? The official and unofficial arms of the United States government, the

Israeli government, the OLPP; and you can probably think of a few others."

Von Marbod sat very still. "Are you quite finished, Mr. Kane?"

"No, not quite. I'm staying at the Dolder. Room 422. Thank you for the drink, Mrs. Tivoli." She did not respond. "I'll show myself out."

In the taxi, all the way back to the hotel, Darius replayed the conversation, wondering if he could have handled it in a better way. After a light dinner, he went to bed, but he could not sleep. He lay awake, still wondering.

For one panic-stricken moment, Darius forgot where he was. The darkness was absolute, and a shrill bell rang intermittently near his head. Darius groped for the sound and felt the phone under his hand. He lifted the receiver just as the bell was beginning a new assault.

"Hello?"

"Mr. Kane?"

"What?" His hand searched the night table for the light switch.

"Anna Tivoli. I'm sorry to wake you."

"Hold on a minute, Mrs. Tivoli, will you?" Darius finally found the switch. The sudden brightness caused him to blink in momentary pain. There was an inch of beer left in a Lowenbrau bottle standing next to the lamp. Darius took a quick swallow and shuddered. He looked at his watch; it was not quite three.

"Mrs. Tivoli?"

"Yes. I'm sorry to call at this dreadful hour, but I couldn't sleep and I wanted to talk to you as soon as possible."

"Go ahead."

"First of all, I never want to see you again. I'll tell you whatever I can, but then I want your promise that you'll leave me alone. Do you agree?"

Darius was rubbing the bridge of his nose. "Mrs. Tivoli, if you can convince me that you've really told me everything you know, I have no interest in bothering you again."

"Do I have your word?"

Darius hesitated for just a moment. "Yes, all right, you have my word. Look, would you hold on for just a minute; I'm still half asleep. I only want to splash a little water on my face. OK?"

"I'll wait."

Darius jumped off the bed, threw back the curtain that sealed off his sleeping alcove, and stumbled over to the desk. He picked up his notebook and pen and started back toward the bed. He stopped in mid-track, ran into the bathroom, washed his face and ran back to the phone. "Go ahead." He flipped the notebook to a clean page.

"I think you should know that Gustav and I were about to get a divorce."

Darius said nothing.

"Are you there?"

"Yes. I'm listening. Go on."

"I tell you that only because I don't want you to believe that you're talking to a grief-stricken widow. I long ago lost interest in Gustav's affairs. I mean that in both senses of the word."

"I understand."

"He was not a wealthy man. I mean, not really rich. He had an excellent salary from the bank, but not enough for us to live in this style. Then, a few years ago, Gustav started bringing Arab visitors to the house. That wasn't unusual in itself. We entertained a lot of his banking customers here. He even got some kind of entertainment allowance. But these men weren't like his usual customers. They never came for dinner and I was never allowed to take part in the conversations. Gustav said the Arabs felt uncomfortable discussing business around women. Anyway, from that time on, we had no more financial problems. Gustav and I never talked about it. Money just wasn't a problem anymore. Ironically, that's when our marriage started . . ." She was groping for a word.

"Falling apart?" Darius suggested.

"Yes. He went on trips without telling me where he was going, and I know there were other women."

"I'm sorry."

"No, it doesn't matter; we both pursued our . . . respective lifestyles. I only wanted you to understand that in many ways I know very little about what Gustav did during the last few months."

"I understand."

"A few days ago one of these Arabs came here again."

"Do you remember what day it was?"

"No, not exactly. I think . . . Friday morning."

Darius wrote "Arab visitor—Friday morning," and underlined the notation several times. "It doesn't matter," he said. "Go on."

"Gustav was very disturbed after the visit. He was unusually bad-tempered. He locked himself in his study for several hours. Then he came out and he seemed quite subdued. He took me into the study and showed me a package, which he put in the wall safe. He said that if anything happened to him, I was to give the package immediately to Kurt von Marbod."

"He didn't tell you what was in the package?"

"No. But after what you said last night, I'm sure it was the tape."

"Didn't you discuss it with Von Marbod after I left?"

"Yes. He said the less I knew, the better."

"Couldn't you demand to see the package?"

She laughed, but there was no humor in it. "I'm afraid you still don't understand, Mr. Kane. I'm not the executor of the estate. Von Marbod is. At this moment I don't even know if I'm named in my husband's will. I'm in no position to demand anything, except the right to begin a new life. That's the only reason I'm talking to you at all. I don't know what my husband was involved in. I don't *want* to know. Whatever it was, I'm sure it's nothing but trouble. I don't know what contacts you have here in Switzerland, but use them. The sooner this thing is cleared up, the sooner I can start breathing again. Von Marbod has the tape, Mr. Kane. How you get it from him is your problem, but I want nothing more to do with this matter." She sounded drained.

"You've been very helpful, Mrs. Tivoli. I mean that. I won't bother you any further; but if, for any reason, you want to get in touch with me again, let me give you a number in New York. They'll always know where to find me." Darius gave her the main switchboard number for NNS and one of the extensions for the assignment desk. He had the impression that she didn't even write them down.

Darius was too excited to sleep. What *were* his contacts in Switzerland? His memory was a blank. He read and reread his notes from the telephone conversation. How could he get that tape? His mind was still a blank. He got out of bed and unpacked, distributing his belongings with uncharacteristic care. He shaved, with elaborate preparation. Then he took all his suits into the bathroom and suspended them on their hangers from towel racks and the hook on the back of the door. He took a long, very hot shower, simultaneously steaming himself and the suits. Darius wrapped himself in the terrycloth robe provided by the hotel. It was still only five-fifteen.

He wandered over to the door and retrieved his breakfast order from the handle outside. It resembled a contract more than a menu. Everything was in three languages: *"Zu servieren um —— Uhr; Ser-*

vir à —— heures; To be served at —— o'clock." Darius crossed out
the 9 he had earlier written and wrote 6. Then he saw some of the fine
print. "We are ready to serve you from 6:30 A.M." Darius put the
colon and the 30 after his 6 and wandered back into the room. It was
still dark outside. He began thumbing through his address book,
which lay on the desk. He had listed all foreign addresses under the
appropriate country or city, rather than by name. The only name
under Zurich was that of the concierge at the Dolder. There was nothing of interest under Geneva. He found Berne. "Baden, Karl. Of
course!" Karl Baden had been on the Stanford tennis team with
Darius. They had retained only occasional contact over the years, but
they were still friends. He dialed the operator.

"Are you busy?"

"Pardon?"

"Do you have a few minutes to help me find a telephone number?"

"Of course."

"The name is Karl Baden. It should be listed in the Berne direc-
tory."

"A minute, please."

Darius could hear the operator flipping through the phone book.

"Sir," she said at last, "there are more than fifteen Karl Badens in
Berne. Do you have an address?"

Darius consulted his book. He had no address. Then he remembered reading a few months earlier that Karl's father had been appointed Minister of Justice.

"Operator, my friend's father is the Swiss Minister of Justice. Now
his name is obviously Baden also, but I don't know the first name."

"A minute, please."

Darius heard the operator consult with someone else at the switchboard.

*"Thea, weisst Du wie der Justitz Minister Baden mit dem Vor-
namen heisst?"*

"Ich glaub' Otto."

She was back. "Sir, I think it is Otto Baden. I have two numbers for
him. Do you want the ministry or the home?"

"Let me have both, please."

Darius stretched out on the bed and, shortly before six, dozed off.

Breakfast came promptly at six-thirty. With it, the hotel delivered a
copy of the *Swiss Review of World Affairs.* By seven-forty-five, Darius
could restrain himself no longer. He called the Baden home.

Mrs. Baden seemed cool at first; but as soon as she remembered Darius' connections to her son, she bubbled over with cordiality. Karl, she told him, was married and had just recently opened his own law practice. He was, at the moment, in Paris, but was due back in Berne that afternoon. Would it be possible, she asked, for Darius to come to her home for dinner that evening? She would see to it that Karl and his wife would be there.

It was barely eight o'clock when Darius hung up. He felt as though he'd already put in a full day.

The evening proved to be something less than a triumph. Karl's father seemed largely preoccupied throughout the meal. Darius was having trouble focusing on the Badens' favored topic of discussion—inflation. Karl's wife, Lieselotte, spoke only the most elementary English; but, Darius suspected, she probably did not contribute a great deal in any language. "A pair of shoes, *ja?* Simple shoes, not beautiful. A hundred and eighty, a hundred and ninety, two hundred francs." Lieselotte clasped her hands before allowing them to fall dramatically on the table. "And dresses!" She let the full horror of what dresses might cost sink in without further embellishment.

"It's true," Karl agreed. "The cost of living has become unbelievable." He turned to Darius. "Do you have any idea what it costs here now for a one-bedroom flat?"

"No," Darius allowed, "I can't imagine."

"For a decent place, nothing spectacular, three hundred, three hundred and fifty dollars." Darius must have looked unimpressed. "You've got to remember, we don't earn American salaries here."

"It must be brutal."

"Shall we have our coffee in the living room?" Otto Baden was already halfway out of the room as he spoke.

"Good idea," said the elder Mrs. Baden. "Liesel and I will clean up, and the men can talk."

Lieselotte pouted prettily. "Always the men they talk, the women they work." She followed her mother-in-law into the kitchen.

"What brings you to Switzerland, Mr. Kane?" Otto Baden wandered over to the fireplace and leaned against the mantel. He lit a cigar, offering one to Darius. "Karl doesn't smoke," he explained. Darius declined.

"Mr. Baden, I'd feel a lot better if you called me Darius. After all, Karl and I were at school together."

Baden bobbed his head in agreement. "Fine, fine. What brings you to Switzerland, Darius?"

"A tape. An audio tape."

There seemed to pass across Otto Baden's face a look of more than passing interest.

"You've of course seen the account of that secret meeting between Secretary Vandenberg and Jamaal Safat?" Darius allowed the question to hang for a moment.

Both Badens nodded.

"The transcript of that conversation was taken from a tape, which may very well have been made without the knowledge of either Vandenberg or Safat. What makes it even more interesting is that the tape was apparently edited and the sense of the conversation was changed. To what degree, I can't say. As you may know, the story was first broken by *U.S. News* magazine. Their correspondent heard the tape here."

"In Berne?" Otto Baden was now decidedly interested.

"No, in Zurich." Darius lit a cigarette. "A banker by the name of Tivoli acted as the intermediary. It seems he played the tape for the man from *U.S. News* and then, a short time later—possibly even the same day—he met with an unfortunate accident."

"You mean he was killed?" Karl seemed incredulous.

"Hard to say. In any event, he's dead."

Darius was about to continue, but Otto Baden, with an unnatural show of joviality, stretched both arms in the direction of the door. "Ah, the coffee."

Even Karl seemed amazed by this sudden display of paternal solicitude. The elder Baden seemed determined, however, to control the conversation. He had taken the tray from his daughter-in-law. "Enough of these unpleasant subjects. Let's talk about something else. Do you hunt, Darius?"

"No, sir." Darius was thoroughly confused, but one thing was quite clear: the subject of the tape was not to be raised again.

After half an hour, Darius consulted his watch and made a great show of how long it would take him to return to Zurich.

"I'll drive you," Karl volunteered, but he sounded unenthusiastic.

"That's awfully nice of you, but I rented a car. Now, if someone could just find my coat for me; and, of course, I'd like to say good night to Mrs. Baden."

Karl began to get up, but his father was already standing. "*My* wife, *my* house." He walked over to Darius and took him by the elbow. "*My* guest," he said with a note of finality. "Come."

Darius turned back toward Karl and Lieselotte. "I'll call you before I leave Switzerland. Perhaps you can join me for dinner."

Otto Baden maneuvered Darius into the hallway that separated the living and dining rooms. "Can you be in my office tomorrow morning at ten?" He spoke in a low tone so that he would not be overheard.

"Of course."

"*MUTTI!*" Otto was booming again. "*Der Darius will sich von Dir verabschieden!*"

Mrs. Baden was drying her hands on a kitchen towel. "Just finished," she said, smiling.

"I'm sorry I have to leave so soon." Darius gave the woman a kiss on each cheek. "You've been very, very sweet, and I'm sorry to have been so much trouble."

"What trouble? For a friend of Karl's? Any time you come to Berne, you call; you make this your home."

Otto Baden was helping Darius with his coat. Karl stood by the door with one arm around his wife, the other on the door handle. "*Servus*, Darius."

"*Servus*, Karl."

Darius felt a little sad as he got into his car, thinking how far apart he and his friend had grown. Then he thought about his appointment with Karl's father the next morning and Karl drifted out of his mind altogether.

Darius overnighted in Berne. It was a short walk from his hotel to a complex of government buildings, one of which housed the Ministry of Justice. At nine-fifty-five he presented himself at Justitz-Minister Baden's outer office. At ten, precisely, a secretary showed him into the inner office.

Otto Baden's manner was pleasant but briskly businesslike. He remained seated behind his glistening walnut desk, motioning Darius to take the chair directly in front of the desk.

"Please," he began, "go on."

Darius was momentarily confused. "I beg your pardon, sir?"

"You had reached the point where you were telling us about the death of Gustav Tivoli."

Darius felt a surge of excitement. Baden's interest in the subject *had* been far more than passing. "That's exactly right. I think I also told you that Tivoli played a tape of the Vandenberg-Safat conversation for Desmond Castleberry and that Castleberry wrote his story in *U.S. News* based on the tape."

Baden nodded.

Darius hesitated for an instant. "May I assume, sir," he asked, "that this conversation will be kept in strictest confidence?"

Otto Baden actually smiled. "You may assume, Darius, that this conversation never took place at all. Go on."

"Apparently, Gustav Tivoli got the tape from Arab sources. According to his widow, he had several contacts in the Arab world that had no direct relationship to his banking business. An Arab, I don't know who, or whom he represented, apparently brought the tape to Tivoli's house last Friday. Tivoli seemed to have been very frightened by what he heard, because he put what I assume to be the tape in his private safe and told his wife that if anything happened to him, she was to give it to their family lawyer."

"You've talked to the lawyer?"

"Yes, sir, I have."

"And?"

"And that's about as far as I got. I tried to explain to the lawyer that there's a great deal more at stake here than he seems to realize. He may have thought I was exaggerating; but I really believe that if the true nature of that tape isn't unraveled, we may have another war in the Middle East."

"I think you've done Mr. von Marbod a slight injustice."

Darius was startled. He was sure that he had not mentioned the lawyer's name. If Baden noticed Darius' surprise, he paid no visible attention.

"He didn't feel that you were exaggerating the situation at all." Otto Baden peered at the ornate ceiling of his office for a moment. "I'm curious, though, Darius. How could you be so sure that Von Marbod would come to me?"

In spite of himself, Darius began to laugh. "Mr. Baden, I don't know if this is the right thing to say at all, but it's the truth. I had no idea that you even knew Kurt von Marbod. I certainly didn't know that he was going to consult you. I called your home yesterday because I was desperate. Karl is one of the few people I know in Switzerland; and I didn't remember until after I tried to find Karl's phone number that his father was the Minister of Justice."

Baden stared at Darius, all the while pulling on his lower lip. "So."

"Look, Mr. Baden. Anna Tivoli called me the night before last at three o'clock. She was terrified. All she wants is to be left out of this affair. All I want is to be able to prove whether or not that tape was altered. Once we know that, we may be able to find out to what extent the conversation was altered; possibly even who did it. Mrs. Tivoli is prepared to let me have the tape, but she doesn't control her husband's estate. She was the one who suggested to me that I contact anybody I know in Switzerland who might be able to influence Von Marbod."

"Who else have you told about this?" Baden snapped.

"No one. I told you. You and Karl are the only people I know here."

Baden seemed to relax a little. Darius had been unaware of the imposing grandfather clock that stood in a corner behind the Minister's desk; but during the long pause that followed, the ticking of the clock seemed unnaturally loud.

"I don't have to tell you, Darius, what Switzerland's principal resource is." Baden did not seem to be waiting for an answer, so Darius remained silent. "It's not banking or milk chocolate or watches or even tourism. It's neutrality." He repeated the word, drawing it out for emphasis. "Neutrality."

Darius sat motionless.

"Switzerland seeks, wherever and whenever possible, to avoid becoming involved in the internal affairs of other countries. It particularly seeks to avoid becoming involved in the conflicts of other countries. If I may say so, we have been remarkably successful in this regard. *If* I were in a position to help you, Darius, it could only be on the condition, with the *absolute guarantee*, that Swiss neutrality would not be compromised. Do I make myself clear?"

"Totally."

"You find me, my young friend, on the horns of a dilemma. But that's my problem and possibly your good fortune. Mr. von Marbod is no more interested in becoming involved with his late client's Arab friends than is Mrs. Tivoli. If the Swiss government were to come into possession of the tape, it would be forced into the position of making a very difficult decision. It would be forced either to suppress the tape —but then, as you very correctly point out, it might contribute to another war in the Middle East, which would not serve Swiss economic interests at all—or it could hand the tape over to its counterparts in America or Israel or possibly one of the Arab governments. By satisfying one, it would surely alienate all the others." Otto Baden gave a small sigh. "No. All things considered, it might be best if the Swiss government never had the tape; if it was, in fact, totally ignorant of its existence. Now that would entail placing an extraordinary degree of confidence in your discretion, Darius."

Darius reflected in silence. The ticking of the clock again filled the room.

"I'm prepared to protect my sources," he said flatly.

"But you're still a journalist. Wouldn't you feel a commitment to explain how you obtained the tape?"

"Under certain circumstances, yes."

"And in this case?"

Darius phrased his reply carefully. "In this case, I have to weigh the relative merits of telling most of the story, while protecting the identity of my source; or telling everything I know, and thereby jeopardizing the cause of world peace."

Baden permitted himself the whisper of a smile. "You should have been a lawyer, or a Jesuit."

Darius bit down on his lip. "You may regard that as sophistry, sir. I'm dead serious."

"Well, I hope so. For my sake, more than yours." Baden reached into the center drawer of his desk and took out a small package wrapped in plain brown paper. He placed it carefully on top of the desk. "Darius, it's been a great pleasure meeting you. You'll forgive me if I don't see you out, but an old man's kidneys . . ." He left the thought trailing in midair as he pushed back his chair and disappeared into a private bathroom.

Darius took the hint and the package.

Darius placed his call to Bill O'Conner from the Berne Central Post Office. It was six in the morning, New York time.

If O'Conner was asleep when the phone rang, his mind cleared the moment he heard Darius' first words. "I've got it, Bill!"

"Are you saying what I think you're saying?"

"I've got it."

"Have you listened to it? Are you sure it's the right one?" O'Conner's voice was alive with excitement.

"It's the one."

"Jeeesus! That is *great!* That is sensational! We'll bird out of Geneva tonight."

"Bill, if I might suggest, you're not thinking clearly. We've got to check this thing out for edits. I think I ought to catch the first flight to New York."

Darius could hear O'Conner's wife in the background. "Can't they do anything at that place without waking the whole house up in the middle of the night?"

"Hold it down, will you? Listen, Darius. You're right. Get here as soon as you can. Call the desk as soon as you've got your flight. I'll have a car waiting for you. You did all right, m'boy." O'Conner sounded exultant.

Darius sat in the first-class lounge of a Swissair jumbo jet savoring his triumph. The steward had placed a dish of hors d'oeuvres on the arm of Darius' chair. Darius had decided to allow himself the luxury of one drink before listening to the entire tape and reading the letter that was also enclosed in the package. He set his watch for Eastern standard time. That would make it eight-forty-five in New York. With luck, he'd be in New York shortly after four in the afternoon.

He reviewed the crowded two hours after his call to O'Conner and his boarding the flight to New York. One frantic telephone call after another: booking the flight; calling the crew at the Dolder, asking them to pay his bill, pack his bags and send them to New York. Then he had called the television assignment desk. Finally, he had driven to the airport, checked in the car and caught a flight to Geneva, where he had just barely made the connection to New York.

Darius remembered finishing his drink and hearing the Swiss pilot's precise, reassuring voice. "Good afternoon, ladies and gentlemen. This is Captain Lustinger welcoming you aboard Swissair's Flight 483. We anticipate a smooth flight. The weather en route is excellent. Our flying time will be a little under eight and a half hours." At that point Darius dozed off.

Darius was dreaming that he and Katherine were giving a barbecue for Jamaal Safat in Redwood City, California. Katherine was asking whether someone (Darius thought she was referring to Safat) was ready to have some dinner. He was stroking her hand, but the voices seemed all wrong.

Darius looked up and found himself holding the hand of a bemused stewardess. "Would you like some dinner? It's very good."

Darius held on to the hand an instant longer and smiled at the stewardess. "Do I have to eat first?"

She smiled back. "I'm afraid so. We have a very strict schedule.

Would you like me to serve you here or would you rather go back to your seat?"

"What's easier for you?"

"It would be easier downstairs."

"That's what we'll do then." Darius picked up his flight bag and made his way down the circular stairway that led to the lower section of the first-class compartment.

Darius took out his Sony TC55 and inserted the tape cassette that had been in Otto Baden's package. He reached in his pocket for a thin, neatly rolled cable. It had a single prong at one end and an earplug at the other. Darius inserted the prong in the tape recorder's monitor outlet, stuck the plug in his ear and depressed the play button on the recorder. He heard the voices of Vandenberg and Safat. There was no doubt about the voices. Darius followed the conversation in the *U.S. News* text that lay on his lap. They matched identically. He put the magazine aside and rewound the tape. Darius nodded at the stewardess as she placed a tray of food on the fold-down table before him. This time, as he replayed the tape, he listened carefully for the telltale signs of a careless edit. Once, he detected a slight "blip" between the end of one Vandenberg thought and the beginning of another. Two or three other times, Darius thought that Vandenberg's voice ended on a slightly "up" note, as though he'd not been allowed to finish a sentence. There were, in short, signs of editing, but Darius was forced to concede that it had been a very professional job.

He reached into his flight bag again and pulled out the letter. It was in German. Darius couldn't decipher the precise text, but he did understand the general thrust. Tivoli had been instructed to play the tape for Castleberry only once. "I decided," he had written to Von Marbod, "to make a copy of the tape . . . *ALS GARANTIE.*" Tivoli did not indicate why he needed a guarantee; but his worst fears had obviously been confirmed. Tivoli emphasized in the letter to his lawyer that he had been specifically instructed not to copy the tape, so that his "clients," as he put it, did not know of the existence of any but their own copies. Then came a startling admission. Tivoli had written to Von Marbod that he had once been instrumental in transferring a considerable sum of money from a secret account, which he knew to be Libyan, to his own Arab contact, whom he believed to be connected with the OLPP. That money, Tivoli said he had later discovered, was used to finance the terrorist attack at Lod Airport. He had been so advised by his contact, who threatened to make that information known to the bank's Jewish customers if Tivoli failed to co-operate in the future. The letter ended on a self-lacerating note. *"Glaub' mir, lieber Kurt*—Believe me, dear Kurt, I would do anything to change the course that events have taken. However, I fear for my life. Should anything happen to me, this letter and the enclosed tape will come into your possession. Do with them whatever is best."

Darius reread the letter, folded it and put it in the inside pocket of his jacket. He placed the tape recorder in his flight bag. For the next four hours, Darius alternately dozed and wrestled with the growing dimensions of his story.

23

National News Service was the broadcasting phenom-enon of the late 1960s and early 1970s. It had been spawned and bankrolled by Edward Langston, whose only previous display of ge-nius had been limited to the merchandising, and later the franchising, of an enormously successful chain of hamburger and fried-chicken res-taurants. A native of Utah, Langston was a devout Mormon who knew little or nothing about television news, except that he despised it. He was a frequent and vociferous critic of what he called the "liberal media," although this did not prevent his spending tens of millions of dollars annually on radio and television advertising.

It was in the late 1960s that Langston was first approached by Bill O'Conner, himself a man in need of a network. O'Conner had ex-hausted three of them, moving twice for better jobs, and most recently for having voiced his ambitions too clearly. O'Conner had proclaimed his intention of becoming president of his network's news division; he was, he maintained, genuinely surprised when the incumbent became resentful.

Since there were no other networks, O'Conner, an accomplished TV executive, decided that it was time to start a new one. His approach to Edward Langston was three-pronged, and in retrospect no one could argue that O'Conner had lacked vision. There were enough disgruntled radio and television station owners throughout the country, he had reasoned, to form a viable constituency for a new network. What did they want? A more flexible approach to programming, a more conservative approach to TV news. O'Conner proposed a unique solution, which, at the time, was extraordinarily daring. News, which generally lost money for the networks, could be fashioned almost immediately into a profitable foundation for a new communications empire. Instead of supporting an immense and costly staff of correspondents, technicians, producers, directors, office personnel and management whose output would be squandered basically on one half-hour broadcast a day, O'Conner proposed that television news imitate its less costly but more profitable cousin—radio news.

There would be no major news broadcast in the new Langston network—no *NBC Nightly News*, for example. In its place, O'Conner envisaged a modest plant—one studio, a small staff of reporters, writers and technicians—producing ten or twelve "news minutes" a day. These would be fed to affiliates around the country on lines purchased by the network from AT&T. The lines were literally coaxial cables, which carried image and sound, supported, on occasion, by microwave relay stations, depending on the remoteness of a particular market. Line charges were expensive, but these would be partially absorbed by slowly attracting independent producers to the Langston network. National News Service, a "news network" that expanded as it marketed its time and facilities to retail producers of entertainment shows, sprang from this relatively modest beginning.

O'Conner had proposed another idea in addition to low-cost budget and flexible operation. "We've got to establish instant recognition and credibility," O'Conner had explained. "We don't want to start with the rejects. We've got to pirate at least two or three of the heavy hitters from each of the other nets. Offer'm each a hundred grand and you can get some of the best-known names in the business. It'll cost us a million bucks a year; but those are the people who'll bring in the clients, and later bring in the profits." Langston had become a quick convert to the O'Conner plan.

The blueprint had been successful for a variety of reasons. Initially, ABC, CBS and NBC had not taken their new competitor seriously. Then, there was the attitude of the Nixon Administration. There were suggestions of a Justice Department investigation—ostensibly, because it appeared that the Big Three might choose to gang up on their only competitor; actually, because Nixon liked Langston's approach to news.

The NNS stations were, on the whole, the weakest in any given market. Still, within the first three years of operation, almost a hundred and seventy local stations had joined the new network—some of them breakaways from the giants. Then, a wholly unpredictable, but vitally important, economic factor developed. Despite mounting advertising costs, the available supply of network time became inadequate to meet the growing demand of the sponsors. ABC, CBS and NBC were still the first to be approached by advertisers, but the spillover of advertising dollars fed the expansion of NNS beyond anyone's expectations. NNS assumed, gradually, the recognizable aspects of every other network: continuous programming from early morning until late at night, a full and thoroughly professional news staff, and a major newscast early every evening. The "news minutes" alone produced an annual income of close to forty million dollars, making the NNS news operation the only profitable one in network television. The Langston quick-food empire funneled the lion's share of its advertising budget into its broadcasting subsidiary, thereby, at one and the same time, providing a constant and solid financial underpinning for NNS, while assuring its corporate headquarters of its accustomed tax break. Nixon's people at the Justice Department ruled that there was no conflict of interest.

During its early years, NNS made a minor-league effort to espouse a more conservative editorial policy, but it was scarcely discernible. Though Bill O'Conner paid lip service to the policy, he had known from the beginning that the format of a sixty-second newscast would leave no room for ideology of any kind. It was the most basic kind of headline service. Later, as NNS expanded its news coverage into the more traditional areas, there was little to distinguish it from the other networks.

Ironically, it was the fate of the Nixon Administration that locked NNS into a rigid pattern of ideological impartiality. In the early days of the Watergate scandal, Langston had exerted considerable pressure on O'Conner to break with the pattern of "mudslinging," which, he said, marked the coverage of the other three networks. O'Conner had almost lost his job. Indeed, it was then that he gained the title of senior vice president, a title that represented a de facto demotion. Previously, he had been in charge of the entire news division, though without benefit of formal title. In mid-1973, Langston named a Utah crony to be president of the news division. O'Conner, by virtue of his experience, retained active control; but, once again, he had a boss. However, when it became clear that senior members of the Nixon Administration had indeed engaged in illegal activities, Langston hesitated. When Nixon resigned, Langston stopped calling O'Conner for their daily consultation; indeed, he rarely called at all. He began to redirect his energies into expanding the corporation's holdings by purchasing a baseball franchise, then an amusement complex and finally a sprawling new Mormon college. Within limits, National News Service under the day-by-day direction of Bill O'Conner had gained an enviable degree of autonomy.

Darius, who had risen to international prominence as a diplomatic correspondent for educational television, had been acquired by NNS in 1973. He was from the very beginning one of the network's senior correspondents; but he had never met Edward Langston, nor, in his years with the company, had he ever been met in New York by a chauffeur-driven limousine. The network's film expediter, whose influence with the U.S. Customs Service was legendary, greeted Darius at planeside, whisked him through Immigration and Customs, and delivered him, with a flourish, into the hands of the chauffeur. "Whatever you done, pal, they love it." The expediter winked and disappeared into a crowd.

Darius settled himself comfortably in the back of the car. "Where am I staying?"

"I've been told to take you to the Essex House, sir." The driver was threading the car through the congestion of the Kennedy Airport complex. "The way I hear it, they got you staying in the company's presidential suite. Half the brass in the company's waiting there for you."

That proved to be a modest exaggeration; but the president of the news division, Matt Donnigan, was there, so was O'Conner, and so were two of the corporation's top lawyers.

Donnigan and the two lawyers were cordial but restrained. O'Conner still retained his early-morning exuberance. "You look gorgeous. Go take a leak. I'll fix you a drink. Then let's get to work."

Darius peeled off his jacket, handing O'Conner the Tivoli letter in the same motion. "You might as well read this first. It's from our late banker friend to his lawyer."

Darius had barely closed the bathroom door when he heard O'Conner's voice rise in mock rage. "Get your ass out here and translate this garbage."

Within a half hour, Darius had given the group a rough translation of the letter; played the tape, without comment, for the simple effect; and then ran and reran those sections where, he suspected, the tape might have been edited.

O'Conner viewed Darius with genuine admiration. "That, my boy, is an absolutely first-rate piece of investigative reporting."

"Excellent," agreed Donnigan.

"Congratulations," said one of the lawyers.

"How do you plan to use it?" asked the second lawyer.

Darius looked at O'Conner, who nodded his permission to respond to the question. "Well, the first thing we have to do is determine exactly how many edits there are in the tape."

"I'll put one of our top radio engineers on to it as soon as we finish this meeting," O'Conner announced.

Darius was skeptical. "We could certainly do that, Bill; but I think we might leave ourselves wide open to criticism if we handle it ourselves."

"What are you suggesting?" asked Donnigan.

"Well, we're the ones who came up with the tape. I'm not going to be in a position to reveal *how* we got it. So I think we can expect a certain amount of flak if we depend on one of our people, no matter how good he may be, to confirm that the tape was edited. Now remember, during the Watergate affair, the Rose Mary Woods tape was given to a panel of experts."

"It took 'em weeks, Darius!" O'Conner interrupted. "I just don't think we can afford that kind of time."

"No, I agree. I'm simply recommending that we find one expert, hire some kind of outside consultant, to examine the tape and pinpoint the edits, and have him give us a notarized deposition. Pay him a bonus to finish the job as quickly as possible. Then, at least, we've got a line of defense against charges that we concocted our own story."

"That's a very sensible idea," agreed one of the lawyers. "What do you think it'll set us back?"

"Who gives a shit?" flared O'Conner. "This'll be one of the biggest stories of the year. What the hell can it cost? A few thousand bucks at most." He turned to Donnigan. "Can we get half an hour from the network for a special?"

The president of the news division nodded. "I think that can be arranged. How soon you want it?"

O'Conner shrugged. "Depends on how fast our expert can do the job. Once we have his report, we'll need a day to put it together."

Donnigan got up. "Call me in the morning. I'll let you know about the special. Before we put anything on the air, though, I want to see it, and I want Marty"—he pointed at one of the lawyers—"I want Marty to see it too."

By now they were all standing. Each of them shook hands with Darius and all but O'Conner left the room. O'Conner was already on the phone with the NNS Washington bureau. "I don't care where he is. Find him. I want to hear from Stein in the next half hour, is that understood?" Sandy Stein had been the network's principal Watergate reporter. O'Conner hung up. "How many tape recorders do you have with you?"

Darius held up two fingers.

"Good. Can you make a dub? *Without* screwing up the original?"

Darius grinned. "I think I can handle it."

"You might as well do that right away. I'll feel a lot better when I have a copy of that tape in my safe." O'Conner watched Darius rummage in his flight bag. "What do you think, does this clear Vandenberg?"

"I don't know, Bill. It seems to, doesn't it?" Darius placed his two Sonys on a coffee table. "The main problem with this story is that we really don't have enough evidence to pin the blame on anyone for sure."

"What the hell are you talking about?" O'Conner exploded. "You've got it in black and white. Safat's your man."

Darius shook his head. "It doesn't say that, Bill."

"Oh, come off it. Tivoli admits in that letter that he's been working hand in glove with the OLPP for years."

"Yes. But it doesn't say anything about Safat specifically."

O'Conner threw up his hands in despair.

"Just listen a minute, Bill. I'm not saying it couldn't have been Safat. I'm simply pointing out that it didn't have to be. The OLPP is among the most fragmented political organizations in the world. They've got more splinter groups than you can imagine. Just because some turkey identifies himself to Tivoli as representing the OLPP—or Safat—doesn't necessarily make it true."

"Well, at least you can say it was the Palestinians."

"I don't think we can even take that for granted."

O'Conner looked at Darius with disbelief. "All right. Go on. I'm listening."

"I admit, the letter looks pretty convincing, but I still have my doubts about Safat's personal involvement. Look, take it backward for a minute. Who gains the most from making it look as though Vandenberg was selling out the Israelis? I mean, not just a few minor concessions but giving the OLPP the *whole* ball of wax?"

"You're gonna tell me the Israelis."

"Sure, the Israelis. Not necessarily the Israeli government, although I wouldn't rule that out either. Look at it objectively, Bill. Vandenberg pulls the ultimate fast one on the Israelis. Not only does he agree to meet Safat, something he's sworn he wouldn't do until the OLPP explicitly recognizes Israel's right to exist, but he does it in Jerusalem, of all places. Now maybe he didn't give away everything, but what guarantee do the Israelis have that he isn't about to?"

"So they bug the meeting, fly the tape to Zurich and hire Tivoli's contact from the OLPP to deliver it. Come on, Darius! Make sense, will you."

"What if the Israelis already had a mole inside the OLPP? Someone who's been tipping them off all along?"

O'Conner considered the possibility. "You think they might?"

"Why not? They've got one of the best espionage networks in the whole world. It only makes sense that they'd try to penetrate the most influential Palestinian group in the Middle East."

"What do they gain?"

"They delay the inevitable. The very fact that Vandenberg even *met* Safat—for a substantive exchange of views—is enough to scare the hell out of them. Bugging the meeting, distorting the tape, leaking it—you think that's going to make a Palestinian state more likely or less likely?"

"But they also destroy Vandenberg."

"That's not necessarily going to break every heart in Israel."

O'Conner was silent.

"Bill, I've been giving this a lot of thought. Ever since Helen was kidnapped, the Israelis have been acting strange. First they meet the OLPP ransom demand. Then they encourage Vandenberg to do the same when the Palestinians up the ante. They learn about the Vandenberg-Safat meeting and they're furious, but after a few hours Ben-

Dor calms down again. They've been acting out of character from the beginning."

"Can you say that on the air?"

Darius slumped back in his chair. "No. I think we have to tell this story one step at a time. Clean. The only thing we can say for sure, once we find ourselves an expert, is that the tape has been edited. It's still a helluva story, Bill. First of all, *hearing* the tape is a lot more dramatic than simply reading the transcript; and then, being able to prove that the damned thing was doctored, that's going to be a bombshell."

O'Conner seemed subdued. "Maybe you're right."

"Bill, as soon as we've finished with this thing"—Darius nodded at the tape recorder—"I'm heading back out to the Middle East. We've still got a pile of information that no one else knows about."

The phone rang. O'Conner picked it up.

"Sandy? . . . Yeah, listen. I need the name of a first-rate audio consulting firm. You know, like one of the outfits that checked out the missing eighteen and a half minutes on the Rose Mary Woods tape. . . . No, I can't tell you what it's about. But I need a name right away, and I want to talk to the head man—tonight! . . . I know it's after business hours. You're supposed to be my best investigative reporter. Investigate! And call me back—or have the guy call me back. . . . Yeah. You're a prince of a fellow."

Darius had begun dubbing the tape. O'Conner walked into the suite's kitchenette and poured himself a drink.

It was after eight P.M. when the call came.

"Mr. O'Conner?"

"Yeah."

"Your Mr. Stein asked me to give you a call. My name is Silas Windsor. I'm president of the Windsor Sound Studios and Audio Consultants in Boston."

"That's excellent, Mr. Windsor. I'm very grateful that you could call at this late hour." O'Conner grimaced at Darius. "I'll tell you why I needed to talk to you, Mr. Windsor; but, first of all, I need your assurance that this project will be kept in the strictest confidence."

"Oh, absolutely. We pride ourselves on our discretion."

"Good. I have a tape, Mr. Windsor, that may have been edited. Actually, it's a cassette, a copy. It may even be a second- or third-generation copy."

"That could complicate matters somewhat."

"Well, there's another complicating factor. Time. I need your analysis of this tape as soon as possible. I'd like a rough estimate from you on how long it would take and how much it would cost."

"It's difficult to say, Mr. O'Conner. I'd say it'll take us approximately a week and it could cost you . . . somewhere between two and three thousand dollars." Windsor had sized up his prospective client quickly and pegged the price accordingly.

"I have no problem with the price, Mr. Windsor; but I need your analysis in twenty-four hours."

"I'm afraid that's absolutely—"

"And recognizing the additional pressure that this would put on your staff," O'Conner continued, simply overriding Windsor's objections, "I'm prepared to offer a bonus of *five* thousand dollars if you can have a notarized copy of your analysis in my hands by tomorrow evening."

O'Conner leered at Darius. He could almost hear Windsor calculating. "Can you have the tape in my hands this evening?"

"We'll charter a plane." Pause. "Oh, and Mr. Windsor, in all probability you will recognize the importance of this tape as soon as you hear it. If, for any reason, the existence of this cassette becomes known, I will assume that the leak originated at your end."

"You can rely on our discretion, Mr. O'Conner." Windsor seemed almost offended. "I've already told you."

"I know I can, Mr. Windsor. It's been a pleasure talking to you." O'Conner dropped the phone with an elegant flourish. "We can go on the air in forty-eight hours."

The network preempted a half hour of its regular programming time immediately after the *Evening News*. Silas Windsor had submitted a notarized affidavit testifying to the existence of at least seven edits in the tape. The possibility existed, according to Windsor, of several other edits; however, the quality of the tape itself was questionable, and he felt that he could not put his reputation on the line with regard to any additional editing.

Darius' report was the lead story on the *Evening News*. It opened with him sitting behind a studio desk. A tape recorder had been placed next to the microphone. Two larger-than-life photographs of Vandenberg and Safat appeared behind him.

"Ever since *U.S. News and World Report* published the transcript of a secret meeting between the Secretary of State Vandenberg and Jamaal Safat of the OLPP, Vandenberg has maintained that the substance of that conversation was distorted and totally inaccurate. NNS has now obtained a copy of that tape. What you're about to hear is an excerpt."

Darius pressed the play button. The camera zoomed in to a close-up of the tape recorder. Superimposed on that picture, visible on television sets across the United States, was a printed text of the conversation, crawling up the screen line by line, synchronized to the voices.

SAFAT: You are not my enemy. America is not my enemy. There should be understanding between us.

The camera tilted up until Vandenberg's photograph filled the screen. The text of the conversation continued to crawl up the screen, disappearing into the tops of millions of television sets.

VANDENBERG: Mr. Chairman, what you say has great merit. The Palestinian people must and will have an independent sovereign state. Neither one of us can ignore reality. Does my wife's safety enter into the equation? Yes. You want formal recognition from the United States? Done. You want to become party to the negotiating process? We'll impose it on the Israelis.

At this point, the picture widened to reveal Darius holding three sheets of paper stapled together.

"What you've just heard is only an excerpt. We'll play the entire tape in a special report following this newscast. What I have here, however, is a notarized affidavit from one of the country's leading audio specialists testifying to the fact that this tape has been edited; that it is, itself, only an excerpt of the conversation that actually took place between Vandenberg and Safat. NNS has irrefutable proof that this tape has been edited at *least* seven times, and very possibly more than that. The voices are certainly those of Felix Vandenberg and Jamaal Safat; the substance of the conversation, however, has been altered. Altered enough times to raise serious questions about the very nature of the original conversation. This is Darius Kane in New York."

The special, which followed the newscast, began in much the same way—except that Darius played the entire tape. That was followed again by the revelation that the tape had been edited. Then, using an eight-minute film montage, Darius recounted the entire story, beginning with the attack on Amman Airport, the kidnapping of Helen Vandenberg, the initial ransom demand, reports of a second, harsher demand, and film of the Venezia restaurant, where the meeting between Vandenberg and Safat had taken place. As the partition inside the restaurant was closed (O'Conner had called Tel Aviv and ordered that particular scene to be re-created on film), the cover of *U.S. News* was superimposed on the bare partition and a forty-five-second excerpt of the conversation was played again. Darius had initially objected to the re-creation, but he was forced to concede, once he saw it on film, that the effect was electrifying.

The report closed with a point-by-point analysis of where the tape had been edited. In each case, Darius quoted from the findings of Windsor Audio Consultants.

"It is clear," Darius concluded, "that this report raises almost as many questions as it answers. We cannot deduce, for example, the nature of an original conversation from an edited version. We are unable to report, at this time, who is responsible for the editing, or, for that matter, why the tape was edited in the first place. There appears to be no doubt that it was the OLPP that kidnapped Mrs. Vandenberg and then, following the Secretary of State's meeting with Safat, released her; but it is not altogether certain that the OLPP is responsible for bugging the meeting, editing the tape, and then making that altered version public.

"One final point. Secretary Vandenberg has maintained all along that the substance of his conversation with Jamaal Safat was distorted. That much, we now know, is certainly true."

Phone calls had begun inundating the NNS switchboard within minutes of Darius' initial report on the *Evening News*. The wire services were among the first to call. Representatives of several embassies insisted on speaking to Darius personally. The State Department called; so did the White House. Colleagues from every major newspaper in the country wanted "just a word" with him.

Shortly before nine P.M., New York time, one of the assignment editors held a telephone receiver high above his head and shouted to Darius, who was sitting in a corner talking by phone with a friend from the *Washington Post*. "You may want to take this one right away. It's Vandenberg."

"Which line?"

"He's on eighty-two."

Darius punched the appropriate button. "Mr. Secretary?"

It was one of the secretaries. "Hold a second, Mr. Kane; I'll put him right on."

"Wait a minute. Where are you, anyway?"

"We're in Aswan."

"OK, thanks." There was a click on the phone and thirty seconds later the Secretary of State was on the line.

"Darius?"

"You don't give up easily, Mr. Secretary. I thought you might be on your way back already."

There was a brief pause, and Darius could visualize the Secretary thoughtfully nodding his head. "You're closer to the truth than you may know. Listen, I just heard about your report. It's an extraordinary piece of journalism."

"That's very kind of you, sir." Darius looked up at the row of clocks above the assignment desk that were set to different time zones around the world. It was four A.M. in Aswan. They must have gotten the Secretary out of bed.

"No, I mean it. It hadn't been announced yet, but I was preparing to come back to Washington within the next twenty-four hours. The atmosphere of distrust generated by that goddamned tape was becoming too much of an obstacle to continue negotiations."

"And now you're going to stay?"

"Well, I'll have to talk with several of the leaders out here, but it's much more likely, yes."

"Do you know what your schedule is yet?"

"No. Listen, I've almost decided to dedicate this chapter of my memoirs to you." Vandenberg paused. "But I don't want to totally ruin your career."

"Thanks anyway. It was very gracious of you to call."

"I'm a very gracious fellow. You bastards just never give me credit."

Darius chuckled. "That's right. Well, good night."

A short time later, Darius called out to one of the assignment editors, "Hey, Wes, I'm calling it a night. If anything important comes through, leave a message for me at the Essex House, will you? I'm going to get some dinner."

The editor raised a thumb.

Darius, two other correspondents and a proud Bill O'Conner took a cab to the East Side and dined at the Sign of the Dove. Their mood was ebullient, the atmosphere, at times, approaching the wild abandon of the opening-night party of a successful Broadway play. Darius was reluctant to admit it, even to himself, but he felt a nervous sense of anticipation, wondering how the papers (especially the *Times*) would handle his story. O'Conner, obviously, harbored the same curiosity. He summoned a waiter, gave him five dollars, and asked if he could send someone to a nearby newsstand for the bulldog editions of the morning papers.

"MYSTERY TAPE!" bannered the *Daily News*.

The story was the right-column lead in *The New York Times*, but that paper's treatment was characteristically more subdued. "VANDENBERG–SAFAT TAPE FOUND," read the headline; the subhead continuing, "Multiple Edits Raise Questions About Contents of Conversation." Both stories, however, were an undiluted triumph for Darius Kane and National News Service.

By the time Darius reached his hotel, after midnight, he was exhausted but exuberant. He reread both news stories and fell into a dreamless sleep.

O'Conner was very nice about it. "I don't want to push you," he had said. "If you need the rest, by all means stay on for another day." O'Conner was not too surprised to learn that Darius was impatient to get back to the Middle East. He had already booked himself on a late-afternoon flight to Rome with a connection to Beirut.

His story continued to dominate the news; however, the first negative rumblings were beginning to be heard. A Mary McGrory column in that afternoon's *Washington Star* raised the first sour note. "Darius Kane," she wrote, "is a professional, and it would be unworthy to suggest that he allowed himself to be used, or, in fact, that the substance of his remarkable scoop might be inaccurate. It is, nevertheless, unfortunate that the apparent vindication of Felix Vandenberg should come from one of the Secretary's so-called 'acolytes.'"

An old friend of Darius' at the *Times* called to read him the text of an Anthony Lewis column that would appear in the next morning's edition. After a searing attack on "'Vandenberg's proclivity for secret diplomacy,'" Lewis had concluded on a similar note. "'It is unfortunate that so many news organizations continue to assign particular men and women, many of whom have been thoroughly co-opted, to cover the Secretary of State. The revelations concerning this tawdry incident would be infinitely more compelling were Darius Kane not widely known in Washington circles as a confidant and personal friend of Secretary Vandenberg's.'

"I suspected that you'd be going back to the Middle East pretty soon," the friend told Darius; "I thought you might want to write a response."

Darius seethed but tried to sound casual. "I appreciate the call. I think I'd better sit on it for a couple of days though. Anything I write now, I may regret tomorrow."

On the first leg of his return flight to Beirut, Darius composed an angry rebuttal to the Lewis column, but then on reflection tore the paper into small pieces and stuffed them into an ashtray.

Whit Traynor was nervously toying with a paper clip. "We don't know, Mr. President."

President Abbott stared out the window of the Oval Office, clasping his hands behind his back. "We don't know," he echoed. "A goddamn reporter finds that someone's been bugging my Secretary of State, screwing around with the tape, making it look as though we're flushing the Israelis down the john, and the entire U.S. intelligence community just stands around scratching its balls. Who do you *think* it is?"

Traynor shrugged. He looked miserable.

"Well, I'll tell you who *I* think it is." The President was shouting. "I think it's some of those right-wing nuts in Israel!"

"I can't agree, Mr. President."

"Why the hell not? They had the motive; they had the opportunity; and they'd like nothing better than to force me to dump Felix."

Traynor dropped his paper clip in a wastebasket and picked up a fresh one. "I grant you, sir, there's circumstantial evidence that could point to the Israelis; but even if it were true—and I don't think it is," he hastily added, "even if it *were* true, we couldn't afford to admit it."

The President turned around very slowly. "Run that one by me again, will you, Whit?"

"Just for the sake of argument, let's assume that the Israelis were responsible. Do you think *they'd* ever admit it publicly?"

Abbott sat down in his executive chair. "Probably not."

"That's right," Traynor continued. "Now, just from a purely political point of view, do you want to get into that kind of a pissing match with the Jewish lobby?"

The President looked uncomfortable.

"Then there are the international repercussions." Traynor was picking up speed. "Israel's the only rock-solid anti-Communist ally we've got in the Middle East. Even if some of their fringe elements are trying to stick it to Felix, we still need the Israelis almost as much as they need us."

The President picked up his pipe and knocked some of the dead ashes into the palm of his hand, dropping them in a big ashtray.

"Look, sir," prompted Traynor, "*who* did it has become irrelevant. Vandenberg's in the clear. The negotiations can probably pick up again." Traynor was warming to his theme. "The key to our Middle East policy rests on three points: guarantee Israel's security, ensure a continuing oil supply from the Arab world and push the fucking Russians back into the Black Sea. We're still on track, right across the board. Why don't we finger the Russians? They're probably tied up in this thing somehow, anyway."

"Are you out of your mind?" The President's jaw muscles were knotted in anger. "U.S.-Soviet détente remains one of this Administration's greatest assets. Do you think I'm going to start playing games with the Kremlin because you *think* that they *might've* had something to do with this mess?"

"I believe there's a very real possibility that they *did* have something to do with it, sir."

"Well, you goddamn well find out before you make another move. I want to know who bugged that meeting, and I want to know pretty damn soon."

Traynor flushed, but said nothing.

"I'm sorry, Whit." The President's face was creased by an amiable and slightly embarrassed smile. "I didn't mean to yell at you. But it wouldn't hurt if you gave your friends over at the Agency a little bit of heat. I want to know who's responsible."

Traynor had risen to his feet. "Yessir. I'll get right on it."

Traynor sat behind the closed door of his White House office, having given his secretary instructions to hold all incoming calls. He was on the direct and secure line to CIA headquarters in Langley, Virginia. George Tipton was at the other end of the line. "Do you think he really wants to know who bugged the meeting?" he asked.

"Who the hell knows what he wants?" exclaimed Traynor. "We've got to protect that dumb son-of-a-bitch from himself."

"He's right about the Israelis. They could be mixed up in this."

"Don't you have *anything* hard yet?"

"Yeah, I think we know where Kane got the tape. One of our guys in Switzerland was on to a Zurich banker who got himself mixed up with the OLPP a few years back."

"Yeah?"

"Well, Kane was in Zurich just before he came up with the tape. So was that *U.S. News* guy, the one who broke the story."

"What about the banker? Where is he now?"

"He got himself killed." Tipton was seized by a coughing fit.

"You oughta quit smoking." Traynor was doodling on a legal pad.

"It's only a matter of time," continued Tipton. "We have a few friends in the Swiss police who'll make the connection any day now. Once we find out who passed the tape to the banker, everything'll start to fall into place."

"What if it *is* the Israelis?" asked Traynor.

"Yeah. Well, that'd be a problem, wouldn't it?"

"It just can't be the Israelis; that's all there is to it."

Tipton cleared his throat with a sharp, rasping cough. "That's a risky game, Whit."

"Well, you're not running a local sheriff's office over there, George. The name of the game is screw the Russians. You know damned well they'd do it to us if the roles were reversed. You got someone over there you can trust?"

"Beirut?"

"Yeah."

"I got someone. In fact, she and Kane are getting pretty chummy. That could be a help."

"Sounds like it could also be a disaster."

"No," said Tipton. "She's good."

24

"Kat?"

Darius was in a phone booth at Beirut's International Airport. The Embassy operator, who spoke English with a French accent, had made the connection to Miss Chandler's private extension.

Katherine's reply was almost a squeal of joy. "Where *are* you?"

"I'm out at the airport."

"Here? Beirut?"

"Yes, but . . ." Darius paused.

"But what?" Disappointment had already seeped into Katherine's voice.

"I've got a question."

"Yeah?"

"Where's Safat?"

Katherine now sounded fully disappointed, and somewhat resentful. "No one's ever going to accuse you of being overly sentimental."

"Come on, Kat." Darius' voice softened perceptibly. "This is important."

"I'm going to hate myself for telling you, but your friend's in Damascus."

"Kat, you're an angel; and because you are, I'm going to come back to Beirut in a day or two."

"Couldn't you come into town now for a few hours?"

Darius squirmed. "Listen, Circe, you and the rest of the Rhine maidens go comb your hair somewhere else, will you?"

"You don't mean Circe; you mean Lorelei."

"Whoever. Are the roads open to Damascus?"

"Yes." She was pouting again. "Next time, why don't you call the triple A?"

"My membership lapsed. Anyway, automobile clubs don't turn me on the way you do."

"Well, that's reassuring. Darius, you caused a helluva stir with your story."

"With any luck, the next chapter'll be even better."

"Is that why you have to go to Damascus?"

Darius was on the edge of giving an evasive answer, but he remembered the scene they'd had at the St. Georges bar. "That's right."

Katherine must have remembered too, because her voice had turned mellow. "Be careful, all right?"

"She *does* care."

"Of course she does; and don't make fun of her, either."

"I'll call you the minute I get back."

"You'd better. Oh, I almost forgot. Your friend Felix is due in Damascus late today."

"If I run into him, I'll say hello for you. Love you, Kat."

"I love you too."

Darius hung up, grabbed his suitcase and looked around for the nearest car rental desk.

He settled for a Volkswagen; he was more concerned about refueling problems on the road to Damascus than he was about comfort.

The drive, at first, was uneventful. The road climbed into the hills above Beirut, past sparkling white villas and lush gardens, and for about fifteen minutes Darius enjoyed a series of breathtaking views of the blue Mediterranean far below. Gradually, the landscape changed, and Darius found himself in the dry hill country of Lebanon. It seemed untouched by the twentieth century. He drove through small villages that still showed the scars of war, and through others that had survived in remarkably good shape. Darius was pleased to discover that Shuturah, one of his favorites, had been lucky. The stone palace built by the Emir Bashir II in the early 1800s was still standing. As he drove through the main square, he saw, sitting alone at a café, one of the devout men of the Druze, identifiable by his tarboosh, a white headdress, which signified his access to the secret scriptures that had been fiercely guarded for almost a thousand years by the followers of this Islamic offshoot. Darius waved at the old man, but he did not respond; he merely turned his head, following the car's path out of town.

There were guardhouses on both sides of the border, but the Syrian security forces who manned them waved Darius from one country to the other with a minimum of formality. Darius had expected some degree of trouble. There was none.

Darius was in Syria, barreling along the main highway toward Damascus, for fully fifteen minutes before he noticed that he was being followed by a black Mercedes. For a moment, he felt a sense of relief. After all, incidents of banditry were not altogether unknown along this road. But after a few more minutes, Darius, on an impulse, depressed his accelerator and pushed the Volkswagen into a sharp curve, almost doubling its speed by the time it broke into a straightaway. The Mercedes had no trouble keeping pace. It was almost as if the two automobiles were joined by an invisible towrope; the distance between them always seemed to remain the same. Darius tried another tack. He slowed down to twenty-five miles an hour, then to a crawl. The Mercedes made no effort to pass. Darius began to feel a touch of perspiration on his forehead, and, for the first time, he began to wonder whether he was not getting in over his head.

Suddenly, Damascus loomed ahead, a skyline of modern buildings and old minarets framed by white-capped mountains in the distance. Damascus, Darius reflected, was probably the oldest inhabited spot in the Middle East—and it had always been a center of political intrigue. For centuries, its strategic location at the crossroads of ancient trade routes had attracted merchants from every direction, and, with them, the armies of rival empires and desert tribes. Now Damascus was in the midst of a building boom. New hotels, restaurants and gambling casinos were transforming the look of the city.

Darius headed into the blaring, wild traffic. For more than ten minutes, he drove down narrow winding streets, unable to recognize a single landmark. Finally, he broke into a broad square where he spotted the squat, imposing Ministry of Security, guarded by machine-gun-toting troops and topped by rolls of intersecting barbed wire. Now he knew that he was no more than ten minutes from the New Omayyad Hotel. Darius had been so absorbed in finding his way to the hotel that he had forgotten about the Mercedes following him. He looked back; there was no sign of it. By the time he reached the hotel, the Mercedes was no more than an unsettling memory.

Darius parked his Volkswagen about twenty feet from the entrance to the hotel. As he was retrieving his suitcase and flight bag from under the hood of the VW, Maurice D'Anty found him. Although taller and certainly handsomer than Peter Lorre, Maurice strongly resembled the late Hollywood star. His eyes were restless, distrustful, appraising all who moved around him in terms of their potential usefulness or danger. His voice was syrupy, ingratiating. "I didn't expect you until this afternoon." He stood on the curb, shielding his words from passers-by with the back of his hand. "Why do you have your own car?" Maurice did not like surprises.

"I drove in from Beirut."

Maurice smiled in sudden, painful comprehension. "Of course. You were just in New York. I heard about your story." He whispered, as though he were breaching a confidence. "Everyone here has heard about your story."

Darius closed the hood. "Any official reaction yet?"

"Not from the Syrians; but Safat released a statement here this morning. He says it was Israel that taped the meeting and that he expects Vandenberg to confirm that." Maurice kept his hand in front of his mouth. "There are rumors that there's going to be a second meeting here this evening."

"Safat and Vandenberg?"

Maurice nodded.

"Let me check in," Darius said; "then I want to talk to you about something important."

Maurice D'Anty was a stringer, a journalist not employed by any particular news organization, but one who sold his product to a number of newspapers, NNS, one American wire service and a French newsweekly. He was believed to be an informant for Syrian security (this was less an economic undertaking than a question of survival), and he was also rumored to be in the pay of at least one foreign intelligence service (the French).

As soon as Darius had checked into a modest room, he led Maurice to the roof of the hotel, where there were several rows of laundry drying in the sun. They leaned against a waist-high wall. Darius looked down six stories and saw two Arabs playing tennis on a poorly tended outdoor court.

"Maurice, I need to see Safat."

Maurice sighed, as though to underscore the immensity of the problem. "It's difficult; but perhaps in a day or two."

"No. Today. This afternoon."

"That's impossible!" The force of his own voice startled him. Maurice repeated the statement in a tense whisper. "That's impossible. Safat never sees American journalists on short notice. I'm not sure that he sees them at all anywhere but in Beirut; anyway, his security people will have to check you out. That takes time."

"This afternoon, Maurice." Darius stared intently at the stringer. "Tell your contacts that I'm carrying a message from Vandenberg; that it's absolutely crucial that I see Safat before Vandenberg arrives here. Oh, and Maurice"—Darius put his hand on the stringer's arm—"try to limit the number of people you sell that information to. I don't especially care, but Safat might." He pulled away from the wall. "I'll be waiting in my room."

Darius was, of course, carrying no message from Vandenberg, and he was far from sure that he knew what to tell the Palestinian leader if Maurice's mission was successful. He returned to his room, ordered two chicken sandwiches and a beer, and waited.

An hour later, Maurice called. "In fifteen minutes a green 1969 Chevrolet will pick you up in front of the hotel. The driver's name is Mohammed."

"That's great, Maurice."

"Darius, when you talk to New York, tell them that inflation in Damascus is terrible."

"I understand; I'll take care of it before I leave."

The car must have been waiting in one of the side streets. The moment Darius appeared in front of the hotel, the Chevrolet pulled up to the curb and Darius got into the rear of the car.

Not a word was exchanged. Both Darius and the driver seemed content to proceed in silence. The streets were becoming narrower, more crowded. Traffic noises were deafening. Darius realized that they were approaching the souk, or marketplace, that dated back to Biblical times. Mohammed stopped the car.

"Should I wait here?" Darius asked first in English and then in French.

Mohammed gestured toward the door. If he understood either language, he gave no sign of it. Darius shrugged and decided to get out of the car. There was no one there to meet him. Mobs of people swarmed through the alleyways: veiled Moslem housewives; Bedouin tribesmen, wearing black-and-white kaffiyehs, many of them fingering their worry beads; and hundreds of other men dressed in a more conventional European style. A few people glanced at Darius with mild curiosity. The Chevrolet did not move from its spot at the curb.

Darius began sauntering down the street, past numerous stalls laden with rugs, hats, secondhand suits and dresses. The scent of peanuts and coffee became stronger as he cut into the "straight street" of which the Bible speaks. The street itself was cobblestoned and crowded with shoppers, donkeys and carts. It was covered by a glass arch that spanned the short distance between the roofs of the ancient houses on either side of the street, so that neither the rain nor the sun could interfere with the intense commercial transactions that composed the lifeblood of the souk. Darius passed endless rows of rugs and shoes, of fruits and meat. Soon he came upon the Omayyad Mosque, a huge structure that had been deliberately built to cover the church that, according to legend, contained the remains of John the Baptist. Darius continued his baffling but not altogether unsatisfying walk. The sounds and smells of the souk had always fascinated him. Just as he was about to enter the mosque, he felt a hard, metal object poke him in the ribs. "*Suivez-moi.*" Darius turned slowly until he saw a stumpy, grizzled coffee vendor carrying a coffee urn slung over his shoulders. When Darius appeared to hesitate, the vendor repeated, in English, "Follow me."

The old man hobbled past the entranceway to the mosque and entered a web of dark alleyways where finally he descended a flight of worn stone steps leading to a subterranean carpet shop. Darius followed his guide through the shop into what appeared to be the proprietor's living quarters and then up a flight of stairs that led to an open courtyard. Waiting in the courtyard, stubbing out a cigarette with the toe of an elegant loafer, stood Safat's Chief of Intelligence, Moussa el-Saiqa. He extended a hand. "I'm most happy to see you again, Mr. Kane. I apologize for having to play such elaborate games." He gestured vaguely in the direction of the disappearing coffee vendor.

"Not at all," said Darius, smiling. "I'm most grateful that the Chairman agreed to see me on such short notice."

Moussa pursed his lips but said nothing as he led Darius into the rear of a mattress shop, up a flight of rickety wooden stairs and into a small office. Seated behind a desk was the squat figure of Ibrahim el-Haj, the OLPP's Chief of Operations. Ibrahim wasted no time in formalities. "You have a message for Chairman Safat?" His English was heavily accented.

"Not just *for* the Chairman," Darius corrected Ibrahim in a gentle manner. "My message has to be given *to* the Chairman."

Ibrahim shook his head. "Impossible."

Moussa interceded quickly. "Of course your message will get *to* Chairman Safat. What my colleague means is that it will be impossible for us to arrange a meeting just at this time."

"No," continued Darius. "I think we understand one another perfectly. The message that I'm carrying must be delivered *by* me *to* Chairman Safat."

"Impossible," repeated Ibrahim.

An uncomfortable silence fell over the room. Darius decided to light a cigarette.

"Perhaps," Moussa began tentatively, "perhaps if you gave us some idea of the nature of your message. Then we could decide if it's important enough to interrupt the Chairman's other meetings."

"I'm sorry." Lacking any message at all, Darius decided he had nothing to lose by being intransigent.

Neither Moussa nor Ibrahim made a move to end the meeting. Darius continued to wait. Again, it was Moussa who broke the silence, holding a silver cigarette case in his hand. "Secretary Vandenberg must be very pleased." Moussa lit a cigarette. "You appear," he continued, "to have convinced the world that the Secretary of State acted in good faith."

"It certainly appears so, doesn't it?"

"Chairman Safat also acted in good faith. Don't you agree?"

Darius gave a noncommittal shrug.

"Mr. Kane"—Moussa's voice carried a note of reproach—"you're a fair man; a journalist. You deal in facts. Your own tape demonstrates beyond any shadow of doubt that the Zionists were responsible."

"I'm just not prepared to discuss that with any precision, Mr. Saiqa." It was a deliberately ambiguous answer. Darius was treading water.

Ibrahim el-Haj was holding his right hand, rubbing the stumps of his amputated fingers. Moussa also seemed to be getting agitated, lighting a fresh cigarette even as he stubbed out the old one in an ash-tray. "Please, Mr. Kane. I don't wish to be rude, but you have a message for Chairman Safat. Mr. Haj and I are his two most senior aides and counselors. We have been instructed by the Chairman to accept your message."

"I understand what you're saying, but *my* instructions were quite specific. Under no circumstances am I to give the Secretary's message to anyone but Chairman Safat." Darius spread his hands in a gesture of helplessness. "No, I'm sorry. I wish I could be more helpful." He addressed himself to both men. "Look, I can't tell you any more than I've already said." Darius was torn by conflicting instincts. Having gambled to this extent, he had little to lose by continuing to be obsti-nate, but he wondered what he would say to Safat if a meeting did suddenly materialize. However, he couldn't help feeling that both Moussa and Ibrahim were anxious, for their own reasons, to make sure that the meeting did not take place. Once again, Darius decided to gamble. "I'm sure the Secretary will find it very curious that two of Chairman Safat's most trusted comrades have been so unwilling to co-operate at such a critical point in a relationship as delicate as this one."

Moussa and Ibrahim exchanged a glance, but they seemed less eager to communicate than to observe each other.

Moussa broke the silence. "I'll see you out, Mr. Kane." He wore a slightly forced smile.

Ibrahim said something in Arabic. Moussa replied swiftly, but Darius sensed that they were disagreeing about something. Ibrahim emerged from behind his desk and walked over to the door, opening it for the other two men. He followed them downstairs. When they were in the mattress shop, Ibrahim shouted instructions to a boy. Then he turned to Darius. "You can wait here. The boy has gone for a taxi."

Ibrahim once again addressed Moussa in Arabic, but Moussa only shook his head, almost imperceptibly; then, without saying another word to Darius, he walked out of the shop and disappeared into the crowded street. Ibrahim hesitated for a moment, stared at Darius as though he were about to frame a question, and then turned and left by the same door.

Darius spent a long, puzzling ten minutes waiting for the boy to return with a taxi. Darius gave him a Syrian pound. The boy beamed and opened the door to the cab, bowing several times. "*Shokran!*" Then, as he closed the door, he uttered a faintly remembered piece of information, "Seenk you."

Darius sank back into the rear seat of the cab. "The New Omayyad Hotel, please."

The driver pivoted in his seat. "*Parlez-vous français?*"

Darius repeated his destination in French.

Maurice D'Anty was waiting for him in the lounge next to the bar. "What happened?"

"I don't want to talk about it here." Darius perched on the arm of Maurice's overstuffed chair. "Anything happen while I was gone?"

Maurice looked at Darius curiously. "Didn't Safat tell you?"

"What?"

"He's calling on Vandenberg to issue a joint statement of condemnation with him."

"Condemnation of what?"

"The Israelis—for taping their meeting. Didn't he say anything when you talked to him?"

"I didn't talk to him, Maurice, I'll explain later. Listen, what time is Vandenberg due in at the airport?"

D'Anty looked at his watch. "In about two hours."

"If I drove out there, would they let me in the airport?"

"I don't think so. Security's very tight."

Darius tapped the stringer on the shoulder. "Well, come on, we're going to try it anyway."

Maurice looked uncomfortable. "You want me to come too?"

"You speak Arabic, don't you?"

Maurice nodded.

"Let's go."

They had begun to pass through a residential section of Damascus, near the presidential palace, when Darius first spotted the green Chevrolet in his rearview mirror.

"Maurice," he said quietly, "try not to be too obvious about this, but look out the back and see if that isn't the same Chevrolet that picked me up at the hotel."

D'Anty turned in his seat so that he appeared to be talking directly to Darius. Actually, he was glancing out the rear window. "I think so," he said excitedly. "Yes, it's the same car."

"All right. Maurice, keep your eye on it and hold tight. I'm going to be making a couple of fast turns."

Darius jerked the steering wheel hard to the right and accelerated up a side street, scraping alongside a wagon.

"They're right behind you." Maurice sounded terrified.

"We're going to have to try to lose them. How the hell do I get to the airport from here?"

"Darius, don't! It's crazy. You can't play games with the Palestinians."

Darius had circled the block, dodging traffic and donkeys; suddenly he was back on a main road again. "I'm not playing games, Maurice; just tell me how to get to the goddamn airport!"

"Oh, my God!" D'Anty was cringing in the seat. The VW was racing toward a busy traffic circle. Darius joined the flow of traffic around the circle, doing more than fifty miles an hour. The VW's tires screamed in protest.

"Maurice," Darius yelled, "for Chrissake, which road to the airport?"

"You passed it." D'Anty had one hand on the backrest; with the other, he was bracing himself against the dashboard. The Chevrolet was four cars behind them. "The next right! The next right!" Maurice was almost hysterical.

Darius cut hard, swerving in front of an oncoming truck. The Volkswagen was swaying violently back and forth.

"Oh, my God; oh, my God!" Maurice was rigid with terror. "They're too fast."

Darius had the gearshift in third and was alternately easing up slightly on the accelerator, as oncoming traffic blocked his path, and then slamming his foot down so hard that the gas pedal, flat against the floor, forced the engine to shriek in pain. Darius glanced quickly in the rearview mirror. Someone in the passenger seat of the Chevrolet was leaning out the window. "The other guy, Maurice, the passenger; does he have a gun?"

D'Anty's fear had entered a new phase. His voice was barely a whisper now. "Yes."

Darius gauged the traffic ahead. The car directly in front of him was slowing down to allow a donkey cart to make a left turn. An open truck was heading toward them in the opposite lane. Darius floored the accelerator again, heading straight at the truck. He could see the driver of the oncoming vehicle looking at him with a mixture of horror and disbelief. The truck driver swerved to the right, onto the sidewalk; the Volkswagen just barely made it through the opening between the donkey and the rear of the truck. They were approaching another traffic circle.

"The airport, Maurice. Where, dammit, where?"

"Second right." Maurice's nose had begun to bleed. He leaned over very slowly and wiped it on his shoulder.

Darius looked in the mirror again. He had gained no more than two or three hundred yards on the Chevrolet. The road was straight and almost empty. Darius rubbed the palm first of one hand, then the other, on his trouser legs. His hands were sweating badly. Up ahead was another traffic circle and the walled perimeter of a Palestinian refugee camp.

Maurice was staring vacantly out the back window. "It's no use," he whispered. The Chevrolet had again pulled to within fifty yards of them; it was gaining steadily. "He's going to shoot." Maurice moaned softly and buried his nose in the shoulder of his jacket.

Darius heard a single shot as he cut against the traffic in front of an oncoming bus, slowing down slightly to avoid hitting a passing motorcyclist. The VW engine went from a howl to a whine and abruptly back to a howl again as Darius turned onto the approach road to the airport. A policeman was so startled by Darius' maneuver that he didn't move.

"It's no use." Maurice was whimpering now. "It's a straight road to the airport, more than ten miles without a single turnoff." They were traveling at more than eighty miles an hour; the VW was being pushed to its outer limit.

Suddenly, Darius began whistling. Maurice looked at him in astonishment. "Are they still with us, Maurice?"

"You're crazy."

"Look out the back, Maurice. Are they still with us?"

D'Anty seemed unwilling to believe what he was seeing. "They're falling back." He spoke in the awestruck tone of a man witnessing a miracle.

"Damn right," snapped Darius. "They don't want to get killed."

Maurice was watching the window in silent reverence. Finally he turned to Darius. "Why?"

Darius had shifted into fourth gear. "Look around you, up and down the road. What do you see?"

D'Anty started to giggle. It had begun as a snort, the air passing noisily through his nostrils. It evolved into a moan, then matured gradually into a grateful, full-throated roar of laughter.

Standing on either side of the airport road, with their backs to the refugee camp, were Syrian security guards, each no more than fifty yards from the other. Lying at the feet of each man was a rifle. It was common practice in Syria, prior to the arrival of any distinguished visitor, but particularly a high-ranking American, for the entire airport road to be guarded by security personnel. So rigid were the precautions requested by the U.S. Secret Service that none of the Syrians was permitted to hold his weapon. Indeed, the Syrian government had given its approval to the Secret Service to shoot any man violating that order. They were to pick up their weapons only in the event of an incident, following specific orders. Their presence, however, had been more than enough to discourage the Palestinians in the green Chevrolet.

Maurice had finally stopped laughing. He was leaning back in his seat with his eyes closed, so that he did not see the look of alarm that suddenly crossed Darius' face.

"Maurice," Darius said quietly.

D'Anty grunted. "What now?"

"I don't want you to get nervous, but I think we've got company again."

Maurice's eyes opened with a start and he jerked around in his seat. He relaxed almost immediately. "It's not them. It's a black car, a Mercedes."

Darius floored the gas pedal again. "I know. It's the same car that followed me into town from the Lebanese border this morning."

Once again, the driver of the Mercedes seemed content to keep a certain, constant distance behind the Volkswagen. Darius slowed down to seventy, then to sixty-five. The Mercedes slowed accordingly.

As they approached the airport complex, Darius said, "Wipe the blood off your nose, Maurice. We're going to act as though we belong here." They were on one of the smaller access roads that skirted the terminal building. There were few commercial flights in and out of Damascus, and the front of the terminal was almost deserted. Darius stopped in front of a red-and-white-striped barricade that blocked access to the airport. He lowered his window, held out his vinyl-covered State Department and White House passes. "Vandenberg." Usually the name itself was enough.

The young soldier manning the guardhouse peered into the car at Maurice, who was blowing his nose. He stepped back and raised the barricade. The Mercedes followed the VW onto the airport tarmac. Both cars parked at the rear of the passenger terminal. The man who got out of the Mercedes was tall, solidly built; he had the slightly pigeon-toed gait of an athlete. He walked over to the Volkswagen, keeping both hands thrust in the pockets of a sheepskin-lined denim jacket.

"Mind if I see your license and registration, sir?" His accent was Southern; his face wore a thoroughly disarming grin.

Darius dropped his head onto the steering wheel for an instant. "You with the Embassy?"

A large, open hand reached in the window. "Jasper Hammond. Sorry if I scared you a mite."

"A mite?" Darius laughed. "You scared the shit out of me. Why have you been following me?"

"Well, we heard you might be coming, and some people thought maybe we ought to keep an eye on you."

Darius got out of the car. He was beginning to get a little annoyed. "Some people thought that, did they? Did it ever occur to some people to let me know what the hell you were doing?"

"Yessir, it did," replied Hammond. He was still smiling. "Only some people weren't so sure you'd be all that tickled by the idea."

Darius was so relieved that he was having trouble keeping his anger at a high boil. "Well, they were right on all counts, weren't they? Where were you when I needed you most?"

"Back of the Chevy. It wasn't all that easy keepin' up with you, you know."

"Yeah." Darius grinned. "Well, come on, Jasper Hammond. I'm gonna buy you a drink."

"I'd like that, Mr. Kane, seein' as how we're gettin' along so nice and everything; but maybe I'd better take a rain check. There's an

Embassy courier flight leaving for Beirut in just a few minutes. I think we can get you a seat on it."

"I'll bet you can, but I wasn't planning to leave just yet."

Hammond gave a small, indulgent sigh. "Look, Mr. Kane, you seem like an awfully nice fellow, but for some reason you're none too popular back in town. So, unless you're planning to settle in out here at the airport—"

"As a matter of fact," Darius interrupted, "that's exactly what I was planning to do. I'll wait here for the Secretary and then fly out with him again when he leaves."

Hammond nodded thoughtfully. "Yessir, well, you can do that; but Miss Chandler said she really had to talk to you."

"Miss Chandler said that, did she?"

"Yessir, she did."

"You and Miss Chandler work for the same company, do you?" Darius paused a fraction before the word "company."

"Yes, we do; the U.S. government." Hammond fixed Darius with a guileless stare.

"Have you ever thought of becoming a spokesman for the State Department, Mr. Hammond?"

"Sir?"

"Where's the courier flight?"

Before boarding the plane, Darius put two hundred dollars in an envelope. He wasn't sure whether Maurice would have problems when he got back to Damascus, but there wasn't a whole lot more Darius felt he could do for the stringer.

He gave the envelope to Maurice as he handed him the keys to the Volkswagen. "You come into Beirut every once in a while, don't you, Maurice?"

"Sure."

"Well, see if you can bring the car back some time within the next few days. I'll have New York send you another couple of hundred plus expenses."

D'Anty still looked concerned but not unhappy. "You'll tell them about the inflation, too?"

"I'll tell them."

They shook hands. Darius followed Hammond to the courier plane.

PART
THREE

25

Darius was standing outside the terminal building in Beirut looking for a taxi when the single honk of a blue Peugeot 204 attracted his attention. Katherine was leaning out the driver's window. "Come on!" she yelled. "I've got a roast in the oven."

Darius tossed his suitcase into the back of the car and slipped into the passenger seat. "You expecting someone for dinner?" He leaned across the seat and pecked Katherine demurely on the cheek.

Katherine turned slowly and looked at Darius with regal disdain. "How would you like someone to stuff an anchovy up your nose?"

"Come here!"

"It's my car. You come here."

"I'm a guest."

"I'll meet you halfway."

Darius grinned. "I don't know why I'm so good to you." He slid across the seat. She flung her arms around his neck with such obvious passion that for a moment Darius was startled. Then he smiled maliciously. "Can't keep your hands off me, can you?"

"Bast—"

She never finished her epithet. Darius had cut her off in mid-word with a kiss that sent both of them groping for each other. The sustained blast of an automobile horn brought them back to reality. The Peugeot was blocking traffic.

Katherine shook her hair into place, glancing into the rearview mirror, and started the car.

Darius felt an unnatural tightness in his throat. "Screw the roast," he said hoarsely.

"That," replied Katherine, "would be unnecessarily wasteful on at least two counts."

They barely talked during the ride into Beirut. Darius sat with his left leg tucked beneath him, studying Katherine's profile, occasionally stroking the side of her neck with the back of his hand. Once, keeping her eyes on the road, Katherine tilted her head and kissed his hand, touching it lightly with the tip of her tongue. Their unspoken assumption was that they would have the rest of the night for each other. For the first time in days, Darius felt comfortable.

The silence had become almost natural, as though each realized that there was no need to talk. Katherine brought the car to a halt in front of a four-story apartment building, dousing the lights and cutting off the ignition simultaneously.

"We're home," she said simply.

Darius pulled his suitcase from the rear of the car and followed her up two flights. Katherine unlocked the door to her apartment and flicked on the hall light. "Drop your stuff anywhere. I'll be right out."

She disappeared into the kitchen.

There are certain characteristics common to most Foreign Service apartments. The usual combination of modest salary and educated taste leads a large number of diplomats to buy Scandinavian furniture. Its simple lines are elegant and easily adaptable to the varied mementos and souvenirs that the Foreign Service officer picks up in a succession of assignments. Katherine's apartment was no exception. Her mementos were Middle Eastern in origin. One wall was decorated with a Persian rug. Several large copper pots engraved with the figures of animals occupied key positions around the living room. A mother-of-pearl chess table and an olive-wood magazine rack flanked a beige couch.

"What do you drink?" Katherine called from the kitchen.

"Scotch and soda's fine." Darius walked toward the kitchen. "You're really serious about eating first."

"Listen, Mr. Hotshot Television Correspondent"—she was bending over the oven—"I don't think you know how hard it is to get an honest-to-goodness, American-style standing rib roast in this country." Katherine was turning the potatoes.

Darius, who was now in the kitchen, placed both hands around her waist. "If you're going to keep my mind off sex, you might as well tell me why it was so important that I leave Damascus so urgently."

She turned to face him with a sigh. "You're going to spoil a wonderful meal."

Darius kissed her on the forehead. "Kat, was it really important?"

She studied him gravely. "Yes," she responded, kicking the oven door shut and leading him into the living room. They sat down on the couch, holding hands. Darius started to pull Katherine toward him, but she shook her head. "Do you remember our fight?" she asked.

"Of course I remember it."

"You were right," she explained. "At least partly right."

Darius didn't interrupt.

"I'm not just a political officer. I also work for the Agency; in fact, I'm station chief."

"Congratulations."

"Don't. Obviously, we've been trying to find out who bugged the meeting and why; but as long as we were able to operate quietly, things weren't being forced to a head."

"And now?"

"Well, your story. It's complicated things. It may have cleared Vandenberg, but it has also forced Safat to overplay his hand."

"The joint statement of condemnation that he wants Felix to sign?"

Katherine nodded. "He can't sign it; and obviously he's not going to."

"I think he's right."

"Who?"

"Safat." Darius pulled out a cigarette. "I think the Israelis were responsible."

Katherine said nothing.

"It all fits. Releasing the Palestinian prisoners; urging Vandenberg to pay the ransom for his wife; and then, when the *U.S. News* story broke, Ben-Dor was far too willing to accept Vandenberg's assurance that the conversation was distorted."

"How about the tape itself?" Katherine asked. "Who'd you get it from?"

"I can't tell you that."

"I'll tell you, then. I don't know exactly who gave it to you, but indirectly it came from a Swiss banker named Tivoli."

"All right." Darius didn't betray any emotion. "What does that prove?"

"Tivoli got it from the OLPP. We've known about his contact with the Palestinians for some time."

Darius shrugged. "Doesn't prove a thing."

"Oh, come on, Darius." Katherine sounded impatient. "You're saying the Israelis bugged the meeting and gave the tape to the OLPP?"

Darius hesitated. "Look, without getting into a big argument now, I want to know on what basis we're talking. Come to think of it, I want to know just how you see our relationship."

Katherine was very calm. "That's fair. You have a right to wonder." She held both his hands. "I love you as I've never loved anyone before." Her eyes never left his.

"You've been told to find out what I know." Darius delivered it as a flat statement.

"You're partly right. Look, you're into something that may be much more complicated or dangerous than even you know. I'm supposed to make sure that you don't go off half-cocked."

"Meaning what?"

"Meaning we know the Israelis didn't do it. Meaning that someone's trying to get things stirred up; meaning maybe another war."

"Are you speculating or do you know?"

Katherine got up. "I'll be right back."

When she returned, she was carrying a briefcase. She unzipped it, spread it open on the coffee table and removed several documents. Then, placing her thumbs at each end of the spine, she pressed down on a pair of unseen catches, as though she were opening a loose-leaf notebook. The spine of the briefcase snapped apart, revealing two large pockets. Katherine pulled several sheets of paper out of one pocket and handed them to Darius. "Read this!"

Darius' eye was instantly attracted to the TOP SECRET classification stamped across the top of the first page. He quickly understood he was looking at the full English-language text of the Vandenberg-Safat conversation.

"Where'd you get this?"

Katherine shook her head. "Never mind where I got it. D'you see where it's going?"

The destination was marked at the top. "Moscow!"

"You still think it was the Israelis?"

"I don't know what I think." Darius read the cable carefully. Then reread it. Finally he asked, "Do *you* know who sent it?"

"I'll tell you this much." Katherine was all business. "The transmission originated here."

"You think it was Safat, then?"

"No, I don't think it was Safat. I think the Russians have penetrated the OLPP; at least they have someone in the upper echelon of the organization. There's no way of knowing for sure whether they were behind the kidnapping of Helen Vandenberg; but once the secret meeting in Jerusalem was set, they decided to get maximum mileage out of it."

Darius dropped the document on the table. "Well, that would narrow it down to the other two people who were at the meeting."

"Your friends Ibrahim and Moussa." Katherine nodded.

"That's right. One of those bastards tried to have me killed today, did you know that?"

"I heard."

"It almost hangs together." Darius lit another cigarette.

"Why only almost?"

"I tried to bluff my way in to see Safat today. I passed the word that I had a message for Safat from Vandenberg."

"And?"

"And I got as far as Moussa and Ibrahim. They were interested as hell in the message, but they weren't about to let me see their boss."

"*Both* of them?"

Darius paused. "Yeah, it's funny. Neither one of them wanted me to see Safat, but I had the feeling that each of them had his own reasons."

Katherine shrugged. "It still points to the Russians."

"It seems to," Darius agreed.

"You're still not convinced."

Darius had slipped off his shoes and he was resting his feet on the coffee table. "I'm not disagreeing with what you've said. It all makes perfectly good sense. If you're right about Moussa or Ibrahim being a Russian agent, that would certainly have given Moscow the opportunity; and, God knows, after the shafting Felix has been giving them here in the Middle East, you don't have to look far for a motive."

"But what?"

"But it still doesn't explain Israel's behavior in the past week or so."

Once again, Darius ticked off Israel's known inconsistencies. "Ben-Dor simply doesn't deal with terrorists. He's never done it for the sake of saving Israeli lives, and I can't see him doing it for the sake of saving the American Secretary of State's wife. That's bothered me from the beginning. And nothing he's done since then has made a helluva lot of sense either. Look, when it comes to compromising Israeli policy, that guy's heart is as cold as a well digger's ass."

Katherine seemed troubled. "I don't know." She was shaking her head. "Everything you've said is true; but the Israelis also know that they've gotten more out of Uncle Sam since Felix took over at State than they ever got before. They bitch about him a lot, but I think they also know that they'd be worse off without him."

Darius bit his bottom lip. "No," he said with an element of finality, "I just don't buy it. Helen was out; she was safe when the story of the Safat meeting broke. Ben-Dor hollered like a stuck pig . . ." Katherine smiled and Darius grinned. "All right," he continued, "bad allusion—like a gored ox—when he first heard about it. Felix goes in and holds his hand and Ben-Dor purrs like a pussy cat."

Darius removed his feet from the table and sat erect. "Kat, even now, when it's clear that someone is trying to screw our esteemed Secretary, Ben-Dor goes out on a limb again. This is the *third time* he's done it. Now you tell me that the Israelis aren't mixed up in this thing somehow?"

"The Israelis aren't mixed up in this thing somehow." She said it without conviction, giving Darius a rueful smile. "I'm going to check the roast."

"Anyway," Darius shouted after her, "why are you being so good to me?"

"What do you mean?" Her voice bounced out of the kitchen, sounding preoccupied.

"I mean," said Darius, lowering his voice as he approached the kitchen, "I mean that if you're the chief spook around here and expect to hold on to the job for very long, you're not going to feed me classified documents because you think I'm such a swell fella."

Katherine was spooning juice from the roast over the potatoes. "I told you," she answered without looking up, "it's not in anyone's interest that you go off half-cocked on this story."

Darius leaned against a counter, watching Katherine thoughtfully. "Were you authorized to show me that cable?"

She straightened up, brushing a strand of hair out of her eyes with a forearm. There was only a moment's hesitation. "Yes."

"In other words, Washington wouldn't be too upset if I put the finger on the Russians?"

"I think that's a fair assumption."

Darius grunted and folded his arms. "Tell me something. Are you completely satisfied that the Israelis had nothing to do with this?"

"I've only got the one cable."

"I didn't ask you that."

"I don't know." She seemed to sense that her answer wouldn't do. "Honestly, Darius, I just don't know."

"It doesn't smell right, though, does it?"

"No," Katherine replied very softly, almost as a whisper.

"Thank you," said Darius. He bent down, holding Katherine's face in both hands, and kissed her very tenderly on the mouth.

For the moment, at least, both of them knew that they could shelve the subject; that they could abandon their professional interests and be lovers once again. Darius helped carry the roast and its fixings to the candlelit table in a small dining alcove off the living room.

"You like Sinatra?" Katherine asked rhetorically, delicately placing the needle on a record. Suddenly the room was filled with soft music. "I've never gotten over him."

They ate in silence, savoring the food and relishing the tranquility. For the first few minutes, Darius tried to think of something to say; but nothing came to mind, and he did not want to break the mood that enveloped them. Soon the silence seemed to develop a mesmerizing, erotic force of its own, almost as though a gentle gravity were drawing them together.

When they finished eating, they sat quite still, sipping what was left of the wine, and reaching across the table until their fingertips touched. Finally Darius stood up and walked around the table. He extended both his hands; Katherine slowly got up and pressed her face against Darius' shoulder.

"I love you, Kat."

They walked into the bedroom, holding each other around the waist. Each felt a sense of tranquil harmony as they embraced at the foot of Katherine's bed. They stood there for a long time, cherishing the moment.

Darius kissed the top of Katherine's head, and she began to unfasten the buttons of his shirt, nuzzling his chest as he reached under her blouse to undo her brassiere. A sense of urgency gripped both of them at roughly the same moment, so that neither was the aggressor, even as they became entwined on the bed in the timeless struggle to hasten, delay and ultimately prolong their climax.

Some time later, Darius lay on his back, his legs crossed at the ankles, cradling Katherine's head in the crook of his shoulder. She rested against his side, one arm across his chest.

"I love you so much," she murmured.

"This much?" Darius asked. He was holding his hands about a foot apart.

"Uh-uh." Katherine threw her arms wide, until her fingers extended past the sides of the bed. "*This* much."

"As much as all that, huh? I'm not sure I can handle a whole bedful of love."

Katherine lifted her head so that she was smiling down at Darius. "Oh, you did all right."

"Just all right?"

Katherine's smile widened.

They lay together in silence. Then Darius said, "I've got to go down to Jerusalem in the morning."

"I know."

Darius wanted to talk. Katherine offered no impediment.

"I can't shake it, Kat. I think the Israelis are up to their ears in this mess."

"It could be a double."

"What do you mean?"

"A double agent. An Israeli who's working for the Russians."

Darius considered the possibility for a minute. "That's possible," he conceded; "but wouldn't the Israelis have been the first to catch on when the tape was leaked?"

"Not if he gave them the edited version to begin with." Katherine doubled a pillow behind her head. "Look, I'm going to tell you something I didn't tell you before. Both of your friends—Ibrahim *and* Moussa—stopped off in Europe on the way back from Jerusalem with Safat."

"How do you know?"

"Because I met the flight in Rome and they split. Only Safat came back to Beirut with me."

"It could be both of them."

"Could be," Katherine agreed. "One of each."

Darius blew out a long stream of air. "Wouldn't that be a kick in the head! That would explain a helluva lot, wouldn't it? Safat's clean; the Russians are trying to screw Vandenberg; and all the while, the Israelis are trying to cover their own man." Darius was sitting up in excitement. "You know something else? That would explain why Ibrahim and Moussa were so worried when I talked to them this afternoon. Each of them must've thought I was going to blow the whistle on him to Safat, but neither one would've been able to tell the other."

"Are you going to do the story?"

"Not yet. I've got to talk to Vandenberg first."

"First flight to Cyprus isn't until morning."

"I know," said Darius, easing the pillow out from under Katherine's head. "Ain't life beautiful?"

26

Issel David approached the half-open door of the Israeli Prime Minister's residence carrying a battered satchel and a raincoat. A Shinbet agent recognized the slight, wrinkled figure. Inside the Israeli intelligence community, David's exploits were legendary. Outside, he was hardly known. David was head of Mossad, Israel's Central Institute for Intelligence. Up until the 1973 war, it had won a reputation for being one of the best intelligence services in the world; after the war, its reputation had dimmed, but it was still highly regarded. David had personally led the Israeli team that captured Adolf Eichmann in Argentina and brought him back to Israel for trial on charges of war crimes.

The Prime Minister and the chief of Mossad were old friends who had shared some of Israel's most difficult and triumphant hours together.

David tossed his raincoat on a chair in the hallway and walked into the Prime Minister's den.

"*Shalom*, Ya'acov."

"*Shalom.* How bad is it?"

"Worse."

Ya'acov Ben-Dor drew his hand across his eyes, stretching the lines of fatigue. "You've heard from Chai?"

David was pulling papers out of his briefcase. "From Chai, from the Americans, from the Golan; it's all bad."

"Chai" was the code name for Israel's most valued undercover agent. Chai, which in Hebrew means life, good luck, or simply the number eighteen, was known to only a handful of top Israeli officials. Chai's penetration of the OLPP had been shared with no foreign government.

Chai, or Ibrahim, was forty-two; born in Jaffa, he had spoken Herew and Arabic with equal fluency since childhood. In 1964, Mossad had assigned him to Beirut with the enormously difficult task of penetrating the Palestinian movement. Chai had gone about the task with a cold-blooded efficiency that horrified some of the very men who had placed the burden upon him. He formed his own commando unit in one of the large, festering refugee camps. He trained young men and women in the use of *plastique,* small arms, land mines and mortars. He ran numerous raids against Falangist outposts inside Lebanon; and, on more than one occasion, Chai led commando teams across the border into Israel in attacks against police stations, where more weapons and ammunition were captured.

Chai's reputation as a terrorist leader became so notorious that by the late 1960s his name and description had been widely distributed within Israeli military and police circles: he was a prime target for elimination. Those who knew his true role made no effort to protect him, or even to contact him. For more than six years, Chai operated on his own.

In 1970, Chai was approached by Jamaal Safat, who offered him a place on the OLPP's ruling committee. Chai refused. Six months later, Safat tried again; and Chai, with a considerable display of reluctance, joined. Once a member of the OLPP, however, Chai made himself indispensable, offering shrewd political advice that gave Safat increasing influence within Palestinian circles, and sound operational judgment whenever the OLPP embarked on a military adventure.

By 1974, Safat had promoted Ibrahim el-Haj to the post of Chief of Operations for the OLPP. Only on the rarest of occasions did Chai jeopardize the hard-gained role of Ibrahim el-Haj by communicating with Issel David, his boss.

Chai's most recent message had reached Jerusalem by way of Frankfurt, West Germany. David himself had decoded it, and he was having some trouble reading his own writing.

"I'll give you the precise text later, if you still want to hear it. But there are three main points." David spoke quickly in a high-pitched voice. "Safat is going to decide within three days whether or not to remain with the Rejectionist Front. The Front itself has decided to launch an attack against Israel within *a matter of days*. Chai doesn't know when for sure, but he says definitely less than a week."

David paused to consult his notes again. The Rejectionist Front, at this point, consisted of Iraq, Libya, Algeria and certain elements within the Syrian government, headed by the Defense Minister, who bitterly opposed the Syrian President's recent policy of moderation.

"Now this is fascinating." David was back on track again. "'Moussa el-Saiqa appears to be a Soviet agent.'" David was quoting directly from Chai's message.

"*Appears* to be?" asked Ben-Dor.

"Chai's careful, you know that. But here's something else, while we're on this point." David pulled another handful of papers out of his briefcase. "The CIA gave me this a couple of hours ago." He passed the full text of the Vandenberg-Safat conversation across the desk.

Ben-Dor puffed out his cheeks. "Our friends in Moscow must be getting very nervous to play this kind of game with Washington." His face was furrowed with concern. "There's more?"

"There's more," said David. "Chai thinks his cover's been blown."

"Safat?"

David shook his head. "No. Not yet, anyway. The American reporter, Kane. Chai's not sure whether Kane's on to *him* or Moussa; but in either case, it's trouble."

"Anything else?"

David began stuffing the papers back in his briefcase. "You've seen the reports from the Golan?"

Ben-Dor nodded. "I put the armed forces on Red Alert just before you came." Red Alert was the highest state of military preparedness short of war, and Ben-Dor had reached his decision based on the latest intelligence reports, which indicated a massive military buildup by mixed Arab forces east of Kuneitra, on the Golan Heights.

"Do the Americans know?" asked David.

"I'm sure they do," the Prime Minister replied; "but let's just say that they haven't been in any rush to share their latest intelligence with us." Ben-Dor sighed. "I'll tell you one thing, Issela." When particularly ominous situations developed, the Prime Minister tended to use the affectionate form of his intelligence chief's name. "With the

Americans, without the Americans, as long as I run this government, Israel will never be surprised by the Arabs again."

"War." David said it simply, without theatrics.

"Do I have a choice?"

"Not just war, Ya'acov. You're talking preemptive strike, right?"

Ben-Dor was kneading his temples with his fingertips.

"How much time before you have to make that decision?"

"Forty-eight hours," said the Prime Minister. "Seventy-two at the most."

"Give me twenty-four."

Ben-Dor looked up with a sad smile. "Issela, Issela. What else do you have in that briefcase?"

"Nothing new, Ya'acov. We considered it once before; but times have changed, conditions have changed; and if you're considering preemptive action anyway, it won't make things any worse."

"I'm listening."

"The conversation between Safat and Vandenberg, it's fascinating, no?"

There was an expression approaching boredom on Ben-Dor's face; but David knew his friend too well. He had the Prime Minister's full attention.

"Without all the other pressures"—David waved in the general direction of his briefcase—"Safat's moving in the direction of moderation. He wants to deal. He wants to see how much the Americans can get for him."

Ben-Dor nodded.

"All right. How about the Syrians? Al-Bakr has been very restrained, even useful to us in Lebanon. *He* wants to go on using the American connection." David paused for a moment. "If we attack on the Golan, the war will spread; you know that. Maybe the Jordanians will stay out; *maybe*. The Egyptians? Houssan would try, but I think he'd be drawn into it too. So we're back to where we were in '73."

Ben-Dor's nerves were strained. "Yes, I think I understand both the political and the military picture, Issel. Get to the point!" He sounded testy.

"The point is that we want to divide the Arabs, not reunite them. You go to war; they have to forget their differences. We push them all back securely into the Soviet camp. But if we apply surgical tactics—isolate the troublemakers—we prevent war; we strengthen the hand of the moderates, and the world congratulates us for our enormous restraint."

"Go ahead."

"The Rejectionists are meeting in Damascus tomorrow. I need a handful of commandos, nothing more. Chai will be at the meeting with Safat. He'll give us all the support we need from that end."

"And what?" Ben-Dor was disappointed. "You cut off a few of Hydra's heads? You know how quickly they grow back."

"Ya'acov! Sometimes the heads you leave in place are more important than the ones you eliminate."

"Who?"

"Without the Syrians and the Palestinians, the Rejectionist Front is toothless. Agreed?"

"For the sake of argument," sighed Ben-Dor, "agreed."

"We kill the Libyan, the Iraqi, the Algerian. It might not be a bad idea if we can eliminate Moussa in the bargain. We spare the Syrian and Safat. We make it unambiguously clear to al-Bakr that we refrained from killing his Defense Minister deliberately. That we want to avoid war with Syria. At the same time we make it equally clear to Safat that we're ready to talk business *if* he disassociates himself from the Rejectionists. That way we keep all our options clear. If it goes badly, you can still make your preemptive strike." David leaned back in his chair. He had finished his brief.

The proposal must have appealed to Ben-Dor from the first. He wasted no time on agonizing.

"Do it," he ordered.

Snoring, with his mouth wide open, Frank Bernardi lay on a couch in Secretary Vandenberg's King David suite. It was two-thirty in the morning, and he was now entering his fourth hour of sleep in the past two days.

Vandenberg stood near his hotel window. He was looking at the Old City, but he did not see it. They had returned to Jerusalem an hour earlier after eight enormously frustrating hours in Damascus. Syrian President al-Bakr was a master at the art of diplomatic stonewalling. He took perverse delight in spinning out old Syrian folktales to make obscure points. He had been hospitable, gracious and inflexible.

The flight from Damascus to Tel Aviv had provided no respite. The National Security Agency and the National Reconnaissance Organization in Washington had clogged up the aircraft's communications center with a nonstop stream of intelligence, including satellite reconnaissance that pointed unmistakably to a massive Israeli buildup on the Golan Heights. Vandenberg had already confirmed an Arab buildup on the other side of the border.

Vandenberg had been toying with the idea of waiting until morning. But he knew there was no time. "Get Ya'acov." He hadn't even turned away from the window. There was no response; only then did the Secretary of State become aware of Bernardi's snoring. "Frank!" There was still no response. Vandenberg's anger was one of his least predictable qualities. He viewed his Under Secretary with a mixture of compassion and concern. Aware of his own exhaustion, he was genuinely reluctant to wake his colleague. He walked over to the coffee table next to Bernardi and shook him gently by the shoulder. "Frank."

Bernardi awoke in a state of confusion. "I'm sorry," he mumbled. "I must have dozed off."

"Throw some water on your face, Frank, and then call Ya'acov for me."

"Now?"

"Now."

Vandenberg knew from the Israeli Prime Minister's voice that he had not been sleeping. Nevertheless, he apologized for the late call. "I have to see you, Ya'acov."

Ben-Dor had been expecting the call. "You want to come over now?"

"If it's possible."

"It's possible. I'll ask Esther to make us some coffee."

Both men were coatless. Vandenberg had even removed his tie. Ben-Dor wore a turtleneck sweater and a rumpled pair of slacks. They sat side by side in armchairs that rotated on a swivel base. The Secretary of State had outlined what he knew about the Israeli buildup. He made no mention of the fact that Arab forces were engaged in a similar buildup.

"I need to know, Ya'acov. If you're planning a preemptive strike, I have a right to know."

Ben-Dor held up a hand. "Not so fast, Felix. I could argue that I had a right to know about your meeting with the Palestinians. After all, the relations between our governments are extraordinarily close. But," he added with a sigh, "I've learned to appreciate that there's a difference between close and identical. You're an excellent Secretary of State, Felix; but you're the *American* Secretary, and I'm the Israeli Prime Minister. We know all the arguments against preemptive strikes. We knew them in October of 1973 also. So we listened, and we followed the counsel of our American friends; and"—he took a swallow of coffee—"we all know what happened."

Vandenberg conceded the point. He nodded slightly over the rim of his own cup. "I understand what you're saying, Ya'acov. I also know, as you do, that any future war may be beyond anyone's capacity to control; and that Israel's ability to act in a unilateral fashion, on any . . . lasting . . . scale"—Vandenberg spaced these last words carefully for additional emphasis—"would be extremely limited." The Secretary took off his glasses and rubbed his eyes wearily. "Let's try to avoid rhetoric, Ya'acov. If you launch an attack, we're involved, whether we approve or not. I want to know what your plans are."

Ben-Dor turned his chair on its axis so that he was facing Vandenberg. "Felix, I'm going to share something with you that no one outside the Israeli government knows. Even *within* the government, there aren't more than five people, including me, who are aware of this. For some time now, Mossad has had a . . . what do you call it . . . a 'mole' inside the OLPP. Not just inside. At the highest level. I'm giving you this information so you'll know that what I'm about to tell you is not speculation or guesswork. We *know* it to be fact. The Rejectionist Front is holding a meeting in Damascus today."

Something, a flickering of the eye, a slight shifting of Vandenberg's position in his chair, caught Ben-Dor's attention. He had become very adept at reading the Secretary's body language.

"You knew about the meeting," he said flatly. Vandenberg nodded. "All right; doesn't matter. That's only the beginning. The Rejectionists are planning an attack on the Golan within a matter of days"—Ben-Dor paused pointedly—"unless something happens to change Safat's mind."

Vandenberg gave a painful laugh, "No, Ya'acov, I'm not planning to issue any joint statements of condemnation with our friend."

"Fine. In that case, it seems unavoidable, as things now stand, that the OLPP would join in such an attack. What is particularly troublesome to us is that the Rejectionists appear to have Soviet support, that al-Bakr could be overthrown and that Hassan could take over the Syrian government. I don't have to spell out what that would mean.

So, if the Israeli government seems a little nervous, a little trigger-happy, as you would say, perhaps you can understand the reasons."

"Nervous? Yes. In fact, from a tactical point of view, I can even understand the value of a preemptive strike. But strategically, Ya'acov, I think it would be an enormous mistake. First of all, you put *me* in an impossible position. Not the man; not Felix Vandenberg. But how can the Secretary of State return to Washington and ask Congress to appropriate more money if Israel launches a massive attack on Syria in the middle of an American peacemaking mission? In point of fact, why *should* I go back and twist arms at the Pentagon to break loose matériel that you *are* going to need if you totally ignore not just my advice but my presence in the area. You put me in an unthinkable position with respect to the Arabs—at least those moderates who've placed a degree of trust in me. How will I or any successor of mine ever be able to present himself again as a mediator in this region if I openly or tacitly give my country's approval to this venture? And that doesn't even begin to take American public opinion into consideration. It's total insanity, Ya'acov."

Ben-Dor spread his hands apart. "Who said anything about a preemptive strike? I've put our forces on alert," he conceded. "What do you expect me to do? Wait until the Arabs are in Tel Aviv?"

Vandenberg was still suspicious. "You give me your personal guarantee that there will be no preemptive strike?"

"Guarantee? What's guaranteed in the Middle East? I give you twenty-four hours, Felix. Then we'll have to examine everything again. I'll even promise you enough time to get out of the area. If you decide to stay, it'll be your decision. But don't try to dictate policy to me, my dear friend. Talk to the Syrians; talk to the Russians; talk to Safat again, for all I care; but don't expect me to wait passively for an Arab attack to spare you any further embarrassment."

The mention of Safat's name struck a chord in Vandenberg's mind. It reminded him of the Israeli Prime Minister's initial revelation—that the Israelis had succeeded in planting an undercover intelligence agent inside the OLPP. The same thought must have crossed Ben-Dor's mind.

"It's true. I know what you're thinking. We still have some unfinished business to discuss. Did we know about Helen's kidnapping?" He answered his own question. "Not until it was too late to do anything about it. Felix, as a friend, please believe me, there was *nothing* our agent could do about that. But once it was under way, he took personal charge of everything, including the operation. There was never any danger to Helen."

Perhaps it was the realization that Ben-Dor had withheld so much information from him at a time when he needed it so badly, perhaps it was just the early-morning hour, but suddenly Felix Vandenberg felt terribly cold and dispirited. He got up to get his jacket.

Ben-Dor misread the move. "For God's sake, Felix, I did everything within my power. Why do you think I released the terrorists? Why do you think I urged *you* to pay the ransom demand?"

Vandenberg said nothing. He put on his jacket and sat down again. His mind was racing. He had already decided to suspend judgment on Ben-Dor's failure to inform him. He was sorting and analyzing the new information that was now available to him. It explained the Israeli Prime Minister's abrupt change, from fury to tolerance, after the story of his meeting with Safat had appeared.

"Ibrahim," he said, almost to himself.

"Yes, Ibrahim." Ben-Dor echoed the name with unintended reverence.

Vandenberg gnawed on a knuckle. "Is it possible that the Russians could've turned him?" He was thinking of the text of his conversation with Safat that had been sent to Moscow.

The same doubt had occurred to Ben-Dor, but he had quickly dismissed it. "No chance," he stated. "But I think we know who the Russian agent is."

"Moussa?" the Secretary guessed.

Ben-Dor nodded.

In spite of himself, Vandenberg chuckled. "Admit it, Ya'acov. Even you must feel a particle of sympathy for the poor bastard."

"Who?"

"Safat! Whom does he pick as his right-hand men? A Russian spy and an Israeli." The lightness passed immediately. "The question is, now, what the hell do we do about it? Is there some way we can use either one of them to prevent war?"

Both men fell into a period of silence. Ben-Dor tapped a palm against his forehead. He was troubled. "Felix, you've got to do me a favor." Vandenberg looked at Ben-Dor. "Darius Kane. Our agent thinks Kane may have somehow figured out who he is. He's not sure. See if you can find out. And if he does know, you must find some way to keep him quiet."

Vandenberg looked at Ben-Dor with a trace of amusement. "What do you expect me to do, shoot him?"

"Felix, this is no joke."

"Damn right, it's no joke. Ya'acov, you can't even control your own press, and your laws are infinitely more rigid in that respect than ours."

"Ask him. What do I know? Appeal to his sense of decency, humanity, patriotism. I mean, it's no small thing when any man's life is at stake, but *this* man . . ." Ben-Dor's voice had begun to rise. He stopped himself. "Do what you can," he added quietly.

"I'll try," Vandenberg promised. "Just understand, I may have less trouble heading off the Arabs than keeping an American newsman from publishing classified material."

It was five o'clock in the morning when the Secretary of State's limousine pulled under the archway in front of the King David Hotel. By five-ten, a groggy Frank Bernardi was sitting in the Secretary's bathroom, wearing pajamas, a bathrobe and slippers. Vandenberg shaved as he briefed his colleague. "I don't know what the hell Ya'acov has up his sleeve, but he's given me twenty-four hours to get the Arabs to pull back from the border on the Golan."

"Are you going to let the Russians know we intercepted that cable from their agent?"

"No." Vandenberg had his upper lip stretched over his teeth as he ran the razor under his nose. He dabbed off the excess shaving cream with a hot washcloth. "There's no point to it. The more ignorant they stay of what we know, the better I like it. Anyway, if we call them on it, we'll have to take some action. But I do want you to draft a cable to the Kremlin telling them that we hold them responsible for whatever those maniacs on the Golan decide to do; and don't mince words, Frank. I want the hair to rise on the neck of every Politburo member."

Bernardi jotted a note on a file card. "What are you going to do about the Israeli mole?"

"Nothing; and I do mean absolutely nothing. If the President gets hold of that, he'll blurt it out to a senator at one of those confidential White House breakfasts. And that senator will tell the Israeli Ambassador as soon as he gets back to Washington; and before you know it, I'll have another crisis on my hands with the Israeli Cabinet. No, sir, we're going to keep this mole business to ourselves."

"What about Kane?"

"Well, that's going to be a problem; but if I know my friend Darius, he's going to be looking for me pretty soon. Just make sure he finds me."

"What are you going to do next?"

"First, I'm going to catch a couple of hours' sleep. Have somebody wake me at eight. You have that cable to the Russians ready for me by then. I also want you to contact al-Bakr and Safat. Tell them I want to return to Damascus as soon as possible. Stress the urgency, but don't explain why."

Vandenberg disappeared into his bedroom.

Darius Kane flew into Ben-Gurion Airport just before eleven that same morning. His first act, even before picking up his suitcase, was to call the King David Hotel to be sure that Vandenberg was still in Jerusalem. Darius simply wanted to avoid an unnecessary drive; but when he asked the hotel operator for the Secretary's whereabouts, he was immediately connected to his sixth-floor office. The secretary on duty had been instructed to get Darius through to Vandenberg without delay. Vandenberg was on the line in a flash. "What took you so long?"

"I didn't realize you missed me so much."

"I don't. What's up?" Vandenberg tried to sound busy.

"I'd like to see you for a few minutes."

"Can you come right up?"

"No, I'm still in Tel Aviv. I could be there by"—Darius consulted his watch—"by twelve-thirty."

"Fine; but no later."

Darius had forgotten the long, dreary agony of clearing Israeli customs. Security precautions were so tight that he finally decided to leave his suitcase at the airport. He had no trouble finding a taxi, and even less convincing the driver that he should attempt a new land speed record between Lod and Jerusalem. This he achieved by the simple expedient of tearing a fifty-dollar bill in two, laying one half on the seat next to the driver and promising him the other half if they made it to the King David in an hour or less.

At twelve-thirty, precisely, Darius was ushered into Secretary Vandenberg's suite.

An elaborate brunch had been set on the coffee table. Vandenberg sat on a couch munching a muffin while skimming a cable.

Normally, it was Vandenberg's custom to keep Darius waiting for at least a few seconds; then he would look up, as though the visit had been totally unexpected. This time, however, he got to his feet immediately and extended a hand in welcome. "I owe you a lot, Darius. I'm really very grateful."

Darius shook hands with the Secretary. "I'm glad it worked out well."

Vandenberg gestured vaguely in the direction of the table. "Help yourself." Darius knew he was being massaged. "So, what new bombshells do you have to drop?" The Secretary's tone was casual, conversational.

Darius tried to keep his voice at roughly the same pitch. "Well, I think I know who bugged your meeting." He looked up at Vandenberg to see if there had been any effect. The Secretary was buttering a croissant. "But then," Darius continued, "you've already got that information yourself, haven't you?"

Vandenberg added a layer of orange marmalade.

"Nice friends you have over there in Moscow."

The Secretary bit into the croissant.

Darius poured himself a cup of coffee. "What's the procedure now? I eat and you talk, or do you want me to keep talking?"

"Keep talking." The Secretary's voice was muffled.

"You know about the Israeli agent, too?" Darius watched the Secretary's eyes intently. On occasion, they registered distress, even when Vandenberg successfully smothered all other reactions. There was now a passing suggestion of discomfort.

The Secretary of State picked up a plate of rolls. "Would you like one?"

"I'd prefer an answer," Darius said, but he took a brioche anyway.

"We're facing the imminent danger of war, Darius. I may still be able to prevent it." Vandenberg paused, and Darius became conscious of the fact that what had been intermittent showers had become heavy rain. The room had darkened perceptibly. "I'm sitting on top of a powder keg," Vandenberg continued, "and you're waving a lighted match at me." The Secretary leaned back on the couch, as though he were sizing up Darius. "You're an enormously able man," he went on, "and I only wish I could convince you to come to work for me. You need government experience, you know. Sooner or later you're going to have to do it." Vandenberg seemed to be rambling, but he had merely been circling for the final approach. "Can our conversation be off the record; I mean, totally off the record?"

Darius had been so impressed by the Secretary's intensity that he nearly agreed. He had the almost physical sense of teetering at the brink of a long fall.

"No, sir," he said finally. "Not in this case."

Vandenberg emitted a melancholy sigh. "Then I can only tell you that you are lacking some critical facts. I don't want to sound melodramatic, but you have the capacity to make any further peacekeeping efforts on my part superfluous. It is no exaggeration to suggest that if you write your story, which I'm telling you is incomplete, a war will be unavoidable."

"You certainly know how to fashion a classic dilemma."

Vandenberg raised an eyebrow.

"If I go ahead and write what I know, I'm putting out an incomplete story, one that you tell me will have terribly dangerous consequences. But if I allow you to fill in the blanks for me on an off-the-record basis, I'll have committed myself, in effect, not to use any of it."

"Look, I can't stop you. You can write anything you want to write, but I'm telling you—and this is on deep background—that we have photo intelligence showing massive troop buildups on both sides of the Golan border. War could break out in the next twenty-four hours. You do what you have to."

The telephone rang before Darius was able to answer. Vandenberg said, "Yes"; and then to Darius, "I've got to take this call. I can't talk to you any more now."

The Secretary waited until Darius had left the room, and then, watching the heavy rainstorm lash against the walls of the Old City, he began talking to the President of the United States.

27

It was a minor news item: "Due to heavy rains in the Jerusalem area, the airport at Atarot has been closed for the day." The item had been slipped into the newscaster's file only a few minutes before he sat down in front of his Kol Yisrael microphone to read the eleven A.M. news.

"Do I have to?" he asked, shuffling through his script.

"Read it and don't argue," replied his editor, pointing a finger to the ceiling, suggesting it was an order from the government, not the whim of a producer.

The newscaster grimaced and loosened his belt. "Wonder what they're up to now."

Six men in a truck heard the news item as they drove through sheets of rain that obscured their vision of the Jerusalem-Ramallah road. The driver squinted and rubbed the fogged-up window with his right hand. A small man, wearing a soaked beret, turned to the other four men in the rear of the truck. "With rain like this, they might have had to close the airport anyway."

The four men were wearing khaki ponchos to conceal their uniforms, which were identical to those of President al-Bakr's special force of twenty-five thousand Praetorian Guards. "Just as well," one of them said; "surer this way." He was a handsome man with graying hair and cool blue eyes. Colonel Ori Elad glanced down at his boots. "David, there will be no communication." His voice barely rose above a whisper. "You should hear from me by fifteen hundred. If you don't . . ." He didn't finish the thought. There was no need to elaborate.

The truck splashed through the main street of Shuafat, a predominantly Arab suburb of Jerusalem. There was a local legend that the Hebrew prophet Samuel had been buried in Nebi-Samuel, a small, now virtually deserted town on a hill overlooking Shuafat. A mosque covered the site, considered holy by the Moslems as well as by the Israelis.

A few minutes later, through the mist, the driver could begin to make out the shape of the control tower at Atarot. Although the Israelis had lengthened and hardened the runway so that Atarot could accommodate even the Boeing 707, the airport had not become a busy center of commercial travel. Now it was extraordinarily quiet, except for the relentless pounding of the rain. A sentry popped out of the mist and stopped the truck at one of the rear approaches to the airport. The driver cursed and lowered his window. David flashed his identification card. The sentry examined it, then the face of its bearer, and pulled back in disbelief. He had never before seen the chief of

Mossad. "Excuse me," he stammered, and quickly raised the steel barrier.

The truck rumbled toward the far end of the runway, where a Soviet-built helicopter waited in the rain, its rotors spinning gently in the wind. The Israelis had captured many helicopters during the '73 war. They had re-equipped several with a sophisticated computer guidance system that permitted helicopter pilots to fly at extremely low altitudes in near-zero visibility, avoiding radar detection in a flight pattern that followed the contours of the terrain.

The truck stopped a few feet from the helicopter, which bore the markings of the Syrian Air Force. David stepped into the rain. He was quickly followed by Elad and his three commandos. For just a moment, David stood before his men as though he were in silent prayer. "I shall wait for you here, not at headquarters," David said. It was clear from the tone of his voice that there was to be no further discussion. "Good luck." David saluted his men. They returned his salute and boarded the helicopter.

Within seconds, the rotors roared into action, cutting through the rain in a blur that sent David scurrying back into the truck. Slowly, the helicopter rose, making a broad circular sweep through the clouds before proceeding in a north-northeasterly direction. The ride was rocky for the first thirty minutes, but the commandos were too busy to notice. They shed their ponchos, polished their boots and checked their Kalashnikov automatic rifles. Each commando carried a specially equipped pistol. It looked like an ordinary Colt, but it was electronically triggered. It was able to fire poisonous darts up to a distance of three hundred yards. The advantage of the weapon, which had been developed by the CIA, was twofold. It was almost completely noiseless; and its effect, even in the case of a minor flesh wound, was invariably fatal.

The helicopter carried its unusual cargo through breaking clouds. Elad studied the landscape: a patchwork of brown hills and terraced farms; small villages with minarets and busy marketplaces; fields where the soil was rich enough to produce harvests of tomatoes, watermelons, grapes, olives, oranges, even tobacco; wadis where shepherds tended their flocks. Almost a million Palestinians lived on the West Bank, once the heartland of Biblical Judea and Samaria. Elad was born in a Jewish settlement near Tiberias, which looks down on the Sea of Galilee. His playmates were both Jews and Arabs; and although he had fought in all of Israel's wars, including the war of independence in 1948, and had risen through the ranks to command an elite force of paratroop commandos, he had never developed a hatred for the Arabs, and he cherished the day when he could return to his kibbutz. He knew that that day would signal the start of genuine co-existence between the Israelis and their Arab neighbors. But until that day came, he would fight in his unorthodox ways.

The helicopter lost altitude while flying over the western rim of the Sea of Galilee. Elad sat in a canvas seat staring at the passing clouds with unseeing eyes. He recalled a series of exploits that his commandos had accomplished, but he suspected none would be more significant than the one on which he was now embarked. The raid against Beirut's International Airport in December 1968 had destroyed two-thirds of Lebanon's commercial air fleet, but it had not stopped the Palestinian terrorist attacks against Israeli settlements. The snatching of an entire Soviet-built radar station at Ras Gharib, 125 miles south of the Suez Canal, in February 1969, from under the noses of the Russians and the Egyptians, had possessed all the earmarks of a Hollywood extravaganza, and it had provided valuable military information; but it had little practical effect on the balance of power in the Middle East. The rescue of the passengers of an Air France jumbo jet, hijacked to Entebbe, Uganda, in July 1976, had won international acclaim for Israeli daring and ingenuity—it was Elad's favorite operation —but it had not put an end to terrorism. Elad glanced at his young colleagues. This mission to Damascus was different: it could accelerate the drift toward yet another war in the Middle East, or it could stop it.

"Once more," Elad said, "let's go over the plans. There's not much time left."

The helicopter shuddered as it crossed over the disputed border territory connecting Israel with Syria and Jordan. To avoid enemy radar, it twisted and turned, suddenly losing altitude, then regaining it; but it continued on its general course, flying across the Golan Heights south of Kuneitra and, on a bead, toward a lonely hilltop three kilometers west of the Syrian capital. At the landing site, nothing was visible from five hundred feet except an empty Soviet-built armored car. Elad smiled. His ground support, so far, was perfect. The helicopter bounced to a stop not more than five feet from the car, and the commandos jumped out. The young pilot, who was also dressed in a Syrian uniform, checked his watch. "Pickup time exactly one hour from . . ."—he paused—"now!"

The commandos synchronized their watches.

"*Shalom*," the pilot whispered.

"*Salaamat*," Elad responded with a wave.

Elad got into the driver's seat of the armored car; his friends got into the rear. The engine coughed once, twice before kicking into full power. Elad then drove the car at a measured pace along a narrow mountain byway toward al-Bakr's hideaway, perched on a mountain peak overlooking an army camp and, below it, Damascus itself. The hideaway, which resembled a Swiss chalet, was accessible only by a winding road with security checkpoints interspersed along the way. It was a heavily guarded road at all times. Now al-Bakr's Praetorian Guard had supplemented the normal contingent of police and regular army troops, and the entire operation had been placed under the personal control of General Rifaat al-Bakr, the President's younger brother. The reason for the special security precautions was simple: the hideaway was to serve as the site for an unusual gathering of military leaders from Syria, Algeria, Libya, Iraq and the OLPP. They were making their final preparations for a surprise attack against Israel.

Not far ahead, Elad could see the point at which the rarely used byway intersected the main road. He checked his watch. Timing was extremely critical. At what he believed to be precisely the right moment, Elad cut into the honking traffic heading toward a checkpoint on the approach to the chalet. He waved wildly, as though apologizing to the driver behind him. A guard, wearing the same uniform as Elad, raised his hand. Elad braked to a stop and handed his security pass to the guard.

"Days like this we don't need, brother." Elad tried to sound casual. "Is the General here yet?"

The guard looked at Elad, a trace of suspicion crossing his dark face. One of the Israeli commandos reached very slowly for his Kalashnikov gun, his colleagues bracing for trouble. A few endless seconds passed.

"None of your business," the guard snapped. But before he could pursue his suspicion, he heard the singsong horn of an approaching black Mercedes. The guard nervously waved Elad toward the chalet. "Move quickly. It's Safat!"

Elad rammed his stick into first gear, and the armored car resumed its ascent. The Mercedes did not even bother to slow down at the checkpoint. From the back seat, a burly man waved at the guard, who noticed that he had only three fingers. Then the Mercedes proceeded toward the chalet, directly behind Elad's armored car. Not by coincidence, Elad had become Safat's advance escort.

The caravan did not stop at the last checkpoint. Elad merely lowered his window and shouted, "Safat, Safat, brother; out of the way!" The two cars rolled into the circular driveway of the main house and stopped in front of an arched entranceway. The four Israeli commandos jumped out of their car and formed a makeshift honor guard for Safat, Ibrahim and Moussa, who walked into the house. Safat waved perfunctorily at the commandos. Ibrahim shot a glance at Elad. Nothing more. Then, as though they had been assigned to protect him, the commandos escorted Safat through a large foyer to a second-story conference room. Elad nodded to a Syrian officer who guarded a heavy oak double door.

The conference room was crowded with uniformed officers from various Arab countries. Aides in mufti scurried from one group to another, carrying attaché cases and papers. A large map of the Middle East stood on an easel behind a long, rectangular table covered with green felt. Bottles of mineral water and trays of fruit were placed at neat intervals along each side of the table. Safat shook hands with the leaders of each delegation, showing special deference to General Abdul Hassan, the Defense Minister of Syria. It was no secret that Hassan was challenging President al-Bakr for control of the Baathist party. He was a tough, ambitious hard liner who totally opposed an Arab-Israeli accommodation. As the acknowledged leader of the Syrian hawks, he had cleverly maneuvered al-Bakr into a position of reluctant support for his plan for a preemptive attack against Israel. Al-Bakr had sent a message of welcome, explaining that he could not attend the meeting because he had to prepare for his next session with Vandenberg.

General Hassan took his seat at the head of the table. The Deputy Defense Ministers of Iraq, Algeria and Libya and the Chairman of the OLPP seated themselves behind their respective flags. The heavy doors were shut and locked. Two guards stood at attention, flanking the door. Elad positioned himself opposite Safat and Ibrahim. One commando stood about ten feet from Elad. The other two braced for action.

"'Brothers, we are gathered here at a solemn hour in the history of the Arab family.'" Hassan began reading al-Bakr's message. "'The Zionist entity is planning a new war of aggression, aided and abetted by American imperialism. This is not a new circumstance, and we must prepare for every eventuality.'" Hassan continued reading al-Bakr's boiler-plate welcome; and when he had finished, with just a trace of disgust, he dropped it on the table. Hassan pushed back his chair, placed both hands on his knees, stared at each delegation head with deliberate care, and then boomed, "Brothers, we are here to plan the final details for a holy war against the Zionists. That war will start at dawn tomorrow, when the sun will glaze into the eyes of the enemy, by Allah's will, and he shall be blinded." Most of the men around the table nodded. Safat, who shared al-Bakr's reservations, sat motionless. Hassan then launched into a detailed rundown of his plans for war.

When Hassan had completed his statement, Elad glanced at his three colleagues and quickly at Ibrahim. Then, with sure-footed care, he approached Hassan and whispered in his ear.

"I am Ori Elad, head of a special Israeli paratroop unit." Elad spoke in perfect Arabic. He poked a Colt into Hassan's back. "If you wish to stay alive, I would strongly advise you to say nothing, to do nothing, merely to sit where you are and watch." Hassan broke into an icy sweat.

Each of the three remaining commandos had already unsnapped the protective flap of his holster, having transferred his Kalashnikov to his left hand, and rested his right hand on the butt of his electronic dart gun. Each man had a preassigned primary target. Within the space of five seconds, three almost inaudible ripping sounds punctuated the stillness of the room. The noise was no more than the slitting open of an envelope.

Moussa was the first to die, a tiny dart embedded in the base of his neck. The personal bodyguards of the Iraqi and Libyan Deputy Defense Ministers seemed more surprised than injured. Each man gave a small gasp, clutched at his back and collapsed.

The first apparent sign of panic in the room came from Ibrahim, who, with surprising speed, pushed his own chair back and, tearing at Jamaal Safat's sleeve, pulled Safat under the table.

The Algerian delegate's bodyguard had managed to rise to his feet; he was fumbling for his pistol when he took a dart in the chest.

The Israelis seemed to pick their targets with casual ease, pivoting slightly toward each new sign of movement. The two Syrian guards flanking the door died within two paces of where they had stood. Only one managed to emit a muffled cry before crumpling to the floor.

The Iraqi Deputy Defense Minister reached for a spot just below his right ear, even as he tried to slide under the table. His colleagues from Algeria and Libya remained rooted to their chairs. The Algerian had managed to place both hands on top of his head in a gesture of surrender when he too was shot in the neck. The Libyan was the last to die.

Within less than sixty seconds of efficient slaughter, the Israeli commandos had killed everyone in the room with three exceptions: Safat, Ibrahim and Hassan.

"Yankel"—Elad pointed at Hassan—"tie up this bastard." One of the commandos pulled a spool of special cord from his boot and tied Hassan's feet to his neck tightly, arching his back in the process. If Hassan tried to move or stretch, he would choke himself to death.

"Lie still and say nothing," Elad warned, while stuffing Hassan's mouth with heavy gauze. Elad then pounced on Safat and grabbed him by the collar. "I'd kill you too with great pleasure," he panted, "but for some reason, my government wants you to live. You will walk out of this room with us and this fat pig of yours." Elad grunted at Ibrahim. "My orders are not to kill you unless I have to. I am told you are an intelligent man, a leader of the Palestinian people. If you wish to remain their leader, you will do exactly what I say. One word, one false step—you're dead. You understand?" Elad was gripping his collar so tightly that Safat felt as though he couldn't breathe. Safat nodded. "You will leave this building, walking between us. You will get into your car." Elad shot a glance at Ibrahim. "You understand, pig?" Elad punched him in the stomach. Ibrahim doubled up in pain. "You will drive directly to your headquarters in Damascus. You will not look back. We shall be directly behind you."

Elad checked the bodies quickly, making sure all were dead. He kneeled next to Hassan. "Good luck in the morning, General. We'll be waiting."

The Israeli commandos rearranged themselves as an honor guard, surrounding Safat and Ibrahim, and opened the door, quickly shutting it behind them. A Syrian officer saluted Safat, but the Palestinian leader paid no attention to him. Elad returned the salute. Trying to affect an unrushed and yet military appearance, the honor guard walked down the stairs and into the foyer. Syrian troops snapped to attention when they saw Safat. Elad paused for a moment to tell a Syrian officer that General Hassan was engaged in detailed discussions and he did not wish to be disturbed. Then, as though confiding a secret to the officer, Elad added, "Safat has to return to Damascus, but he has left his Chief of Intelligence upstairs. We shall all be back in about an hour." The officer escorted Elad's group into the courtyard.

Elad waved for Safat's car, while one of the Israeli commandos rushed to get the armored car. Safat got into the Mercedes, along with Ibrahim, and the four commandos hopped into their car. Slowly the two cars pulled away from al-Bakr's hideaway and headed toward the first checkpoint on the way down the road to Damascus.

The Syrian officer was puzzled. Years of arch-flattening duty had sharpened his senses. One question rattled through his mind: Why had an officer of al-Bakr's special guard bothered to talk to him at all? That was most unusual. He decided to check the conference room. From the outside, everything appeared to be normal. But he turned the elaborate iron knob just for good measure and the door opened. It should have been locked. He unhooked his pistol and pushed open the door. He stood in momentary bewilderment, still unsure of what had happened. Then, at the far end of the room, he spotted Hassan, lying, as though paralyzed, in an awkward position. He raced toward him and cut his bonds. Hassan pulled the gauze out of his mouth. "Stop them," the Defense Minister shouted. "They've kidnapped Safat." The officer, filled with a mixture of pride and panic, ran down the stairs, screaming out an alert to all checkpoints.

Without any challenge, however, the Safat procession had passed through the first checkpoint and then the second. At that point, the Mercedes began picking up speed as it careened down the mountain road toward Damascus, with Ibrahim, a human shield, spread-eagled over Safat on the floor of the car. Their driver, ignorant of what was happening, rose to the occasion by keeping a heavy hand on his horn and scattering a few peasants and goats that had somehow managed to get onto the road.

Elad, meantime, had turned his armored car off the road and onto the unpaved byway that would lead him to the hilltop where he hoped the helicopter would be waiting. Within seconds after he turned, a Syrian guard at the nearest sentry point got word of the attack and fired his rifle into the air. He rushed toward a jeep that was parked nearby. Elad was driving at a brisk pace when he saw through his rearview mirror that he was being followed.

He increased his speed. In the distance, he saw the helicopter. Its rotors were already turning. The four commandos leaped out of their car and into the helicopter; even before the fourth commando had hit the deck, the helicopter was airborne, zigzagging into the sky in an evasive pattern to avoid the blast of machine-gun fire coming from the pursuing Syrians. The Israelis returned the fire, but it was merely a reflex action. They were already out of range.

28

Darius sat at his desk in his hotel room nursing a bleeding knuckle. He was staring at a mark on the wall where, in growing frustration, he had just slammed his fist. He had known instinctively the moment he had left Vandenberg's suite that his story on Soviet and Israeli penetration of the OLPP would have to wait. Vandenberg had, for the moment, provided a more pressing alternative. Darius started typing the lead of a radio report.

NNS News has learned that U.S. intelligence satellites have picked up alarming evidence of massive troop buildups on both sides of the Syrian-Israeli border. Secretary of State Vandenberg is known to be deeply concerned that war could break out on the Golan Heights, possibly within the next twenty-four hours.

Once Darius began typing, he felt better. It was the story of the hour; no question about it. The other material could, quite legitimately, wait.

When he had finished three versions of the "war" story, Darius placed his call to New York. When the phone rang, Darius asked to be connected with a recording studio. He gave them a voice level, but no preliminary comment. It was only after he had finished that Darius asked to speak with the editor.

"I'm already on." It was Vic Lazlo. "Hey, Darius, guy; that's a helluva story!"

"Yes, it is."

"Does anybody else have it?"

"Not to my knowledge."

"Well, we'll give it a real ride, guy!"

"I think you should."

Lazlo seemed to sense that something was wrong. "Can I get anyone else for you?"

"No, thanks, Vic. Just tell TV what I've got, and tell them I'll be in touch a little later."

"Will do."

Darius hung up quickly. He had been concerned that the Israeli censor might not allow him to complete his reports. He wasn't far from wrong. The phone rang again.

"Mr. Kane?"

"Yes."

"This is the military censor's office."

"What can I do for you?"

"Would you mind telling where you got the information for your report?"

"Yes, I would."

"Pardon?"

"I said I would mind; very much."

"Oh." The Israeli sounded surprised.

"Well, nice talking with you." Darius hung up before the censor could respond.

It took less than an hour for Darius' reports to rebound from NNS Radio back to Jerusalem. Every wire service in the U.S. had tried to confirm his story independently. When they failed, they began quoting NNS. Israeli radio and television were not far behind.

By three o'clock, the Israeli Foreign Office, under enormous public pressure, released a statement confirming half the report. Arab forces, the statement conceded, were massing on or near the Golan Heights.

At three-thirty, a limousine carrying the Secretary of State pulled up in front of the Prime Minister's office. A top-heavy battery of microphones had been set up, and a chorus of insistent questions enveloped the Secretary the moment he stepped out of his car.

"What about the satellite photographs?"

". . . true that you expect war within twenty-four hours?"

". . . said to be deeply concerned!"

The questions were interwoven, one with another; only fragments were clearly audible. Vandenberg picked the least damaging fragment.

"I'm always concerned that peace, which is a very fragile commodity in this part of the world, might be in jeopardy; but I don't believe that it would serve any useful purpose right now for me to engage in speculation. Thank you."

Vandenberg turned away from the microphones and walked into the hallway and up the stairs that led to the Prime Minister's office.

Ben-Dor greeted him with a broad smile.

"Don't look so glum, Felix. Things can always get worse."

Vandenberg smiled, a tight, professional smile. "In this part of the world, Ya'acov, I think there's a law to that effect."

Ben-Dor drew his colleague into his private office. "Sit down, Felix. Can I get you something?"

"You can relieve my curiosity. What are you so bloody cheerful about?"

"I've given you some cards, Felix. Trumps."

"I don't play bridge. What are you talking about?"

Ben-Dor pulled a cigarette from the pack that lay on his desk and tapped the filter end against the glass cover of his watch. "Late this morning, a team of Israeli commandos flew into Damascus. I won't bore you with details, but they engaged in a degree of . . . selective elimination. The Pentagon would like that term, don't you think?"

Vandenberg sat as though frozen to his seat.

"The principal members of the Iraqi, Algerian and Libyan delegations were eliminated; but the Syrian Defense Minister was spared, and so was Safat. Our men made it absolutely clear to them that they too could have been killed, but that they were being deliberately spared because Israel wants to prevent war and to continue moving toward a settlement. Our men went in and out without suffering a single casualty."

Vandenberg had turned pale with fury. He was obviously having trouble controlling his voice.

"You're saying that after giving me your solemn pledge of twenty-four hours of negotiating time, you launched an attack in the heart of Damascus?" Vandenberg looked frantically around the room, as though searching for any vestige of solace that might help him regain his self-control. He found none. "You have in all probability destroyed whatever infinitesimal chance I might have had of preventing war. How *could* you have put me in this position? What do you imagine the Arabs will do now? What *can* they do except attack you? Their honor's at stake!"

Ben-Dor assumed an air of almost patronizing formality. "*Mr.* Secretary," he began, "you seem to have overlooked the fact that we are not totally inexperienced in dealing with the Arabs. Whose pride are we talking about? The Iraqis'? The Libyans'? Even *you* don't like dealing with them. The only ones whose pride could be involved are the Syrians, and we've taken care of that. I told you that Hassan was left deliberately unharmed. *Honor.* Is that the word you used? Do you really believe the Syrians are going to admit that a handful of Israeli commandos was able to penetrate al-Bakr's most tightly guarded home, break up a meeting that no one in the world is even supposed to know about, and then escape without a single casualty? My God, Felix, they don't even have a scrap of evidence that we were ever there!"

The Secretary had regained his composure. "From what you've told me," he noted dryly, "the corpses of those people that you—what did you call it? . . . 'selectively eliminated'—those corpses could provide some fairly convincing evidence."

Ben-Dor adapted himself to the change in mood. "I don't believe, Felix, that they're about to advertise that." Resting his elbows on the desk, the Israeli leaned toward Vandenberg. "Believe me, they won't say a word. I'll even go one step further. This may be the best possible time to approach the Arabs for a settlement. Safat knows that he could've been killed. Al-Bakr knows not only that we spared his Defense Minister, but humbled the most dangerous adversary that he has. They won't attack us now, Felix. They've lost whatever element of surprise might have existed. They know we're on full alert; but even more important, we've also let them know in unmistakable terms that we're ready to negotiate. Talk to them now, Felix. Go to Damascus and talk to them."

Vandenberg shook his head. "I don't even know if they'll see me now."

"They'll see you," Ben-Dor said firmly.

"Let me think about it," responded Vandenberg. He had already made up his mind to go.

Frank Bernardi was stunned at the news of the raid. His pessimism about its consequences filled the room. "I don't see that we have any options, Felix."

Vandenberg watched his Under Secretary without expression.

"If we stay here or go back to Washington, we forfeit any ability to influence the outcome. The only thing you *can* do is go to Damascus, Felix."

Vandenberg issued a thin smile of approval. "I agree," he said. "Any word yet from the Syrians?"

"No," Bernardi said, scowling, "and I don't think there will be. After all, to them it's got to look as though you knew about the whole operation."

"That's what worries me more than anything else," Vandenberg agreed. "Even if al-Bakr sees me, how the hell do I convince him that the Israelis pulled this stunt without our knowledge?"

"You don't." Bernardi was crushing a throw cushion between his hands. "He's not going to believe you anyway. Ben-Dor's got to give you something; a concession, something tangible."

Vandenberg viewed his friend with open approval. "I think there's hope for you yet, Frank. Get Ya'acov on the phone for me, will you?"

The conversation was brief and deceptively simple.

"Ya'acov, I don't have time to argue, and I don't have time to play games. You're the one who got me into this mess, and you're the one who's going to help me get out of it. I want your authority to tell al-Bakr that Israel is ready to engage in a serious West Bank negotiation *if* he can get Safat to publicly acknowledge 242 and 338."

This was a reference to a pair of United Nations resolutions that, among other things, confirmed the right of "all nations in the area" to an independent existence. A Safat acknowledgment of resolutions 242 and 338 would amount to an indirect OLPP recognition of Israel's "right to exist"—an issue that lay at the core of the Arab-Israeli dispute.

"Not enough, Felix." Ben-Dor's voice was flat and final.

"What the hell do you mean, 'not enough'?"

"Not enough." Ben-Dor paused, searching for the right words. "If they want our cooperation"—he raised his voice—"if *you* want our cooperation, Safat is going to have to get his friends to rewrite the OLPP Covenant that calls for Israel's destruction. Otherwise, putting aside my own feeling, there'd be no chance of getting such an agreement through the Knesset."

"Supposing they just drop the phrase calling in effect for Israel's destruction. That, plus explicit acceptance of 242 and 338?" Vandenberg was holding his breath.

Ben-Dor reflected for a few moments in silence. Then he said, "Felix, we Israelis are modest people. We're not asking for the moon."

Vandenberg decided to press his case. "In that case, Ya'acov, I also want to be able to say that you're willing to accept Safat as a legitimate representative of the Palestinians."

"Absolutely not!" The Prime Minister's voice rose in outraged indignation.

"You're not listening to me, Ya'acov. I said *a* legitimate representative, not *the*."

There was silence at the Prime Minister's end. While the raid against al-Bakr's headquarters was in progress, Ben-Dor had held an extraordinary meeting of his Cabinet, during which he had advised his colleagues of the attack and warned that Israel would have to be prepared to make concessions in the event that negotiations did materialize subsequent to the raid. He had already requested—and had already received—authority to proceed essentially along the lines that Vandenberg had just outlined. Ben-Dor confided none of this to the Secretary of State.

"You know what you're asking, Felix?"

"I do know, Ya'acov; believe me."

"Even if it works, my opponents will introduce a no-confidence vote against me in the Knesset."

"I understand that; but you're exactly what Israel needs now, Ya'acov—a statesman, not just a politician."

"Don't start flattering me, Felix. I may change my mind."

"I have your permission, then?"

"My very reluctant permission."

"Thank you." Vandenberg hung up. His father had once told him, "When someone gives you what you want, don't press your luck. Take it and run."

By late afternoon, Darius' story was being graphically confirmed throughout Israel. Military reservists were seen in the large cities and the small kibbutzim rushing to active duty, hitchhiking rides to their units. Israeli housewives were stocking up on staples in a frenzy of panic buying. Even members of the Israeli Cabinet, summoned to Jerusalem by the Prime Minister earlier in the day, were now confirming, confidentially, that they had been ordered not to return to their offices in Tel Aviv but to stay close to the Knesset in the event of an emergency meeting. There was an almost palpable air of crisis.

At seven P.M., a grim-faced Prime Minister appeared unexpectedly at the King David Hotel. He refused to talk with reporters, but he did deliver a short, ominous speech to a largely American gathering of the

United Jewish Appeal. Ben-Dor, speaking in English, said, "Israel always has and will continue to exercise restraint in the face of provocation, but it would be a tragic miscalculation if anyone were to confuse restraint with the inability to act. The government of Israel does not seek confrontation, but neither will it shrink from it. Israel is dependent on the help of others, but our course of action will never be controlled by that dependency. We have the strength and the daring to inflict a crushing defeat on anyone who plans or tries to carry out our destruction."

The speech, although delivered in a flat monotone, brought the audience to its feet. The applause continued even after the Prime Minister left the hotel.

At seven-thirty P.M., Darius was just about to leave the hotel himself, on his way to the satellite facilities in Herzliya, when spokesman Carl Ellis cornered him in the lobby. "The Secretary's flying to Damascus tonight."

"What time?"

"The press buses leave here in half an hour."

Darius raced back to his room and called Jerry Blumer at the NNS office at Herzliya. "Jerry? Now don't interrupt me and just listen. I've got to leave here in just a few minutes. Vandenberg's going to Damascus tonight. I'll need a crew at the airport. Did you hear about Ben-Dor's speech?"

"Yeah. Kol Yisrael carried it live."

"All right. We've got that on film. Now, I suggest we handle the story this way. We can use the film you've got of the reservists hitchhiking to their units. We've got some good footage here of housewives and panic buying. I'm going to start voice-over with the same stuff I used on my radio spots—the satellite intelligence material. Cover that any way you can. Then the reservists; then the housewives. Then we go to a big chunk of Ben-Dor, here, this evening; and I'll do an on-camera close at the airport. If you want to, you can cover part of that with the Vandenberg departure footage. Any problem?"

"No. I'll see you at Ben-Gurion."

Darius threw his toilet kit, some fresh socks, underwear and a clean shirt into his camera bag. He zipped his typewriter back into its carrying case and rushed downstairs again. The first of the three press minibuses had already departed. "Lefty" Shulberg, an ex-newsman who now served as head of the United States Information Service in

Tel Aviv, was shepherding the last of the Vandenberg newsmen onto the remaining two buses.

There was little conversation on the ride to the airport. No liar's poker. Most of the reporters were busily typing new stories, or "adds" to stories already filed. Each bus had taken on the qualities of a jarring newsroom racing toward an imminent deadline. Darius rewrote his television report; and when that was completed, he wrote three fresh radio reports. Everything would have to be recorded at the airport for Blumer to feed to New York.

By nine-fifteen P.M., the newsmen arrived at the airport. By nine-thirty, Darius had filmed his on-camera close, twice, and recorded his three radio spots. He was about to hand Blumer copies of all his scripts when a small black-and-white Israeli police car, flashing a blue light on its dome, led the Vandenberg motorcade to the side of the Secretary's waiting Boeing 707. There was no departure statement, not even a *pro forma* wave in the direction of the cameras. Vandenberg got out of his limousine and strode purposefully up the front ramp of his aircraft.

"Gotta go." Darius gave Blumer a pat on the shoulder, picked up his camera bag and typewriter, and ran to the rear of the plane.

The Boeing's engines had already started. Carl Ellis was standing at the head of the stairs waving frantically at Darius, like a third-base coach. "Let's go, let's go, let's go!"

A member of the flight crew waited at the foot of the stairs, holding a clipboard with the manifest. He nodded at Darius, and the pair of them bounded up the steps, taking them two at a time.

There was no briefing on the flight to Damascus.

Syrian President al-Bakr thumbed an endless succession of amber worry beads across his forefinger, past the palm of his right hand. He had accorded the proper protocol to the Secretary of State, but there was not even a suggestion of warmth. The interpreter was a Syrian, a member of al-Bakr's personal staff; his English was flawless, though lacking in elegance. Vandenberg had the uneasy feeling that certain subtleties, shadings, nuances, eluded the man and therefore evaporated without ever reaching the Syrian President. Vandenberg, believing that diplomatic flexibility decreases in direct ratio to the number of people involved in a negotiation, had proposed that he and al-Bakr meet alone. The Syrian President, however, had insisted that his Foreign Minister join them, so Vandenberg had included Bernardi too.

The four diplomats sat in a semicircle in one of the presidential conference rooms, which resembled a Victorian parlor, the windows shrouded by heavy velvet drapes, the conference area dimly lit by brass sconces.

Al-Bakr seemed to be in a sour mood.

"There is only one issue to be discussed: Israeli aggression." The interpreter reduced the Arabic to stenographic notes and repeated the sentiment flatly in English. It was the third time in less than ten minutes that al-Bakr had returned to the same theme.

"Mr. President," retorted Vandenberg, "I don't minimize the gravity of the situation. But unless both sides are prepared to exercise utmost restraint, simple inertia will carry us into a war, the consequences of which are impossible to anticipate, except that I think we can confidently predict that it will bring untold anguish to *all* peoples of the Middle East."

Vandenberg felt it was time to break the cycle of platitudes. "Mr. President, what I'm about to say carries with it the risk of grave misunderstanding, and I'm sure you'll believe me when I say that I do not lightly violate diplomatic confidences. However, I think it's vitally important that we grasp the opportunities as well as the obvious dangers of the current situation."

The progress of the worry beads was momentarily stalled.

"During the past few hours, acting under instructions from my President, I have communicated with the leaders of the Soviet Union. We have proposed an immediate and total halt of arms shipments from the United States to Israel against the assurance of a similar halt in Soviet war supplies to Syria."

The proposal had, in fact, been tacked to the end of a blistering cable that Vandenberg had sent to the Kremlin early that morning. There was little or no chance that the Soviets would even respond. The Secretary did not expect al-Bakr to be favorably impressed either; but he wanted to underscore the probability that if war broke out, America's role as a mediator would be finished. The Arab world would fall once again into the Soviet orbit. Israel, with U.S. backing, would oppose them. Since al-Bakr had in recent months thrown his personal influence behind a policy of moderation, such polarization was not, for him, a promising prospect.

"Our actions, Mr. Secretary, as you well know, have always been those of an independent nation. While we value the support of our Socialist friends, we pursue our own policy, if I may say so, sometimes with the encouragement of parties who are not always able to live up to their commitments." The U.S. Congress had yet to authorize all the economic aid that Vandenberg had pledged to al-Bakr seven months earlier. "Also, it is my impression that U.S. generosity to Israel has been at such an extraordinary level for so long that its capacity to wage war would hardly be affected by a *temporary* break in the supply line." Al-Bakr paused before adding, "Even if the American Congress were to permit such an interruption."

The meeting was not going well. Al-Bakr's tone was getting angrier. Bernardi leaned over to Vandenberg and suggested a fifteen-minute break.

The Syrian President, inclining his head politely, placed his right hand over his heart. If his guests required a short rest, then of course they would take a break.

Vandenberg and Bernardi walked out of the conference room, down a flight of stairs and outside into the garden. The Secretary of State was depressed, almost morose. "We're getting nowhere, Frank. Maybe we should just pack up." They walked in figure eights around the rosebushes. "I think I'm going to tell al-Bakr that I feel my usefulness has been exhausted. If I put Ben-Dor's proposal before him now, he'll piss all over it. He's not in a mood to negotiate."

Bernardi had been exposed to the Secretary's fluctuating moods on more than one occasion. He brushed aside Vandenberg's pessimism. "You're only reacting to what he *said*, Felix. Did you hear what he *didn't* say?" Bernardi didn't wait for an answer. "He didn't even mention the Israeli raid." He smiled. "Ben-Dor was right. He's not going to bring it up. Give him something to salve his pride, Felix, and I think the man's ready to deal."

They continued walking through the garden, almost brushing shoulders, their voices lowered. Vandenberg had his hands clasped behind his back. "It's possible," he conceded. "You could be right." Vandenberg's voice had taken on a faintly more optimistic tone. "I don't have to let him know that Ben-Dor's proposal is firm. I could raise it as a possibility."

"Exactly."

"And if he doesn't bite?"

"You can still threaten to leave the area."

"I'm not very hopeful, Frank."

Bernardi placed a big hand protectively around his friend's shoulder. "You never are, Felix. Let's go upstairs."

They returned to an empty conference room. Al-Bakr had left, as had the interpreter and the Foreign Minister. The Secretary and the Under Secretary of State sat down and waited. Several minutes passed before a young man, whom they both recognized as a mid-level functionary of the Syrian Foreign Ministry, entered. "The President asked if you would be kind enough to come and join him upstairs."

Vandenberg and Bernardi exchanged glances, but said nothing.

Al-Bakr greeted them at the entrance to a small second-floor dining room. He was as openly effusive now as he had been grim before. "Mr. Secretary!" He took obvious pleasure in the look of surprise that involuntarily crossed the faces of both his American guests. A splendid Arabic meal had been arrayed on a long wooden table, and standing before the table, almost in a receiving line, were the Syrian Defense Minister, Abdul Hassan; the Foreign Minister, who had participated in the earlier session; the Chairman of the OLPP, Jamaal Safat; and his Chief of Operations, Ibrahim el-Haj.

"I believe you know all my Arab brothers." Al-Bakr was enjoying the scene.

Vandenberg was still somewhat nonplussed, but he walked down the line, regaining a little of his composure with each handshake. By the time he reached Safat, he even permitted himself a warm smile, grasping the Palestinian's elbow firmly with his left hand, enclosing Safat's hand with the other. "What disturbed me the most about that tape, Mr. Chairman, is that you sounded so much more impressive than I did." Then, still holding Safat's elbow, Vandenberg turned toward the table and a huge roast lamb, which occupied center stage. "Which end of the lamb should I talk into?"

There was a burst of nervous laughter.

Vandenberg then shook hands with Ibrahim. "We always seem to meet over food." He grinned.

"Please," gestured al-Bakr, speaking in English for the first time, "help yourselves."

The seven men seated themselves around a circular table. Only the Syrian President seemed to be eating with genuine enthusiasm. The Defense Minister was distinctly subdued. Vandenberg, who had an extraordinary capacity for small talk, even under the most trying of circumstances, had launched into an analysis of the American fondness for sports that rewarded tactical flexibility over strategic planning.

"What I find most astonishing," Vandenberg was saying, "is the enormous postwar popularity of baseball in Japan. Next to the Chinese, I don't believe there's a people in the world who place a greater emphasis on long-range strategy than the Japanese; and yet baseball places a higher premium on the ability to make rapid tactical changes than any sport I know."

Vandenberg was filling time. The next move was up to the Syrian President, but the Secretary of State was taking great pains to avoid a misstep, while at the same time giving the appearance of nonchalance.

There was a momentary lull in the conversation. Al-Bakr and Vandenberg had consumed a complete meal; the others had eaten no more than was required by good manners. Al-Bakr picked up his water glass.

"I would like to propose a toast. For some time now, with the help of our inexhaustible friend"—he nodded in Vandenberg's direction—"and his distinguished predecessor, we have been moving slowly in the direction of a just and lasting peace in the Middle East. We have long known that final settlement would not be possible unless it takes into account the legitimate interests of the Palestinian people. This issue has been too long deferred, and the wholly justifiable indignation of our Palestinian brothers has been too long contained. We are at a crossroad, and we may not pass this way again. If we fail in our efforts to achieve political ends by political means, the alternative is obvious. The alternative is war, and war is a tragedy for mankind. The tragedy may be unavoidable, but we owe it to history—to our children and to our children's children—to summon up every last remnant of good will that is within us before the dogs of war, which even now are restrained by nothing more than threads, are finally and irrevocably unleashed."

It was a remarkably moderate statement, which all but begged Vandenberg to prevent a new war. It was the kind of opportunity for which the Secretary of State had been silently praying. Al-Bakr was inviting him to deal directly with Safat. Beyond that, in the oblique language of diplomacy, he was telling Vandenberg that he had expended every last vestige of his own prestige in bringing Safat this far and in overriding the objections of his own Defense Minister. Vandenberg had to indicate that the message was clear and that the obligation was accepted.

"Mr. President, Chairman Safat, distinguished colleagues," he began, speaking very slowly, "every confrontation has within it the seeds of opportunity. Wars are not begun because of events, but because of the ability or inability of men to perceive the nature of the opportunity inherent in those events. If war, which has already brought so much suffering to all the peoples of this region, is avoided, it will be because of the vision of statesmen like you, Mr. President.

"Those of us whom history has chosen to play the role of intermediaries can act only in the context of leaders whose perceptions transcend the facile solutions of brute force."

Vandenberg turned slightly, as he said those last words, so that he was facing Safat.

"We stand ready to lend our support to all those who favor peaceful solutions, and the United States will always exert its influence in that direction. I propose a toast, therefore, to the vision of President al-Bakr, and to the courage of those who are prepared to join with him in the search for a just and lasting peace in the Middle East."

The stage had been set. Al-Bakr and his ministers of defense and foreign affairs withdrew silently from the room. Only the interpreter, Safat, Ibrahim el-Haj and the two Americans remained behind.

Vandenberg was more than a little discomfited by the presence of Ibrahim, knowing that every word of his conversation with Safat would be transmitted to the Israeli government; but he proceeded nevertheless, explaining his perception of Israeli thinking with meticulous care.

A major roadblock developed during their long discussion about a single word: "*a*."

Safat had been expounding his views.

"The Arab summit conference of 1974, at Rabat, named Yasir Arafat as *the* legitimate representative of the Palestinian people. Since the OLPP now occupies the role among the Palestinian people once held by the PLO, I, Jamaal Safat, am the rightful inheritor of that responsibility. If I agree to accept U.N. resolutions 242 and 338, I must insist that the Israelis accept my leadership of the Palestinian people."

Vandenberg felt seriously inhibited by the presence of Ibrahim. "Frank," he said, turning to his Under Secretary of State, "I think you and Mr. Haj should examine the question of how we're going to implement this exchange of understandings."

Bernardi understood immediately and rose to his feet, but Ibrahim remained seated. Safat nodded to his deputy. "It's premature," whispered Ibrahim in Arabic. "There is no understanding yet."

"Go with him." It was an order.

Ibrahim looked sullen, but he complied.

Safat gripped both arms of his chair in a show of mock apprehension. "Am I to be subjected now to the full force of the Secretary's renowned persuasive powers?"

Vandenberg smiled deferentially. "From what I've heard, the Chairman's powers of resistance are certainly more than equal to the challenge. However," he added quickly, "my powers of persuasion have been grossly exaggerated. If I have any abilities in this field at all, they lie in the capacity to find areas of common understanding and interest. For example, in our first meeting, you impressed me with your conviction that the OLPP would benefit from recognition by the United States government. As I indicated to you then, and I repeat now, that would be feasible only after the OLPP concedes Israel's right to exist. What we're discussing, therefore, would seem to transcend the importance of one word."

Safat began to interrupt, but Vandenberg overrode his objections. "Especially . . . especially, since the perception of reality is sometimes far more important than objective reality itself. Recognition by the United States, which could flow out of this agreement, would confer upon you, Mr. Chairman, the last remaining vestiges of international legitimacy. I'm not insensitive to the distinction that exists in being *a* representative or *the* representative of the Palestinian people; nor would I insult your intelligence by suggesting that the Israeli government would not prefer to deal with another representative. But, if you'll forgive me for being blunt, Mr. Chairman, that is purely an internal Arab problem. You've pointed out, quite correctly, that the Rabat conference of 1974 indirectly conveyed to you the authority to speak on behalf of the Palestinian people. You either retain that authority or you don't. The United States can neither confer it upon you nor take it away. If the Arab world regards you as *the* legitimate spokesman for the Palestinians, then you are. If, on the other hand, the Arab world believes that you must share that authority, then you will share it. What you will have to consider, Mr. Chairman, is whether your position will be undermined or enhanced by an additional degree of international legitimacy."

Safat sat, tugging thoughtfully on a ragged tuft of hair. "And how," he asked finally, "does the United States view King Mohammed's role?"

"As I said, Mr. Chairman, ultimately that becomes an Arab question. Certainly in the initial stages of contact between the OLPP and the Israelis, King Mohammed may play an invaluable role. But, I repeat, eventually the question of who represents the Palestinian people will have to be resolved by the Arab world. *That* discussion is premature."

"I think," Safat said slowly, "that you are somewhat too modest, Mr. Secretary, in your assessment of American influence. Whom will Washington back in this matter?"

"The question," Vandenberg repeated, "is premature. It depends on far too many variables. In the course of the next few years, Jordan and the OLPP will create their own realities. The United States is not inflexible. We adjust to a changing world. Look at China, look at Vietnam, Cuba, Syria."

"Why should I trust you?" Safat was beginning to yield. He needed one more gentle push, one more measure of encouragement.

"I'm not asking for your trust, Mr. Chairman. I'm asking you to make a cold, clinical evaluation of the world, of your own interests as you see them. By becoming a recognized participant in future negotiations, do you damage your position or enhance it? That's the issue, and only you can decide it."

Safat sat silently for a few minutes. "Is that all?" he asked finally.

"No, Mr. Chairman. I would be less than candid with you if I didn't raise one more point."

"And that would be what?"

"That would be dropping a certain phrase from the Covenant of the OLPP." Vandenberg paused. "I would have hesitated even to raise the issue if it hadn't been suggested to me that you were already going to consider it at the next meeting of your National Council." The Secretary was smiling.

"It is too late to engage in games, Mr. Vandenberg. Your intelligence is extraordinarily good. That has already been decided, as you indicated, but I must tell you now that we have no intention of substituting any explicit recognition of Israel." Safat looked at Vandenberg. "Certainly not now."

"Nor would I expect you to"—Vandenberg barely hesitated—"now."

The silence that followed must have lasted several minutes, but neither man moved or spoke. Finally Jamaal Safat stood and extended his hand to the Secretary of State. Vandenberg took the Palestinian's hand. One of the most troublesome logjams in the Middle East had cracked.

"I think," suggested Vandenberg, "that we should ask our colleagues to join us, don't you?"

Safat nodded.

It was four o'clock in the morning by the time the final arrangements were concluded. Safat would return to Beirut, where, later that morning, he was scheduled to give an interview to the British Broadcasting Corporation. In the course of that interview, which was to be released at noon, he would reveal the OLPP's willingness to recognize U.N. resolutions 242 and 338. He would say nothing at that time about changes in the Covenant. At the same time, he would announce his understanding that the Israeli government was prepared to recognize him as "a legitimate representative of the Palestinian people." That announcement would be confirmed by Israeli Prime Minister Ben-Dor. At noon, precisely, the governments of Israel and Syria would announce the simultaneous easing of the alert status of their troops. Secretary Vandenberg would then announce the impending release of an important statement by the White House at eight A.M. Eastern standard time. The Washington statement would contain the American guarantee of the understandings reached by the Syrians, the Israelis, and the OLPP. The United States would also announce, for the first time, that the U.S. government was itself giving serious consideration to recognizing Jamaal Safat as "a legitimate representative of the Palestinian people." By six P.M., Middle East time, the governments of Israel and Syria would begin pulling back their forces along the Golan front.

The subject of the Israeli commando raid on Damascus the previous day was never broached.

Vandenberg had been prepared to raise the subject of Soviet penetration of the OLPP; but since the raid itself was never discussed, he decided to withhold that information. In any event, he assumed (correctly) that Ibrahim had already conveyed the essence of Moussa's double role to the Palestinian leader.

By four-fifteen A.M., Vandenberg instructed one of his Secret Service agents to get word to the press corps that they would all be leaving Damascus within the hour. At four-twenty-five, an officer of the U.S. Embassy woke up the fourteen newsmen. They had spent the night gambling, reading, exchanging rumors and, finally, falling into fitful slumber on an assortment of couches and armchairs in the reception room of the New Omayyad Hotel.

During the course of the night, Darius had obtained from his Armenian cameraman, whose sources were legion and frequently reliable, some tantalizing pieces of information. The previous day, Darius learned, there had been either an attempted coup or an Israeli raid near Damascus. The sources differed on that key point. They agreed, however, that there had been casualties at President al-Bakr's mountain hideaway. Several ambulances had been seen leaving the area, and there had been an exchange of gunfire on the outskirts of Damascus. Darius had struggled for much of the night to put that information into the larger context of his knowledge. Shortly before three, though, he too had fallen asleep.

The Syrian government had provided five official Mercedes cars to take the reporters back to the airport. They reached the Secretary's aircraft well before five A.M., prepared for a long wait. It was not uncommon for overanxious Embassy officials to get them to the airport several hours before Vandenberg arrived. This time, however, a scant fifteen minutes had passed before the flashing lights and howling sirens of the Syrian police escort signaled Vandenberg's imminent departure.

The Secretary's limousine pulled up to the front ramp of the aircraft, so close, in fact, that none of the reporters could gain access to Vandenberg.

Herb Kaufman yelled, "Shall we wait for you here, or do you want us to come back with you?" But the plane's engines had already been started, and if Vandenberg had heard the question, he gave no sign of it. The reporters scurried to the rear of the plane. Within three minutes, the Secretary's plane was airborne.

Again, there was no briefing on the plane. At one point, Frank Bernardi walked down the aisle on his way to the bathroom. Darius waited a minute and then took up a position in the galley. He caught Bernardi on the way back.

"Did the Secretary see Safat?"

Bernardi placed a hand on Darius' shoulder. "If the Secretary knew that I even stopped to say 'good morning' to you, he'd string me up."

Darius held his ground, fixing Bernardi with an unwavering stare. "The heat's out of it, isn't it, Frank?"

"Let's just say we've made progress; and that, you bastard, is all you're getting out of me." Bernardi literally elbowed his way past Darius, ignoring the hands that plucked at his sleeves as he made his way up the aisle to the sanctuary of the forward cabin.

It was not quite six o'clock in the morning when the Secretary's plane taxied to a halt in front of the main terminal at Ben-Gurion Airport. Felix Vandenberg had slept exactly two hours out of the past forty-eight, and it was beginning to show. He stood for a moment at the head of the El Al ramp, took a deep breath, and picked his way slowly down the stairway and toward the knot of Israeli officials and security men who awaited him on the tarmac.

A crowd of Israeli and foreign journalists was trapped in a distant press enclosure, shouting questions to no avail. The traveling newsmen tried to hear snatches of conversation between Vandenberg and the Israeli ministers who had come to welcome him.

Darius walked toward the Secretary's limousine. He approached one of the agents. "Which side is he getting in?"

"Right here," murmured the agent.

Darius intercepted the Secretary some ten feet from the car, falling in stride with him. "Congratulations," he said quietly.

Vandenberg hesitated for only an instant, looking at Darius with the trace of a smile. "One of these days, Kane, I'm going to tell you about these last forty-eight hours."

"I'm glad you got it."

Vandenberg made no effort to discredit Darius' assumption of success; but just before he got into the car, he warned, "Don't go overboard, yet. I still have to talk to Ben-Dor."

"When do you do that?"

"As soon as I can change my shirt." Then, just as the door was closing, Vandenberg leaned forward in his seat. "I want to see you for a couple of minutes after I talk to Ben-Dor."

Darius knew what was troubling the Secretary. The man's power to concentrate on a wide variety of problems simultaneously was extraordinary. He was still engaged in the process of nudging the Middle East almost single-handedly back from the brink of war, but one small part of his brain was still occupied with Darius' story about the OLPP penetrations. Darius shook his head in grudging admiration.

29

Ya'acov Ben-Dor was solicitous. "You're tired," he observed, helping Vandenberg off with his coat.

"I'm fine," remarked the Secretary of State, heading for the Prime Minister's study.

Ben-Dor poured two cups of coffee and pushed a plate of buns across his desk. "Have one. Esther made them herself."

Vandenberg reached first for the coffee.

"So," began the Prime Minister, "how did it go?"

"I thought you'd know already." Vandenberg looked up with a slightly malicious smile. He knew that there was little chance that the Israeli agent could have summarized and transmitted the substance of the all-night meeting in the brief time that had elapsed.

Ben-Dor pouted. "No. That fast it doesn't go."

Vandenberg reached for a bun; he took a large bite. "In that case, I feel a little better. I don't like to bore you with stale news."

Ben-Dor tapped impatiently on his desk with a letter opener. "Come on, Felix. Don't play games with me."

Vandenberg rubbed his eyes wearily. "All right. It went well. I'll tell you the part you'll like least first. I finessed your agent out of the room during the key part of my conversation with Safat. He may be a first-rate spy, but I don't know how much he understands about diplomatic language. I didn't want him fouling things up at the last minute."

Ben-Dor shook his head from side to side. "I'm not so sure how well I understand your diplomatic language either."

"You understand it, Ya'acov, better than anyone. I had to convince Safat that he was only *a* legitimate representative. I told him that's all that you or we could accept, and if he wants any kind of recognition from either one of us . . ."

Vandenberg hadn't really expected to slip it past Ben-Dor that easily, but the Israeli didn't even let him finish the sentence. "Wait a minute. When did U.S. recognition become a part of the deal?"

"I didn't promise him recognition. I promised him a statement from the White House, if everything else goes according to plan, saying that the U.S. government is giving *serious consideration* to recognizing Safat as *a* legitimate representative of the Palestinian people."

"You had no right to go that far, Felix."

Vandenberg smiled solicitously. "Ya'acov. My old and dear friend Ya'acov. For years now, we have withheld recognition from the OLPP on the specific grounds that they persistently refused to recognize *your* right to exist. Now, if everything goes according to plan, Safat is going to make that policy shift public during the course of a BBC interview about three and a half hours from now. If he doesn't do it, there won't be any U.S. announcement; but for God's sake, Ya'acov, you can't expect the United States government to take a more rigid posture toward the OLPP than your government does."

Ben-Dor conceded the point reluctantly. "You still shouldn't have done it without discussing it with me. What about the rest of it?"

Vandenberg ran his hand briskly over the rough stubble on his face. "The quid pro quo for the BBC interview is that you make a similar announcement, any way you see fit, that you're prepared to recognize Safat as *a* negotiating partner if the OLPP goes along with 242 and 338. Unless you have some other preference, you may want to leak it to Kane. It'll keep him off the penetration story until I have a chance to talk to him again." Vandenberg paused. "And, by the way, Safat confirmed what we already knew about the OLPP changing its Covenant again."

Ben-Dor nodded. "What about the Arab army on the Golan?"

"Twelve noon. You and al-Bakr will release a simultaneous statement that the alert is being lifted and the troops on both sides are being pulled back."

Ben-Dor leaned back in his chair. "It looks like you've done it, Felix. *Mazel tov!*"

Felix Vandenberg gave an audible sigh of relief and dropped the bun he'd been holding onto the floor.

Eight-fifteen A.M. The lobby of the King David Hotel was jammed with tourists, security men, reporters, cameramen and a dozen or so members of the hotel staff. Jerusalem continued to be gripped by war fever. There had been no indication from any quarter that there were grounds for relaxation. An expectant hush enveloped the lobby as Secretary Vandenberg passed through the main entrance. Everyone had been pushed unceremoniously behind the rectangular boxes of plastic plants, and the entranceway in front of the registration desk was empty. A dozen hand-held floodlights bathed Vandenberg and his security escort in a harsh brilliance. Lines of fatigue were etched on the Secretary's face, and he seemed, quite literally, to have trouble walking. He ignored everyone.

Darius was waiting on the sixth floor, near the elevators.

"You're going to have to wait a few minutes," Vandenberg grunted as he moved toward his suite. He turned, trying to see past his security detail. "Frank, I want you with me."

As he entered the suite, Vandenberg stripped off his jacket, tie and shirt, flinging them onto a chair. He turned abruptly, motioning Bernardi to follow him into the bathroom. "First thing we've got to do is cable al-Bakr and Safat. Repeat the details of the understanding and tell them Ben-Dor agrees on all counts." Vandenberg started to shave. "What time is it in Washington now?"

Bernardi calculated quickly. "One-thirty in the morning."

"Well, that's too goddamn bad. If I can't sleep, why the hell should they? Get Stewart and the President for me. I want them both on at the same time. Someone's going to have to be able to answer questions for the President after I get off."

Vandenberg finished shaving; he turned on the hot water until steam began to fog the mirror. He immersed a washcloth in the water, wrung it out and then carefully covered his face with the hot, moist cloth. A moment later, he turned on the cold water and repeated the process. The Secretary snatched a towel from the rack, patting his face and neck dry as he walked into the bedroom. He quickly got into casual clothes.

By the time he re-entered the living room, Bernardi had already dictated the text of the cables to a secretary and he was on the line to the White House. "No," he was saying, "I want you to get General Stewart on the line first, *then* get the President."

Vandenberg disappeared into the bathroom again.

"Felix!" Bernardi was calling from the couch. "I've got the President."

The Secretary of State moved with unaccustomed speed. "Mr. President?" He was still adjusting his trousers. "It's very good news, sir."

The scrambler had been activated on the phone; each man's voice was badly distorted and slightly delayed, so it was necessary to pause at the end of a thought before the other party could reply.

"You have no idea how delighted I am to hear that, Felix." The President sounded as though he were under water. "When I heard you were calling, I was afraid we might be going to war."

"No, sir." Vandenberg sketched out the terms of the agreement he had reached with the Arabs and the Israelis. "I'll be happy to answer any questions you might have, Mr. President; and then I'll dictate the rough draft of a statement to Harlan. If you approve, sir, we can have the White House release the text at eight A.M., your time."

"I don't have any questions. I'm just damn pleased that it worked out so well. You're to be congratulated, Felix."

"Thank you very much." Vandenberg had an uneasy afterthought. "Mr. President, I know this is probably unnecessary, but you know how things sometimes go awry in this part of the world. I wouldn't represent this to Congress as too much of a triumph just yet."

"I know what you're saying, Felix. Well, I'll leave you and Harlan to it then."

Vandenberg covered the phone with his hand and turned to Bernardi. "He's not even sticking around to listen to the White House communiqué that's going out over his name." He shook his head in disbelief. "Harlan?"

"I'm here, Felix."

"Is the President still on?"

"No, he's gone back to bed."

"All right. I want you to go over this draft very carefully. Frank and I are so goddamned exhausted that it may need reworking. If you make any changes though, call me back."

Vandenberg consulted the text and then read it to Stewart.

"It sounds fine, Mr. Secretary, but I'll go over it carefully. You've really done an incredible job." It was an unusual compliment from the normally reticent National Security Adviser.

"Thank you, Harlan. I'll be in touch with you later. We'll probably overnight here."

"Fine, sir. I'll talk to you later."

Vandenberg collapsed on a couch. He started to say something to Bernardi, but then he saw that his Under Secretary of State had just dozed off in an upright chair. Vandenberg nudged Bernardi into embarrassed consciousness. "You're sleeping while history's being made."

Bernardi was beyond any kind of response.

"Go to bed for a few hours, Frank. You've earned it. Send Kane in on your way out."

Vandenberg made no effort to conceal his own exhaustion as Darius entered the suite. "You can imagine," Vandenberg droned, "how eager I am to engage in a protracted discussion of First Amendment guarantees; but before I take my allotted hour's sleep for the night, I wanted to determine whether National News Service can survive the deferral of another war."

Darius grinned. "It's a good thing you're tired. I was afraid you might indulge in some hyperbole."

The Secretary pushed out his lower lip thoughtfully. "Tell me what you think you've got."

Darius recognized that there was to be no further bantering. It was time to lay out everything he knew and, where possible, to fill in the gaps with educated guesses.

"All right, Mr. Secretary. Let's take it in order. I don't know whether the Russians initiated the kidnapping of your wife, but I am sure that one of Safat's top lieutenants is a Soviet agent. So at least they knew about it, and played a key role in it. In any event, they've tried to make the most of it by undermining, in fact, by trying to destroy, your role in the negotiating process out here.

"For the longest time, I couldn't understand the Israeli connection in all of this. Nothing Ben-Dor's done these past several days has made much sense. For a while, I thought the Russian agent might even be an Israeli, or vice versa; some kind of double agent. But now I'm convinced that there have been at least two high-level penetrations of the OLPP. The Israelis have got a man in there too. Just what part he played in your wife's kidnapping, I don't know.

"Now, just twelve hours ago, everything here spelled war. You spend the night in Damascus and the whole picture's been turned around. Why?" Darius answered his own question. "I can think of two reasons. I know that there was some kind of military operation in Damascus yesterday, before you arrived. If it was a coup attempt, it had to be unsuccessful. If al-Bakr had been overthrown, you wouldn't have any kind of deal now. But I'm more inclined to think that the Israelis pulled one of their John Wayne stunts. They've got a man on the inside; so if there was a war council meeting of the Rejectionist Front—and they're the only ones who'd really be pushing hard for a military showdown these days—the Israelis would have known about it and could've broken it up. I can't see al-Bakr getting too upset over anything that undermines the influence of his Defense Minister's friends."

Darius was waiting for some kind of reaction from Vandenberg, but the Secretary of State hadn't moved.

"So, in that context," Darius continued, "you fly into Damascus and meet with al-Bakr and Safat. You blow the Soviet agent's cover and deliver some kind of conciliatory message from the Israelis. Al-Bakr figures he's never going to be in a stronger position domestically and puts the arm on Safat." Darius paused again, but there was still no reaction. "That's it," he added.

Vandenberg stared blankly at Darius for a long moment, struggling to understand how the reporter could have constructed a scenario so close to reality. Finally, he responded in a voice heavy with gloom. "Don't you think we have enough problems already?"

"You're not denying any of it?"

Vandenberg exploded. "For Chrissake, Darius, you don't really believe that I'm going to respond point by point to that patchwork of speculation and hypothesis, do you?" Lowering his voice, the Secretary confided, "Look, you're right about one thing. We're on the verge of an historic agreement. Within the next few hours, the Israelis and the OLPP are going to announce a modified recognition of each other, and that's going to be followed by an immediate pullback of forces along the Golan border. Now, I'm telling you this, off the record, to impress upon you the incalculable harm you could do with your exploration of the dark corners of rumors about raids and penetrations. I mean, there has to be *some* outer limit where the requirements of a free press are subordinated to matters of peace and war."

Darius could feel a tightness in his chest. "I'll hold the story, Mr. Secretary, but I won't kill it."

Vandenberg sighed with exhaustion and exasperation. "I'm too tired to argue now, Darius. Just promise me that before you write anything about what we've discussed you'll talk to me again."

Darius gave the pledge reluctantly. "All right." He frowned. "What about the OLPP-Israeli recognition story? When can I use it?"

Vandenberg picked up the phone, depressing a button that connected him with one of his secretaries. "Get the Prime Minister for me." He replaced the receiver. "I don't know how you feel about being involved in history, but since Safat is making his end of the announcement in a BBC interview, I suggested to Ben-Dor that he might want to deliver his part through NNS."

The buzzer on the phone interrupted him.

"Ya'acov? I've got Darius Kane here with me." Ben-Dor seemed to be raising some kind of objection.

"No, of course," Vandenberg concurred. "It would have to be on a hold-for-release basis for noon." The Secretary looked at Darius, who nodded his agreement. "I'll put him on."

Darius found himself, five minutes later, standing in front of the elevators outside the Secretary's suite in a state of utter confusion. On the one hand, he had, scribbled in his notebook, the text of an extraordinary Israeli announcement. Despite the qualified nature of the language, the Israeli Prime Minister had acknowledged his archfoe, Jamaal Safat, as "a representative of the Palestinian people." Darius alone had just been handed one of the major stories of the year. On the other hand, he recognized that he was being used as an instrument of high-stakes diplomacy.

"Screw it," he muttered to himself. "What the hell's the difference if he gives it to me alone or announces it at a press conference?" There was a difference though, and Darius knew it. By limiting the announcement to a single news agency—and a foreign one, at that— Ben-Dor had retained a margin of deniability in the event that anything soured in the interim. Furthermore, Vandenberg had once again maneuvered him into a position where the story of the penetration and the raid would have to be deferred for at least a few more hours. Darius Kane felt dirty, resentful, and yet excited.

As the elevator took him down to the fourth floor, Darius did some quick calculation. Noon, Jerusalem time, was five A.M. in New York. The television network was not yet on the air. The radio network was still extremely limited. If he reported his story much before noon, it would leak. Still, it was a hell of a story; and, for what it was worth, it was all his.

At seven minutes after noon, Middle East time, the first "snap" ran on Reuters, out of Beirut. It was followed, within seconds, by almost identical bulletins over Associated Press and United Press International.

The agency sequence was slightly reversed in New York, but news of the dramatic switch in Israeli and OLPP policies hit the wires minutes after five A.M., Eastern standard time.

By five-fifteen, a New York editor for the AP connected the two stories and issued a separate bulletin on the coordinated announcements coming out of Beirut and Jerusalem.

Forty-five minutes later—one P.M., Jerusalem time—a spokesman for the Israeli Defense Ministry announced that the Red Alert had been reduced. There was no similar announcement from Damascus, where such information is never made public; but the Israeli spokesman announced that he had "indications" that Arab forces along the Golan front had also lowered their alert status.

A string of announcements and leaks punctuated the rest of the afternoon, but they were all anticlimactic.

One announcement from State Department spokesman Carl Ellis, however, intrigued both American and Israeli newsmen. He quoted Vandenberg as confirming the Israeli and Palestinian agreement to accord a measure of recognition to each other, adding that the White House would have further news at three P.M., Jerusalem time.

There was an outburst of right-wing opposition to Ben-Dor's concession; and following the White House announcement that the United States was giving "serious consideration" to recognizing Safat, the opposition became bitter and vitriolic. Likud leader Shlomo Dubin called for the Knesset to meet in extraordinary session for the purpose of voting no confidence in the Israeli Prime Minister. Dubin charged that Ben-Dor and Vandenberg had "hatched a plot of abject betrayal."

War-weary Israelis were willing to give the agreement a chance, however. There was a general feeling of relief that a new round of fighting had been averted. Many Israelis, sophisticated in the art of diplomatic communiqués, seized immediately on the qualification in Ben-Dor's recognition of Safat and the OLPP. They conceded that sooner or later one concession or another to the Palestinian problem was inevitable.

The satellite report had gone smoothly.

"Piece o' cake" was Blumer's verdict, although his screams had echoed throughout the building when it appeared for a while, earlier in the evening, that film of the Defense Minister had been misplaced.

Darius had discovered long ago that the big stories are generally the easiest to do. Besides, there were no late developments.

By seven P.M., Secretary Vandenberg had emerged from the Prime Minister's office exuding a sense of accomplishment and satisfaction.

"I will," Vandenberg had told the crowd of waiting reporters, "be returning to Washington tomorrow. Immediately upon my return, I'll be meeting with President Abbott. It's possible that I will be back here in the Middle East in two weeks to engage in a more intensive search for a West Bank settlement based on the OLPP's acceptance of resolutions 242 and 338 and the decision of the Israeli Cabinet to allow me to proceed on that basis."

With that piece of film securely in hand, Darius had reached Herzliya before eight-thirty, and he had been able to spend more than three hours composing his report.

Now, it was approaching two o'clock in the morning, and Darius had passed beyond simple exhaustion. As Paul eased the car into the King David driveway, Darius wanted nothing more than an uninterrupted half hour soaking in a hot tub.

The lobby was empty. The bar was closed. Darius took the elevator to the fourth floor, unlocked the door to his room and stepped over a pile of messages and communiqués that had been gathering since late afternoon. He was tempted to ignore them all. He had already stripped down to his shorts and was making his way into the bathroom when he gathered up the harvest of paper, glancing quickly at one sheet after another. Then he found the message from one of Vandenberg's secretaries. "Come up to the Secretary's suite whenever you return." The word "whenever" was underlined.

Darius closed his eyes. He didn't feel up to another confrontation with Vandenberg, but he knew that one was unavoidable.

At two-thirty, after a quick cold shower, he was escorted into the Secretary's suite once again.

Vandenberg was standing by the window, holding a glass of soda water. He motioned in the direction of the bar. "Help yourself."

Darius poured himself a glass of ginger ale before joining the Secretary. "It's an impressive sight, even at night." He inclined his head in the general direction of the Old City.

Vandenberg's manner was preoccupied; his expression, mournful. "It's ironic, isn't it?"

"What's that, sir?"

"Here I am on the verge of reaching a breakthrough of almost inconceivable proportions between the Arabs and the Israelis, and the whole thing may be jeopardized by the nature of our own adversary system."

Darius tried to find a suitable response but couldn't; a brief period of silence followed.

"I can't argue this with you, Darius. I'm genuinely trying to understand it. Perhaps you can explain it to me."

"Aren't you being just a little disingenuous, Mr. Secretary?"

Vandenberg turned on Darius without anger. "No. I'm absolutely serious. I know that you, and several of your colleagues, believe me to be insensitive to the democratic process, but perhaps you can explain how the cause of democracy will be served by destroying the only real chance for peace that the Middle East has known."

Darius was feeling dizzy with fatigue. "I'm sorry, Mr. Secretary, but you're misrepresenting the issue. It's not a journalist's responsibility to consider the consequences of a story that he writes; only to judge its accuracy. You might even be able to convince me of the merits of your argument in this case. That would still be irrelevant. Eventually, you'd be putting every reporter in a position where he's forced to make impossible decisions with regard to almost every story that he writes." Darius was struggling to think of a good example. "Look, for the sake of argument, let's say that your value to the United States was beyond question."

Vandenberg forced a grim smile. "Now you're really grasping at straws."

Darius softened his tone. "I said 'for the sake of argument.' If I found that you were being paid off by some multinational corporation, would you expect me to suppress that story because of the consequences that it might have on perfectly valid, but unrelated, negotiations?"

"Of course." Vandenberg still smiled, struggling to keep the conversation from degenerating into an argument. "Darius, all theoretical discussions are simple because theories are uncomplicated by reality. You wouldn't expect me to believe that journalism is the one unsullied field of man's endeavor, that no reporter has ever compromised his own ideals or integrity."

"No."

"Then why do we have to conduct this discussion on a hypothetical plane? If you broadcast a story saying that the Russians and the Israelis have succeeded in planting agents in the OLPP's upper echelon, what do you think Safat's chances of survival would be?"

"Slim."

"Exactly. And even if he did hang on somehow, do you seriously believe that he'd still be in a position to conduct a policy of moderation toward the Israelis?"

"Probably not."

"And if there were an Israeli agent who had managed to penetrate the OLPP, how long do you think he'd go on living if you wrote your story?"

Darius said nothing.

"Darius, it was *my* wife who was kidnapped. *I* was the one who was slandered by that tape. Don't you think it would give me enormous personal satisfaction to point the finger at Moscow, to publicly slap the Russians around? What would that accomplish? At the next SALT negotiation, I'd still have to sit down at the same table with the same people."

Darius' head was throbbing. He put his glass on the window ledge and leaned against the back of a chair.

Vandenberg apparently decided that he had pressed his argument to maximum advantage. "I can't tell you what to write and what to withhold; but please, Darius, I ask you as a friend to consider carefully what you're doing."

Darius nodded. "You know," he acknowledged, "I was planning to get a couple of hours' sleep tonight, but I think you've just taken care of that."

Vandenberg looked at Darius sympathetically. The Secretary realized that Darius was in the grip of an impossible dilemma.

Darius was thoroughly engrossed in his thoughts as he left the Secretary's suite. He decided to walk down to his own floor. He barely noticed the armed Israeli soldiers standing watch on each landing, but they scrutinized each step he took. A soldier on the fifth floor called down to his buddy on the fourth floor, telling him to check Darius' pass.

The guard's English was heavily accented. "Your pass!"

Darius fumbled in his pockets until he realized that he must have left the pass in his room. "It's probably on my night table," he explained.

The Israeli Army wastes little time training its soldiers to be ingratiating with foreigners—invaders or tourists. "Key!" the guard demanded.

Darius patted his pockets. Apparently he'd left the key in his room too.

"Come!" The Israeli pointed his Uzi down the stairs.

Darius stifled his mounting frustration; he walked with the guard down the remaining four flights.

The desk clerk recognized Darius, but he pointed out that the duplicate key was also missing. The clerk spoke quickly to the soldier, apparently explaining who Darius was. Without a working knowledge of Hebrew, Darius caught only the word "Vandenberg." If his prominence in the clerk's eyes rested on his association with the Secretary of State, it seemed to have precisely the opposite effect on the guard.

"I'm sorry, Mr. Kane," the clerk apologized. "I'll have to come up with you myself." He nodded in the direction of the soldier. "He says he doesn't want you wandering through the hotel alone at this hour."

Darius was too tired to argue.

During the elevator ride, the clerk pumped Darius for information about the latest prospects for peace. They were standing in front of Darius' room, the clerk showing no signs of opening the door, when Darius' patience finally evaporated. "Look," he said, "you've been very nice; but it's past three, I'm tired as hell, and I still have a lot of work to do." His voice had begun to rise as the clerk nervously pushed the key into the lock.

"You're quite right, Mr. Kane. I'm sorry. I shouldn't have troubled you, only"—his voice seemed to break, but then he regained control—"only I have a son serving on the Golan . . ." He didn't complete the thought, leaving Darius standing in front of the half-open door feeling terrible.

"You're all I needed," Darius muttered to himself, slamming the door behind him. He strode across the room to the French doors that opened onto his balcony. He was fumbling with the thumb-bolt when he heard a familiar voice. "You really know how to win friends."

Darius spun around in the dark, slamming his knee into the corner of a chair. A light clicked on, and there, lying fully clothed on his bed, was Katherine.

Darius was quivering with anger. "Goddammit! Don't you ever do that again!"

Katherine swung her legs over the side of the bed and joined Darius at the French doors. She brushed a strand of hair away from his forehead and kissed him softly on the mouth.

"I'm sorry. I really am. I wanted it to be a surprise, but not"—she suppressed a smile—"not like this." She took Darius by the hand and led him onto the balcony. Below, beyond the manicured gardens of the hotel, lay the Valley of the Lepers, shrouded in dark shadows. Out were the tourist lights that earlier in the evening had bathed the walls of the Old City. Nevertheless the night was so clear that moonlight was reflected off the swimming pool, directly beneath them; and the rocky slopes, rising from the valley to the base of David's Citadel, were etched in colorless light.

Darius had said nothing since his flare-up of anger, and Katherine adapted herself to his mood, slipping her hand under his arm and drawing next to him.

Almost five minutes passed in total silence, and a new sense of calmness was evident in Darius' voice when he spoke. He put his arm around Katherine's shoulders, drawing her closer. "I'm glad you're here."

She smiled at him. "I'm glad I'm here too."

They turned to face each other. Darius could feel Katherine trembling as they kissed. "Are you cold or are you thinking unclean thoughts?"

Katherine leaned back, spacing her words with great care. "What I'm thinking doesn't have a single, solitary, redeeming social virtue."

"Good. That's just what I was thinking." Almost as an afterthought, Darius asked, "Why are you here, by the way?"

"You."

"That's flattering, but didn't the Ambassador want a more compelling reason?"

"He doesn't ask anymore."

A slight edge crept into Darius' voice. "Well, maybe I should rephrase the question. Is this trip business or pleasure?"

"A little of both."

Darius pulled back, feeling the beginnings of a new surge of anger. "Look, my company has a strict policy against being debriefed by the Agency; and if you're here on business, my hours don't start till ten."

Katherine leaned against the balcony railing. "I could've lied to you. I could have given you any number of half-assed reasons for being here. But you asked me, so I told you."

Darius had turned away from her; he was staring out into the garden.

Katherine's voice was flat. "Darius, I do get awfully tired of apologizing for working for my own government. *Our* own government," she added.

"I'm not asking you to apologize. I just don't like being used. Not by you, not by him"—Darius jerked his head in the direction of the sixth floor—"not by anyone."

"All right," Katherine conceded. "In a sense, I'm using you; but only in the context of confirming what you've been trying to find out all along. If you hadn't uncovered the basic information by yourself, I wouldn't have been able to tell you anything."

Darius was still staring out into the garden.

"Listen to me," Katherine whispered. "Are you listening to me?"

"I'm listening."

"The Agency's been taking a real beating over the past couple of years. The whole world . . . No, forget about the world; it knows better. The American *public* is convinced that dirty tricks were patented in Langley, Virginia. People are beginning to think that covert operations are some kind of American obsession; that if we'd only quit, everybody else would. You know the Russians tried to start another war out here. Now that the Russians have had to abort their plans, I'm just supposed to let you know that Washington wouldn't be too unhappy if our Soviet friends were featured in an unfriendly headline or two."

"*Washington* feels that way, does it?" There was no warmth in Darius' smile as he played with the word. "Which part of Washington? The Washington Monument? The armory? The Redskins? Or did they take a vote?" He paused. "Listen, Katherine, I just spent half an hour with someone else who claims to represent Washington. He swears that if I run this story, I'll be plunging the world into disaster!"

"And you?"

"I don't know what the hell I think."

Katherine hugged herself against the early-morning chill. "'You cannot hope to bribe or twist/Thank God, the British journalist;/But, seeing what the man will do,/Unbribed, there's no occasion to.'"

"Is that supposed to be funny?"

Katherine shrugged. "You're creating an unnecessary dilemma for yourself."

"Is that a fact?"

Katherine nodded.

"Well," said Darius, "you're an old friend. Help me down off the horns."

"Now you're getting sarcastic."

"I'm *not* getting sarcastic." Darius' voice rose well above a whisper. "Shhh."

Darius lowered his voice. "I'm not being sarcastic. Go ahead. What were you going to say?"

"As you've pointed out, Washington is made up of many parts, and they're pulling you in different directions. You're especially upset with me because you're not sure if I really love you or if I've been using you all along."

"So far you're right on target."

"All right, then. Analyze the problem objectively. Not too long ago, you gave me a very convincing lecture, right here in this room, about your father's dedication to journalism, about how being a journalist really made a difference."

"So?" Darius knew where she was heading.

"So, he was talking about a commitment to truth. What do you care what Vandenberg thinks, or what I think? Tell the truth."

"Would you advise me with quite as much conviction if it was one of your agents I was going to blow out of the water?"

Katherine didn't bat an eye. "No. But why should I ignore the best argument there is just because I happen to agree with the outcome?"

"You want to throw Safat right back into the Russians' arms?"

"Of course not. But I don't think that's going to happen, and you don't *know* it for a fact, either. Your friend Felix wants to save détente. That's the only thing on his mind. He knows that if you expose the Russians for the cold-blooded bastards they really are, people aren't going to be so all-fired eager to play games with them anymore."

Darius found himself arguing Vandenberg's case. "What if it leads to another war out here? Will you still feel I've done the right thing?"

"Whoa. Wait a minute." Katherine held up her hand. "What are we talking about now? Darius Kane taking the weight of the world on his shoulders? Who elected you? You're a journalist, Darius. Nothing more, nothing less. Where were you when the White House was trying to muzzle *The Washington Post* during Watergate? I don't recall hearing you dump all over Daniel Ellsberg or Dan Schorr when they were passing classified material around. You may not like hearing it from me, but you're the wrong fellow to be yelling national interest."

Darius didn't say anything for a long time. Then he smiled ruefully. "Now I know what they mean about the devil quoting scripture."

They had seated themselves on a pair of wrought-iron chairs. A ribbon of light was beginning to appear on the horizon. Darius took

Katherine's hand. "What'll you do if I don't run the story?" It was his own way of testing her.

"Nothing." She read the skepticism in his eyes. "Really. Nothing."

Darius Kane had reached a decision. Two decisions. "Let's go to bed."

Darius didn't sleep at all that night. He was up at seven. He showered, shaved and pulled on the clothes he would wear on the plane later that morning.

Katherine watched him from the bed with an air of proprietary pride, her head propped up on an elbow. Darius was seated at the desk, his back to her, trying to fashion his lead sentence. It took a long time before he began typing; but once he started, his fingers flew across the keys of his typewriter.

By the time Darius completed the story, all his self-doubt had vanished. He *knew* he was doing the right thing. He pulled the last carbon book of paper out of the typewriter, stacked it with two others on the desk, and turned toward Katherine.

"Want to see it?"

Katherine shook her head. "No. Anything else you write; but not this one."

"You're not getting cold feet, are you?"

She didn't respond to the question directly. "I wouldn't have given it to anyone else, you know."

"I believe you."

"I hope you do."

Darius walked across the room and seated himself on the edge of the bed, stroking Katherine's hair. "When this thing breaks, I don't know if I'll be traveling with his eminence anymore."

"I didn't know he could keep you off the plane."

"Oh, I suppose it'd be difficult if NNS wants to make a real stink about it, but I don't know how heroic the brass is going to feel when it really hits the fan."

Katherine kissed the palm of his hand. "Come on. They're going to love it. It'll be the story of the year."

Darius wasn't convinced. "It'll be a blockbuster all right, but networks aren't all that crazy about being too far ahead of the pack. They get lonely. It makes them nervous."

"Are *you* having second thoughts?"

Darius picked up the phone. "No." He dialed the press room, just off the lobby. "Morning. This is Darius Kane. What time are we leaving for the airport?" Pause. "And do you know what time we're scheduled to get into Andrews?" He scribbled on a hotel memo pad. "Where are we refueling?" Another note on the pad. "OK. Thanks very much." Darius hung up and then leaned over the bed to kiss Katherine. "I'll tell you one thing I *do* have second thoughts about. Leaving you here alone in this bed." He touched her face tentatively and got off the bed.

In less than ten minutes, Darius had packed his suitcase and garment bag and placed them outside the door. They would be picked up, taken to the airport and fluoroscoped by security personnel. The bags would reappear on the tarmac at Andrews Air Force Base.

Darius telephoned Blumer at the bureau. "Jerry, I'm going to go downstairs in about five minutes to film a stand-upper. It's a very good story and I can't tell you anything about it over the phone, but it's very, very big. I'm going to film it twice. I want one version to go to London for a possible bird for tonight's news. The other one I want you to ship to New York. . . . Now wait a second, don't interrupt. I know it won't get there in time for the show if you send it on a regular commercial flight. What if we chartered to Athens? . . . All right, I'll let you worry about it; but believe me, money is not going to be an object on this one, and it's got to get there in time for tonight's show. . . . OK. I'll see you at the barricades."

Darius grabbed his typewriter and scanned the room for papers, pens, tape recorders, or money he might have left. He made a conscious effort not to look at Katherine, who had not moved from the bed, but he felt her eyes following his every movement.

"Your toilet kit," she reminded him.

He retrieved it from the bathroom. "Thanks."

"Darius?" She propped herself up on an elbow.

"Yes."

"Darius?" Her voice was a barely audible whisper.

Darius looked at her and smiled. Both of them knew that they had no idea when they would be seeing each other again. "I love you, Kat. That's something to remember."

Katherine nodded, but couldn't speak. Tears formed in her eyes. "Darius." This time there was no question in her voice. She smiled through her tears. "You better get moving, Hildy Johnson, or I'll call the Shinbet and tell 'em you stole my watch."

Darius left without another word.

He filmed his report against the backdrop of the Old City. His Israeli cameraman, Gregor, couldn't believe his ears. "You sure about all that, Darius?"

"I'm sure." Darius took him by the arm. "Gregor, for a few hours anyway, please don't say anything to anyone about this story."

Gregor shrugged. "My English, you know, is not very well. I no understood what you said." He pointed his thumb in the direction of his soundman. "He speaks even worse English than me."

"Than I." Darius corrected him with a grin.

"You see?"

30

At the airport, Darius conveyed the essence of his story to Blumer, who merely whistled. "Too risky to try satelliting that stuff out of Herzliya," Jerry agreed. "The censors'd kill it in a flash. Better to ship it out your way."

Even though Darius was conscious of the roar of the airplane engines, he still lowered his voice. "Call O'Conner and tell him he's got a bombshell flying his way, but don't spell it out. Tell him I'll call him from Torrejon when we refuel."

"Darius?" Blumer looked at his protégé with pride. "You're one hell of a reporter."

"I know." Darius whacked Blumer across the back. "Not bad yourself," he said, grinning. He picked up his typewriter and camera bag, walked slowly across the tarmac and boarded the Vandenberg plane.

He sat down next to Brian Fitzpatrick, whose Irish imagination had been sprung by exhaustion.

"I'm starting to feel like one of the ancient Visigoths," Fitzpatrick growled, "doomed to wander endlessly around the earth."

"Yeah," added Kaufman, "but at least *they* got to rape and pillage. All we get is briefed."

"Not on this leg." It was Carl Ellis. He squatted in the aisle next to

Darius. "Try not to be too conspicuous about it," he whispered, "but the Secretary'd like to see you up front as soon as we take off."

Darius barely moved his head in agreement. He delayed as long as he could, waiting until his colleagues had settled into their customary "long flight" pattern of reading, sleeping and liar's poker. After they had been airborne for about thirty minutes, Darius sauntered up the aisle, stopping briefly to chat with one of the secretaries. Then he slipped into the forward cabin, noticing that Bernardi was making a conscious effort to avoid him. Ellis motioned Darius into the conference cabin. "He's waiting for you."

Secretary Vandenberg sat on one of the couches that were attached to the inner cabin walls. He made no pretense of being otherwise occupied. Darius seated himself a few feet away.

Vandenberg's expression was impassive. "What have you decided?"

Darius tried to keep his voice calm. "I filmed the report in Jerusalem. It's already on its way. It should be on the air tonight before we get back."

There was a flicker of panic in Vandenberg's eyes, but it was almost immediately replaced by a look of fathomless sorrow. The Secretary stared vacantly at a bank of high clouds. "Our capacity for self-mutilation knows absolutely no bounds." He seemed to be fighting to control his anger. "It's a tragedy, Darius. There's no other word for it. You and your friends in the media think of yourselves as the guardians of our way of life. You know what you are? You're the gravediggers of democracy!" There was icy contempt in his voice. "There *is* no such thing as absolute freedom. As soon as a society moves too far in that direction, it invites repression. There *has* to be a limit; and if the press refuses to govern itself, then sooner or later someone else does it for them. That's not a threat. That's one of the immutable laws of history, from which the United States is not exempt. It happened in Germany; it happened in Hungary and Greece and everywhere else in the world where people believed that you could have limitless freedom without responsibility." Vandenberg regained a measure of self-control. "Could you still keep the story off the air?"

"I could," Darius responded coldly, "but I won't."

The Secretary exhaled deeply. "Then there's nothing more to be said."

Darius hesitated for a moment, then got to his feet. "I'm afraid you're right."

As Darius left the conference cabin, he almost collided with Bernardi in the aisle. There was no consolation from that quarter. "I thought you had a little more brains than the others."

Darius had anticipated the reaction, but felt stunned, nevertheless.

The other newsmen were more than a little resentful of Darius' access to the Secretary. Their feelings were couched in humor though.

"Are you briefing on this leg, Darius, or is the Secretary gonna fill us in on what *you* told *him?*" Kaufman was smiling, but nervous.

Darius ignored him. He didn't feel up to it.

In the forward cabin, Bernardi was just being summoned by the Secretary of State.

"I want that story killed, Frank."

"What did he do? Film it and leave it in Israel?"

Vandenberg pounded his fist on the couch. "I don't know."

"Look, it may not be all that bad, Felix. We can call the Israelis and have them confiscate the film. If he sent it somewhere else, we can find that out quickly enough. Film cans have a way of getting lost."

Vandenberg shook his head. "No. What good does it do if we get the film? All we gain is a couple of hours. He'll just do the story when he gets back to Washington."

"We don't get into Andrews until after the evening news shows are off the air."

"Goddammit, Frank, talk sense, will you? I want the *story* killed. I don't want it on tonight or tomorrow night or a week from next Tuesday." Something occurred to Vandenberg. "Isn't Ed Langston the board chairman at NNS?"

Bernardi nodded. "Do you know him?"

Vandenberg was wiping his glasses with a paper napkin. "I've met him a couple of times. What's more important, though, is that he knows me. Also, I think he's the kind of man who'd be suitably impressed if he thought he could do his country a service." The Secretary made his decision. "I want to talk to Langston."

"I'll have communications get him for you right away."

"Not from the goddamn plane!" Vandenberg exploded. "We'll have every intelligence service in the world listening in. Set up a secure line at Torrejon; and cancel my appointment with the Spanish Foreign Minister. I don't have any time for his aristocratic bullshit anyway."

Arrangements had been made for the Secretary of State to use the American base commander's office at Torrejon. Communications already had Edward Langston on the phone; the network chairman had been advised that the nature of Secretary Vandenberg's business with him was a matter of urgent national security.

"That means," a U.S. official had explained apologetically, "no recording devices, no secretary on the extension."

"I understand," Langston had answered softly; but he really didn't understand, and he was nervous, wondering what in God's name could have prompted the Secretary of State to be calling *him* in such dramatic fashion.

Vandenberg did nothing to diminish the sense of drama.

"Ed, I'm calling on you as a friend and as a patriot." Vandenberg knew his man. "I'm counting on you to keep the essence of this conversation in the strictest confidence."

"I think you know me well enough for that, Felix." Until that moment, it would never have occurred to a man like Edward Langston to address the Secretary of State by his first name, but Vandenberg seemed to invite the familiarity.

"Good. I want you to know, first of all, that I've never made this kind of request before; and if I didn't believe that world peace was at stake, I wouldn't make it now."

Langston's mouth had begun to feel a little dry.

"One of your reporters, Darius Kane."

"Yes?"

"He's a first-rate journalist, but he's stumbled on to part of a story that could have devastating consequences if it's broadcast prematurely."

"What's the nature of the story?"

Vandenberg repeated the main points of what Darius had told him the previous day. Aware of Langston's right-wing reputation, Vandenberg concluded, "As long as the Russians are unaware of what we know, Ed, we have an edge on them; but most important of all, if the Middle East explodes because of this story, it'll drive the Palestinians and possibly the Syrians and the Egyptians right back into the Soviet camp. You can imagine what kind of pressure that'll put on the Saudis, and what that's going to mean, in turn, to our oil supplies. We've worked damn hard to get the Russians out of the Middle East. I don't think it's worth one television report to let them get their hands back on the area again." Vandenberg waited for a response. "Ed?"

"What are you asking me to do, Felix? Kill the story?"

Vandenberg picked his way through this minefield very carefully.

"I wouldn't put it that bluntly, Ed. I'm asking you to delay it. Give us a chance to get things rolling in the Middle East. A few weeks from now the situation could be radically changed."

Langston gazed at the Manhattan skyline from his fifty-second-floor office. He had never before felt so close to the shaping of his nation's destiny. He was elated, but controlled, responsible. He phrased his answer with the instinctive caution of a successful businessman. "Whether or not I decide to help you, Felix, one thing must be understood. This conversation never took place."

Vandenberg leaned back in his borrowed swivel armchair. "I understand totally, Ed. I'm very much indebted to you."

The transatlantic line died. Langston felt a little short of breath. He looked at the phone, hoping it would ring again. He wanted desperately to be able to talk to someone; anyone. He was, he mused, in the awkward position of the apocryphal pastor who, having squeezed in a few holes of golf on Easter Sunday, shot a hole in one and couldn't tell anyone about it.

He pressed down a button on his intercom connecting him with his secretary. "I want O'Conner up here right away."

O'Conner, at that very moment, was being briefed by Darius, who was calling from a staff sergeant's office at the Torrejon Air Base. He had responded in exemplary fashion.

"They'll really put the screws to us, but it sounds to me as though you've got it cold."

"There's no question about it, Bill. If I had any doubts before my meeting with Vandenberg this morning, I don't have any now. He didn't even *try* to convince me that the material was inaccurate."

"All right. We'll order up the bird from London, just in case the Athens flight gets in late. You might as well try to get some sleep on the flight home. You're gonna need it."

Darius felt a mixture of melancholy and relief as he hung up. For good or ill, it was now out of his hands.

Bill O'Conner was given no time to reflect. His secretary craned her head around the door of his office. "Bill, Mr. Langston would like to see you right away."

Intuitively, O'Conner knew why.

O'Conner found Langston in an expansive mood. Langston harbored no doubts about his ability in the business world, but news had always been a slightly different matter. His distaste for journalists had matured over the years, and the fact that he now ran his own stable

had never relieved him of the suspicion that his subordinates considered themselves members of an elite to which he could never aspire.
Langston savored the unfamiliar intoxication of having just been absorbed into the Establishment. He was about to participate in "making policy"; and onerous as the burden might be, there was no doubt
in Edward Langston's mind that he was acting in the national interest.

"Have you talked to Kane yet?" Langston asked.

"I just got off the phone with him, Ed. How'd you hear about it so
fast?"

Langston ignored the question. "I want the story killed."

O'Conner had expected more of a preamble. "You're joking." He
hadn't intended to say that. It had just slipped out.

"I want it killed," Langston repeated.

"Do you mind telling me why?"

Langston was very much in control of the situation. "I'd like to,
Bill." He sounded genuinely regretful. "I'm simply not in a position to
discuss it."

"Well, I'm sorry, Ed; I can't accept that. You don't just pretend that
a story like this doesn't exist."

Langston interrupted. He adopted an avuncular tone. "Bill, before
you say something that you may regret later on, I think you should
know that I do not consider this matter open to debate. There are
larger issues at stake here than you know about. The story is to be
dropped. That's an order."

Bill O'Conner was not a coward, and his commitment to news was
genuine. "Don't put me in this position, Ed. I don't want to resign, but
you're not leaving me much of an option."

"I hope you don't mean that; and for both our sakes, I'm going to
pretend you didn't say it. I think there are a few factors you should
consider. I want to assume first off that my executives have some faith
in my integrity. If I don't give you a specific reason for my decision,
it's not because I don't choose to, it's because I'm not able to. Then too
I think you ought to give some thought to the quixotic reaction that
your resignation might have. You have a home, a family. You're at the
peak of your career, but you're not a young man, Bill. I don't think
any of your former employers would trip over themselves to rehire
you. Anyway, your financial stake in this company is not inconse-
quential."

The company's stock option plan had just crossed O'Conner's mind
too.

"But most important of all, Bill," Langston continued, "is the fact that your resignation wouldn't alter my decision one bit. The story would still be killed."

"Kane'll leak it." The argument seemed suspended in midair, lacking any potency.

"That's a very real possibility," Langston conceded. "But if he does so, I hope you'll impress upon him that he would be taking the action in his capacity as a private citizen of this great democracy, not as an employee of National News Service."

O'Conner sighed. He knew now that he wasn't going to resign. He was trying to salvage a grain of self-respect. "Can't you even leave open the possibility of re-examining the story?"

Langston was feeling magnanimous. "Of course!" He waited a beat. "But not today."

O'Conner left the executive suite without a further word. By the time he reached his office, he was in a helpless, seething fury. He hovered over his secretary's desk for only an instant. "I don't wanta *see* anyone. I don't wanta *talk* to anyone. No phone calls, no messages, nothing! Is that clear?" He had slammed his door before she could reply.

Katherine Chandler's message had been sent from the U.S. Embassy in Tel Aviv through a back-channel communications system. It would not appear in the State Department's cable traffic or in that of the White House. It was so selectively routed that not even the official file of the Central Intelligence Agency would carry a record of its existence. It was a simple one-line message: "STORY TO RUN AS DISCUSSED." George Tipton received the message shortly after eight in the morning, Washington time. He was unable to reach Whit Traynor at the White House until almost nine-thirty.

"That's fine," Traynor had remarked. "That'll take care of a lot of things." A passing concern had crossed his mind. "What are you going to do about the Israeli agent?"

Tipton indulged in a rare moment of humor. "Better you shouldn't ask," he quipped.

Just before nine, Tipton had initiated a series of actions that would ultimately lead to the release of an American intelligence officer who had been kidnapped by one of the more radical wings of the OLPP six weeks earlier. It was a decision that Tipton had reached with the greatest reluctance. He did not enjoy any part of the process of eliminating a friendly foreign agent. But, in his mind, Ibrahim el-Haj was within nine hours of having outlived his usefulness to any government. Kane's story would have that effect, but it would yield no advantage to the Agency. Tipton believed that the Agency had to extract every ounce of advantage from any given situation. By three P.M., Washington time, Tipton's men had secured the release of his own agent. Chai was already dead.

Bill O'Conner had half hoped that the executive producer of the NNS *Evening News* would force a showdown. It would have given him an opportunity to reconsider his own decision. But O'Conner's grip on the news division was so tight that producers argued with him only on rare occasions. In this case, the producer resisted, but not seriously.

"What are you, crazy, Bill? It's one helluva good story. We plan to lead the show with it." The producer held a copy of Darius' script that the London bureau had telexed to New York.

O'Conner had ignored the script. "I know what kind of story it is. That's exactly why we have to be so damned careful with it. Put your White House guys on it first thing tomorrow morning. I want a double confirmation on this story." O'Conner knew he didn't need one in this case, but it was the proper excuse.

The producer had shrugged. "You're the boss."

And that had been it.

Darius sensed that something was wrong the moment he stepped off the plane at Andrews Air Force Base. There was nothing in the air of impending crisis, no electricity that usually precedes a big story, no restlessness among the reporters waiting behind steel barricades, no live camera units, nothing. The usual lineup of State Department officials, wives and diplomats waited near the ramp of the giant Boeing. Several hundred Air Force men and their families waved paper American flags from behind a fence near the VIP lounge. The tower, with its rotating beacons, was white against the dark sky. The President's "doomsday" plane, a massive 747, was parked at the far end of the apron.

Darius descended the ramp, trying to contain his anxiety. He approached the bullpen, hoping for a barrage of questions from his colleagues. There were none. Several friends waved; a few others shouted "Hello." The AP's Ken Dawson hung in mock fatigue over a steel barricade. "I see Felix has made the world safe for democracy again." Now Darius *knew* that something was wrong. He checked his watch. It was seven-forty-five P.M., Washington time. NNS should have released his story to the news agencies at least two hours before.

"There he comes!" one TV reporter bellowed over the whine of the dying engines. "Start rolling."

Vandenberg walked happily down the ramp, waving in the general direction of the TV lights. He shook hands with a succession of diplomats and dignitaries, enjoying the compliments and congratulations. He stopped to kiss Linda Bernardi. "Without his help," Vandenberg said, pointing to his Under Secretary, "we might have been able to finish this job a week earlier." Vandenberg grinned and continued his handshaking walk down the receiving line. When he had run out of hands, he paused and then slowly approached a cluster of microphones positioned on his side of the barricade; he tried to look reluctant, as though with each step he were fighting the pull of an invisible magnet.

"Really, I have nothing to say." Vandenberg smiled at several familiar faces on the other side of the barricade.

"Could you move just a little closer to the microphones, Mr. Secretary?" It was a young reporter, who spoke with a proper mix of reverence and eagerness.

The Secretary turned serious. "I'm delighted, of course, to be back again in . . ." Vandenberg turned, in a convincing imitation of confusion, to Bernardi, who dutifully played his straight man.

"This is Washington, Mr. Secretary."

"I'm delighted to be back here in Washington. As most of you no doubt know by now, we've made considerable progress these last few days in averting another war in the Middle East. I understand that the President is holding a news conference in a little more than an hour. So I hope you'll understand if *I* don't take any questions now. The President has asked that I return to the White House as soon as possible. Thank you all for coming out here."

Vandenberg turned toward a waiting helicopter before anyone could ask a question.

Darius grabbed Dawson by the sleeve. "Ken, what the hell is going on here?"

Dawson was puzzled. "You heard your friend. The President's holding a news conference. You didn't expect him to let Felix take *all* the credit, did you?"

Darius felt a wave of nausea sweep over him. "What about my story on the OLPP?"

Dawson was under deadline pressure. "I don't know what you're talking about. Why don't you get your bags while I file this junk and I'll drive you in to the White House."

"OK," Darius grunted. "I'll meet you in the VIP lounge. I have to make a call myself."

Darius found his suitcase and garment bag among the pile of luggage stacked near the plane's tail section. He carried his bags across the tarmac and into the VIP lounge. Darius dialed double 8 for an outside line, and when he heard the dial tone, he called the NNS Washington bureau. The operator seemed genuinely pleased to hear his voice. "Darius! Welcome back."

"Thanks, Mary. Do me a favor, please? Get me Bill O'Conner. If he isn't in the office, try him at home."

"Sure. Hang on."

Somehow, the operator's warmth was reassuring. Perhaps, Darius told himself, he was just overreacting. Maybe the film hadn't reached New York or London in time. He could hear the phone ringing and then O'Conner's voice.

"Mr. O'Conner," Mary said, "I have Darius Kane on the line for you."

Darius was in no mood for preliminaries. "What happened, Bill?"

"What do you mean, 'what happened'?"

"You know what I mean. What happened to my piece?"

"I made the decision to hold it until we can get a double confirmation. Jackson's checking it out at the White House."

Darius felt dizzy. "You mean you got the film and you didn't use it?"

"Yes. We got the film. It looked fine. I screened it myself."

"Well then, Bill, for Chrissake, why the hell didn't we use it?"

O'Conner was being uncharacteristically patient. "I told you. I think we need to check out some of the details."

It had suddenly become very clear to Darius. "How'd he get to you, Bill?"

"How did *who* get to me?" Now there was a note of irritation in O'Conner's voice.

Darius was beyond caring though. "*Who?*" he flared. "*Vandenberg,* that's who! I had this goddamn story cold, and you know it. Don't give me this bullshit about checking out details."

"Look, Darius, you're tired. I can understand you're upset, but why don't we talk about it in the morning?"

Dawson had arrived and he was impatiently pointing at his watch. It was, Darius knew, pointless to continue the argument. The *Evening News* was already off the air.

"All right," he agreed limply, "in the morning."

Dawson helped carry Darius' luggage to his car. They were on Suitland Parkway, heading toward Washington, before Dawson brought up the subject. "What did you start to tell me before about the OLPP?"

Darius felt torn. If he gave the story to Dawson, it would probably appear, in weakened form, on the Associated Press wire. If there was any chance, though, of still getting the story on NNS, there were two good reasons why it made little sense to leak it to the AP. It would dilute the effect of the report and it would infuriate O'Conner.

"Forget it. I'll tell you about it later."

They parked near the Washington Monument and walked to the Executive Office Building. Uniformed guards examined their White House press cards at the southwest gate and then again as they entered the EOB.

The auditorium was already crowded. Live television cameras blocked every aisle. Darius found a seat near the back row.

At exactly thirty seconds after nine P.M., President Abbott entered the auditorium, looking serene and dignified. Nothing became him more than a public ceremony. He walked with a confident stride toward the lectern, which had been decorated with the Presidential seal. Secretary Vandenberg and Harlan Stewart sat down on the only two chairs on the thickly carpeted stage. The President motioned to the reporters to be seated.

"Ladies and gentlemen," he began, "I have a brief opening announcement, and then I'll take your questions"—Abbott paused theatrically—"if you have any." The reporters laughed despite themselves. The President smiled. He loved his prime-time performances.

"First, I would like to extend my sincerest congratulations to the Secretary of State." Vandenberg nodded deferentially in the President's direction. "Were it not for his untiring efforts, we might find the world in a far different condition this evening, and it would certainly not have been possible for me to make the following announcement. I will be leaving Washington in early March for a six-day visit to the Middle East. Some of the specific dates have yet to be worked out; but I will be meeting with the leaders of Israel, Egypt, Syria, Jordan, Saudi Arabia"—here the President paused—"and it is also my intention to meet with the Chairman of the Organization for the Liberation of the People of Palestine."

The senior AP correspondent had already jumped to his feet, but the President raised his hands. "I haven't quite finished." The reporter sat down. "Secretary Vandenberg will, of course, be accompanying me to the Middle East; and it is my plan that he will remain there, following my own discussions, for the purpose of establishing at least the framework of a solution to the festering problem of a Palestinian state. Now, Mr. Wilmington, I'll be happy to take your first question."

The AP reporter stood, glancing down at his notebook. "Mr. President, you've just announced your intention to meet with the Chairman of the OLPP. Would it be correct to assume that the United States has now granted official recognition to the OLPP?"

President Abbott stole a quick glance at the "guidance material" that had been drafted under Vandenberg's direction only minutes earlier. "Within certain limits, Mr. Wilmington, yes, that would be correct. As you know, the United States has withheld any recognition of the OLPP for as long as that organization refused to acknowledge the existence of the state of Israel. We consider Chairman Safat's acceptance earlier today of the appropriate U.N. resolutions to be a reversal of that policy; and therefore, within the same terms enunciated by the Israeli government today, we are prepared to recognize the OLPP."

Darius knew that his own story was being masterfully and deliberately smothered; that if he failed to raise it now, it would be so overtaken by events that it could never be revived. He jumped to his feet. "Mr. President!" In his sense of mounting frenzy, Darius had overlooked the traditional sequence of Presidential news conferences. President Abbott was pointing at the woman from UPI. Darius fought to restrain his impatience during the string of questions that followed from the respective White House correspondents from ABC, NBC and CBS.

The news conference was more than fifteen minutes old before President Abbott began recognizing outstretched hands beyond the first row. The President's eyes never seemed to stray in Darius' direction.

It is not easy at a White House news conference for any reporter to gain recognition, especially when the President chooses to ignore him. It is not, however, impossible. The technique has been perfected over the years by such insistent White House gadflies as Clark Mollenhoff and Sarah McClendon. It calls for a carefully timed combination of volume, breath control and a steely determination to complete a question no matter what interruptions threaten to cut it short.

Darius got to his feet just as the President was coming to the end of his answer to a previous question. "Mr.-President-you've-avoided-all-reference-here-this-evening"—Darius strung his words together in a continuing stream until he was sure that his voice had overridden all challengers—"to-the-events-that-led-the-Middle-East-to-the-brink-of-war."

A number of heads had turned in his direction, and Darius was now confident that he would be able to complete his question in a more normal cadence.

"There is indisputable evidence that both the Soviet Union and Israel succeeded in planting intelligence agents at the highest level of the OLPP."

Almost every head in the auditorium had now swiveled toward Darius.

"Furthermore, there is evidence that the Soviets, in particular, knew about, may have initiated, and certainly tried to exploit the kidnapping of Secretary Vandenberg's wife to lead the Middle East toward another war, and that the principal reason that war did not break out was the secret raid by an Israeli commando unit in the heart of Damascus some forty-eight hours ago. My question, sir, is this: Was your sudden announcement here this evening—that you are going to the Middle East—prompted by a desire to keep those facts from becoming public?"

President Abbott's expression turned grim; he gripped the lectern with both hands. "Mr. Kane," he pronounced evenly, "I must say that I find both the tone and the substance of your question offensive. I understand that where the Middle East in particular is concerned, any President must expect that not only his actions but even his motivations will be subjected to intense scrutiny. And it's perfectly proper that this should be so; but to suggest, as you've just done, that the President of the United States would travel to the Middle East for the express purpose of saving the Soviet Union from embarrassment is, to put it very bluntly, absurd." The President very deliberately turned away from Darius, inviting another question; but Darius had remained standing.

"Mr. President, a follow-up question, if I may. First of all, sir, without intending any disrespect, you've ignored the substance of my question, that is, both the Israeli raid and the dual penetration of the OLPP. Secondly, isn't it a fact that the decision to hold this news conference within an hour after Secretary Vandenberg's return—before you could even discuss the implications of his trip—that that decision was made at Secretary Vandenberg's suggestion for the specific purpose of overshadowing the other events I've referred to?"

"Mr. Kane, you seem to be laboring under the misapprehension that the only time the President can talk to his Secretary of State is when the two of them are in the same room at the same time. We have been in constant touch by both telex and telephone, and the decision to hold this news conference was made a number of hours ago. Now, as to all of your other allegations, I hardly know where to begin. In fact, it might be best if Secretary Vandenberg himself addressed these incredible charges. Come on up here, Felix."

Vandenberg cleared his throat nervously as he approached the lectern. "As the President has just told you, the decision that he would visit the Middle East and that the announcement would be made at this news conference was reached several hours ago. But that is only a circumstantial denial of all the points that Mr. Kane has raised." His right hand chopped at the air, giving his words additional emphasis. "I am not aware that any foreign government has succeeded in penetrating the OLPP. I am not aware that the Israeli government launched a commando raid in Damascus; nor, I might add, is it clear to me how such a raid could have been instrumental in preventing a war." Vandenberg's eyes moved slowly up the rows of seats until they settled on Darius. "I have always regarded Mr. Kane as a serious and responsible journalist. I can only assume that he has fallen victim to a condition that at one time or another plagues the most careful and well-intentioned among us—bad information."

Secretary Vandenberg started to return to his seat, but Darius exploded with one more question. "Mr. Secretary, are you flatly denying the raid and the penetration by Soviet and Israeli agents of the OLPP?"

Vandenberg returned to the lectern. His voice and his eyes were cold. "Mr. Kane, I just have."

Darius sank into his chair, overcome by waves of shock, disbelief, frustration and finally fatigue. He was vaguely aware of another reporter's question about what kind of Congressional reaction the President expected.

Abbott's voice seemed to be coming from another planet. "It is the requirements of global peace that dictate our trip; not politics. I am confident that all members of Congress, Republican and Democratic, will recognize that it is in the national interest of the United States that I undertake this effort. The Congress will respond accordingly."

At nine-thirty, almost to the second, the AP correspondent rose to deliver the traditional "Thank you, Mr. President," ending this news conference. Across the noisy auditorium, filled with rising or departing reporters, Vandenberg caught Darius' eye and held it for a moment before falling into Abbott's wake.

31

Whit Traynor's reclining chair was at a precarious forty-five degree angle, his feet clinging to the edge of his desk. Through the open curtains of his floor-to-ceiling windows, he had just caught a glimpse of Darius Kane walking along a White House path toward a Pennsylvania Avenue exit. Kane looked very dejected. Traynor, never one to let an opportunity escape, was already on the phone to his CIA liaison.

Edward Langston was lying on a couch in the den of his Connecticut home nursing a pale Scotch and water. NNS never carried "instant analysis" so the network had already begun showing a rerun of *Gunsmoke*.

Annabelle Langston poked a face covered with cold cream around the door. "President say anything interesting, dear?"

Langston pulled himself into a sitting position. "He's going to the Middle East." He reported the fact without any apparent interest.

"Is that good or bad?"

"I suppose it's good." Langston cleared his throat. "The President ought to know what's best."

"Of course he does," his wife agreed.

Bill O'Conner was still sitting behind his office desk gazing at a silent, flickering image. He had killed the sound but not the picture on the NNS monitor. He didn't feel like talking with anyone, including his wife. After fifteen minutes, he picked up his briefcase and left his office, walking past the closed doors along executive row. His colleagues had all gone home hours earlier.

O'Conner wandered downstairs to the TV assignment desk, which was staffed twenty-four hours a day. He narrowly avoided a collision with one of the motorcycle couriers who was hurrying down the corridor on his way to Kennedy Airport to pick up a film shipment.

"Hey, Mr. O'Conner! Howya doin'?"

O'Conner ignored him. Only two people were on duty: a young desk assistant, who was eating a hero sandwich while reading a college sociology text; and the duty editor, who was on the phone, momentarily unaware of O'Conner's presence. O'Conner cleared his throat.

"Mr. O'Conner, I'm sorry," the editor apologized, "I didn't see you standing there. What can I do for you, sir?"

O'Conner felt a wave of helplessness and disgust. What he needed was an argument, a forum in which he could justify his decision. He looked again at the editor's docile, apparently frightened, face.

"Nothing," he mumbled mechanically. "Nothing at all."

Secretary Vandenberg was in the private office of the President's National Security Adviser. Most of the White House staff, Harlan Stewart among them, had gone home shortly after the news conference. President Abbott had retired to the family quarters.

Vandenberg had accepted an incoming call from the Israeli Prime Minister; he would have preferred delaying this confrontation, but he decided to get it out of the way.

"Ya'acov, why aren't you asleep?"

Ben-Dor's voice registered a chilly monotone. "You'll forgive me, Mr. Secretary, if I dispense with our usual pleasantries."

Vandenberg sounded resigned. "Of course, Mr. Prime Minister."

"Don't you think it would have been courteous, to say the least, if the government of the United States had seen fit to inform the government of Israel that the President was planning to meet with the Chairman of the OLPP?"

Vandenberg looked out at the front lawn of the White House and sighed. "Mr. Prime Minister, sometimes the exigencies of a situation leave little room for courtesy or even formalities. My principal concern, as you should know, was to override Kane's story before it destroyed everything that you and I had worked toward these past few days. Believe me, that announcement was, quite literally, a last-minute decision."

"And the sacrifice of an Israeli agent. Was that a last-minute decision also?"

"I'm sorry, Ya'acov. Now I really don't know what you're talking about."

The Israeli Prime Minister hesitated for an instant. "Very well," he snarled finally. "I assume you've taken whatever steps are necessary to avoid any personal implication or embarrassment. But believe me, Mr. Secretary, I wasn't born yesterday. An American agent was released by the OLPP in Beirut this evening only an hour or two before our own man was killed. I'm not so naïve as to believe that we could ever find proof of your complicity in this affair, but you believe me, Mr. Secretary, I won't forget it." The line went dead.

Vandenberg stared at the phone in helpless rage. Then he picked up an ashtray and hurled it across the room. "Goddamn this fucking job!"

A second later, a secretary knocked tentatively at the office door just as it was flung open. "Is anything wrong, Mr. Secretary?"

Vandenberg stared at her for a few seconds and shook his head slowly. "No," he muttered, "not a thing."

Darius Kane was sitting in his cubicle in the Washington bureau of NNS. Several editors and technicians were still on duty; but when Darius entered the newsroom, they all had seemed preoccupied. Not a word had been exchanged, though the night editor, an old friend, had nodded. Darius knew of no formal communication from New York, but the grapevine had carried the message of executive displeasure. It was enough. Darius' story was submerged but not ignored in the wire service reports on the Presidential news conference, and he had little doubt that it would become the source of heated debate in Congress within a day or two. He also had little doubt that as the debate intensified it would embarrass NNS.

If the story was accurate, why had NNS ignored its own correspondent? A reporter's error was forgivable. The reporter who underscored the error of his network was not. Within National News Service, Darius Kane was already a pariah.

Darius tugged open a drawer of his desk; he took out a blank interoffice memorandum. He rolled the sheet of paper into his typewriter. "FROM: Darius Kane. TO: Bill O'Conner. SUBJECT: Kane's status." Darius advanced the paper four spaces. Then he typed out a terse note of resignation. "In the immortal words of Ernest Hemingway: 'Upshove job asswards!'"

He slipped the note into an interoffice envelope and dropped it in his secretary's out basket.

It took him only a moment to decide on his next step. He consulted his airline guide and called Pan American Airways. "I'd like to get on your next flight to London, with the first available connection to Beirut."

"Will that be first class or economy?"

"First class," he answered. "And I'll be paying for it by Air Travel Card." NNS would absorb the cost without a murmur.

Then Darius dialed the overseas operator. "I'd like to place a call to Beirut, please." He looked at his watch. It would be five-thirty in the morning in Beirut. Katherine could catch up on her sleep later.

It took the operator ten minutes to place the call. Katherine's voice was muffled with sleep.

Darius felt a surge of exhilaration. "Kat?"

"Yes."

He knew that she was now fully awake. Darius could picture Katherine sitting up in bed, brushing the hair out of her eyes and doubling the pillow behind her head. "Did you get the text of the press conference yet?"

"No. But I heard it on VOA." Her voice sounded troubled. "I'm sorry, Darius."

"Yeah, well"—he tried to lighten his own tone—"what can you do?" He was filling time.

"What *are* you going to do?"

"I just quit."

There was a long pause. Katherine asked, "Did you have to?"

"No. Not in the sense that they would've fired me, but Vandenberg got to them and they caved."

"That bastard!"

Darius was surprised at the anger in her voice. "Who, Vandenberg?"

"Of course Vandenberg!"

For a moment, Darius examined his feelings toward the Secretary of

State. "Yes," he agreed. "Him too; he didn't have to screw me the way he did. But at least that sonovabitch acted in character. He lied like a bandit." Darius paused awkwardly. "But he did what he had to do, and I did what I had to do. That bunch of heroes I work for, though; they don't even know which side of the fence they're working."

"What about you and me, Darius?" Her voice sounded apprehensive. "What about *us?*"

"What *about* us?"

"We're not really on the same side of the fence either."

"But it doesn't have to be that way forever, does it?"

Katherine misunderstood. Her voice brightened perceptibly. "No, not at all. I know a lot of people here. You'll like them." She began to speak very quickly. "You can rest for a few days. Maybe we could even go to Rome for a week or so; and then when we're back, I could introduce you to them."

Darius felt a sudden, awful chill, a feeling of almost total aloneness. "No, Kat, I don't think that would be a very good idea." He slowly lowered the phone to its cradle, disconnecting the overseas line to Beirut even as Katherine continued speaking. He stood by the phone for a few moments; then he picked up his typewriter and left the office.